G000129063

Sweethearts and Swan Songs

A heartfelt and copiously researched tribute to the author's great grandfather, *Furze Sweethearts and Swan Songs* is a gripping tale for avid readers of First World War fiction and research alike. Wilberforce combines a talent for conveying camaraderie through dialogue with the ability to conjure suspense and atmosphere in his portrayals of Furze's engagement with the Great War. Friendships and relationships alike are built up thoughtfully throughout the story, and it is embellished with a fascinating array of photographs, original hand drawn maps and letters to remind the reader of the real life story being retold. The love of mothers for their sons, and the wartime letters between Furze and his sweetheart Daw, are communicated with understated sensitivity. A story of love, loyalty, humour, heartbreak and heroism, it is not to be missed.

William Tink - Head of History - Charterhouse School

Furze

Sweethearts and Swan Songs

Copyright

This paperback edition published 2021 by Jasami Publishing Ltd
an imprint of Jasami Publishing Ltd
Glasgow, Scotland
https://jasamipublishingltd.com

ISBN 978-1-913798-41-3

Copyright © B.D. Wilberforce 2021

All rights reserved. No part of this publication may be reproduced, stored in a retrieval system, or transmitted, in any form, or by any means (electronic, mechanical, photocopying, recording or otherwise) without the prior written permission of the publisher except for brief quotations used for promotion or in reviews.

This novel is based upon true events and the diary of a British Officer during World War I. Some names, characters, incidents, and dialogue portrayed in this are fictitious, and so identification with actual persons (living or deceased), places, buildings, and products is not intended or should be inferred.

The moral rights of the author have been asserted.

Visit JasamiPublishingLtd.com to read more about all our books and to purchase them. You will also find features, author information and news of any events, also be the first to hear about our new releases.

Publisher's Note

B.D. Wilberforce is one of those rare talents whose writing will captivate and enthral you as it takes you on an emotional journey to another time. Furze Sweethearts and Swan Songs was written in the poetic and lyrical language of that time, and should be read and enjoyed as the reader is wrapped in those moments.

Jasami Acknowledgements

The Jasami team is integral to the production of all of our titles, as they are talented, creative and hardworking. I especially wish to thank our Executive Editor May Winton on this project, as she has been elemental in her support and editing of this novel.

Editors

May Winton
Joanne Tahaney
Emma Toft

Marketing

Videographer - Kirsty Lawson
Social Media - Cassidy Smith

Cover Design

Joy Dakers

Lieutenant Edward Keith Byrne Furze

This novel is based upon the hand-written diary Lieutenant Furze kept between 13th January and 27th June 1915

Dedication

This novel is dedicated to my grandparents: Lynette Furze and Michael Wilberforce, David Ritchie and Jennifer Prentice. Lynette and Michael, I knew in my early life and were the very epitome of staunch dedication to family, friends, duty, and each other. David I never met, although his admirable intellectual character and strong moral grounding live on in my own father Andrew. Jenny has been a bedrock of my life and is someone I continue to learn from, look up to, and feel proud of every day. Grandparents represent lives and memories both wondrously distant and intimately connected to our own. They can impart wisdom to the young that cannot be gleaned from many other sources, as long as we pause, and listen. Without these four lovely souls, I would never have had the patience and understanding to discover the meaning contained within the pages of Furze's diary.

Contents

A Young Furze

B.D. Wilberforce

Furze at Primary School

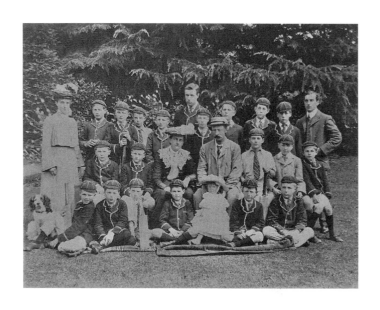

Charterhouse Hodgesonites Mr Paige Cricket
Quarter Summer Term 1905

B.D. Wilberforce

2nd Lieutenant Commission 1912

The Queen's Regiment
Dinner in Bermuda 1913

B.D. Wilberforce

The Queen's Regiment
Bermuda 1913

Preface

This novel is based on the hand-written diary kept by Lieutenant Edward Keith Byrne Furze from January to June 1915. At the time of writing, our protagonist was a twenty-four-year-old junior officer serving in The Queen's Royal Regiment (West Surrey), one of the senior line infantry regiments in the British Army. The Queen's still exists today as the Princess of Wales's Royal Regiment, an amalgamation of various British infantry regiments.

Although this novel is a work of fiction, it is rooted deeply within the factual foundations contained in Furze's diary. Every character, event, and battle that you encounter is based on historical fact and I have ensured that, where possible, I remain as true to Furze's account as feasible whilst constructing a compelling narrative. The purpose of the story is to map Furze's development as a soldier, as a son, as a friend, and as a lover, highlighting the similarities that remain between individuals today and those who trod our societies over a century ago.

There are many accounts dealing with the First World War, and innumerable novels approaching the topic of love, so this story attempts to represent Furze's war, and Furze's journey when it comes to these two intimate and challenging topics. We all face difficulties in life, whether physical, emotional, or moral. Furze's account of this brief six-month period, during which he stands toe to toe with the seemingly insurmountable obstacle of the Great War is, regardless, infused with hope for a life many of us can relate to. A life involving someone he loves.

Before you begin reading, I ask that you picture this scene: a young man thrust into what would turn out to be one of the bloodiest wars mankind has ever engaged in. Life is turbulent enough in one's twenties without the call to fight, lead, inspire and, if need be, lay down one's life, and it is this cacophony of tribulations that Furze has to attempt to balance. Troops and siblings look up to him, commanders and parents place their trust in him, the Germans attempt to kill him, whilst his sweetheart Daw holds his heart. This novel picks up at a point in Furze's journey where he has recently recovered from serious injuries sustained during an incident in the First Battle of Ypres that he can barely remember.

Returning to the Western Front is a terrifying prospect.

B.D. Wilberforce

Excerpt from Furze's Diary 13th January 1915

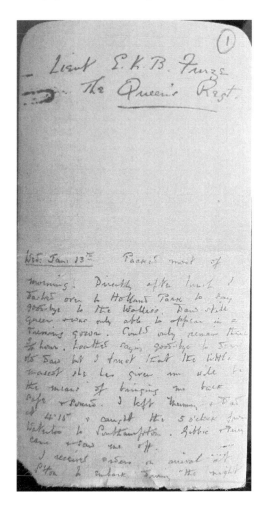

The Departure

I

March 1915

Furze shuddered and stood deadly still, the letter in his hand. It was the unmistakable crack of an enemy sniper's round, followed seconds later by the gut-wrenching thud of a bullet penetrating a soldier's skull just behind him.

Initially his reaction was one of relief. *Thank goodness I was on the move, and not standing where I had been a few seconds ago.* Then a stronger, darker thought took hold of him. *Please God, not him.*

Thoughts of his injuries during the first Battle of Ypres made him quiver. He had had a lucky escape then, so what was preventing that same luck from saving another innocent soul now?

At last Furze got a grip of himself, turning slowly. The mud in the trench made his boots heavy, as though pleading with him not to turn around, not to face the nightmare that was sure to present itself when he did. No amount of mud, however, could have held Furze in position, and no amount of experience ever prepared him for these, horrible, appalling moments when they barged their way into his life.

The sight he had most feared reared its ugly head, grinning at Furze in putrid satisfaction at the pain it caused him.

II

January 1915, two months earlier.

"Loathed having to say goodbye to dear old Daw, but I trust the little mascot she has given me will be the means of bringing me back safe and sound."

Wednesday January 13th, 1915.

Lieutenant Edward Keith Byrne Furze, known as 'Furzzy' to his friends, looked out of the window of 57 Avonmore Road in Kensington, London, and smiled. Although he was due to head back to his Regiment in France, and thus the Western Front, Furze acknowledged that it was an absolutely beautiful day. It was calm, crisp, and cool; the winter sun dancing delicate rays across the panes of glass separating him from the frosty elements. It was as though nature was holding her breath, conscious not to disturb his peace prior to the clamour of war. He began quietly musing over all of the other things he would have liked to do, had he not been stuck inside packing his kit and equipment.

Lost in contemplation, his mother's voice chose that moment to come hurtling up the stairs, thoughtlessly interrupting his moment of solitary reflection.

"Are you done packing yet, Keith? The pie is getting cold!" Mary called from the dining room.

He started, nerves on edge, and snapped back into a routine of alert awareness of his surroundings. The unexpected call from below had ripped him from a rare opportunity to disconnect from the world, from the expectations that others had for him. Furze realised he had inadvertently tensed his shoulders, bending his knees slightly to lower his profile against the parapet of the windowsill.

Calm yourself, he thought, steadying his breathing, *that's a window, not a trench wall, and that's your mother's voice, not a Commanding Officer.*

12

His left knee, injured in November, started aching and he eased himself onto his bed, massaging it as he did so. Angry at his reaction he didn't think before snapping back to his mother's quite ordinary request. "I've more important things to consider than the temperature of a pie, I shan't be rushed!"

There was a prolonged silence from the kitchen before he heard his mother's deflated response. "Of course, Keith, sorry… I wasn't thinking." Mary's voice sounded as though it was weighed down with a lead anchor and Furze kicked himself at the unnecessary harshness of his reply. He realised that she was only acting out of care for him, wishing to provide a hearty meal before his return to the War.

"No, you're quite right," he quickly added, looking down at the pile of neatly stacked bags he had finished packing and re-packing to perfection. "I'll be down presently, it smells delicious."

"Lovely," his mother's voice rang up once more, buoyed by this more positive response. "I'll plate up right away!"

Furze strode downstairs and instantly felt ravenous at the sight of his mother's spread. Although most food produce was in very short supply, Mary had a knack for making the blandest vegetables delectable to sight and taste. As he sat down at the table, his mother's glance spoke volumes.

"Is everything alright, Keith, you seem a little pensive?" As she said this, Mary realised the naivety of her comment, but who could blame her for voicing the deep-rooted concerns she held for her son.

Furze looked up impatiently, of course he was pensive. He had been recovering at home for two months after narrowly escaping death at the hands of a war neither he, nor his friends, had asked for. A war he was now being ordered to return to, leaving the life he actually wanted far behind him. Thankfully, empathy held its ground as he registered the concern on his mother's face. Before he could think he blurted, "I'm frightened…" then turning back to his food in embarrassment whilst adding, "because of this darn wound to the knee, it's playing hell with my nerves."

Mary studied her son, torn between a desire to discuss his fear and move on from a topic that was evidently a source of great disturbance for him. She knew Furze was an immensely emotional individual at heart, although she knew that discussions on the topic had to be on his terms. With that in mind, she changed the subject to one she knew he would appreciate.

"Will you be visiting Daw before you depart?"

Her intuition was not misplaced, and Furze's complexion moulded effortlessly into one of expectant pleasure. Daw Wallis was Furze's sweetheart; a delightful woman he had been spending a great deal of time with even though they had yet to share their first kiss. The War complicated such matters of the heart given its requirement for a clear head.

"Indeed, I intend to visit her directly." Furze responded, glad of the change of subject.

He had not voiced it to anyone up until that point, but his frank admission of fear to his mother had somehow solidified its reality. He was scared about returning to the Front, that much was now clear, whether that would hamper his ability to do his duty was yet to be seen.

Swallowing down his food, he finished off the pie and rose to dash over to 48 Holland Park where Daw lived with her family.

"Keith! It's so good of you to drop by and see me, especially given the fact you are leaving today. You must have a thousand other things to be focusing on." Daw surveyed Furze with a keen gaze that was both concerned and pleased for him taking time to come and see her.

"How could I have not!" exclaimed Furze. The surety of his statement bringing a flush of colour to her cheeks. He took Daw's hands in his own, and looked into her delicate face, the hint of a smile caressing his thin lips. "I just wanted to let you know that everything will be fine. I'll only be away for a few months and, in that time, I will be thinking about you every day and shall write as much as I can."

"I should like that very much, your letters always bring such warmth to mother and I. Rest assured that I shall write to you even more, describing all of the wonderfully mundane happenings at home."

They both smiled, pressing one another's hands.

"Your letters are never mundane," he reassured her, "hearing about your life here reminds me of real life, allows me to remember, even for a brief moment, that the War is only a temporary state." Furze held Daw's gaze, taking in the variety of colour that made up the deep hazelnut hue. They had an earthen warmth to them, drawing Furze deeper into their embrace every time he stole a glance.

"Don't be a tease," she smiled, "do you really care for them that much?"

"Truly," Furze pressed her hands in his, "my life on the Front would be far less bearable without them." He paused a moment, observing the woman he held such a deep care for. Thinking to his unintended admission of fear that morning, a thought crossed his mind. "Daw," he continued tentatively, watching her expression as he spoke. "I feel as though I can talk to you freely, about anything, in a way that only you could understand."

Daw noticed the emotions behind Furze's question, and responded with a nod, not wishing to interrupt his flow.

"I'm scared," he admitted, feeling both relieved and horrified at the admission. "Not in a cowardly way, you must understand, more in a tense, anxious way." He thought about how best to articulate how he was feeling. "My friends are out there, fighting the Germans, and I'm to return having only just escaped death during my last visit. I'm afraid for them, I'm afraid…" suddenly the words caught in his throat, hooked as though strung on a fishing line.

"Go on Keith," Daw encouraged softly, willing him to continue.

"I'm afraid, that the man who returns to you won't be the man you know now." He almost gasped this last sentence, suddenly aware of its implications.

"Oh Keith," Daw smiled adoringly, wondering how such a large heart beat within the thin chest of the man in front of her. "You needn't give that a second thought. It's natural to be afraid of war, of what's out there when it's so uncertain. But one thing you needn't concern yourself with is how I feel. Leave that to me, you have enough to think about."

Something inexplicable passed between the two consciences before Mrs. Wallis, Daw's mother, arrived with the tea. The fragile thread snapped. Daw looked away, but Furze had noticed a feeling within him that he hadn't felt before. It made him both strangely uncomfortable and utterly at peace.

"Excellent tea Mrs. Wallis," Furze complimented, eager to uphold a good reputation within the Wallis' household.

"Well then," Mrs. Wallis replied, settling contentedly into her armchair, "it appears I still have some uses. Daw, my dear, have you told Keith about your plans to contribute to the war effort?"

"Well," she murmured avoiding Furze's look, "it's really not much, and many others are doing far more. The other week, whilst dining at the Savoy, I heard a group of American women talking about a fund they had set up to support their husbands who were fighting on the Front. I couldn't help myself, so I asked what it was they were doing, and whether I could be of assistance."

"Very admirable." Furze nodded.

"It turns out that these American women, who are all expatriates and married to English men, hold rather vast fortunes from the States, and wished to put their combined funds to good use. They have set up an organisation called the American Women's War Relief Fund which has been in operation almost since the outbreak of the War."

"There can never be too much positive intent in the world," Furze smiled. "What does this fund aim to contribute to?"

"Well, it initially wished to sponsor an ambulance ship," continued Daw, becoming ever more animated at Furze's reception of her account, "but this proved to be an incredibly costly and time-consuming affair."

"Time and finance, two great enablers of progress," Furze added thoughtfully.

"Quite so! Therefore, in the interest of simplicity, they are looking to sponsor motor ambulances instead. Although they are a group of highly notable and reputable ladies, I offered any help they required from within my own social circles, to gather funds and expand knowledge of their cause."

"It couldn't be a better use of your time," Mrs. Wallis expounded proudly.

Furze couldn't agree more, and admired Daw's eagerness to contribute. She could quite easily have attempted to forget the War and the horrors of the Front. Instead, this wonderful woman was playing her part, contributing in whatever way she felt she could.

"It's an admirable plan," he reassured her, his words supporting her initiative with the strength of a cathedral's foundations. "If there is one thing we need more than anything else out on the Front, apart from good quality tea," Mrs. Wallis gave a wry smile, "it is medical support. If you and your friends can enable the provision of some motor ambulances, you will be making more of a difference than you can ever know."

Furze glanced at his watch and stood up to take his leave. As they made their way to the front door, Daw noticed his light frame. "Are you sure you're quite well, Keith? You could always request further time off, to ensure you return to the Front with your whole strength recovered. Is that not what your commanders would want?"

Furze adored her care for his wellbeing but knew he could stay in England no longer. "I'm quite recovered, don't you worry. Retain your focus for the War Relief Fund, something tells me that will be rather a time-consuming initiative."

Daw looked at him, her face flushed, remembering the fear he had expressed earlier and committing to supporting him as much as possible in her letters. Nothing she said could stop him from returning to the Front, but she would provide what light relief she could through her accounts of life at home. Unable to grasp the words to express how she truly felt, she released him to the War saying nothing at all, leaving a simple mascot in his grasp for good luck.

Furze walked home, picked up his kit, and said his good-byes to Herbert and Mary. His parents had done this time after time with both him and his older brother, Douglas, but that didn't mean it was any less painful.

"Be strong Keith," Mary bid, carefully embracing her son. She wished with all her heart to hold him close to her for the rest of time, safe and protected from the world.

"We'll keep things in order until you return son," Herbert added, "remember, if there's anything you need out there, just let us know."

As Furze's taxi departed for Waterloo station, he turned to catch a final glimpse of the two people who had raised him. Herbert held Mary tightly in his arms, her head pressed into his chest, her shoulders heaving with heavy sobs. Furze thought about telling the driver to stop to return to his mother and tell her everything would be fine. But he knew he could not. The only way to bring his mother peace was to live out this war, to win. The only option he had was to fight. He tore himself away from the tiny figures dwindling into the distance behind him, tiny needles of pain puncturing his heart, and sped towards the Western Front with Daw's little mascot clutched tightly in his hand.

Charterhouse Hodgesonites Cricket XI 1905

The Soldier

"Stayed in bed all morning as I was tired and the sea was rough."

Thursday 14th January, 1915.

To Furze's dismay, the water in the Channel kicked up a devilish surge that night as he crossed from Southampton to Le Havre, jolting him back to consciousness whenever he managed to drift off. His patience was tested every time he was jarred back to reality, the morning sun drifting into his tiny cabin only to be met with a grimace and a few expletives.

"Why, of all the short crossings one has to make," muttered Furze, his head rolling with the swell, "is the English Channel so God-awful…"

By 2:30 pm the mail boat finally arrived at Le Havre where Furze, relieved to be on a platform that wasn't throwing him about like a rag-doll, disembarked and made his way to the nearest British Army office.

"Good afternoon!" Furze flung into the air as one would a cricket ball. Attempting to stroll through the front porch of the little office he, instead, swerved into the doorframe.

"Good afternoon, Sir," replied an orderly, ever so slightly taken aback at the young officer's uncoordinated entry, but catching the ball nonetheless. "Everything alright?"

Furze, steadying himself and collecting his thoughts, attempted a smile but found his head spinning.

"Ah, choppy crossing was it, Sir?" Nodded the orderly knowingly. "Here take a seat and I'll get your papers. What's the name?"

"Thank you kindly, the name is Lieutenant Keith Furze, 3rd. The Queen's, Royal West Surrey Regiment," he murmured, grateful for the seat. "Choppy doesn't begin to cut it...the journey was dire."

"I guess that's why there's a Navy, Sir, we don't all have sea legs," quipped the orderly, as he hurriedly checked through some papers.

Smiling a little at this, Furze raised his head. The room began to sway uncomfortably once again.

"Any news?" Furze asked, to mask his discomfort.

"A little, Sir. The French offensive in the Champagne region is still raging on, apparently the Germans are well entrenched. Oh, and H.M.S Formidable was sunk in the Channel on the first of this very month." A file flew across the room. "Headquarters has been pumping as many troops across the channel as possible recently. They all arrive at a number of different ports, but we have borne the brunt of it this past week. You're lucky to have come during a moment of relative peace."

As the orderly communicated this, a flurry of other young officers burst through the front entrance and started rambling their respective requests. Handing Furze his next set of orders, the orderly gave him a wry smile which Furze returned. "First stop, Rouen."

"We've halted the Germans," noted the Adjutant at the holding camp just outside of Rouen, "but only with a constant stream of fresh troops flowing through camps such as this one."

This news both encouraged and worried Furze. As pleasing as it was to know that the Germans had been halted, he wondered at the sustainability of pumping ship after ship, train after train, of reinforcements to a front line where they seemed to disappear as silently as morning dew in summer. Were the Germans having to do the same, simply to maintain their seemingly unstoppable advance? The Adjutant directed him to his division's depot, reminding him to remain there and await further orders. It was here that his thoughts were interrupted by the welcome voice of an old friend of his, Lieutenant Alexander Garmin, an officer Furze had served with before he was injured.

"And how is Daw? Still as sweet as ever?" Enquired Garmin.

"Sweeter," replied Furze. "It was simply rotten having to leave her this time, especially given how much she looked after me when I returned from the Front. It's strange Alex, when I'm with her the world seems clearer, I understand things with greater ease. I feel I have a purpose in this war to protect her from what's out there, and to return to her, if I can." These words brought a wealth of memories flooding into Furze's mind, of Daw's concerned look as he departed, of his parents' embrace, and these caused a flood of emotions to resurface.

Garmin smiled warmly at his friend's words, and also observed the concern behind each one. He had always admired Furze's positivity, and if there was one thing Daw had done to help Furze during this ghastly war, it was to increase that positivity to entirely new levels. With greater peaks come greater troughs, though, and he prayed his friend would be able to handle the lows that were sure to come.

In his room that evening Furze wrote a letter to Daw, informing her of his safe arrival in France and sending her Garmin's best wishes. Although there was little to encourage her of his safety whilst at war, he was sure that the news of his friend being close at hand would give her some strength. Lying in bed a little later, staring at the blank grey ceiling above him, he suddenly found himself questioning his own strength of mind. How weak, how feeble he appeared to himself when he considered the enormity of existence, the scale of the war he was a tiny part of. *I feel as though I am running with my arms tied behind my back towards a precipice, my only escape being a ledge I will be incapable of grabbing.* He shivered nervously, uncertainty seeping through his veins and chilling his bones.

There was the fear he had expressed to his mother, expressed to Daw, centred around his seeming inability to alter what appeared to be the inevitable demise of some, or all, of the opportunities present in a life without conflict.

He sat up in bed and rubbed his face violently. "Pull yourself together man." He muttered, and as he ran his hands up and down his thighs nervously, he came upon the little mascot Daw had given him. He pulled it from his pocket and stared at it. Slowly, mercifully, he allowed warmer thoughts of their time together to gently, soothingly, massage his concerns into oblivion.

The next day Furze was immensely pleased to find that two further friends of his, Lieutenants Charles Leader and Eddie Brookes, had also just arrived in the holding camp.

"Glad you have deigned to return to work, Furzzy," Leader jibed, as they tucked into lunch together. "Although we've been doing quite well without you."

Furze smiled. "So I hear, in fact, as you're doing so well on your own, I've already booked my return ferry home."

The group chuckled. "How did you get here?" asked Leader.

"On the postal boat, of all things," Furze replied. "It was an awful journey."

"That brings a whole new meaning to the phrase, being posted out to France,," grinned Brookes. "You never did have an affinity for the sea and I've only just returned from leave myself," he reflected. "The family send their regards Furzzy, of course, they never fail to ask about you. I must admit, I do tend to feel terribly at odds with things when at home, knowing so many of my friends and fellow officers are fighting over here. It just doesn't sit right with me to take too much time away, as challenging as things are on the Front.

"I know what you mean," nodded Furze.

The group continued their conversation until Leader and Garmin were both called away, leaving Brookes and Furze alone to discuss more personal topics. Although Furze had a great deal of time for his other two friends, it was Eddie Brookes he was closest to, both of them having been close since their time together at Charterhouse School.

"Do you recall your time there?" asked Furze.

"Vividly," responded Brookes, "it was a mix of terror and blissfully distracting activity. Do you remember those ghastly runs the school made us do?"

"Pontifex!" Recalled Furze. "A short race, all things considered, but that dastardly hill at the end made one wish to simply bury oneself and be done with it."

"Death drop…" Brookes added.

"That's the one, it led straight up from the valley surrounding the school, almost vertically. The taller runners sprang up it like whippets, whilst the rest of us clawed our way to the top as though scaling a fortress wall. I could have sworn our legs got shorter the higher we got."

"When one got to the top, though, and saw the bell-tower of Gownboys House from across the cricket pitch, you didn't half feel proud," Brookes said.

"Those events certainly helped us understand how to push through our limits," mused Furze, "we can count ourselves lucky on that front given our current situation." He looked over at his friend, who appeared lost in the memories. "I was thinking about our time there just before returning from leave, a large part of who I am today was moulded at Charterhouse."

"I'd agree with you there," murmured Brookes, casting his thoughts into a whirlpool of memory. "It's certainly the reason why I try and appreciate the little treasures life hands to you."

"You have always been calm and composed," Furze responded, "I can't recall a single moment when you haven't seemed in control."

"Façades are a powerful ally," sighed Brookes, the laughter lines to the sides of his eyes revealing a wisdom far beyond his years. "I think I have been petrified for most of my life."

Furze was perplexed, he had never considered such a calm, reflective man as Brookes to be frightened by anything. Yet, this dramatic realisation suddenly exposed one of life's indubitable truths: fear knows everybody's name.

"I had no idea...to me, you were the person I looked to precisely because you seemed to take everything in your stride."

"I know, Furzzy, and that's exactly what I wanted you to do," sighed Brookes. "I found meaning in supporting others by acting indifferent to challenging situations. You could say that it was the strength you found in my apparent character that gave me the determination to keep going when things were tough. In reality, the strength you thought was mine was always your own. It was simply reflected back at you."

Furze was unwilling to allow his friend to deny his own abilities. "You know that not everyone could have done what you did. That strength of character was not a façade, it was always your natural state. You just hadn't realised that at the time, so it appeared as though it was something false, a simple overlay to deflect life's challenges."

"I'm glad you're back Furzzy," Brookes almost whispered.

"I'm glad you're here," Furze replied, "there are only a few people I know who I can have such unfeigned conversations with."

As enjoyable as these conversations were, the War was never far away and, a few days later, Furze received a letter detailing his posting to the 2nd Battalion The Queen's. Soon after, Garmin and Leader left the camp for the Front with a draft of forty men.

"I'll see you out there," Brookes stated as he ordered his draft towards the station. "It won't be long until we're all enjoying the hospitality of German rounds, instead of the French locals."

"Always an event I look forward to." Furze grimaced, as his friend departed. "Look after yourself my dear fellow, try not to get killed before I catch up with you."

"I'll do my best," laughed Brookes, although the way in which he surveyed Furze expressed darker fears. "We'll be okay Furzzy, think of the War as death drop at the end of Pontifex. It may take the wind from our lungs, but we'll get through it. England is our Gownboys bell-tower, and we'll see it in no time."

There was never very much more to say during these moments. One man may be ordered sooner to the Front than another, but all knew that their arrival at this brutal destination was inevitable. Fate, not time, was master there.

Eventually, after a week of waiting impatiently at the reserve encampment, the remaining portions of the 7th Division, under Furze's command, caught the train to Le Havre before marching a further four-and-a-half miles to their new camp.

"Sir, what's the next encampment like?" asked one of the soldiers marching next to Furze.

"Better than the trenches," replied Furze with a smile, as he looked back at the soldier and his nearby fellow officers. "If you're lucky, you might even get breakfast in bed."

The experienced soldiers grinned, the fresher ones grinned expectantly, both encouraged by his joviality for different reasons. Furze had learned the invaluable importance of keeping morale high on the way to the Front. Many of the young soldiers around him were going there for the first time, their minds ripe with stories of horror, for those seemed to be the only stories men brought back.

As the troops settled into their new surroundings, Furze's mood positively bloomed with the unexpected arrival of his closest friend, Captain James Fuller. He had been serving alongside Furze in the 7th Division and the two were practically inseparable when posted anywhere together. Having both grown up in the same neighbourhood in London, they had known each other for as long as either could remember, forming a bond that transcended description. Perhaps as a result, Fuller was very similar to Furze. A positive mindset, even in the most testing of times, he was one of those individuals who seemed impeccably dressed for every occasion, a trait Furze shared, further deepening their respect for one another. It was true that there were those who took Fuller's qualities and self-confidence for arrogance, and Furze often feared where his friend's 'overcome all odds' attitude might lead him. However, first and foremost Fuller was a loyal and fierce friend, Furze and he being men after each other's hearts; two beings seemingly forged from one and the same metal.

"My goodness, it's good to see you," resounded Furze, as they embraced for the first time in months.

"Likewise, Furzzy," Fuller responded, examining his oldest friend. "I'm very pleased you've recovered, I was incredibly worried about you when I last saw you. One never likes to see anyone carted off on a stretcher, and you looked…spectral."

"You were far too kind, checking in on me so often. Although I appreciated every visit as the hospital is inexorably dull."

"Well, you looked so unbearably miserable cooped up in that bed, and misery doesn't become you. I felt it my duty to remove such emotion from your face."

Furze smiled; he hadn't realised how much he had missed Fuller's company.

"Do you remember much from the event?" Fuller enquired.

"Not really." Furze contemplated a moment. "My memory is patchy at best, it's one of the reasons I keep a diary, but I remember less than usual about that period. One moment I was bedding down for the night in the Headquarters building, the next I was being carried to the field hospital on a stretcher. I remember I was in agony, but other than saying I had severe shrapnel wounds the medics wouldn't divulge any more."

"I imagine they didn't want to worry you," Fuller suggested.

Furze returned his comment with an appreciative smile. "You always look for the positive, don't you? Well, regardless, it took me a long while to get back onto my feet. I must have appeared a haggard husk of a man to my parents when I limped off the train."

"Poor Herbert and Mary, we think we have it rough but I cannot imagine being a parent during this period. I pity your parents especially, given how loving they have always been, they never failed to make me feel welcome in your home," Fuller reflected.

"You're a surrogate son to them, they'd likely adopt you if they hadn't their hands full already with my four siblings and I!" The pair chuckled jovially. "Anyway, how have you been?"

"As well as one can be." Fuller then dived into his activities since Furze's departure. "The men were a handful without your help, but they pulled through. The rest of the battle at Ypres was a sordid affair, that's for sure. As much as we are currently holding the Germans at bay, we are very much on the defensive. Each time we gain ground on one section of the line, we lose ground on another. Calling the situation a stalemate doesn't quite cut it. You've seen the number of reinforcements being pumped to the Front?"

"I have," Furze assented, "fresh drafts every day."

"Quite, and that is characteristic of our current situation. The Germans are like a large boulder, rolling downhill. We are the structure holding the boulder in place, for now, but we are a structure requiring constant repair. Take the structure away, and the boulder will cascade onwards; that's what the Front is currently like."

Furze quietly studied his friend's face. Within it he still saw the same remarkable untapped enthusiasm, but also seemed to have been tempered by his recent experiences. "Are you alright, Fuller?"

Fuller thought for a moment before replying. "I think so Furzzy, at least in comparison to most. Nobody can spend time out here without being affected in some way, and you know me, ever trying to be the optimist. The last few tours in the trenches have been horrid, though, I guess I'm struggling like so many others, to see an end to this bloody engagement. Anyway, how are things at home?"

Furze thought about delving deeper into Fuller's musings, then decided instead to shift the conversation on to happier topics and explore them again at another time. He mentioned his time with Daw and Fuller's face lit up.

"Well, let me know when you and Daw decide to tie the knot," Fuller said with a grin, "and I'll send a letter to the German High Command ordering them to pause the war."

Furze blushed. "Don't suggest such things, Daw and I... well...it's far from that."

"I'm joking, dear fellow." Fuller smiled, striking his friend on the back as he rose from his seat. "Though your reaction is fascinating."

"What does that mean?" Furze exclaimed, following his friend out.

"Nothing at all, nothing at all, just hold onto that happiness, Furzzy, for the both of us."

Eventually, Furze received orders to take a draft of the 1st Battalion South Staffordshire Regiment up to the Front with Fuller, from where they would both join The Queen's. As fate would have it, their departure was accompanied by an unwelcome flurry of sleet and snow. The officers reluctantly proceeded onto the parade square, where the soldiers from the 1st Battalion S. Staffordshire Regiment looked cold, wet, and miserable.

Furze and Fuller were rather cold and miserable themselves, hardly looking forward to the long journey ahead of them and worrying over what this grim weather would mean for conditions on the Front. *The trenches are going to be appalling.* Furze thought to himself as he surveyed the shivering troops in front of him. Some of them stood stock still, snow resting upon their unmoving shoulders, their grim faces turned in his and Fuller's direction. These were the veterans, the soldiers who had already seen the horrors in store and either knew how to face them or were already too dejected to care. Others shivered, stamped their feet, and struggled to get all their kit on. These were the new soldiers, fresh from basic training and utterly unaware of the hell they were slowly pitifully being marched towards.

Fuller was also surveying the waiting troops, a similar look on his face. "They look as though they could use some encouragement," he suggested.

"I think we could use some encouragement," Furze responded, before gathering himself, "but, I guess we don't get that luxury."

"Better snap to it then, authority or humour?" quipped Fuller.

"Humour." Returned Furze, as they locked glances, knowing precisely what was needed. "The time for authority will be upon us soon enough." Back on operations, the two friends revelled in each other's company, and dashed towards the soaking soldiers.

"How are we this morning men? British High command has decided that one Christmas was not enough for us this year, so they have sent in some snow to mark the occasion," blasted Furze, attempting to wipe away the chill of the morning with enthusiasm which he hoped would be infectious. The soldiers turned their attention to him, perking up as they began engaging with the young officers they were to follow to the Front. Although dripping wet, the sight of Fuller and Furze, equally sodden but still smiling, brought them some comfort.

"I would have preferred a supply truck of warm socks and gloves," rejoined one.

"Socks and gloves!" mocked another. "What use would they be against the German guns?"

"More use than your sodding aim," quipped a third.

"Speak for yourself," the second soldier retorted, "you try aiming at a German with frostbitten fingers."

Marching the three miles to Montevilliers the draft boarded the awaiting troop train and prepared for their twenty-four-hour journey. It would take a number of days before they reached their Regiments.

Fuller grimaced. "Well, it's a good thing I foresaw such a journey and prepared for all eventualities!" As he said this, he opened up a crate that had just been delivered to their compartment, revealing a copious quantity of supplies to keep them content during the long journey. Furze had no idea how Fuller managed to do it, but whatever the situation, no matter the cost, he made life bearable for those around him.

The Friend

"The train was the longest I have ever seen, containing 41 carriages and about 1,500 troops."

Sunday 31st January.

The train trundled onwards through Montevilliers and Le Havre, allowing its cargo a brief moment of respite at Rouen before ploughing on into the night.

"I feel as though we're cattle..." grumbled Furze, his head jolting against the side of the carriage.

"Meat to the slaughter," Fuller responded dryly, "come to think of it, cattle may have it better."

"How so?" queried Furze.

"They don't have to march as much as we do." The pair let out sarcastic laughter.

"Transport does seem to be in short supply here," Furze contemplated, "after all this time I had hoped we would have better ways of travelling across the Front."

"It doesn't bode well, does it..." Fuller agreed. "It's hard enough remaining strong and motivated when one is in the trenches. Arriving tired and demotivated after marching for miles and miles doesn't help."

"We can only hope that the Germans have it worse," Furze suggested, "just think, we're operating over friendly ground, they're attempting to do the same over enemy territory."

At Merville, Fuller and Furze detrained and marched their drafts of the 7th and 8th Divisions the twenty miles to their next destination.

"Do you know where The Queen's are currently located?" queried a weary Furze, as he handed the Stafford's draft to its Adjutant.

"They're currently in the trenches, but will be relieved tomorrow for a four-day rest," the Adjutant replied, "so you'll be able to link up with them then. For now, you should get some sleep, you look no better than the men."

This, Furze determined to do. As luck would have it, Fuller and he had been billeted in the transport barn for the night, and the individual in charge, Transport Sergeant Lea, had kindly lent Furze a horse to use on the two-way journey to hand over the Stafford's. As he stuck his left foot into the stirrup and attempted to haul himself onto the horse, a searing pain shot through his knee.

"Blast," he muttered, lowering himself down again, "not quite healed yet, have you?"

Clutching the horse's reins in his right hand, he massaged his knee with the left, attempting to soothe the pinpricks of pain pulsing from it. It made him uneasy. *If this is how you react to a march, I dread to think what you'll be like in the trenches.* A part of him desperately wanted to learn about what had occurred that night, in part to understand the potential extent of his injury, and partially to seek the justification for such a potentially deadly inconvenience. He might have escaped death once, but the irony of this injury taking his life because he was unable to move swiftly enough under enemy fire was not lost on him. Slowly, the discomfort began to ease, *I'll have to be careful.*

Mounting successfully on the second attempt, he made his way back, registering muck and mud in every direction. News from the Front was that the trenches were absolutely wretched, and Furze didn't get much joy from being back in the thick of it. He could not help feeling that both sides were mustering their strength for something monumental.

Something's coming, he brooded, *and I'd hazard it won't be pretty.*

Whatever was in store, Furze's spirits continued to be bolstered by every friend he re-encountered upon his return. At Fleurbaix, Furze and Fuller ran into Lieutenant Bobbie Ross who was close to them both. Incredibly well-read, Bobbie had a penchant for retaining knowledge, and Furze enjoyed his friend most of all when he was recounting a dash of epistemology he had picked up from a recent novel. Generally, this occurred over a glass of single malt whisky, Bobbie oozing the passion he had felt from reading the compelling narrative, and Furze playing Devil's Advocate to encourage some heated debate.

What Furze lacked in learning, Bobbie more than made up for and when it came to leadership, Bobbie took great pleasure in absorbing more than a thing or two from his friend. In fact, this was one of his main discomforts. Although a highly capable leader, Bobbie didn't like taking command of large bodies of troops, being far more comfortable surrounded by a small, select group of soldiers he could manage individually. Perhaps underlying this was a lack of trust in anyone being able to live up to his exacting standards. Alternatively, being a perfectionist, it might have been a fear of being unable to live up to them himself.

"Quite the journey, it seems," Bobbie commented, turning to Furze, "you must have taken the scenic route."

"It's quite a sight, seeing so many troops being moved across such large distances," agreed Furze. "You're lucky you caught us at the time you did, turns out we made better time than we anticipated."

"For that, I'm incredibly grateful, as it has given us the chance to see one another, if only for a moment."

"Ever generous with your hospitality as well, Bobbie," Fuller added, raising his tea cup in thanks.

"Always a pleasure," Bobbie raised his cup in return. "It's immensely good to see you all looking so well, especially you, Furzzy. We were all rather concerned when we heard you had been shipped home."

"My thanks, I shan't say it's good to be back, but I am glad to be with you all once again. I hate the thought of leaving you here, reaping all the glory!"

"If only there was glory to be reaped," snorted Fuller, "that would make things more bearable."

"Come now, Fuller, don't be a pessimist," chuckled Bobbie, "I can think of no greater glory than wallowing in the mud for King and Country!"

The group enjoyed the jovially ironic conversation for a while longer before Fuller and Furze took their leave. They headed to the Adjutant, Captain Bates, who expressed evident relief at their arrival.

"You couldn't have come at a better time, chaps," said Bates, who already knew them. "Although it's been quiet here lately, the men have been working tirelessly building up the trenches and some fresh leadership will do them good."

"I'm glad we can help! Has it really been as quiet as we have heard?" asked Furze.

"Yes indeed, we haven't seen much of the Germans over these last few weeks, but that is making the men jumpy. Mind you, Headquarters isn't much better. We are expecting an attack by the Germans at any time, so we are all on edge, and that is draining morale."

Fuller nodded at these words, "what about our plans Captain, are we likely to head over the top any time soon?"

"Nothing confirmed yet, Fuller, but I shouldn't think it long before we make a move given the number of reinforcements we have been sent recently. Your drafts are some of the last to arrive."

Fuller and Furze exchanged glances as Bates pointed them towards the cottage near Brigade Headquarters where they were to spend the night.

"Some of the last to arrive…" mumbled Furze, allowing his thoughts to voice themselves to Fuller.

"By my reckoning," calculated Fuller, "that means we're likely to be making an attack in the coming weeks."

"Or, we are expecting an attack very soon," added Furze, "and a large one at that. It's not characteristic of the Germans to remain quiet for so long."

"Either way, if we're some of the last to arrive, it means our lines have never been stronger. Whether we attack or defend, we couldn't have arrived at a better time in my view." Fuller smiled, as he and Furze entered the little cottage.

To their mutual pleasure, the two friends had both been assigned to 'B' Company, which was currently in first reserve billets. To better understand the current state of the British trenches, Furze made a visit to that part of the line to which the Stafford's draft had been sent. The mud was absolutely terrible, and Furze got stuck several times on his journey. He marvelled at the fact that, in places, the British and German lines were only one-hundred yards apart, meaning he could quite clearly hear the Germans talking over and above the ominous growling of their incessant troop transport trucks. *Replenishments of food, ammunition, barbed wire, fresh troops...* he pondered, *one can only assume the Germans are reinforcing their lines as heavily as we are.* He turned his ear to the British lines, straining to determine which side's transports produced the greater rumble. Was it his imagination, or did the German lines throw out a stronger discordant mixture of sound?

He spotted an orderly crossing his path. "Any news?"

"Only rumours, I hear that a great number of Allied guns is massing, just as we have seen with the recent troop drafts."

"Interesting," muttered Furze, "their objective?"

"As I understand it," the orderly replied, "to bombard Lille, which is supposedly sheltering a fresh German Army Corps."

Furze entered the tiny room he was sharing with three other officers and perched on a chair to write a letter to Daw.

Dear Daw,

I miss you terribly. Things here are progressing as well as one can expect at present, and I remain greatly encouraged by the presence of Fuller, Bobbie, and Brookes. Fuller sends his fondest regards and I feel things would be far less bearable without his company.

I cannot express too much on our movements, for obvious reasons, but I feel both sides are preparing for something big. At the forefront of my mind is, who will make the first move? Attacks are an inevitability of war, not that this fact makes the thought of them any more appealing.

Do tell me about your happenings at home when you next get the chance to write. When I next see a field ambulance, I shall think of you and wonder if it's one of the ones you and your War Relief Fund has contributed to. Of course, there is no way of telling, but you might allow me the liberty to wonder.

Keep well, dear Daw,
Keith.

This activity gave his troubled mind a moment's respite before, as night made its dark descent, there began the sounds of gunfire from the section of the trenches surrounding La Bassée, to the right of Furze's current position.

Has it begun? he wondered drowsily. *If not yet, then soon.*

The sun shone with a glorious winter force on the next day and it was most welcome, for the Battalion was required to parade at 11:00 am to be inspected by the Commanding Officer.

Without warning, the British guns on their right and left flanks opened up a fearfully heavy cannonade, the shells ripping through silence of the inspection as easily as they ripped through the air. The chatter of rifle and machine gun fire followed from the direction of Armentiers.

A young Lieutenant rushed over to the officers making the inspection. "Orders, gentlemen, from Headquarters," he stated, breathless, "the men are to be made ready to move at a moment's notice."

The disturbance turned out to be nothing more than a minor firefight and not the attack that every man in The Queen's expected. They all gratefully returned to general duties for the next few days and Captain O'Connor, the Brigade Signaling Officer, asked if Furze could cover for him in a few weeks' time when he went on leave. Lying in bed on Friday night, Furze listened for the sound of gunfire in the distance, wondering if he would get any sleep. *Not a sound,* he thought, immensely comforted as, the next morning, The Queen's was to relieve the Staffords in the trenches at 6:00 am.

As soon as he stepped outside the following morning the heavens opened and rain poured down upon the waiting troops. *Just my luck,* shivered Furze to himself, wrapping his overcoat more tightly around him. The Front seemed to drain his energy, for no matter how much sleep he got, no matter how much food he consumed, he lived in a perpetual world of physical and mental strain.

Interacting as little as possible whilst still retaining a commanding presence, he led his platoon to a small trench slightly detached from the rest of 'B' Company and separated from 'C' Company by about twenty-five yards of swamp. It felt rotten being back, the surrounding mud and grime helping to wrap him in a blanket of damp chill. As he wandered through his men, checking they had settled in as best they could and taken up their defensive positions, he caught snatches of disdainful conversation.

"Trust 'em to give us the worst trench..." growled one soldier.

"The other lads must 'av it better, the stench in 'ere is horrid," spat another, attempting to wipe mud from his already caked sleeves.

Although he did his best to console them, he could hardly disagree with their observations. Their proximity to the swamp on their right did little to make conditions any better, the mud getting deeper and the stench hanging more heavily the closer one got to it. Walking up and down, surrounded by such a foul environment, he huffed and plunged his hands deep into the pockets of his trench coat. The left one met an object he had not expected to find there, and he drew out, as if by design, a neat little letter. Intrigued, he hopped into cover, and pulled the paper from the envelope. It was from Daw, he recognised the writing instantly and his soul sprang as though touched by an electric charge.

Although he had already read it, touching the page he knew she had touched brought him both energy and peace as his eyes caressed the words she had intended only for him. Refolding and returning it carefully into the pocket which had now become a vault of great importance, he trudged onwards, feeling emboldened.

Furze stood his platoon to at 6:15 am, but nothing much occurred all day. Every now and then, a German sniper took a pot shot at the men but, thankfully, disturbed only the soil it struck. As the day progressed, a letter arrived with orders that required him to call a sergeant he trusted.

"We're to conduct a reconnaissance party," he announced, watching the Sergeant's reaction closely.

"Now, Sir?" asked the Sergeant in a fashion so matter-of-fact it was almost blunt. This was just the sort of attitude he was looking for. Conducting a reconnaissance over a trench parapet and towards the German lines called for no room for error and no questioning of orders.

"Precisely, this evening," Furze replied with surety. "We aren't far from the German line, you can hear their conversations from behind our current position, and Headquarters want us to see what intelligence we can gather." In his mind, Furze had already come to the conclusion that an assault was inevitable and, although his gut squirmed with nerves, gaining a greater understanding of the German position would only help his men carry out their attack.

The Sergeant nodded. "How many men should I gather?"

"Two others, we shall move more quickly in a small group and four will be plenty."

"Yes, Sir, I'll gather them now," the Sergeant saluted as he moved to depart. Suddenly he stopped, his commander's words sinking in. "We, Sir? You comin' with us?" Forgetting his formality, he added, " 'pologies, Sir, meant no disrespect."

"As you were, Sergeant, I shall be leading the reconnaissance," Furze smiled. "I would never ask anyone under my command to do something I wouldn't do myself."

"As you like, Sir," responded the Sergeant, saluting with an inquisitive look before departing to fulfil his duties.

After sundown, having briefed the small body of troops and handed command over to one of his subordinates, Furze and the three soldiers crept quietly up and over the side of the trench. The night was, thankfully, dry and the air cool and crisp. Every sound seemed to echo across the entire Front in that moment as he placed his boots carefully and deliberately on each rung of the wooden ladder. Progress, even out of the trench, was delicate and slow, each man aware of the importance of maintaining a low profile as they approached the parapet. At the top of the ladder, Furze slid onto his belly and waited, immobile, peering into the black in front of him, barely breathing.

Nothing. Not a sound.

"Clear," he exhaled almost inaudibly, and the other three soldiers followed him up one by one. Although the stench from the nearby swamp still groped their lungs the air was instantly clearer. Lying side by side, bellies to the ground and facing the German lines, the small party proceeded to crawl tentatively forwards. Their progress was painfully slow, bodies flush to the floor as they inched across the boggy potholed ground. Within minutes, all four men were completely filthy. Furze's hands had become numb, yet his forehead was dripping with sweat. His lungs were working hard, pumping air to the muscles in his arms that were pulling him, and those in his legs that were pushing him forwards. His left knee hit something hard, possibly a rock, hopefully just a rock, and pain javelined through to his spine. Water seeped from his eyes as he controlled himself, trying hard not to curse at the unexpected shock of pain. He stopped crawling, focusing all his attention on controlling his breathing; head low, fists clenched, staring brutally and spitefully at an indistinguishable point on an unintelligible horizon. The men either side of him watched for his movement, having stopped when he stopped, wondering what he had seen.

Blasted shrapnel, Furze thought, picturing the German shell that had originally caused his injury, *you didn't kill me then, and you won't kill me now*. The crawl resumed, yet he paused every few minutes to slow his breathing and refocus on the moment so as not to be heard by the German troops in the still night air. After a couple of hours, he brought the whole group to rest and peered into the dark ahead of him.

That's it, he thought, silently, *that's the enemy's barbed wire. We can't be more than forty yards from it.* He gestured carefully towards the wire, signalling to the others to wait and observe. One by one, each man carefully settled himself into a more comfortable position and watched in the threatening gloom for about half an hour. A single noise too loud, a single movement too obvious, and the German lines would erupt in mortal response. Silence, however, turned out to be their fifth companion that night and darkness their sixth, for nothing of note was audible nor visible to any of them.

Eventually, given the length of time it would take for them to crawl back, Furze signalled for the group to return to the British lines. He did his best to subdue the severe feelings of dismay and annoyance he felt at having gathered little to no information, and he could feel his temper rise in tune with his body temperature as the painfully slow crawl resumed.

Blast them! Did they know? Did they hear something and lie silently so as to give nothing away? He was incredibly frustrated and became only more so when he realised how irrational he was being.

Of course they didn't know, or they would have shot us, he reasoned, before his mind turned its critical eye to his own actions.

Did I miss something? If the Sergeant had led the party, would it have been more successful? Ripples of self-doubt shuddered throughout his exhausted body, and it was all he could do to focus on inching through the mud instead of leaping up and throwing a rock at the German lines just to encourage a reaction, anything of note from this brooding viper. Eventually, one by one, the filthy, exhausted soldiers slithered over the British parapet and into the trench, immensely grateful to have returned safely.

"Well done men," he nodded to his three grubby companions, "a shame not to have recorded anything but you were all as silent as ghosts."

"Thank you, Sir. Dismissed." The Sergeant nodded to the two soldiers, before turning once more to Furze aware of his obviously suppressed anger. "You led us back safely, Sir, we're all grateful for that." He then saluted and followed the path of the trench.

At midnight the next day, Furze made his way out of the trench and onto the road leading to Fleurbaix to take over as acting Brigade Signalling Officer from Captain O'Connor. It began to rain, but he no longer gave the weather any notice, allowing it to flood over his putrid uniform as he trudged along the lonely, soggy, cold route back to dry billets. The simplicity of the Sergeant's words the previous day had struck a chord with him, and a slight smile formed at the corners of his mouth as he walked, eventually stumbling, head-down, into Bobbie's room at 2:00 am.

"Do us a favour, old chap," he said, shaking Bobbie's huge frame from its slumber, and dropping his kit on the floor, "grab us a bed for the night, would you?"

Bobbie awoke to discover Furze standing over him, wet, shivering, and plastered in mud. He let out a bark of a laugh, his throat dry from sleep. "Been for a moonlit mud-bath have we Furzzy?" he jested.

The ridiculousness of the situation, and the comforting sound of his friend's voice, briefly brought a wild grin to Furze's face before he proceeded to fling off the remainder of his sodden clothing. Meanwhile, Bobbie prepared a bed for him, and Furze limped over to it. Whilst carefully gathering Furze's sprawled kit into a pile, Bobbie noticed Furze's limp and the way in which his friend's hand inadvertently massaged his left knee as he fell into the bed's warm folds.

He was about to speak but paused as he heard Furze let out a light snore. Looking at his friend, Bobbie was struck by Furze's condition, and frowned a little. He knew Furze held himself to the highest standards when it came to keeping his appearance smart and serious, so his turning up in such a bedraggled state concerned him. In addition, although he knew Furze had suffered badly from the wounds sustained at Ypres, he hadn't realised how much those wounds were still affecting him.

Is he unravelling? Bobbie wondered for a moment. Furze had never been a paradigm of physical prowess, but his strength of will was something Bobbie had never questioned. Yet, at that moment, lying muddied and exhausted with a rebellious knee, Furze appeared incredibly vulnerable.

Bringing himself out of his brooding stupor, Bobbie sighed, *the trenches are ghastly, what do I expect from a man who's just spent his night crawling over no-man's land. If the only unravelling Furze does is to take less care over his appearance, then that's hardly a concern.* Heading back to bed himself, he hoped that would be the extent of his friend's pain, but he was far from convinced.

The Window Sill
(5th-6th November)

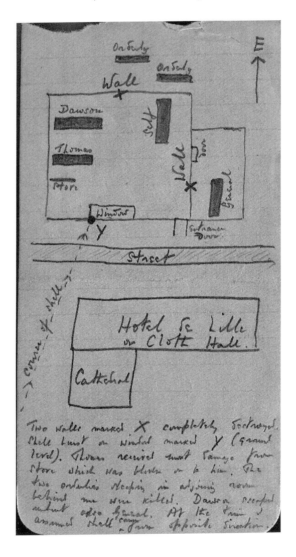

The Window Ledge

"At dinner the General told me in detail the exact happenings on the night of 5th-6th November – It was most interesting, and it made me realise still more what a damned lucky escape I had."

Tuesday 9th February.

Furze yawned in great satisfaction for what seemed like an eternity, before rolling out of bed to be confronted by the pile of a stinking muddy uniform he had deposited on the floor very early that morning. Initially, he was struck by how neatly it was stacked, before realising that Bobbie had likely been the one who had gathered it together. *Dear Bobbie,'* he thought with a touch of guilt, *I wonder where he has wandered off to?*

As if by design, he noticed a note on the side table by his bed.

> *Furzzy, Odysseus himself could not have*
> *awoken you this morning, so I thought it*
> *best to let you rest. I have duties to attend to*
> *in my Platoon, but I shall see you soon. B.*

Furze grabbed the soggy pile of clothing and headed for the wash house. He basked in the feeling of civility and cleanliness that swept over him as he wiped away the mud that caked his body and his clothes. It was as if the hardships of war were being washed away with every clump of dirt that dissolved into nothingness and drifted into insignificance.

Back to his usual presentable self, Furze strode to Brigade Headquarters, and was delighted to hear that he was to share a room with his friend, Charles Blount.

"Well this is a stroke of luck," Furze smiled, as he entered Charles' room.

"Luck has nothing to do with it, my friend," Charles responded, his frown vanishing as he rose in greeting, "when I was tasked with assigning you a room, there was never any question of where you would be."

"Well then, I thank you for it," Furze acknowledged.

"This desk shall be yours," Charles motioned to one by the far wall. "Tea?"

"Please," Furze nodded, taking a seat. "How have you been Charles?"

Charles gave Furze an easy look as he poured a second cup of steaming liquid from the flask beside him. He maintained formalities when on duty, even amongst friends, although Furze knew him well enough to notice how greatly he enjoyed having company.

"I've been well, certainly well enough not to complain about anything. Headquarters has been a hive of activity for weeks, organising the influx of all of these fresh drafts of troops, and that keeps me quite busy."

"That's very good to hear, we've amassed a large force," Furze noted, quite deliberately, taking the mug Charles offered him, and hoping his friend would have some information to share on the British plans.

"We have indeed," Charles assented, "and the General has now formed his complete Staff, meaning we can actually coordinate the Brigade's affairs properly."

At that moment, an orderly arrived and Charles' presence was requested elsewhere. "I'll be back shortly, Furzzy," he said apologetically as he followed the orderly out, "please, make yourself at home."

Furze seemed to have arrived during a bit of a lull as Headquarters was immensely quiet for the rest of the day. He caught up on a number of letters he had been meaning to write, before feeling the insatiably British urge to make himself a fresh brew. On his way back from the little kitchen used by the Staff Officers, Furze's eyes caught upon an object standing in the corner of an empty room.

Well, what are the chances? He smiled, doubling back and entering the room.

There, in perfect condition, was a little piano. His fingers itched; it had been so very long since he had had the chance to play. *Would anyone mind?* he wondered to himself, before deciding that given the current state of things a little light music would do everyone some good.

Presently, the soft chords drifted rhythmically around the building. A number of officers appeared at the doorway, drawn to the sounds as moths to a flame, taking a moment out of their war-torn existence to appreciate a delicate reminder of a life almost forgotten amidst such constant hostility. Eventually, the General appeared seeking the source of such an unusual stir.

Furze held the General in high regard, having served under his command at the 1st Battle of Ypres. The General had taken him under his wing and taught him a great deal in the months preceding, as well as during, that lengthy engagement. Thus, it didn't come as a surprise when the General invited Furze to dine with him that evening, primarily to relate to him the exact events of the night of the 5th of November 1914.

"You're lucky to be alive Furze," began the General. "There were six of us in the building that night. The shell killed two, seriously injured Thomas and you whilst miraculously leaving Dawson and I unharmed, if a little dazed."

"So, it was a shell then?" enquired Furze. "I assumed as much."

"It was indeed, thank God it wasn't a bigger shell with a more accurate trajectory. It hit a window ledge on the west side of the building and that redirected its course. We have that little ledge to thank for our lives…had it come straight through the window it would have detonated exactly in the middle of the room you were in, killing everyone in the building."

Furze shuddered, and the General took a sip of coffee.

"You will recall that you were sleeping in the same room as Dawson and Thomas?" asked the General.

"Yes," agreed Furze, racking his memory for the details, "and there were two orderlies in a room just behind mine whilst your own room was off to one side."

"Precisely," grunted the General. "When the shell hit that blessed window ledge, it fragmented and its trajectory shifted. Some of the shell went north, hitting a store cupboard that fell and seriously wounded Thomas. Other shell fragments flew south-east, these were the ones that wounded you, Furze."

Furze turned the General's description over in his mind, shuddering at the tiny twists of fate which had worked to save his life.

"The majority of the shell burst through the east wall of the building and into the room in which the two orderlies were sleeping. It killed them both."

"Poor souls," murmured Furze, stunned. He had been living with the results of this event for the past few months, cursing his injuries and attempting to understand why it was he who had to suffer such pain. Now, on hearing the General's description of an event which had stolen the lives of two others, he was shocked at how brutally fate chose its victims.

The General watched the reaction on the face of the young man in front of him.

"It should have been me," Furze suddenly articulated. "The window ledge didn't save a life, it just misdirected death to someone else. My life cost theirs…"

Furze stood up at that moment, running his hands through his hair and pacing to the window of the room they were dining in. Reaching out, he silently ran a hand over the window ledge in front of him, the embodiment of the object that had traded their lives for his own.

"Sit down Furze," the General directed calmly.

"One small moment, one chance dice-roll and this unforgiving conflict claims more lives." Furze's mind was racing over the catastrophe of loss. He seemed not to have heard the General.

"Furze!" The General remained calm, but his voice flung authority at the young officer. "Sit down, now!"

Drawn from his consternation, Furze promptly returned to his seat, embarrassed at his loss of rationality.

"Sir, my apologies, it's a lot to take in."

"No need to apologise Furze," responded the General, "simply regain your composure."

He had observed enough young men teetering on the brink of hopeless despair to know when a stern word was required to stop them from plunging themselves into its ruthless abyss.

"You have been through a great deal, and the reality of your brush with death was always likely to cause distress. That was why I asked that the medics spare you the details."

Furze looked at the General, shocked. "So, it was by your orders that I wasn't informed?"

"It was."

A mixture of emotions washed over Furze: anger, confusion, gratefulness. How should he react? He looked into the General's face, at the lines around his eyes and at the corners of his mouth. His thoughts struck momentarily on the fact that the face in front of him was suited far more to laughter than judgement and trusted that the General's furrows had been borne from good humour and kindheartedness, even if they had been deepened by stress and pain. This senior officer had Furze's best interests at heart, and he knew the right decision had been made.

"Thank you," Furze eventually exhaled. "Your decision allowed me the space to focus on my recovery, preparing me to face the event now with you to explain it truthfully. I'm grateful for that."

"Very good Furze," smiled the General, "too many soldiers blame themselves for the deaths of others, even when they had no control over the situation. I refuse to let you succumb to a grief that you don't deserve."

"But such small variables..." began Furze, before the General cut him off.

"Doesn't change the fact that, in this moment, you are here. You are alive." The General studied Furze with feeling. "To dwell on the past is to forget to live in the present. I lost two men that day, and I have accepted that because I'm grateful that the lives of my other three men were spared."

The General rose from his chair and Furze followed suit. "I'm glad you're back. Your life cost nobody else's. Furze, remember that."

Following the General's explanation of the events that had caused his injury, Furze's nerves were placated somewhat, and he went about his duties over the next few days with a greater sense of calm and purpose. After a few days of driving rain, another friend of Furze's, Lieutenant Guy Olliver, appeared as though washed in by the swell. One of the most emotionally intelligent people Furze knew, there was a devious smile glinting from under his friend's dark curls, which had matted themselves stubbornly against his forehead.

"How do you manage it, Guy?" Furze observed, an eyebrow raised in mock suspicion. "You always turn up at the most unlikely of moments. It's great to see you!"

"That would be telling," Guy responded, picking up Furze's overcoat with mischievous ease, his eyes burning with the plan hatching in his mind.

"Surely not today, Guy," sighed Furze, "the weather has been dire..."

"My dear fellow," Guy mocked, approaching his friend with the overcoat poised as a gladiator's net, "if you barricade yourself indoors at the slightest hint of rain you will ruin this jolly getaway for the both of us. Who ever visited France without doing just a little sightseeing? Plus, I know a great cathedral you will simply adore."

"You're incorrigible," relented Furze, his curiosity getting the better of him, silently appreciative of his friend's penchant for activity. He donned his coat with feigned reluctance and followed Guy's lead.

Guy led them to the nearby village of Fleurbaix where they visited a cathedral Furze thought was quite exquisite. The village was eerily quiet, the cathedral standing tall against a backdrop of tiny houses a protective sentinel keeping watch over its surroundings.

"I suppose that's what it was partially designed for," mulled Guy, when Furze voiced this thought. "Given that it represents a higher power, one that supposedly protects those who believe in it. Constructing a building so imposing, so vastly superior to those around it, emulates that sentiment."

"There's laudable logic in that," agreed Furze, "removing religion from the equation, though, it's an impressive piece of architecture nonetheless."

They began to make their departure, deep in thought, moments before the unmistakable roar of the German guns was heard. Shells began dropping into the village.

"Run!" Roared Furze over the noise of the shells exploding just behind them.

Bricks, roof tiles, and shards of concrete sheared off the buildings, as they ran, scything through the air and smashing against their counterparts across the streets.

"Up that road, hurry," panted Guy, "that's the route we took in, get to the top of the hill."

They slammed to a halt, breathless and shaken, but safe upon a nearby ridge. Turning back, they took stock of the damage the little village had sustained wondering whether its stalwart defender would be able to withstand the bombardment. They were glad to see that the damage to the cathedral and the village was minimal, although many of the buildings surrounding it had not been so lucky.

"There's nobody stationed here, why would the Germans bomb it?" Furze was perplexed and angered at the unnecessary damage.

"Inaccurate intelligence, perhaps?" suggested Guy, who was bent double catching his breath. "Still, better they bomb a village with no one in it than one filled with civilians and troops."

"That's certainly preferable," assented Furze, "at least the cathedral wasn't damaged, it's such a beautiful building."

"Perhaps there is something to that faith malarkey after all," teased Guy.

"Given the situation we are returning to," responded Furze, dryly, "it's hard to have faith in anything other than one's friends."

The next few days passed uneventfully, and Friday 19th February heralded the end of Furze's secondment to Headquarters, thus releasing him back to his Company which was billeted in La Toulette. He was pleasantly surprised by the quality of the Company billets and felt very happy to be back with his men, taking the liberty of writing a letter to Daw to mark the occasion.

My darling Daw,

Time passes here with the speed of a gushing river, and I am continually amazed at how long it has been since I last wrote. Tell me, how are your mother and sister, well, I hope? More importantly, how are you? Your last letter described accompanying my sister to decide upon the dress for her wedding, I hope she didn't drag you along to too many stores. You really are a dear for going with her, I know she will have valued your company.

Conditions here are very agreeable currently, the men are stationed in comfortable accommodation, and I have made the acquaintance of the Regimental medic, Doctor Greenleas. He's a capital fellow, and wise beyond his years. I was present when he was dealing with a young Lieutenant whose feet had become frostbitten during his last tour in the trenches. Although nothing serious and something he will recover from, the good Doctor highlighted that 'the best cure is preventing the occurrence in the first place', words that struck me greatly. He was quick to point out that such carelessness for one's person cannot be afforded on the Front, especially not by an officer. What use would we be to our men in such a state! We are lucky to count him among our number, and I feel safer for it.

I miss your conversation, dear Daw, even with all my friends around me the Front can be a lonely place, with comforting words in short supply. I'm more confident in my mind and abilities than I was when I arrived, and the General's description of how I sustained my injuries was both shocking and liberating.

Do write to me soon, your words always bring me such warmth,
   Keith

Back in the thick of front-line duties, Furze was ordered, on the evening of 20th February, to take a working party of forty soldiers to 'Y' Farm, and report to an officer of the Royal Engineers. Gathering his working party, Furze marched them through the dark of night to the Farm, where he was told that a new line of high command trenches was required along the ground just in front of 'B' Company's position. The body of troops toiled for three hours, digging, piling and reinforcing the new high command trenches. Eventually, after an immensely muddy and tiring night, the party was given leave to return to their billets at 3:30 am. Furze returned to his room, grubby and exhausted once again, wishing that he hadn't spent so long playing cards the evening before instead of getting some pre-emptive rest.

It turned out that the digging and building of trenches was to be Furze's main tasking over the next few nights, with troop exercises in new attack formations interspersed throughout the days. Tuesday brought their first casualty whilst working. It had been an absolutely beautiful day and the night was no less so, with a ripping moon. Whilst its light brought speed and efficiency to the work of the British troops, this large and beautiful moon also granted the Germans excellent visibility. Lance-Corporal Wont, much like the rest had been digging vigorously for a few hours straight, taking the occasional moment to pause and gulp down some water. Alas, during one such break, whether through exhaustion or a momentary lapse of judgement, he straightened ever so slightly to stretch, and a sniper's round hit him in the head.

"Down, get down!" The hissed orders spread across the working party, as though echoing the lone rifle shot.

Furze rushed over to the wounded soldier, maintaining a low profile as the rest of the troops flung themselves to the ground. Blood was seeping from the wound in Wont's head but he was, miraculously, still alive.

"It's alright." Furze cradled Wont's head and ordered a nearby soldier to bring up a field dressing. "You're still with us."

"Will he live, Sir?" asked one of the nearby soldiers.

"Shut up and get down!" snapped Furze, angry at himself for having let a soldier under his command get wounded and venting this anger on the questioning soldier. A thought then flashed through his mind. *What if this is a friend of Wont's? Wouldn't I ask the same question if this had been Fuller?*

Furze cursed himself for the automatic reply, then turning in the direction of the voice adding as calmly as he could whilst blood from Wont's head stuck to his hands. "It appears that the bullet only grazed him, he will need to be evacuated immediately and taken to Doctor Greenleas. Grab a stretcher, and a get him to the field hospital." Furze turned to another soldier kneeling nearby. "You, help carry this man to safety!"

Furze considered calling it a night, but his soldiers had already resumed their digging and building, almost in defiance of the German marksman. Impressed with their dedication, he allowed them to carry on with their task for the next few hours, working well whilst suffering no further casualties. As a result, the rest of the week progressed delicately, the presence of the German sniper at the forefront of every soldier's anxious mind.

The troops were right to show such concern for on Friday just before they were to depart, it transpired that one of The Queen's further up the line had raised his head above the trench's parapet for one moment too long and the same sniper, who had shot Wont three days earlier, killed the soldier outright. In the commotion that followed, and after the British troops laid down some return fire, a friend of the soldier rushed at full height over to him without thinking. The sniper consequently shot that soldier in the same position as the first. Furze and his working parties obtained this information from the stretcher-bearers who carried the two still, lifeless, bodies down the line. As the stretchers passed Furze's men, each one stopped his work and lowered his head in silent respect for their fallen brothers.

The Owl

"We managed to supply quite a good meal, madame producing truffles for us."

Saturday 27th February.

Content with the fact that his last tour in support of the Front line had not gone too badly, and thankful that Wont's wound would not be fatal, Furze rose late and presided over inspections throughout the day. Most of the soldiers and officers were in good spirits, with their kit and equipment, as well as their bodies in a clean and an agreeable state.

Furze got chatting to a number of the soldiers he had led during the digging party. "Well done lads, those were long nights but you have worked tirelessly throughout the last week."

A few of the soldiers murmured their appreciation, and Furze realised that although in good spirits the men were exhausted all the same.

"Keep up that level of energy and diligence, and the Germans won't stand a chance when we meet them," he added in an attempt to lift their spirits.

"Do you think we shall meet them soon, Sir?" asked a young soldier timidly, unsure as to whether he had the right to pose such a question to the officer in front of him.

Furze observed the concern on the young man's face; he was scarcely older than nineteen and voiced many of the fears that had raced around Furze's own mind. In addition, the question was sound in every measure. The problem was, he didn't have the answer, despite every part of him wishing he did.

"I cannot say for sure," he replied, choosing his words carefully, aware of how attuned the surrounding soldiers were to his voice, "but we must all be ready to face them at a moment's notice. This is a war of attrition men, during which our courage must remain steadfast and our attention on point."

"It would be helpful to know in advance though, Sir, so we have time to prepare like, you know…" uttered another nearby lad.

Furze realised he had an important role to play in alleviating their concerns, but found it difficult to fault their commentary, given the simplicity of their request. They weren't asking for warmer trenches or tastier rations, as welcome as these would have been, but only the chance to prepare for the inevitable. He considered his reply, aware that although he held the highest rank among them, the young soldier who had posed the question was in command of the conversation.

"You're quite correct, Samuels," Furze began, addressing the soldier by his name, "and were this war entirely of British design then no doubt we would have planned it far better than the Germans, and finished it in time for tea."

Samuels and some of the other soldiers smiled at this outlandish suggestion, aware of the many complications of war.

"However, this is a conflict of German origin and, alas, they have never been ones for flexibility. Once we scuppered their plans concerning France, they simply couldn't get their heads around what to do next. Hence, here we are. We have the stronger position, troops, and moral, and it is our duty to become either the immovable rock or the unstoppable wave."

He paused, allowing the weight of the situation to sink in. "So, gentlemen, we will undoubtedly meet the Germans soon, but we must be patient in the knowledge that it must be at the right time."

Many of the soldiers nodded their understanding, grateful for his words, even though the future was still wholly uncertain.

Such is the delicacy of command, Furze thought, *how to encourage others when one is spending so much energy encouraging oneself.*

As if by design, in response to Furze's thoughts about personal morale, Brookes arrived at his room suggesting they throw a dinner party. As unusual as Furze thought the idea was, given their situation, he had to own that some lightheartedness would do them all some good.

"It's a ripping idea!" Responded Furze eagerly. "One never knows whether the chance will present itself again and I've also been feeling the strain recently."

"I'm thrilled," smiled Brookes. "Do you think Madame will be able to put on one of her spreads if we can find something edible?"

Madame was the bubbly French landlady of the house in which the officers were billeted. As they were so young, Furze and his friends had grown quite attached to her and viewed her as a surrogate mother. In return, Madame had taken them all under her care, providing them with the heartiest of meals that she could muster when they were not in the trenches. On those rare occasions when the officers produced the ingredients she was more than happy to rustle up a larger spread for their dinners, taking great pleasure in ordering them about in the kitchen when they offered their assistance. Of course, being set in her culinary ways, she never let the officers actually do any of the cooking, but they were a great help in peeling, cutting and carrying.

"Well, we can ask her. In fact, let's do so right away and waste no time."

Presently, Brookes and Furze raced off to find Madame, allowing the carefree attitudes that had been stolen from them to surface for the briefest of moments.

Having brought Madame on board, they invited Major Slacke, Commander of 'C' Company, Lieutenant Philpot, who was also in 'C' Company, Lieutenant Hemike, and Doctor Greenleas to dine with them. The evening was a monumental success, not least because Madame cooked up a veritable feast for the group. She had, unbeknownst to them, added some truffles to the soup for the starter, paired with a small but tasty helping of rabbit, for the main course, chicken with green peas, Heinz baked beans and potatoes. Finally, for dessert, stewed fruit and coffee.

"Madame," exclaimed the Major, "that was, quite positively, the best meal I have enjoyed in France."

"Quite so," joined Hemike.

"The truffle soup was a delight," noted Furze, "and quite unexpected, Madame. We certainly did not provide that ingredient for you."

"You flatter me far too much," Madame tutted, but her flushed cheeks gave away her evident enjoyment at the reception of her cooking. "You know I'll always do my best to provide for you, it's the least I can do when you risk your lives in defence of my country."

With bellies full for the first time in a long while, the group retired to an evening of poker and bridge. Bridge was suggested fiendishly by Philpot, who shared a passion for the game with Furze.

"What a good idea that dinner was of yours, Brookes," Furze stated with an immensely satisfied look on his face. "Rather a jolly meal really."

"I agree, Furzzy, made all the better with Madame's addition of the truffle soup! She really is a dear old thing, I simply cannot understand how she remains so cheery."

"Come on you two," launched Major Slacke, "sitting there in your armchairs, one would think you were a couple of retired Generals musing over past victories."

The group laughed merrily, and all moved to take their positions around the card table.

"Now then, Furzzy, we have a game to continue," grinned Philpot.

"Not so fast gentlemen," interjected the Doctor, "poker is the order of the evening, I believe. Once I have beaten you thoroughly at that, we can then move on to a lesser card game."

"A lesser game?" scoffed Hemike and Philpot. "We shall see about that, Doctor. You really shouldn't knock games just because you show no skill in them."

The evening progressed in a most amusing fashion with Brookes playing outrageously and winning everything. This greatly frustrated the Doctor and Philpot but added to Furze's enjoyment at a night spent away from the strains of war. As it turned out, Brookes and Furze were right to take the chance to enjoy such a moment with one another, for Furze received orders the next evening that he was to leave his friends and move to 'A' Company. The Company Commander, Captain Hewett, had been taken ill, and Furze was required to take over command of the Company in his absence.

"Such rotten luck," Furze grumbled as he packed up his kit.

"Chin up, Furzzy," Fuller soothed, though he was equally unsettled by the departure of his friend, "you'll be back here in no time. Captain Hewett is a sturdy chap, he'll recover quickly."

Furze continued to pack his kit in a dejected manner.

"Either way," Fuller continued, "you have been chosen to command an entire Company in the Captain's stead, that's a great opportunity."

"You are right," sighed Furze, "as ever. But I'm immensely sorry to be leaving you, I haven't gotten to know the fellows in 'A' Company in the slightest. Plus, I've never commanded a Company before, what if I make an utter fool of myself, or worse, get someone killed?" This weight of responsibility suddenly descended upon him, and Furze sat back onto the bed, instinctively massaging his left knee out of habitual concern.

"When I was first made a Captain, I was told to get to know my Lieutenants well," Fuller advised calmly, observing his friend's anxiety and attempting to soothe his thoughts. "Remember, a Commander cannot lead a Company on his own." Closing Furze's kit bag and holding it out for him he concluded, "the support of one's junior officers is essential."

Furze looked up at Fuller, noting the sincerity of his features and took hold of the offered bag. As he did so, Fuller heaved him up onto his feet. "You're made for Command, Furzzy, believe me. Your concern for the welfare of your troops testifies to this, just don't try too hard to lead and it will happen naturally."

"When did you become so wise?" Furze asked, in awe of his friend's control over the situation.

"At the same time you did, Furzzy," Fuller smiled ruefully, "when we joined this ghastly war."

With his friend's support broadening his mind to the possibilities of leading a Company, Furze walked confidently over to the building assigned to the officers of 'A' Company, determined to get to know his Lieutenants' characters first and foremost.

"Good evening, gentlemen," he greeted as he entered the room where they were all seated playing cards.

The three Lieutenants looked round and rose to meet him. Could he detect a hint of disappointment, even distain? They had likely been informed that a new Commander would be covering for Captain Hewett in light of his illness, but perhaps they had not thought it would be an officer so close to them in age. His heart rate rose and nerves began to gently grip his throat. Did they believe him too young to take control of the whole Company?

"Good evening," responded the individual whom Furze assumed was the most senior Lieutenant amongst them, "how can we help?"

"Lieutenant Furze, acting Commander of 'A' Company in Captain Hewett's stead," he addressed the group, offering his hand. Would the Lieutenant take it? Furze held his posture, centring the attention of the room on himself and gazing purposefully, yet welcomingly, into the young man's eyes. If he could win over this man, the other two would follow suit he reasoned.

"Well, I'll be darned," the officer replied with a grin, taking Furze's outstretched hand. "Lieutenant Humphreys, Sir." The other two Lieutenants allowed their stony faces to relax and assume expressions of relief.

"Welcome to 'A' Company, it's a pleasure to have you join us and you must excuse our initial wariness." Humphreys lowered his tone ever so slightly, "with the Captain out of action, we wondered if they would send us some desk-bound officer from Headquarters. Instead, if what I've heard is true, you're far from that."

Relief flooded through Furze's muscles and he began to feel more at ease.

"This is Lieutenant Jones," Humphreys gestured to the officer closest to him, who stepped forward and shook Furze's hand vigorously.

"Splendid to have you with us, Sir, splendid," Jones babbled.

"The pleasure is mine," Furze replied, before casting his eye to the third and final of his new Lieutenants. This young man had remained silent since Furze had entered the room, although he had risen to his feet in greeting. He stood a little behind the other two with a look, not of hostility, but of inquisitive contemplation. A small smile played at the corner of his mouth as he watched Furze's interaction with the other two and, when Furze's eyes met his own, he held the gaze with a tenacity wholly unexpected from a man so young.

"Lieutenant Austin, Sir," the young man said, seizing the opportunity to speak for himself.

"The newest officer in our Company," Humphreys added, "but don't let that fool you. Young Austin here is learning with a ferocity the Germans should quake at."

"Excellent to meet you," Furze shook Austin's hand, and the young man offered him his seat at the table, before striding off to source another for himself.

Lieutenants Humphreys, Jones, and Austin, all in their early twenties, seemed incredibly engaging. They welcomed Furze into their ranks warmly, glad to enjoy the company of another young man similar to themselves and proceeded to update him on recent events.

Furze was immediately taken with Austin and made a point to get to know him as well as possible. The opportunity to do so presented itself when Austin agreed to introduce him to a number of the soldiers in the Company. As they went from billet to billet, Austin weaving effortlessly in and out of conversations whilst introducing the new Commander, Furze marvelled at the authority the young man held so effortlessly over the battle-hardened soldiers of 'A' Company.

"How long have you been in the Company, Austin?" Furze queried.

"Six months, Sir," Austin replied, in a tone ever so slightly reserved, "but it didn't take me long to embed."

"I don't doubt," agreed Furze, as he observed a group of corporals saluting them as they strolled past.

Austin shot a glance at Furze as he said this, attempting to read what was behind this comment. His youth was the one feature Austin was acutely aware of and fiercely defensive about. He despised having his capabilities judged purely on his years, rather than his actions, and this occasionally led him to perform acts of sheer recklessness simply to prove, unnecessarily, his worth.

"It's a good Company of soldiers, Sir," Austin continued, wishing to gauge his companion, "if one looks after their interests."

A faint smile appeared on Furze's lips; he appreciated an officer who valued the welfare of his men so highly.

"And how do you manage to balance the interests of your men with the interests of your superiors?" Furze asked, testing the depths of Austin's convictions.

"It's not a balance, Sir," Austin remarked, choosing his words carefully. He had not expected Furze to pay such attention to his opinions. "I see them as one and the same. The interests of my superiors should be the interests of the men, and by association I should be able to cater to both simultaneously."

"Honourable sentiments," Furze mused, "but you are far too experienced an officer to believe that Headquarters always takes this view."

Austin held himself a little taller at this compliment.

"I'd also own," Furze continued, "that you know I am too much of a realist to accept such an idealistic answer."

Increasingly intrigued Austin replied, "idealism doesn't factor into my reasoning. Headquarters takes a strategic holistic view of what is required to win the war and this, I would own, is in the interests of my men. With this goal in mind, I view my superiors' orders as requiring me to achieve that end but granting me the liberty to decide how best to do so when the lives of my men are at stake. Blind obedience is not leadership, Sir."

"Obedience is the bedrock of the British Army," Furze pressed, enjoying the verbal joust.

"Indeed," flashed Austin, "but so is integrity. I have a duty both to my men, and to my superiors' wishes. Should I ever face the situation where, in my opinion, the interests of either misalign with the other, I feel it integral to my role to take every possible action to bring about the best outcome for both sides. I take pride in achieving, especially if it is achieving what others deem impossible."

"That is the duty of youth," Furze smiled, "to convince the generations that have come before to open their eyes to the possibilities they no longer have the energy to contemplate."

"That could be seen as an idealistic observation," Austin quipped.

"Perhaps. Maybe you and I can be allowed one from time to time," Furze observed, lifting his head and peering up at the brooding sky above. "You have a wife, I hear?"

Taken at the sudden change in topic Austin responded automatically. "Yes, Maggie, she's the sweetest person in my life." He blushed at his honesty. For some reason Furze made him feel at ease.

"You evidently care deeply for her," Furze responded wistfully. "Life seems to be smiling on you, Austin."

"Well, I love her dearly, and was being sent off to the Front so thought 'to hell with it' and married her."

The pair nodded simultaneously, as another batch of men saluted them as they passed.

"Thank you, Austin," Furze said, as they found themselves back at the officers' billets, "you really didn't have to go out of your way like that."

"It was a pleasure, Sir, I'm very glad to be serving under you."

Their friendship cemented, Furze requested, "please, call me Furzzy."

On Monday, the first day of March, the Battalion marched off to take over some new trenches, heralding the start of their next tour. The route taken by the troops saw them march down the Rue de Bataille, turning off to the left, just short of Laventie, to Picantin, which was about six miles away. The line of trenches, Furze noted, faced south-east about two-hundred yards in front of Rue Tilleloy, just opposite Aubers. Furze was in an exceptionally buoyant mood, as he was getting to know his eager Lieutenants well, and thought Austin showed real promise as a future Company commander. He had also learnt that 'A' Company would be taking over some of the less sordid trenches on the right of the Battalion's line.

The German trenches were about three-hundred-and-fifty yards away and, that night, 'A' Company worked on the trench parapets until around 3:00 am. Before he turned in, Furze had an insatiable urge to write a letter to Daw.

My dear Daw,

The moon is particularly lovely tonight, casting a mysterious glow on our present position. I have now taken over a Company of troops and am supported in my duties by three exceptional officers. One, a young Lieutenant Austin, I have become quite attached to and could not imagine leading these men without him.

To our great satisfaction, we are residing in what used to be a high command trench, and my own dugout contains a bed, table, arm and ordinary chair, as well as a sweet little fireplace. Regardless, I cannot help but be reminded of the German's swift advance when I consider that this trench was never intended to form our Front line. How much ground we must have lost to find ourselves in this position. Of course, the reality is that it is still muddy and cramped, but I can tell that the men appreciate conditions that are unusually agreeable.

I felt the need to send you something, dear Daw, other than accounts of my life here. Something personal, from me to you, so I wrote the following poem. Perhaps it's silly

*of me, but something about this moonlit
morning called to me.*

*When everything was quiet and rest
An owl stole from her lonely nest
Into the dark and dreary night
To catch and see what she might*

*She had not waited very long
Before Mr Mouse came trotting along
The owl pounced down - it was in vain
And Mr Mouse was caught again*

*The moon on high was shining bright
When the owl returned to her nest that night
The owlets hissed, hooted and screeched
When at last – that nest again she reached*

*The eldest owlet by name was Jack
And before his mamma had returned back
Had told his brothers once and for all
That they should have nothing - but he
would have all*

*Boo hoo! Cried his brothers he shall only
have one
And what's more if he teases us he shall
have none
Then they hissed and cried and set up a
howl
But at that moment in came the owl*

*What's this! Cried the owl with a
tremendous loud hiss*

It seems as though something is wrong or amiss
Has anything happened while I've been away?
Oh! Nothing extraordinary or out of the way

The owl turned away with an ugly sneer
And said that they squabbled when she was not there
Now mind said she - after today
Don't squabble and fight when I am away

It reminded me a little of my own siblings, how silly we all were when we chose to squabble with one another over matters that now appear so trivial.

I look forward to hearing all about your accounts at home very soon.

Fondest,
Keith

Satisfied without quite knowing why, he folded the paper up and placed it carefully in its envelope. Then he blew out the tiny candle which had been licking the walls of his dugout with its feeble flames and listened to the sentries pacing up and down the trench just outside.

Two-and-a-quarter hours later, he was up and standing the men to arms in case of a dawn attack. As this did not happen, he instead set the men to cleaning the trench and improving the pathway that ran all along the floor. At intervals, the Germans lobbed shells over the heads of 'A' Company into some empty buildings just to their rear, sharp reminders that they were never far away. Each night brought only one or two hours sleep for

Furze, being one of the first up in the morning to ensure all the soldiers were at their posts and the last to turn in at night in order to ensure all the trench work was completed properly. He was greatly fatigued and had to muster all his strength each morning to remain energetic. There were moments throughout the day when he would come close to nodding off, so took to wandering up and down the line talking with as many of the men as possible just to keep awake.

Austin became a regular and indispensable companion during these morale-boosting outings. Eager to assist his commander, and now close friend, he regularly awoke before Furze so that he would be ready and waiting to receive his orders.

"You really should get some rest." Furze attempted to scold him the first time he had emerged from his dugout one morning, only to find Austin leaning against the trench wall rubbing his hands together in an attempt to warm them.

"So should the men, and they need our attention," responded the young man without a moment's hesitation. "I'd rather sleep soundly for a few moments knowing they're looked after than sleep restlessly for an age worrying that they're not."

Furze realised then how invaluable such company was and couldn't help but feel a rush of energy when he saw his thoughtful friend every morning thereafter.

On their fourth day in the trenches, one of the British heavy guns opened fire on the German lines with lyddite, a form of high explosive comprised of molten and cast picric acid. The British gunners' aim was on target that morning and Furze observed that a farm in Trivelet, held by German forces was badly hit, as were the German trenches to their direct right. In all, twelve rounds were expended, and Furze was told afterwards that all but one hit their targets, wreaking havoc on the German line.

"That's welcome news!" Jones exclaimed, when Furze related this to his three Lieutenants.

"Those gunners are doing us quite a service eh, Furze?" pitched in Humphreys. "If they keep that accuracy up the Germans will have a hard time holding their position."

"I wouldn't be so sure," Austin brooded, in a low wary tone, "the German lines are deep, well-fortified, and complex. It'll take more than some artillery to dislodge them, even if it is well-aimed."

"What's got you in such a mood today, Austin?" Jones grimaced. "Honestly, sometimes I wonder whether anything will satisfy you."

"I don't disagree with the effectiveness of our bombardment," responded Austin, unperturbed by Jones' comment. "I only caution that the Germans can give as much as they take. We need to keep up our guard, that is all."

"Austin's words hold some truth, even if they are a touch pessimistic," agreed Furze. "We should all be on our guard."

Their concerns were more than warranted as the Germans retaliated that afternoon with some intensive rifle and machine gun fire. Given how silent the past few days had been 'A' Company, along with a few other Companies either side of them, took the chance to respond, creating a small but intense firefight. Although the Germans seemed to get the worst of it one of the soldiers in 'A' Company, Wallis, was shot.

"What's the situation?" Furze asked breathlessly, he and Austin having rushed over to Wallis' body which lay strangely still amidst the surrounding activity.

"I'm sorry, Sir," responded one of the men, "he's gone. Shot through the head and killed outright, quick it was."

"Some small solace," observed Austin, pain contorting his face. Even in the few months he had been there the war's cruelty had already begun to engrave indelible marks upon Austin's complexion.

"Cease fire!" roared Furze at 'A' Company, and his order was copied and multiplied as it was passed down the trench. He didn't want to lose another man to a stalemate firefight based on pent up anger, and wondered why he had allowed his men to rise to the German provocation. As the final few shots rang out through the air that hung thick with smoke, the action was brought to a close. Neither side had lost or gained ground, therefore both had suffered what seemed to Furze unnecessary casualties. Wallis' body was carefully removed on a stretcher and buried later that day. He was the first soldier Furze had lost since taking command of the Company.

"It was a firefight, Furzzy," Austin commiserated, attempting to rationalise the event that evening in Furze's dugout. Casualties of war are an inevitable, if disagreeable, outcome of our position."

"I know that, and Wallis is hardly the first man I have lost," Furze responded, sullenly, "but I had hoped to hand the Company back to Hewett in one piece. We didn't even gain any ground. Why the hell did I order the men to fire back?"

"You can't protect everyone," Austin noted, almost sternly. "We had to respond to the German fire, you know that. It could have been an attack for all we knew and better to respond than to be caught off-guard."

Furze grunted in admission.

Austin refused to have his friend wallow in such unnecessary self-doubt. "Remember what I said when we first met? The end-goal, winning this war, *that* is the best outcome for the men in this Company. Wallis probably took down two or three Germans before he fell, think of it like that. We may not have gained any ground, but we weakened the German forces for certain."

As unsure as Furze was over the truth of this statement, he understood Austin's outlook and appreciated his support nonetheless.

'A' Company's final day in the trenches began with the British heavy guns dropping another deafening bombardment on top of the German trenches in front of them.

"Nine shells by my count," muttered Humphreys, who had been observing the shelling through his field-glasses just next to

Furze. "At least that number struck the German parapet and entered their trenches."

"With each shell containing lyddite," Furze observed, "untold havoc must have been caused." He was thankful that it was not his troops being subjected to such horror at that moment.

Finally, at 7:00 pm, the Warwickshire Regiment relieved The Queen's, and Furze marched 'A' Company back to their new accommodation on the outskirts of Levantie. As he lay in bed, his mind turned to Fuller, Brookes, and Bobbie, sincerely hoping that they had survived the last tour as well. Then, for a moment, the faintest pang of pride struck him when he reflected that he had just successfully led his first Company into, and back out from, the trenches.

The Sniper

I

"I was with him two minutes before he was hit and only just before he had written a note to his wife in case anything should happen to him. It was a terrible tragedy and has made me very unhappy...."

Wednesday 10th March.

Sunday brought with it the usual Battalion kit inspections, which the soldiers attended in good fashion. As they dispersed, Furze managed to catch some time with the Commanding Officer to discuss the events of the last few days, including Wallis' death.

"It is most unfortunate, Furze," consoled the Commanding Officer, "no one likes to lose any man under his command. If it's any help, our intelligence suggests that 'A' Company's response did a damn sight more damage to the Germans than they did to us. Your men performed admirably."

"Thank you, Sir," acknowledged Furze gloomily, "but it's always a dire sight, seeing one of your own lose his life."

"It's the nature of war my boy." The CO continued, aware that Furze had a great deal on his mind, "we may not like it, may despise it even, but we cannot change what has passed. Dwelling on it too long is neither healthy, nor productive. Fight for the future Furze, not the past."

The blunt truth behind the CO's words opened Furze's eyes to the reality of the situation and made him realise that there was plenty more work to be done. Brooding over his actions would have little impact on the outcome of this war. He may have lost a soldier, but many more would be claimed before it was over. He followed the CO to Headquarters and joined his fellow officers for a conference that had been called rather abruptly. The air among the muttering men dripped with nervous anticipation and many conjectured about the topic at hand.

"Do you think the Germans are planning an offensive, or the Allies?" posed one.

"Neither, this will be a mundane routine talk about remaining positive and keeping morale high amongst the troops," drawled another.

"A meeting with all the officers just to remind us of that? What drivel, it's far more serious," scoffed a third. The voices gently died away, though, as the CO and Furze entered.

"Gentlemen, thank you for coming," the CO began. "Now, I know you have all recently been relieved from the trenches, but tomorrow night you shall be required to return there once again."

"What's our intention, Sir?" asked Fuller, who sensed that something big was occurring, and had assumed the demeanour of a pinpoint hunting dog.

"It is this, Captain," replied the CO. "On the morning of the 10th, so in precisely three days, an attack is to be made by the 8th and part of the 7th Divisions, supported by a large French force on our right flank."

There was some murmuring from the officers gathered in the cramped room. This was the attack, Furze assumed, that had been expected since he'd arrived back from leave. Given that the Germans had not attempted an offensive, he reasoned, it made sense for the Allies to do so instead. It seemed the only way to drive the enemy back.

"You are being brought up to the trenches," continued the CO, "in order to participate in or support the attack as necessary. Once in position tomorrow night, ensure that all preparations for a quick and efficient attack are made, and keep the men in good order. We have practiced these attacks a great deal over the last few weeks, so there should be no doubt over how to proceed should the situation call you to action. Any questions?"

The men in the room eyed one another, contemplating the information they had just been given.

"It would have been good to give the men a little more time to rest, Sir," posed a captain.

"As is always the case," quelled the CO, "yet this is the position we find ourselves in. We didn't have too bad a time of it during our last stretch in the trenches, so a day or so of rest should be more than adequate."

"Do we have any further clarity over our part in the attack, Sir?" asked Fuller, who had been sketching a rough layout of the trenches in his small notebook to visualise the plan of attack. Furze had never seen Fuller without that notebook, which he seemed to use for almost everything, and marvelled at his friend's knowledge of the British and German lines. Fuller twisted the notebook slightly, before adding, "by my reckoning, we shall be in a perfect position to offer fire support to both the British and French troops as they advance."

"Not as yet, Captain, but your logic seems sound. Further Company orders will be distributed following this session. Any further questions? No? Well, in that case gentlemen, carry on, and good luck."

The officers filed out, filled with a mixture of eager anticipation and trepidation over the forthcoming engagement. Covering for Hewett, Furze had not anticipated leading 'A' Company through a scenario that could well evolve into an assault on the German lines. Thus, once he had informed his men of the next day's movements, Furze took Austin and spent the evening with his friends in 'B' Company, trusting that time with them would steady his nerves.

"Gentlemen," began Furze, motioning towards Austin, "this is the chap I have been telling you about, I simply would not have settled so well into 'A' Company without him."

"Ah!" grinned Fuller, "we've heard much about you."

"Far too much," Lieutenant Merrow laughed. "Furzzy always needs someone to look after him."

Austin, as was his wont, remained calm and observant at first but shook hands with them both, touched that Furze had already mentioned him to his friends.

"Very good gents, very good," laughed Furze, "now, on to business. The rumour is that over four-hundred generals are currently based in our neighbourhood."

This news brought shivers down the officers' spines.

"It must be a large attack on the 10th," suggested Austin. "There wouldn't be that many high-ranking officers if it wasn't."

"That, or the attack is of great significance needing hands-on management at the highest level," added Fuller.

"Either way, you're in for a treat old boy," chimed in Merrow, not wishing to present too dour a picture to Austin, "any soldier serving under Furzzy here should count himself lucky!"

Austin raised his drink in agreement, he was beginning to ease into such welcome company and had particularly warmed to Fuller.

"Nonsense," countered Furze, "I'd sooner serve under any man here, and feel the better for it."

"To one another, friends both old and new," Fuller motioned, nodding to Austin. They all raised a toast and turned to discussing the potential particulars of the forthcoming attack.

The next day, having settled into the section of the trenches they had relieved from the Warwicks, Furze and his fellow officers were called to a second briefing held by the Commanding Officer at which they expected to receive detailed operation orders for the attack on the 10th. Leaving 'A' Company in the capable hands of Lieutenant Humphreys, who took command without a second thought, Furze approached Headquarters with a rising sense of foreboding about what was to come.

The CO opened the briefing. "Good afternoon gentlemen, I hope everything is in order?" There were general nods and murmurs of assent amongst the officers, who waited expectantly for him to continue.

"Right, here is the order of battle. The 8th Division is to attack and take Neuve Chapelle, whilst the 21st Brigade supported by the 20th is to move up on the left and advance towards Aubers." As he was speaking, he traced the route the 21st Brigade was to take on the map in front of them. Every swoop of his arm commanded the attention of the surrounding officers. "All clear so far?"

Again, the officers nodded.

"The Queen's and the Welsh Fusiliers are to be ready to assist in the attack, and open heavy covering fire as the situation develops. Well done for predicting that Mr. Fuller," the CO smiled. Finally, the Warwicks and Staffords are to act as the Brigade and Division Reserves respectively."

"Sir, that map is incredibly detailed, and the plan makes sense in relation to what it shows. But are we certain that the intelligence we have gathered matches the reality?" This question came from one of the newest officers in the group and called Furze to take a closer look at the map they had been examining. Its representation of the German lines was, indeed, of exceptional detail.

"I'm glad you raised that, Lieutenant," remarked the CO with a sly smile. "This map is a one-to-five-thousand scale replication of the British and German lines surrounding Neuve Chapelle. There exist one-and-a-half-thousand identical copies of the one we see before us today, produced from the numerous photographs our lads in the Royal Flying Corps have taken of the land from above."

There were appreciative whispers at the magnitude of the operation that had been undertaken to collect intelligence for their benefit.

"I can assure you, gentlemen, that no finer, nor more detailed, map of the area can be found."

"How do our numbers compare to the German's, Sir?" asked another officer.

"Given our recent influx of reinforcements, it is my understanding that we outnumber the Germans by at least two to one."

"Building on that, Sir," jumped in another anxious voice, "do you think the Germans are aware of the attack, given all our troop movements?"

"An important point, well asked," responded the CO, turning to the man, "every precaution has been taken to ensure the secrecy of our intentions. Our guns have been moved into position slowly and carefully, and our troops have been rotating regularly to give the appearance of troop refreshment, rather than replenishment."

"Do you think it has worked?"

At this question, searching more for his personal opinion than fact, the CO paused. "I cannot say that the Germans are utterly unaware, in fact, I would say that we would be fools if we didn't expect them to have intelligence networks as intricate as our own. However, given everything we know, and the fact that it appears as though the Germans have not called up their own reserve units, I would say they do not expect us to attack as soon as we intend to."

This practical and honest response addressed the concerns of the group, and they levelled no further questions. The Commanding Officer was well liked and respected by all under his command, and his clear, concise delivery of orders was a trait all the officers greatly appreciated.

"Good, then I shall close with the following: the attack will be preceded by a heavy bombardment from our guns which aims to destroy the majority of the German wire and stun their troops before the assault."

The CO folded his arms, stood tall, and observed the room calmly, commanding the space in its entirety. "Gentlemen, this is the first British offensive of the war. It is our chance to remind not only the Germans, but also our allies, of the power the British military can bring to bear when it is called upon to do its duty. We have been stuck in our trenches, locked in a stalemate long enough, and it is finally time to act. We have greater numbers, more accurate intelligence from the air, and we have a swathe of supporting artillery. The skill and bravery, above all, of you and your men will drive us to success. Serve your country. Serve your men. It is down to you to lead them to a victory that everyone at home can be proud of!"

With that, the officers launched a hearty cheer into the air, and returned to their respective commands to disseminate what they had learnt. Furze returned to pensive looks from Lieutenants Humphreys, Jones, and Austin.

"How did it go, Sir?" asked Humphreys.

"It's going to be quite the attack," announced Furze, before relating the morning's briefing to the three subalterns. On hearing the plan, their anxious demeanours eased slightly. They too, were particularly interested in the depth of the reconnaissance which had been undertaken, as well as the magnitude of the bombardment before the ground attacks were launched.

"You will all perform admirably," Furze reassured them, before considering something else. Observing these three men under his command, his mind returned to the final speech the CO had given his own officers, a speech that had left them feeling more motivated and confident.

Why not give it a go, he thought to himself, *it can't do any harm.*

Furze emulated the CO, folding his arms, standing upright and looking straight into the eyes of his subordinates. "I was no pillar of strength during my first few contacts but remember that we fight with the best troops in the world, and we fight against an enemy that threatens everything that we, our families, our friends, and our country stand for. Lead your men with surety, and they will follow you through the very gates of hell and back. Serve them, and they will be eager to serve you. Place their interests above yours, and you will have the entire Company looking after your own in return. I am honoured to serve with all of you and when we sit back in our billets in a few days time, we will be satisfied that we did all in our power to protect our country. I look forward to sharing that moment with each one of you."

Stuck by such unexpected passion the three young Lieutenants offered further words of agreement and encouragement to one another before separating to relay orders to their men. That night, the mood in the trench was one of intense expectation and anxiety. Underpinning this, however, one could sense an indestructible determination emanating from the friendship and support the troops felt for one another.

II

Wednesday 10th March.

Furze's pocket watch ticked in his hand. He observed it in silence. The men of 'A' Company lined up smartly along their trench, all eyes on their commander.

7:28 am.

In two minutes time, the British guns would open Holy Hell on the German lines; their grim chorus signaling the beginning of the battle. A battle to gain a few hundred yards of soggy, muddy, pot-holed ground.

7:29 am.

The eyes of 'A' Company were on him. The breath of each man hanging expectantly on the cold morning air. Furze turned to his left, nodded, and was met by a number of acknowledgements. He nodded to his right, and caught the eye of Austin, who returned a look of steely confidence, although his hands were shaking slightly with what Furze could only imagine was a mixture of anticipation and fear. He looked back at his watch.

7:30 am.

The silence was shattered by the eruption of the British artillery opening a tremendous fire onto the German trenches, Neuve Chapelle and Aubers. The barrage lasted forty-five minutes, the British soldiers awestruck by the extraordinary roar. Eventually, the thunder ceased, and Furze knew the 8th Division was about to begin its advance towards Neuve Chapelle.

" 'A' Company!" roared Furze, fuelling his lungs with the seriousness of the situation. "Mount the parapets and prepare to lay down covering fire!"

The Company clambered up onto their respective parapets, and Furze poked his head over the top. There was a brief moment, which lasted less than a second, when he observed the dead ground before him. The German lines of barbed wire, stretching for miles to his left and right. The thought flashed through his mind that the wire seemed remarkably untouched by the barrage.

He summoned all his strength and bellowed. "Fire!"

'A' Company unleashed a blistering covering fire on the opposing German lines. The soldiers all along the trench were one unit, connected and inseparable. Protecting one another, as well as their colleagues in the 8th Division who were battling towards their objective. Furze, Humphreys, Jones, and Austin ran up and down the line encouraging, urging, shouting, and directing, ready, at any moment, to give the order to advance in support of the attack raging around them. Though Furze could not be certain, it looked as though the assault was advancing quickly. The 8th Division was well covered by 'A' Company and the rest of The Queen's, who were doing an admirable job keeping the Germans pinned below the parapets of their trenches. Furze could hear the chatter of machine gun fire, the rhythmic crackle of rifles, and the rip and boom of hand-held grenades. He rushed over to the right-hand side of the trench to see how Jones' platoon was doing.

"Keep it up men!" Furze shouted, adding to Jones' encouragement and causing the fire from this section to become even more fearsome. Furze then rushed to the next section, which was putting up a phenomenal rate of fire. It was Austin's platoon.

"Great job men, but you can do better! Jones' platoon has a heavier rate of fire than yours!" Furze yelled at them.

"You hear that, men? Let's show Jones' platoon how The Queen's get things done!" cried Austin, in furious response.

The effect was noticeable, and the soldiers flung rounds at the German lines with a ferocity beyond anything Furze had expected. He slapped Austin on the back as he went past and, as he did so, Austin grabbed his arm, holding out a letter.

"Could you take this for Maggie, Furzzy, just in case…you know." For the first time, Furze noticed raw, unguarded fear behind Austin's youthful bravado. Whether one approached the war quietly, confidently, or pensively, none of them had chosen to be there.

"No need Austin, we'll all see this day through," Furze attempted to smile, hoping his action would bring his friend some measure of confidence.

Austin looked at him imploringly.

Furze assented, "I'll keep it safe for you, and give it back once the fighting is done, I promise."

He carefully took the letter, giving Austin a reassuring nod before rushing onwards. He felt a great deal of tender pride for Austin at that moment. His section of the trench was in good order, the covering fire from his men was consistent and oppressive, and there Austin was at the head of it all. He pictured the moment, back in the safety of their billets following the battle, when he could tell Austin how well he had performed.

War allowed Furze a brief interlude to smile, to hope, before closing its cold, dirty hands around his heart, choking its warmth and shattering his resolve. It was the unmistakable crack of an enemy sniper round, followed seconds later by the gut-wrenching thud of a bullet penetrating a soldier's skull just behind him. He shuddered and stood deadly still, the letter in his hand. Initially his reaction was one of relief.

Thank goodness I was on the move, and not standing where I had been a few seconds ago. Then a stronger, darker thought took hold of him. *Please God, not him…*

Memories of his injuries during the first Battle of Ypres made him quiver. He had had a lucky escape then, what was preventing that same luck from saving another innocent soul now?

At last, Furze got a grip of himself and turned slowly. The mud in the trench made his boots heavy, as though pleading with him not to turn around, not to face the nightmare that was sure to present itself to him when he did. No amount of mud could have held Furze in position, and no amount of experience ever prepared him for these harrowing, appalling moments when they barged their way into his life.

The sight he had most feared reared its ugly head, grinning in putrid satisfaction at the pain it caused him. Austin, the young gentle British Officer, lay on the floor of the trench blood seeping from a bullet wound to his head.

"Austin!" Furze shouted, as he careered back. "You're going to get through this Austin, stay awake! Stay awake! You're going home to your wife, you're going home to Maggie. Medic! Get a medic down here now, we have a seriously wounded officer in 'A' Company! MEDIC!"

9:15 am.

Austin remained unconscious, tended by medics, whilst Furze dutifully led the rest of his Company through the remainder of the battle with no more casualties. By nightfall, the 21st Brigade had taken part of the enemy's trenches and was positioned directly to the front of 'A' Company. Furze ordered his men to cease fire so as not to hit their fellow soldiers but kept everyone on high alert in case they needed to cover a swift withdrawal.

Eventually, Furze felt the Company secure enough to hand over command to Humphreys and tend to Austin personally. He found him still and at peace near where he had fallen.

"He remained with us until 1:15 pm, Sir," one of the medics muttered objectively, they had seen it all before. Furze's anger rose within him; how could they not see the strength it took for Austin to remain with them for so long having suffered such a serious wound? Using all his resolve, he tempered his desire to scream at the medics, focusing on the still figure of his friend. His eyes blurred, his heart bursting with sorrow as his mind registered a tragedy almost beyond belief. To have been standing next to Austin only moments before, to have taken the letter meant for his wife in case anything should happen, to have been so close to the event. All this caused him intense pain, and the death of such a first-rate officer, and dear friend, whom Furze had come to rely upon, hit him hard.

"Any other casualties, Sir?" one of the medics asked.

Furze snapped. "God-damn it man! Isn't one casualty of war enough!?"

The medic was taken aback at such a harsh answer to a reasonable question before a voice behind Furze soothed the situation.

"No further casualties, thankfully, so if you could make the necessary arrangements to remove the Lieutenant's body tonight that will be all." It was Humphreys, his steadfast resolve alleviating the shock coursing through Furze.

"Yes Sir." The medics saluted the two officers and glancing pitifully at Furze before departing.

"There's nothing you can do, Furzzy," consoled Humphreys, resting a hand on Furze's shoulder. The physical contact drew Furze out of his stupor, and he immediately felt disappointed in his reaction to the situation.

"I shouldn't have acted so harshly, I just feel…" Furze looked down at Austin's lifeless body. "Couldn't they have done more? Couldn't I have done more?"

Humphreys studied his Commander. "Nobody can outrun death, Furzzy, it comes for all of us eventually. He died how he would have wanted to, leading his men valiantly."

This comment lifted Furze's spirits slightly, and he marvelled at Humphreys' mastery of the situation. He had a lot to learn from those around him.

"Thank you, Humphreys, you're right of course. As steady a hand as ever. Will you deal with things from here?" Furze asked, gesturing to the body he now couldn't bring himself to look at.

"Leave it to me, you have a Company to look after," Humphreys reassured him, gesturing to a Sergeant who had just raced up requesting further orders.

Furze had lost a friend to the war, and it cut him to the bone. How many more would he lose, before that bone broke irreparably?

Tommy

"Through some grave error our heavy guns dropped lyddite into ours and the Welsh Fusiliers' lines, but thank goodness not for long."

Thursday 11th March.

Furze awoke early and received the day's operational orders with nothing more than a sense of numb duty. He put on as valiant a face as he could for the soldiers of 'A' Company as he relayed to them that the 21st and 20th Brigades were to continue their attack toward Aubers. With blank efficiency, he told them that if the Germans bolted from their position, then 'A' Company would be required to pursue them. Despite the morose delivery, news of the Germans' weakened position and unsteady resolve brought some hope back to the troops, as did the British artillery bombardment that began at precisely 7:00 am. As with much positivity on the Front, this was checked soon enough when the Germans retaliated by shelling 'A' Company's position, putting a couple of 'Jack Johnsons' uncomfortably close to their trench.

"The cheek of it," piped up Jones once the German barrage had subsided, attempting to humour his downbeat Commander. "Time for our gunners to show them what-for eh!" Jones turned to Furze as he said this, smiling, just as Furze flung him to the floor as the British guns opened up.

"Get down!" Furze bellowed, "what on earth?"

"I thought those were our guns?" Jones sputter as he and Furze scrambled into cover, feeling the shock of lyddite dropping close to The Queen's position.

"They are…Good God, they've gravely mis-targeted…"

It transpired that the British guns had indeed miscalculated their aim, dropping their rounds extremely close to The Queen's and the Welsh Fusiliers. Thankfully, the mistake was quickly rectified with minimal damage to the British troops and their position, but no shortage of mistrust was harboured towards the gunners.

The attack thus developed further, and Furze kept 'A' Company ready for an advance at any moment, should the Germans retreat from their position. By nightfall, the 21st Brigade appeared to have covered a great deal of ground, but no information was passed to The Queen's until the next day.

"Apparently our lads captured three-hundred prisoners." Furze heard one soldier say to his companion.

"I heard it was close to eight-hundred," the other replied.

Such rumours seem to circulate through the lines like wildfire, thought Furze. Nevertheless, he was pleased at the solace such small tales of success brought to the troops.

Finally, after three days supporting the 20th and 21st Brigades' advance, Furze was informed that the British offensive had been temporarily abandoned.

"How so?" He enquired of the orderly who had brought the news.

"After our initial offensive, the Germans called up their reinforcements," the orderly replied, looking haggard. He had likely been asked the same question a hundred times on his rounds. "It was a large body, from what I understand, and they went straight in to support Aubers."

"Has there been any information on how the German troops have fared against our attacks?" Furze was more than a little dismayed to hear that the British offensive had been stopped without taking Aubers and sought at least a little reassurance that it had not all been in vain.

"I don't have precise numbers for you, Sir, but command believes they have suffered heavily. Our artillery hit them badly, and our advances certainly left a mark."

Furze thanked the orderly and called Humphreys and Jones to relay the information to the troops.

"Abandoned?!" exclaimed Jones, incredulous.

"Best say halted," chipped in Humphreys, who understood the delicacy of the situation. "We don't want the men to become dejected."

"But all our reinforcements, we outnumbered the Germans. Didn't we Furze?" Jones' questions were well intentioned, but they harassed Furze's already weighty conscience.

"I'm sure we'll get more details soon," Furze replied curtly, "for now, just relay the news to the men. At least we are likely to be out of these sordid trenches soon."

The news was taken as well as could be expected, the soldiers both glad that the threat of assault had been removed, and anxious at the apparent strength of the German line. As a result of this pause, the most notable event over the ensuing days was the departure of Captain Bates, Adjutant of The Queen's, who had been ordered to take over command of the Warwickshire Regiment following the death of its commander. As sorry as Furze was to lose Bates, he made an effort to welcome his replacement into the trenches and the Regiment as warmly as he could.

"Lieutenant Furze, Sir," he began, holding out his hand to the officer.

"Major Kirkpatrick," the new arrival replied, taking the outstretched hand, "the pleasure is mine. I've heard a great deal about this Regiment, and this Company in particular." He eyed Furze keenly, "my condolences for your recent loss, losing someone under your command is never easy, but losing a friend... that is something quite detestable."

Furze was taken aback at the familiarity of the remark yet, noticing the obvious concern upon the new adjutant's face, appreciated the comment. "Thank you, Sir."

"I have a wife at home, Evelyn, for whom I care more than anything in the world," the Major continued, as Furze walked him to his dugout. "She is who I fight for. But here, on the Front," he looked up at the parapet of the trench, "it is the men around us we must fight with and protect. Our friends may command our attention, but we must never forget that it is every man under our command that deserves our time."

Furze nodded his agreement, considering the major's words and finding comfort in the wisdom the new arrival appeared to possess "This is your dugout, Sir."

"Splendid," answered the Major, as Furze turned to go. "Oh, and I'm not one for formalities Furze, so please, call me Kirk."

"Absolutely, Kirk," Furze found himself smiling, "and I go by Furzzy."

Having spent a lengthy ten days in the trenches The Queen's were eventually relieved by the 20th Brigade. Furze marched 'A' Company five miles back to Estaires, where they found their billets clean and warm, and once the soldiers were properly settled, Furze and the other officers moved into their own rooms.

"Furzzy!" yelled Humphreys from an adjoining room, whilst Furze was stripping off his grubby uniform.

"What is it?" he questioned, moving towards the voice.

"Come and see for yourself, I think it'll be worth your while."

Intrigued as to what could have caught Humphreys' attention, Furze felt a surge of delight at the sight of a little piano.

"How neat," pronounced Furze, who couldn't help but chuckle at his musically illiterate friend's attempts to play the instrument.

"I don't know how you manage to make these things sound so good," huffed Humphreys, whose unpracticed fingers had been jamming at the keys.

"My dear fellow, some tasks require delicacy and patience. Qualities that, admittedly, are in short supply here."

"Well, I look forward to watching you 'delicately' beat the Germans, Furzzy," Humphreys retorted, duly shifting out of the way to allow Furze access to the instrument.

Having spent every waking moment of the past ten days either looking to the welfare of his men, executing his orders, or wrestling with his emotions following Austin's death, Furze allowed the soft tones which sprang from the piano to envelope him as his deft fingers floated over its keys. He forgot the strains of the past few days, focusing his mind on the present perfect moment of harmonious collaboration between man and instrument. So rarely were the troubles which swirled around his mind diluted enough to make them palatable, yet music had this welcome effect. As the gentle harmonies drifted around the building, Furze's quivering nerves recovered a sense of calm serenity that had not been present for many days.

Humphreys watched the frame of his friend deflate as gently the joyous melodies became fainter, their speed lessened, and Furze sat at last, silent, elbows on the edge of the piano, fists clenched together, staring before him into melancholy's bleak chasm.

"Austin?" Humphreys asked, his humanity reaching out to embrace such evident pain.

"The Lark Ascending, by Ralph Vaughan Williams. That was his favourite. He mentioned that it was played at his wedding." Furze answered. As soon as his fingers had touched the keys, he had known which piece he had needed to play, and as painful as the recollection of it was, he had wanted to do something to honour his friend.

"He would have appreciated it, Furzzy," Humphreys said, moving up next to him, "I can't think of a more appropriate send-off."

"He gave me this, Humphreys, only a moment before…" The words caught in his throat, sticking like glue and refusing to articulate themselves. Instead, he simply pulled Austin's letter, faint patches of blood still visible upon it, from his pocket and presented it to his friend.

Humphreys drew in a breath, then collected his strength, as much for Furze's sake as his own. "That's some weight to carry, Furzzy," he observed, carefully taking the letter from Furze's shaking hand. "You have a lot to focus on at the moment, men who need you to lead them, and you have held this long enough. I'll deal with it from here."

"Thank you." Furze gathered himself and rising from the piano felt relief flooding through him. "My apologies, for placing this burden upon you."

"Nonsense," Humphreys responded, "he was a good friend, and a great officer, I miss him too, Furzzy, though I may not express it that openly. This is the least I can do."

At long last, Captain Hewett returned, fully recovered, to take back command of 'A' Company and Furze was only too grateful to return him his men. Whilst he had appreciated the opportunity to hold such a position of responsibility, he believed that some distance from his memories in 'A' Company would be beneficial.

"Furze, how has it been?" asked Captain Hewett, as he entered 'A' Company's billets.

"Morning, Sir, you're looking well rested," Furze commented, evading the question.

"I feel well, I must admit," returned Hewett, "that time to recover certainly did me good. There is something about returning home, spending time with the family, walking the dogs. A normal existence, eh?"

"I quite agree, I think everyone yearns for that sort of life when on the Front. I trust you heard about poor Austin?" Furze felt a pang of grief at the mention of his friend, but Hewett had known Austin before Furze took over the Company, and Furze felt a desire to tell him about the loss personally.

"I did Keith, I was devastated to hear of his death." Hewett's face showed deep sorrow as he said this, and he took a seat. He looked at Furze, "your report suggested he died in a manner we should all be proud of?"

"He did, Sir, leading his men from the Front, and setting an example many would do well to take note of. I had come to rely upon him." Furze felt his emotions swelling but held the Captain's gaze. "I just feel it was such a horrible waste of vibrant life."

"War is a waste old chap, but it can sometimes be the only way to combat oppression. Never forget that we fight and die for something far more important than our own selves."

Furze lowered his eyes as he mulled over the Captain's words.

"Austin was a capital fellow," Hewett continued, "and I can see that you had an exceptional connection with him. I am grateful that he spent his last moments with such a capable Commander, let alone a good friend. Learn from this Furze. I'm afraid to say that, as an officer, this will not be the only time you lose someone close to you."

As harsh as those words may have sounded, Furze knew they were uttered with the best intentions and it was necessary to understand the sheer weight of responsibility that came with command.

On Wednesday 31st March, Furze received a delivery he had been awaiting with marked anticipation. Following Austin's death, Furze had written a number of letters to his father and mother, finding the process of placing his pain on paper immensely cathartic. In response to his son's evident distress his loving father had determined to help in whatever way he could, and Furze was shocked at the result, not wasting a single moment to write to Daw about it.

> *Darling Daw,*
>
> *Do forgive my account of more happenings on the Front, but I simply couldn't wait to tell you about a delivery I received today from Father. A horse! Not simply any horse, I might add, but a deep black thoroughbred war horse the likes of which I haven't seen. At seventeen hands, he stood proud and calm when I first approached him, a commanding presence if ever an animal could be. His coat gleamed in the morning light, drawing my attention to it in the same way a deep gorge captures one's focus.*
>
> *Oh Daw, during that first meeting he was so calm, so observant and aware, the very model of composure putting even the best drill Sergeants to shame! My favourite features though, which I hope you shall appreciate if ever you meet him, are his two right legs which have pearly white hair up to his ankles. It gives the impression that he is wearing two dainty white socks and I'm quite taken with them.*
>
> *I couldn't help myself and took him for a ride directly before breakfast, his power is astonishing. For a moment, I feared he might have too much energy, but it didn't take me long to find my flow, and all doubts*

vanished in a heartbeat. We galloped down the country lane with a swathing fluidity that infused me with joy and, as the world rushed past us, I felt as though it took with it all my troubles and concerns. Even fear couldn't keep up with me at that moment, atop such a magnificent beast.

We rested at the top of a nearby hill, and I must admit I was struck with emotion. Father must have spent a fortune on the horse, a strange decision for a man so usually practical. He must have felt utterly powerless to help me when he received my last letters, I own I likely appeared rather distressed in them. Resting atop this living, breathing representation of my father's love was a moment I shall never forget. I made a vow, dear Daw, to return with this horse to him and show him precisely how much this gesture meant to me.

Fondest wishes,
Keith
P.S. I have decided to name him –
Tommy.

Furze couldn't resist taking Tommy out as much as possible over the following few days, introducing him to as many of his friends as possible whilst conducting his duties. On one such day he decided to visit Charles Blount, who had not yet met Tommy and found him, as usual, with the General.

"Lieutenant Furze, ripping to see you," roared the General, "is that a new mount?"

"Looks like it, Sir," chimed Charles, eying Tommy keenly and flashing an approving smile in Furze's direction. "Fit for a General."

"I very much doubt that," countered Furze, rather embarrassed at the presumption. "Nevertheless, I have rather taken to him. This is Tommy, Sir."

"Glad to hear it Furze, and Tommy is a welcome addition to our ranks. Will you join us in riding to Estaires? I should value your opinion on the recent engagement." The General enquired.

"It would be a pleasure, Sir, although 'A' Company only provided fire support in the recent attack, so I may not be able to add much to what you already know."

The General and Charles mounted their own horses, and the trio turned towards Estaires. "I value your opinions highly, gentlemen, and I trust you to be discreet."

"Of course, Sir," said Charles, as Furze nodded in agreement.

"There is to be another attack soon," continued the General, "due to the abandonment of the last action, which gained little in the way of ground."

Charles and Furze glanced at each other, pondering over where the General wished to take the conversation.

"What is the feeling amongst the men at the moment, Furze?" The direct question caused Furze to pause, contemplating his answer. He thought it best to be honest.

"Confused, Sir." He replied, taking care to observe the General's expression as he spoke. "Many wonder how so little could have been achieved by the last attack, given the number of reinforcements we brought up in preparation, outnumbering the Germans at least two to one."

"Indeed." murmured the General. "What else?"

"Well, from my Company's perspective," continued Furze, "our supporting fire seemed vicious. Added to the barrage from our own guns, the scale of which few had experienced before, it's unclear how the Germans withstood it."

"Hmm," nodded the General.

"I think, in all honesty, the attack seemed poorly planned, executed too quickly, and actioned on a whim rather than on solid information." Furze wondered if he was overstepping the mark, but he trusted the General. "True, the aerial maps were impressive but, at one point, our own gunners almost hit my men!"

"Yes, that was too near a miss," agreed the General. "Thank you for your honesty Furze, and it corroborates what I hear from other trusted officers."

"I hold many of the same views Furzzy," Charles added, conscious of his friend's concerned look. "Headquarters was overwhelmed with confusion as reports flooded in that none of our attacks were turning out the results expected."

"Morale was hit, Sir," noted Furze, "but the soldiers are still all behind you."

"That is good to know, Furze," answered the General, evidently lost in thought. They continued for a while in silence, allowing their commander this moment of reflection. "Thank you both. That was only the beginning, and something to learn from. Better communication will be essential in the future, as will greater patience." The General suddenly turned and smiled at Furze. "Anyway, on to lighter topics, tell me more about Tommy!"

The Adjutancy

"In the afternoon the Commander in Chief Sir John French came and inspected us...he addressed us for a few minutes but his words were not at all inspiring."
Wednesday 21st April.

On the evening of 7th April, The Queen's were due to return to the trenches once more, so the Brigade Commander carried out a tedious, yet necessary, inspection all morning after which Furze rode Tommy up to the trenches. He proceeded to Headquarters in 'E' lines, which was where the Battalion was to settle that night and was told that there had been little movement on either side recently. Having repulsed the British assault, reports suggested that the Germans had been working tirelessly, bringing up further reinforcements to replenish their lines and repair their defences. Given the losses sustained by the British troops during the last assault, Headquarters was reluctant to make another push until more drafts of fresh troops had arrived.

On the one hand, Furze was content in the knowledge that another large attack was not due for a while. On the other, he was worried about the underlying 'all or nothing' mentality that he caught glimpses of in the Staff Officers with whom he spoke.

Credit has to be given to the Germans on that front; they played their cards close to their chests and outmanoeuvred our High Command. Next time, it won't be so easy, thought Furze.

Furze was a gentleman and held a careful respect for the soldiers and commanders of the opposing forces. Soldiers and officers who, like his colleagues and he, were fighting because their country and its leaders required it. They fought because those in positions of power believed it was the right thing to do. To respect and understand one's enemy was to give oneself the only chance of overcoming him in battle. It also helped Furze retain his sense of humanity, for, without such rationality, he considered the war little more than a feud between base animals.

At 7:30 pm The Queen's relieved the Bonde Regiment, trudging into their wet and muddy dugouts under torrential rain. It was unsettling being back in such an unwelcoming environment after resting for three weeks, and the officers spent a great deal of time working their way around the men attempting to settle them in. To Furze's surprise, the next day he received orders to leave 'A' Company and report to Headquarters, a lonely building standing in what used to be the village of Favquisart. A somewhat conspicuous target, the British had decided that if the Germans were capable of destroying an entire village without hitting it, Headquarters would be perfectly safe there. It transpired that his assigned duty consisted of writing up the Battalion's war diary, as required by Lord Claud Hamilton, and he undertook this task with keen interest by writing most mornings and inspecting the trenches in the afternoons.

Through his conversations with the other officers while gathering information for the War Diary, he managed to have a long talk with Major Bottomley whom he had not seen since serving together through the 1st Battle of Ypres.

"A dire battle, Furzzy," the Major recalled, perched uncomfortably on a rickety wooden chair one evening, "but I fear we haven't seen the worst of it yet."

"Nor I," agreed Furze, "and I have been pondering the last British engagement."

"What's on your mind?" posed the Major.

"This impasse unsettles me. Yes, the lines shouldn't be changing hands constantly, but I fear that such a stalemate will result in a battle of patience."

"That doesn't sound so bad."

"Not in principle," responded Furze, mulling over this thought. "We aren't the aggressor here, the Germans are. By all accounts, we should just wait until they make attack after attack and wear down their forces."

"And yet?" pressed the Major.

"I feel there is more at stake here than merely defending against an aggressor. I get the sense that national pride directed our last attack, and pride is a raw nerve to the British."

"I value your thoughts Furze, but don't devalue the skill of our commanders," warned Bottomley, "I'm sure they acted upon better reasons than their pride during our last offensive, unless you have any evidence to the contrary?"

Furze looked over at the Major, who eyed him keenly, awaiting his response. Although Furze counted him a friend, he also understood the stark differences in their characters. Bottomley was matter of fact, an optimistic realist and, above all, concerned only with the evidence to hand. If something didn't register with at least one of his senses, then the matter wasn't worth consideration. This made him an exceptional commander from the point of view of following orders to the letter. However, alternative thinking had never been Bottomley's forte, and he certainly wasn't one for heart-to-hearts.

Furze knew not to press the issue and smiled. "No, only a hunch. You're likely right, Major, I'm sure Command knows what it's doing."

On Sunday, The Queen's was relieved from duty and Furze, now attached to the Staff and not to a specific Company, was told that the Regiment was to be billeted at Ft. D'Esquin. Seizing this freedom, he rode ahead with the Company Quartermaster Sergeants to help select the most appropriate billets for the men. As ever, it was a joy to be riding away from the trenches, and Tommy was on particularly good form. He noticed the same looks of tired relief on the faces of the Quartermasters and grinned as a thought crossed his mind to lift their moods.

"Gentlemen, who's up for a little race?"

"We wouldn't stand a chance, Sir," laughed one of the Sergeants, "unless…"

The rest looked at one another before, unanimously, bolting forwards in mutual pleasure. Furze barely had time to register the moment before the billeting party had flung itself in the direction of Ft. D'Esquin. The sergeants, who had been lent horses for the trip, knew their mounts were no match for Tommy and used their numbers and head-start to keep Furze at bay. Their pack tactics succeeded in blocking the route every time Furze got close and thought he had found a gap, enabling the lead sergeant to inch further and further ahead. Impressed, and enjoying the group's tenacity, this equine joust continued until the final moment, when one of the Sergeants mistimed his horse's stride and pulled heavily on the reins to prevent himself from falling. This left a gap momentarily, yet perfectly timed, for Furze to unleash Tommy's full power and surge through the mass, catching the lead Sergeant in seconds and swooping to victory.

The quartermasters steamed to a halt just behind him.

"Thought we 'ad you there, Sir," the lead Sergeant said breathlessly, patting his panting mount, "you've some real power in that one."

"You manoeuvred yourselves splendidly, until the end," grinned Furze. "Now, to business!"

Business, as it turned out, was all Furze would have time for over the next week or so as a result of Major Kirkpatrick going on leave, and Furze being made acting Regimental Adjutant. His first task was to get the Battalion to its new billets in La Gorgue, a short march away. They left Laventie on Wednesday evening and were met with atrocious weather, which made the march incredibly unpleasant. To make matters worse, the new billets were far from agreeable, and the men grumbled at the prospect of spending their well-earned rest in such dire surroundings.

Just my luck, Furze thought, as the men trudged into the new billets, *my first task as their Adjutant and they'll likely blame me for picking the accommodation.*

The next morning, even Furze had to own that he had passed the night uncomfortably. That said, the men were all warm and dry, so they rose, packed up their soggy kit, and marched to Estaires. They paraded on the Brigade training ground where Furze took the chance to hold an inspection. Although each man was responsible for the welfare of his own kit and person, it was the adjutant's responsibility to ensure the group as a whole was fighting fit.

"Pampered rascals!" One of his Sergeants commented to him once the inspection was over, having heard a soldier gripe over the night's accommodation.

"It's only natural," Furze responded. He knew the Sergeant, hard as nails, he was precisely the blunt, to-the-point individual you wanted next to you during a battle. He did, however, lack a little paternal instinct, and delicacy was certainly not his area of expertise.

"Yes, Sir, but they should know better. Serving this long on the Front makes you appreciate the little things, you know? We 'ain't had no fighting, it's made 'em soft."

"I agree with you about the inactivity, Sergeant, but the men need their rest. Don't you worry, we will be back in the thick of it soon enough, and we all perform better when fully rested."

"The sooner the better I say," growled the Sergeant.

"By-the-by, I wish you to relay some good news to the men," Furze mentioned with a slight smile.

"Oh, really Sir, what?" frowned the Sergeant, unaccustomed to good news.

"We will be billeting here, in Estaires, this evening. That will no doubt lift the men's spirits."

"No doubt, Sir, but God help 'em if I hear a single grumble from any of 'em. I'll tell 'em now and get 'em assigned." The Sergeant saluted Furze and powered off, eager to bark at the Company.

The billets in Estaires were of very fine quality and the Battalion had resided there before. On hearing the Sergeant's news, the Battalion's spirits were immediately lifted, and there was a flurry of activity as the soldiers rushed to move into their quarters. Furze observed the humdrum activity with gentle amusement. No matter what situation men found themselves in, they never seemed to lose that sense of competition that made them scramble over one another to secure the 'top bunk' as he liked to term it. He remembered how, as young teenagers, his friends and he had done much the same at Charterhouse when assigned their boarding dormitories each term. As soon as the door to the room had opened, the boys used to rush to get the bed furthest from the door, or nearest to the radiators, flinging their belongings across the room at the mischievous hand of chaos. Here, even amidst the war, a common rivalry existed between all the men as to who would get the 'best bunk'.

Mind you, I'm not much better, he thought, sheepishly, as he approached his quarters with a victorious feeling, for they were situated in a very nice house which formed Estaires' HQ.

The next few days saw some superb weather press down upon numerous Brigade and Company inspections, as well as some route marches and Battalion training. Furze's spirits were elevated further on Saturday by the arrival of a long-overdue letter from his sweetheart, Daw. It had been a long while since he had heard from her, and Furze had been feeling the natural pangs of longing when someone one cares for so deeply falls out of contact. He slid open the envelope, running his fingers over the elegant curves of her handwriting on its front, and began to read.

My darling Keith,

I'm so sorry not to have written sooner. Life here, although nothing compared to yours, has been very busy with Mother and I are helping out with the war effort where we can. My work with the War Relief Fund is growing beyond all reckoning. I have now met the group's president, Leila Paget, who is quite inspirational and has been conducting humanitarian work across a collection of countries for a number of years now. I even made a visit to the Fund's Hospital at Oldway in Paignton and learnt a little about how to look after some of the wounded soldiers that had been brought there to recuperate. But I'm loathe to talk about the war with you, who lives and breathes it every day.

I hope you are feeling better in yourself. Following your last letters, I was so distressed that I paid a visit to your parents, who were very sweet to me. Your mother cooked for me, and we talked about you as a boy! You really did sound such a funny thing back then, and I'm sure I heard stories I shouldn't have.

Your father was a darling, and even invited me to join him on his trip to collect your new horse. Oh, isn't he a beauty? Your last letter to me describing how you felt when you first took possession of him was heartwarming. Your father was simply besotted the moment he saw him and his care for you was beyond compare. I can tell that you make him, and your mother, very proud. 'Tommy' is a name well-suited to such a magnificent mount!

I miss you dearly and wish you every safety until your return. My heart is with you, and I shall be waiting at Folkestone the week you plan to arrive back on leave, whenever that may be...

*Ever yours,
Daw*

The arrival of Daw's letter warmed Furze's heart and he spent the next few days basking in her words. He simply couldn't wait to see her again, dance with her through the halls of the Savoy, listen to her as she recounted stories of a life so far removed from his own, and watch the wind rustle playfully in her hair as they walked in London's glorious parks.

Please God, allow me the chance to see her again, he thought silently.

Closing his eyes and holding the letter tightly to his chest, his mind caught one phrase that brought a shiver of anticipation.

My heart is with you...

Usually, Daw would have written 'my thoughts', or 'my prayers', and the new turn of phrase struck an unusual warmth within him, a hope, perhaps, of something he had not yet dared to consider with so much pain and death surrounding him. As counterintuitive as it was to numb oneself to the compelling calls of love, Furze had always thought it best to cauterise such feelings out of fear; fear and anxiety over the impact they might have on his ability to fight. The more Daw wrote, however, the more Furze was beginning to believe that such emotions might well be a strength, rather than a weakness.

Sunday through to Tuesday saw more fabulous weather, in which the Company progressed with its route marches and training, as well as an impromptu trip to the Division bathhouse.

"They feel like men again," Humphreys commented, as he sat next to Furze, having been assigned to keep tabs on the proceedings. "It seems small, but it's easy to forget the humanity we come from in environments such as these."

"I was thinking the same," agreed Furze, grateful for his friend's company, "all of these men left lives at home and found themselves here, fighting for a cause I'm certain many truly fail to comprehend. It's worth reminding them of the civilisation and freedom awaiting them back home."

Major Kirkpatrick, Fuller, Garmin, Manson, and Brookes eventually return from their respective leave, and Furze was overjoyed to have his friends and colleagues back with him in France.

"You couldn't have returned at a better time." He smiled at them that evening, "the Commander in Chief, Sir John French, will be leading a Brigade inspection tomorrow."

Kirkpatrick snorted into his coffee, "The Commander in Chief?"

"That's what I heard as well," assented Brookes. "Is there a reason for his presence? I would have thought he'd have enough on his mind without carrying out a Brigade inspection."

"I know nothing other than that I'm afraid," responded Furze, looking honestly into the faces of his companions, "but it means everything has to be in perfect order."

"I've met Sir John," Kirkpatrick added warily, "the Commander must be in his sixties by now."

"What's your opinion of him," queried Furze, intrigued.

"Well, he has had a distinguished career for sure, but there are those who feel he lacks the tact to collaborate properly with the French commanders."

"But what do you think of him?" pressed Garmin.

"I've always felt he is a commander with a plan," responded Kirkpatrick carefully, "therefore, old boys, I'll be honest with you. I feel the Commander would only make an inspection like this if he had something in mind for the Brigade."

"So, there's to be another attack..." finished Brookes.

"Precisely," assented Kirkpatrick.

"Better go back on leave then," quipped Fuller, with a wry smile that the group mirrored.

The news soon got round that a number of the Allied High Command would be at the parade, and this led to a restless night as the officers kept their men up late, ensuring they and their kit would gleam the next day.

Furze roused his Regiment early and performed a practice run of the inspection due that afternoon. The usual minor issues were detected, missing kit, unclean boots, soldiers standing in the wrong position, so it took all morning, and many a sharp word from eagle-eyed corporals, before the troops were judged ready to face the Chief. The other Regiments in Furze's Battalion had been doing the same and, by the afternoon, the three Battalions of the Brigade had formed three sides of a square on Estaires' parade ground.

At precisely 3:00 pm, Sir John French appeared, surrounded by a plethora of generals, colonels, and other senior staff officers. The entourage looked resplendent and sent excited whispers around the Battalions, whispers that were swiftly silenced by the steely reprimands of the Non-Commissioned Officers.

Furze stood apart, and to the front of his Company with the other officers, watching Sir John French with great interest. Here was the man who made the final decisions over where his Company would go, where it would fight, where it would kill, and where it might be killed. The weight of the war at that moment rested on his shoulders, and any man in his position, Furze thought, would need such an entourage of advisors just to outsource his thoughts to.

Furze cast his eye over the other generals, and noted that Sir Douglas Haig, and General Sir William Robertson, were also with Sir John. Sir Douglas, standing proud but sullen behind French, had been instrumental in the Battle of Neuve Chapelle, Furze knew. General Robertson was the youngest of the three, and Chief of Staff of the British Expeditionary Force.

The Generals inspected each Battalion in turn, striding purposefully around the inside of the square from Company to Company, and section to section, commenting and talking to the officers and men as they passed. Furze was not spoken to, but presented his men with pride, steadfast in his certainty of their quality. After an hour or so Sir John, seemingly satisfied, moved to address the Brigade. All the soldiers and officers were brought to attention, and eagerly anticipated words of inspiration from the man in whose hands their futures resided.

"I wish to thank you all for your dedication to this fight," French began, without a touch of emotion. "Know that your efforts are noted by King and country, as well as all those at High Command."

Furze was perplexed; the General almost looked bored.

"Continue to fight well, and do your duty, and we shall end this war victorious and head home. Be brave, be bold, and face whatever the future holds. My thoughts are with you."

Sir John only spoke for a few minutes, and then hurriedly took his leave. Furze was greatly disappointed and felt rather deflated. In his opinion, Sir John French's words were not at all inspiring, and he worried about the effect this would have on his men. For Furze, any officer who did not have the full confidence of his troops would make a poor leader and this thought weighed heavy on his mind. As such, when the other Regiments disbanded, he held his own on the parade ground a moment longer and addressed them.

"Men, listen in!" Furze commanded. "You have all done yourselves, the Regiment, and the Battalion proud today. The Commander in Chief was evidently impressed by your dedication, turnout, and professionalism, and for him to give you even a moment of his time is a credit to you all. Were His Majesty here, he would be proud to know you served in his Army, and I know Sir John French felt the same." He paused, looking at the faces of the men in front of him, then continued, strolling up the line. "I have no doubt you will uphold those same standards on the field of battle, as you demonstrated on the parade ground so well today. If you can face the Commander in Chief, you can face the Germans!"

The men laughed heartily, and Furze nodded to the sergeants to disband them.

That's put them in finer spirits, he thought happily, before proceeding to dinner with the officers of 'B' Company.

Apprehension

"The YPRES battle is still raging furiously and it rather looks as though we are suffering a slight reverse. We expect to be called up there but it all depends how things go."
Tuesday 27th April.

Although Major Kirkpatrick took back the Adjutancy after the Commander in Chief's inspection, Furze was asked to stay on at Headquarters.

"Fancy a ride, Furze?" came the voice of the Commanding Officer behind him one morning. Furze turned, and saw Kirkpatrick grinning eagerly behind the CO.

"You'll need to wrap up," Kirkpatrick added, "it's fresh out there."

"Absolutely gentlemen," assented Furze, eager to escape from his paperwork, "I'll join you in a moment."

Furze donned a warm overcoat and went to fetch Tommy. Regretfully, he hadn't taken the poor animal out for a long while, having been distracted by his duties as Adjutant, and Tommy whinnied haughtily at him as he entered.

"It's alright for you, old boy," Furze said with a jovial scold, "you haven't had a Regiment to run!" Then he stroked the horse's nose and neck and mounted up to meet the others.

"Right-oh! Let's make the most of this afternoon," cajoled Kirkpatrick, and the three riders cantered out into the French countryside.

"He's moving well," the CO commented, glancing at Tommy keeping pace with his mount.

"He gets restless, Sir, I haven't a clue where he gets his energy from, but it appears bottomless."

"Horses respond to their owners, Furzzy," added Kirkpatrick, before gesturing at his own thoroughbred, "this one, for example, has a tendency to bowl straight through hedges rather than jump over them."

When the trio got to their intended destination, a place just to the rear of the trenches, the other Regimental and Company commanders joined them. The group then proceeded to a nearby artillery observation post to view, and comment on, the ground over which the Battalion expected to advance in the forthcoming days. After a few hours, the CO, satisfied that his officers had gained enough knowledge of the land to impart to their troops, took the party back to Estaires where they dismounted and joined him in his quarters.

"Listen in gentlemen," the CO began, summoning them to his table. "You've now viewed the ground in front of our lines and, I own, this was not a task undertaken on my whim alone. I expect an attack to be forthcoming, and I wish all of you to understand the situation to the fullest extent before it begins."

"Do you know when we may make a move, Sir?" asked one of the officers.

"I'm afraid not Captain," answered the CO, "but I don't expect it to be long. The Commander in Chief's visit the other day allowed him to inspect our readiness for action, and I believe he was suitably satisfied. All I can say is, be as prepared as you can, and I'll keep you up to speed with any new information I receive."

There were nods of assent amongst the group.

"For now, prepare to move into the trenches tomorrow evening, where we shall relieve The Black Watch stationed around Neuve Chapelle."

The CO bade them all a good evening, and Furze left with Major Slacke to take dinner, discussing the forthcoming attack until late into the night. The next morning, Furze was startled back to consciousness with a shout.

"The Germans have broken through the French, Furze!"

"What?" Furze replied, groggily, in the direction from which the exclamation had come.

"The Germans Furzzy! Come on you rascal, get up."

Furze, having taken a moment to process the news, turned over and flung himself out of bed. It was Major Kirkpatrick who had interrupted his slumber and, given that the Major rarely got so agitated, he dashed to get changed, before following him to find out what was going on. It transpired that there was trouble at Ypres.

"What's the news, Sir?" Furze enquired as they entered the CO's room at Headquarters.

"What we know is the following," began the CO, leaning over his large field map. "Early this morning, the Germans launched a targeted attack on the French lines, here," he gestured to a position on the map. "This attack has, allegedly, broken through the line, and this part of the Allied Front is now under severe threat."

There were murmurs around the room from the startled officers. They had all been preparing for an attack, but not one instigated by the Germans.

"What are your orders, Sir?" queried a staunch Major, always quick to the point.

"We shall no longer be relieving The Black Watch. Instead, ready your men to move at a moment's notice, wherever they may be required."

A collective, "Yes Sir!" resounded around the room, before the officers hurried out to enact the CO's orders.

Every Company packed away its kit, cleaned its billets and, by midday, the Battalion was ready to move. Furze was rushed between Headquarters and the various Company commanders all day succumbing, by the end of it, to a rather rotten throat. The Regiment, however, remained in this state of tense stasis for a couple of days, removing only the essential items of kit from their bags each evening, before packing it all away again each morning. On Monday 26th April, Kirkpatrick returned from a meeting with the CO.

"Any news?" Furze croaked, his throat still giving him grief.

"The situation at Ypres appears to have calmed down somewhat, reports suggest the Canadians are doing a sterling job beating the Germans back."

"Good men," muttered Furze, relieved, "where does that leave us?"

"We are to remain on high alert, for now." Kirkpatrick flung himself onto a chair, "I tell you though Furzzy, this uncertainty is sapping my energy."

Due to the need to remain on high alert, it became increasingly difficult to train or conduct inspections, and Furze worried about how much longer the men could take being held in such suspense. To tell someone they are to face a certain danger, is to present them with fear, uncertainty, and uneasiness. But it is also to present them with a chance to ready themselves for what is to come, taking strength in the knowledge that they have been able to anticipate and prepare for it. But tell someone they will face danger too many times, with no such danger materialising, and they can lose interest in that danger and become complacent instead of empowered. Furze dearly hoped that the men would be given some clarity very soon.

To Furze's deep frustration, the Regiment's situation remained unchanged the next day, so Furze decided to gather the Company Commanders and put a plan to them.

"Gentlemen, thank you for your time. I am distinctly aware that all our soldiers are being kept ready to move at a moment's notice for good reason. However, I fear they cannot be left in such a state of flux for very much longer, without being in danger of losing their sanity."

"I agree with Furze," Kirkpatrick replied, "my Company is positively tugging at the leash to be let loose on the Germans, or be told they can go back to playing cards and talking nonsense to each other all evening."

"Your Company talks nonsense regardless of their situation Kirk." Fuller grinned, a moment of good humour borrowing the spotlight before returning it to the matter at hand.

"As is their right," Kirkpatrick smiled in return. "Nonetheless, they would still like to know whether their nonsense can be put to irritating the German lines, rather than your men. What do you propose Furzzy?"

"Well, this afternoon I thought we could have an inter-company route march. We haven't been able to get much training done in our present state but, if I can swing it with Headquarters, I believe a bit of activity mixed with some lively competition would do the lads some good."

"Capital idea!" piped up Fuller.

"I'm in agreement," responded Kirkpatrick, "plus, Fuller will be able to enjoy being beaten by a Company that does nothing but talk nonsense!"

The officers roared with amusement and nodded in mutual agreement. "I'll return momentarily gentlemen." Furze instantly whisking himself off to talk to the Commanding Officer about his plan.

"You do realise we could be called upon at a moment's notice Furze?" The CO enquired in a measured tone, tapping his pen on the table as he mulled over the suggestion.

"I do Sir," answered Furze earnestly, "which is why a route march is the ideal form of distraction, activity and exercise. The men will be carrying everything that they require, should they be called upon, and we shall ensure we keep up constant communication with Headquarters, ready to act as required as soon as needed."

"You say the men are on edge?" probed the CO.

"They are more than ready to be sent wherever required, but they haven't done anything productive for days, they are restless, and bored. And with boredom follows complacency. They need to be let out, to stretch their legs, much like Tommy the other day."

"Well, I suppose you are right, the men need to be kept active." The CO assented, "but ensure you pick a route that sticks close to the camp and maintain contact with Headquarters at all times."

"Thank you, Sir! The men will welcome the news." Furze grateful for the acquiescence, flew out of the room.

The competitive route march was an enormous success, causing a great deal of amusement amongst the men and acting as a necessary release for their pent-up energy. It also couldn't have been more appropriately timed for, the next morning, no sooner had the Battalion moved out onto the training ground than up dashed the General.

"Get the men ready to move in two hours' time," he commanded to Furze, "and spread the message to your counterparts."

"Yes Sir!" Furze bolted, already moving towards the nearest officers as he did so.

The Queen's, led by their officers and senior Non-Commissioned Officers, rushed back to their billets and frantically got ready to move out.

"Get a move on!" bellowed a Sergeant near Furze, to a group of straggling soldiers.

"We were told we were moving out last time," Furze overheard a young soldier mutter to his friend, "we'll remain here, you'll see."

"Never make assumptions my dear fellow." Furze voiced calmly but with authority, making the soldier jump as he appeared beside him.

"I'm sorry Sir," the young man stammered, "I meant nothing…"

"Don't concern yourself," Furze reassured him. "Just remember, being ready for something that doesn't materialise is better than being caught unawares by something that does."

This time the orders were followed through and, at around 1:00 pm, the Brigade marched twelve miles to Merris. During the march, as Furze rode down the column, he passed the youth he had spoken to that morning, and the soldier nodded gratefully to him. Upon their arrival, the soldiers were told to move into new billets and await further orders, whilst the officers were gathered for a briefing.

"My thanks gentlemen," the Commanding Officer said, "I half expected to remain where we were, but the change of scene is a welcome relief. We are to form the General Headquarters reserve force, whilst the battle continues to rage at Ypres."

"How is the situation there, Sir?" asked Bottomley.

"Developing, is all I have been told," responded the General, "but we have been placed here in support of Ypres, should matters there get any worse."

The tension in the room was apparent, each officer painfully aware that reserve forces of this size were rarely called up on a whim. Although the Brigade was once again on constant alert, with no knowledge of when, or if, it would be mobilised, at least the soldiers had new surroundings to settle into.

The Organ

"In the afternoon I played the organ in the church which I much enjoyed. The organ is too manual, but very nice to play. The church here is like all Roman Catholic edifices – beautiful."
Saturday 1st May

The next few days saw little movement for the Brigade, nor much news from the front. The weather was spectacular, the sun gently increasing in strength as summer dawned on the troops waiting languidly in the usually idyllic town. Merris was a quiet place, commanding the valley beneath it from its position on the top of a hill. On one such contemplative day, as Furze drank in the tranquility of the scene, a thought suddenly struck him. He had heard about this place from Bobbie Ross. After Furze had been sent home to recover in November, his Brigade had taken part in the assault at Klein Zillebeke. The assault was a deadly one, and it was to Merris that Bobbie Ross had fought. Out of the thirty or so officers in his Battalion, Bobbie was the only one who had survived. Furze remembered his friend recounting the dire memory, mentioning the very cottage Furze now called home as the spot he had chosen as his Headquarters. Furze could now fully appreciate why Bobbie had done so.

"It's strange to be back, Furzzy," Bobbie said that morning, as they strolled amongst the troops after breakfast, "seeing this place now, so peaceful, doesn't seem to fit with my memory of it."

"You went through the unthinkable taking it," Furze said, feeling his friend's pain, "and you chose an excellent location as your Headquarters."

"It was a Godsend, and a last resort…" Bobbie replied, thrust into his thoughts, "but I'm glad you think so. When we were fighting up the ridge to the town, and man after man was falling around me, I caught sight of the cottage and remember thinking, 'if we can only reach that building, we can regroup and command the area.' It appeared a fool's hope, but I had to give the men something to focus on other than death. I had to give myself something to focus on, even if it seemed an impossibility."

He paused, and Furze gazed at him in silence. "When we got there, I could hardly believe it," Bobbie continued, "and it was only then that we realised how few Germans we had been fighting against. Once we had won the cottage, we had won the fight. The cost, though, was catastrophic."

"And we now control this position," encouraged Furze, "so imagine the toll the Germans will have to pay if they ever attempt to take it back."

"True," agreed Bobbie, continuing their walk, "how do you think Ypres will play out?"

"At this stage," mused Furze, "I don't think we will be called upon. The Germans would have followed on from their initial success by now if they had intended to push us any further back. The fact we haven't been ordered up in support already leads me to believe they are content with their gains."

"For now, perhaps," nodded Bobbie, "but take it from me Furzzy, the Germans are stubborn bastards when they want to be. I've learnt that the hard way."

On Friday 30th April, Furze remembered it was his brother, Nevil's, 18th birthday, and so he wrote him a letter befitting a boy turned man.

Dear Nevil,

Eighteen, what a sturdy age to reach in a world that is currently so fragile. As I sit here, in France, thinking over how dearly I wish I were back in England with all of you, I think upon what advice I can give my younger brother, now a man. We never know where life will take us, and no measure of preparation can ready us for the challenges that will be thrown at us. Right now, the world is on fire, and men fight for the security, pride, and honour of their country, as well as the safety of the people they love.

Throughout my life, I have always striven to make Mother happy, Father proud, and to inspire you. To be the older brother whose mistakes you can look to for guidance, and who, in time, you can surpass in all things. Know that I'm sorry I have not been there for you more, to walk with you and ride with you, and see you grow into the strong, young man I know you to be. With Doug and I on the front, do not look to your future in the Army with too eager an eye. Your time here will come and, when it does, you must be ready to face it. However, more importantly, no, most important of all, it is your duty, as the last son in the house, to ensure Mother and Father are ready to face your departure. Look to their needs above yours, while you can.

Humour Mother when she fusses over your meals and your attire, respect Father

as he steers you to be a better gentleman,
and spend time with Diddy and Margy, even
if all they want to do is walk in the park and
talk of their sweethearts. Protect them all,
that is your duty now, as a man of eighteen.
No matter your age, remember, you are
always a son, and a brother.

I love you dearly, and hope, with all my
heart, to see you soon.

With pride,
Keith

On Saturday 1st May, May Day, Furze decided to go and take a look in the church situated in the centre of Merris and wandered leisurely towards it. He marvelled at the beauty of the Roman Catholic edifice and took a moment to appreciate the fact that such beauty remained untouched and defiant, even when surrounded by the monstrosity of war. He prayed it continued to stand thus, and duly entered it.

Walking slowly up the aisles towards the pulpit, his right hand drifted gently over the wooden pews, rubbed smooth by the touch of thousands of individuals seeking quiet solitude and guidance. He was perfectly alone, the only sounds being the tap, tap, tap, of his footsteps on the cool stone floor, the rustle of his uniform, and the hiss of his breath as he continued his journey. As Furze's eyes reached a corner of the church, they pulled forth a sight that caused him let out a gentle gasp of longing. There, hidden from most of the congregation, crouched a splendid organ.

He sat in front of it, pausing, the silence around him almost quivering in anticipation.

Then, gently, he let go of the peace and allowed the joy of the organ's tones to sweep over him, soaring Elgar's Enigma

Variations into the air. He spent the afternoon playing a selection of pieces he had memorised, his mind wandering back to days at Charterhouse, where he had spent hours engrossed in the wonders of this majestic instrument.

He had not sat at an organ in a long while, and the moment captivated him.

He changed the tune, for a brief period returning home to memories of Daw leaning over his shoulder, listening to his music and watching his hands. He could feel her arms around his neck, her hair draped over his shoulders, hear her breathing, and smell her perfume. He remembered playing her delicate renditions of the songs she loved on her parents' piano, summer streaming unapologetically though the open windows of her living room. He struck the keys of the organ passionately, pressing his feet against the lower keys with a steely determination, holding onto the glorious memory as though it was his most valuable possession.

He stopped.

His hands were shaking.

His eyes were closed.

He wasn't aware that he had closed them, being so engrossed in the music and the memory. Standing, he took one last look at the beautiful instrument, and turned to leave the church. The organ had made him miss Daw, his home, and his family greatly, but it had also reminded him of who he was fighting for.

Moments such as those, and the memories they recall, as well as create, are not to be looked at with sorrow, he thought, *but treasured.*

As his footsteps faded gently away, the church seemed to exhale, resigning itself to the care of the silence Furze had briefly banished with his musical memories.

Alas, the solace of the church did not follow Furze out, and bad news from Ypres continued to drip in day by day. Heavy cannonading could be heard each night, and it was relayed that the Warwicks at Hill 60 had taken a severe blow. Eventually,

Furze was informed that the Allies had abandoned the Ypres salient, and the Brigade was ordered to move back to La Gorgue on the 5th May to support the repositioned British line.

At 10:00 pm, they set off into the chilly yet clear and beautiful night. Furze, mounted tall upon Tommy and basking in the night's fresh breeze, rode ahead of the column with Belchan in order to arrange their accommodation. On the brow of a nearby hill, he turned briefly to look back at the line of troops behind him, snaking out from Merris. Thousands of men, laden with kit and equipment, forming an unstoppable mass that forged towards its next destination. The scale of the war continually amazed Furze. The sight of this Brigade alone was striking, yet there were not thousands, but millions of troops at war all along the Front. He turned back to Belchan, "they have a long march ahead of them, let's make sure everything is in order by the time they arrive." The men had been saddened to leave Merris, and he wished to ensure they felt valued when they arrived, exhausted, at around 01:30 am.

Rising early, just a few hours after their arrival, Furze and his fellow officers joined their Commanding Officer to ride up to the rear of the trenches. Even Tommy seemed disgruntled to be woken so early after their moonlit march, and he nibbled Furze as he led him out of the makeshift stable block.

"I know, Tommy, I know," Furze soothed, "I'd welcome sleep just as much as you, but we have work to do, my boy."

A captain met them just behind the trenches. "Good morning Sir," greeted the Captain politely to the CO, saluting as he did so.

"Morning Captain, a rather topping one wouldn't you say?" The CO had adopted his commanding air of positive attentiveness.

"Indeed, Sir," the Captain agreed, though it was evident the response was automatic rather than genuine. The Captain had deep-set eyes as it was, but the bags underneath them highlighted the fatigue he was struggling with. Regardless, he held himself tall, focusing on the task in hand. Looking to the wider group, he continued, "Good morning gentlemen, let me show you which trenches you will be taking over in due course."

The officers dismounted and followed the Captain and CO to their trenches. The Brigade was to be in the support trenches initially, but the Captain knew the land well, and showed them the lines of advance which each of the surrounding Brigades, Battalions, and Companies would take during the impending engagement.

Observing the CO and the Captain, Kirkpatrick muttered to Furze, "here are two officers who know what they are doing."

"Agreed," replied Furze, who had been increasingly impressed by the Captain's knowledge of the Allied position and the CO's marked attention to every detail shown to him. As they made their way back, Furze turned to Kirkpatrick who was riding calmly beside him. "What do you make of the plans, top-level as they were?"

The Major chewed over the question before replying, "in general, I am more confident over our next attack than I was over our last."

"You don't think it too simplistic?" pressed Furze, eager to scour his experienced friend's mind.

"Simplicity is never to be frowned upon, Furzzy," countered Kirkpatrick. "The last attack may have had those new aerial photographs, but the next one appears to rest more heavily on the experience of the men on the ground. I'd sooner entrust my life to that weary Captain, who has lived and breathed the situation, than a piece of paper."

That evening, the officers once again attended a conference with the CO.

"I hope today provided you with some clarity about the forthcoming offensive?" The CO queried the group.

"It did, Sir," answered one of the Majors, and the other officers nodded their assent and murmured in agreement. "Top-level though it was."

"Splendid, and point well noted. Rest assured further details will be forthcoming, I promise you that." The CO took a measured look at the faces of his officers, before continuing, "I know that we have been assigned as the reserve for the initial assault, however, let me assure you gentlemen that this offensive will be tumultuous. We should not expect to remain in reserve for very long, so I ask you to prepare your men and yourselves accordingly."

There were some hurried glances amongst the younger officers and one Captain enquired, "has the attack date now been finalised, Sir?"

"Yes Captain, high command has confirmed that the offensive will begin on the morning of Sunday 9th May. However, we shall be moving into our position in the support trenches on Saturday, so be fully prepared by tomorrow evening."

"How are the lines looking, Sir," queried Furze "with all the German advances around Ypres should we expect an enemy emboldened, or one wearied by their recent offensives?"

The CO looked at Furze, weighing his answer carefully. "You bring up an important point Lieutenant, though you may not like the reply I have to offer. There has been grave news from Hill 60."

The officers around Furze shifted nervously whilst he held the CO's gaze, adamant not to react until the full story had been told.

"Whilst our Royal Engineers managed to successfully detonate the mines they had placed under the hill on 17th April allowing our troops to capture the position, our men were then subjected to severe German bombardments and numerous counter-attacks over the next four days." The CO paused, considering his next statement.

The tension in the room bound each man to one another, locking them all in a state of focused suspense.

"Having distracted us with an attack at Ypres, they released chlorine gas onto Hill 60 from positions no more than one hundred yards from our line. The gas arrived so quickly that most of our soldiers were unable to put on their protective gas masks in time. Our casualties were…severe."

"Dear God!" growled Major Slacke, quivering with rage.

"Our troops from the 15th Brigade held out admirably for a few days until the Germans released a second gas attack. This time, by some horrible happenstance, the wind blew the deadly cloud along, rather than across, our line. As you know gentlemen, standard procedure denotes that troops under gas attack move to the flanks of the trenches, but this was impossible, given that the gas cloud hung over the whole line. Although our troops were alerted to the danger, the gas cloud rested so thickly that it was impossible for them to remain in position, even after re-damping their respirators multiple times. Most of our troops withdrew, and those that valiantly remained were eventually overwhelmed by the Germans."

The CO stopped and lifted his head to face the stunned silence in the room.

"So, in reply to your question Furze, I will lay it out as it currently stands. The Germans have been launching major offensives almost every day for the past few weeks. They have faced harsh resistance on all fronts, taken a beating, yet captured some key positions along our lines. Hill 60 will have emboldened them, no doubt, but with their sights trained on that part of the line, we are expecting less resistance at our position. Do they foresee an attack? I doubt it, as they will be expecting us to reinforce our position around Hill 60. However, their troops may have had their spirits lifted by the recent news. Other than that, gentlemen, I have little more to offer on their state of mind."

"Thank you, Sir." Furze attempted to remain calm, though he felt far from it. "Your openness is greatly appreciated. It appears that the enemy, though having enjoyed some measured success recently, is stretched, tired, and pressured. Our offensive may be exactly what is needed to break their resolve, as well as their line, whilst providing some relief to our lads up at Ypres and at Hill 60."

"Quite right, Lieutenant," agreed the CO, relieved that the news he had passed on could be taken in a positive light. "That is, I believe, precisely why High Command has chosen this time to execute the plan."

The intensity present in the room during the CO's talk began slowly to dissipate as the officers asked further questions to alleviate their concerns. Every man was concerned about the offensive, worried about the Germans' recent success and uncertain over the general state of the War. However, the thought that the Germans' recent attacks had stretched their resources and battered their resolve, gave the officers some courage. A taught rope snaps with greater violence when cut than a lax one, and their offensive would be the scissors.

The Plan

"Busy all day preparing for the move at night but at about 17:30 it was cancelled owing, it is thought, to the French failing to attack down South with their half-million or more men."
Friday 7th May

Morning broke with a flurry of activity. Following the CO's talk, each officer threw himself into his duties, rallying the troops with a motivating mixture of determination and trepidation. Thanks to their efforts, and the beautiful weather, preparations ran smoothly.

"A sign of good things to come Furzzy!" Fuller exclaimed as he sprang past Furze to check on some of his troops.

"I wouldn't speak too soon Fuller," retorted Kirkpatrick, lifting his head from the documents he had been bending over to take a wary glance at the sky. The Major had the better of the situation as the weather turned, just after lunch, and a grey and hammering rain hit with a vengeance. Fuller returned from another inspection absolutely sodden and the look he gave Furze spoke volumes.

"Don't say a word…" Fuller growled.

"Ever the optimist dear fellow," smiled Furze, offering his friend a nearby cloth to dry himself.

"It is my firm belief that the weather has allied with the Germans," announced Fuller. "Forget rational thought; if the sun is shining, we should prepare the men for rain. If it is raining, we should prepare the men for...you guessed it, rain. It brings one quite to distraction, I might as well prepare the men in a lake!"

Furze, expecting to begin moving his men off that night, left Fuller to his grumblings and made his way to Headquarters to ask for further orders. He waited patiently as information flooded in and out of the building, held within official letters, upon scraps of paper, and on the tongues of messengers before, at 5:30 pm, he was told that the move had been postponed. Worried that the Germans may have anticipated the British attack and struck first, Furze hurried back to Fuller's Company, and found his friend in deep conversation with Major Kirkpatrick.

"What news from Headquarters?" enquired Kirkpatrick, observing the concern on Furze's face.

"The move this evening has been postponed, dash the Germans! Have you heard anything about why this decision has been taken?" Furze dropped into a seat next to his two friends.

"Your guess is as good as ours Furzzy," answered Fuller.

"I'm afraid we haven't heard anything particularly conclusive," agreed Kirkpatrick, "but it is thought that the French failed to execute their planned attack in the south."

"You don't say?" Furze was aghast. "But they have half-a-million men or more! What could have occurred to prevent them from launching an attack?"

At that moment, Major Bottomley hurried into the room, saw the three officers, and rushed over to them. "Good evening gentlemen, no doubt you're wondering why the move has been postponed?"

"Timing is everything," remarked Fuller. Furze couldn't help allowing a smile to escape him.

Bottomley frowned, before continuing. "Well, I have just come from Headquarters."

"So has Furzzy," interjected Kirkpatrick.

"Indeed, I noticed the good Lieutenant there before I was called to a meeting with the CO. The move has only been postponed by twenty-four hours. Details on why are not yet being passed to the lower ranks, but I have been told to inform you and the other officers of the following rough scheme of attack." With a flourish, Bottomley withdrew a map from his greatcoat, and spread it upon the table around which the officers had gathered.

"The 8th Division is to burst through the German trenches opposite Rouges Bancs." Bottomley launched his explanation, gesturing at the map as he explained the plan. "From there, they are to advance on Fromelles. The 7th Division, once the 8th has broken through and achieved its first objective, is to follow the 8th during its advance. The 22nd Brigade is to form the advanced guard, and The Queen's, the vanguard. When we move off, we will initially head for Leclercq, before proceeding to La Plovich, and finally on to La Cliqueterie. All clear thus far?"

"Absolutely clear," asserted Furze. As Bottomley had been laying out his map, the three officers had, as was their habit, taken out their notebooks and were recording everything with interest.

"Good. At La Cliqueterie, we will meet up with the Indian Regiments and the 1st Corps, which are making a wide turning movement south of Aubers." Bottomley stopped, and looked at his fellow officers.

"Is that all?" questioned Kirkpatrick warily.

"I'm afraid so," responded Bottomley.

"Well, it does seem to make sense," Fuller commented cautiously, "although I have seen more thorough plans in my short time."

"Well, it's what we have so we'd better get behind it!" proclaimed Kirkpatrick, rapping his knuckles on the table. "We'll spread the plan amongst the other officers."

Furze caught Humphreys, Philpot, Garmin, and Pratt on his rounds, and briefly disclosed all that had been explained to him by Bottomley. As the group separated, and Furze headed to his billets, he mulled over the approaching attack. It seemed to him that the Germans had been giving them a hard time recently, and that an attack was wholly necessary if their momentum was to be checked. He just prayed that it was the right time and place for such an attack.

Tomorrow night, thought Furze, *if we do indeed move out, the Brigade will position itself in the support trenches just behind the Front line. Come what may, this is what has been decided.*

The information given to the officers, rationed though it was, would be all they had to work with to make the assault a success. The rest would be up to them, through the snap decisions they would have to make in the moment. Furze had certainly been part of engagements where much more had been known, yet he had also been a part of actions that not been planned at all, and which had resulted in success. With that thought, he laid his worries to rest in the bed of trust he had formed upon the skill, dedication, and experience of the soldiers and officers he fought alongside.

His slumber was interrupted the next morning by a shout, "Furzzy, old boy! Are you awake you dozy chap?"

Unperturbed, for he knew precisely who owned the voice which had bluntly clambered into his room, Furze rose and flung open the windows. It was a glorious day, with beams of sunlight glinting beautifully upon the puddles of rainwater left, forgotten, by the night's clouds. Major Kirkpatrick, already fully dressed, stood below Furze's window grinning from ear to ear. He held not only his own horse, but Tommy as well, fully saddled and chomping at his bit. Furze knew just what his friend wanted, and he couldn't have thought of a more soothing activity before the menace of an impending battle.

"You rascal Kirk! You know how much Tommy likes his sleep."

"Apparently not as much as his master," countered Kirk merrily. "It's a beautiful day Furzzy and, in addition to the supreme pleasure I get from being awake before you, I thought a good long canter before the Brigade moves off would do us both some good."

"Tommy and I understand the need for rest and relaxation. One day, we shall teach you about it." Furze was already dressing himself. "Until then, at least I can count on you to come up with the most splendid plans Kirk. I'll be down presently."

Furze mounted Tommy, finding the horse to be boundlessly enthusiastic that morning. He absorbed the animal's energy, running his fingers up Tommy's neck, feeling the beast's breathing beneath his legs, and soothing him with gentle words. There was a fresh spark to the air that morning, as if the particles of wind carried an electric charge upon them as they brushed past his face.

"Fine morning, can't you appreciate that at least, you little blighter!"

Furze turned to berate his friend's rough comment but burst into laughter on observing that the explosion was aimed at Kirkpatrick's horse, who had become distracted by the taste of a nearby branch.

Eventually, the pair threaded their way out of La Gorgue, and into the surrounding countryside. *It really is a topping day,* mused Furze, allowing his thoughts free rein at that moment. They rode and rode, breathing in their surroundings, galloping along the straights of the roads and forging up to the highest points along their route. They met numerous bodies of troops along the way, chatted to a string of other officers, also making the most of the morning, and were in high spirits by the time they rested at the top of a nearby knoll.

"Reminds me of home, Furzzy," Kirkpatrick proclaimed, as they sat atop their panting mounts, surveying the surrounding countryside. "The fields near to my home look immensely similar, a joy to ride through, with numerous little towns and villages speckled across one's route."

Furze looked at his friend, and thought he detected a solemnity about him that had suddenly surfaced.

"What's on your mind Kirk?"

"Does it make sense to you, Furzzy?"

"Does what make sense?"

"The War. The idea of war, the execution of war, the purpose of war."

"Well," replied Furze, choosing his words carefully, feeling the weight of importance each one held. "War as an idea, no. Fighting for the sake of land, power, money, greed; none of that makes sense nor appeals to me."

"Well, precisely," nodded Kirkpatrick.

"But war in defence of something...that has meaning, that has purpose. This war has but one purpose for us, or at least for me. Protection. Of what we love, and who we love."

Kirkpatrick remained silent, thinking over the words. Furze continued, "We fight so that we don't see these integral aspects of our lives disappear. Our King, our country, our friends, our families, all this is what we fight for, all this is why we serve together, in this country, in this war."

"I know, Furzzy, I know," agreed Kirkpatrick. "And, of course, that makes sense. I think every day about protecting the people I love, and the country I care for. But...I just feel uncertain. I see all these lives set before us, all these young and vibrant individuals branded as 'soldiers', given a uniform and sent to fight. All we hear is this side making gains here and the other side making gains there. Gains won using the blood of young men on both sides, the mortal currency of war."

Furze shuddered.

"I just wonder..." Kirkpatrick was looking towards the Allied lines as he stated this, his gaze transfixed while his train of thought faded away.

Furze wondered what had stirred the Major, who had displayed such a steadfast resolve since joining the Regiment. He thought he had got to know the Major very keenly in that short space of time, but realised he had plenty more to discover about his companion.

"War is never a joyous affair, it is a universal truth that it cannot be so. Although we cannot and do not, wish for it, it nevertheless occurs. All we can do, in our position, is our duty. For that is the only honourable option in this dire landscape. Fight hard, lead well, and support all of those around us. If we are lucky, we will come out of this nightmare unscathed and victorious, but only time will tell. Take heart though Kirk." Furze encouraged warmly, leaning in to grip Kirkpatrick's shoulder, arousing him from his stupor.

Brought back to the present Kirkpatrick stroked his horse's ears, listening intently.

"Soon we'll all be back in England, and you and I will be sitting on a hill just like this, staring over fields remarkably similar in appearance, but without the guillotine of war above our necks. On that day, Kirk, we will not speak, but silently survey a world at peace, knowing we fought to make it so."

Kirkpatrick turned to Furze, a grateful smile on his face. "You have a way with words, Furzzy, and I hope, sincerely, that we can find ourselves on that hill."

"In time, old chap, in time."

"This will be a bloody attack, you know that."

"I know." Furze had wondered whether the scale of the forthcoming attack had brought on the conversation, and this comment confirmed that it had. "I feel that this one will cause us a great deal of grief, but we must be strong enough to get the men through it."

"Do you think we can?"

"What I think doesn't matter. We must, Kirk, we simply must."

That night the Battalion marched off at the head of the Brigade, down to the support trenches they had been shown earlier in the week. The night was cool and crisp, the bright moon shining through the clear sky with an intensity of an immense eyeglass.

The Queen's trenches were far from luxurious, but they were, at least, relatively dry and the soldiers settled in without too many grumbles. The clarity of the night meant it was immensely chilly, and sleep for Furze, was out of the question. Therefore, once all the soldiers were fully positioned by 1:30 am, he occupied himself by strolling up and down the lines, checking on the sentries and holding hushed conversations with the men. They were a close-knit bunch of troops, for serving with another man in such an environment created a bond that was thicker than the mud they fought through. At 3:30 am, Furze started to feel as if the cold was burrowing into his very bones, so he ordered tea to be brewed and spread amongst the soldiers. The silence in the trench was far more chilling than the cold of the morning, and Furze, feeling undeniably anxious, wanted to do anything to shake off his nerves. Most of the soldiers were deep in sleep, but there were enough awake for the tea to be greatly welcomed, and for Furze to feel as though he had company.

Best to resign myself to the facts, he thought restlessly, holding his warm brew tightly. *I shan't be getting any sleep this night.*

Map - The Battle of Aubers Ridge

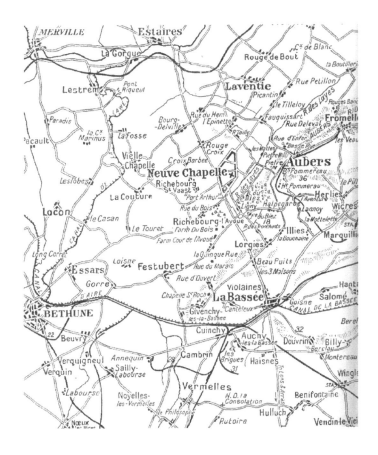

The Battle of Aubers Ridge

"...at nightfall, as far as one could see, nothing had been gained and we had suffered something like 5,000 casualties, which is equivalent to a Brigade."
Sunday 9th May.

The morning's silence was torn apart by the British guns; the explosion from each shell serrating the frosty air like blunt scissors.

5:00 am.

Furze, who had not caught an inch of sleep and had been expecting the barrage, felt a shiver run down his spine as the first thud of the guns shook the ground beneath his boots. *The bombardment is heavy, and certainly fierce,* he thought, and just hoped it was accurate. To his knowledge it was directed at the German trenches in front of Rouges Blancs, and although he trusted the skill of the British gunners supremely, the targeting mistake he had observed during the last engagement made him uneasy. Looking about him, he saw that the men were packed so tightly into their support trench that one mis-aimed shell from their own guns would wreak havoc.

Much of the purpose of these preliminary bombardments was to destroy the wire and defences in front of the German lines, rather than the lines themselves, so that the British soldiers could make their assault more easily. Massacres were far more likely when the troops were tangled in barbed wire, than when they fought the German's eye-to-eye in their trenches.

5:40 am.

The bombardment ceased, signalling that the main British assault was about to take place. As if on cue, the leading Battalion of the 8th Division left their fire trenches in front of The Queen's and charged the enemy's line. As the men scrambled up the ladders, flinging themselves across no-man's-land towards sheer uncertainty, a mighty roar was heard from the assaulting troops. Those in the support trenches emulated this roar; each and every man praying that those who had just gone over-the-top would get through safely.

However, amid all this goodwill and encouragement, every soldier inadvertently winced at the sound of the German machine guns beginning their harrowing chatter as the British troops charged towards them. After twenty minutes of intense expectation, at 6:00 am, The Queen's were told to lead the Battalion out of the support trenches and to the line just to the rear of Rue Petillon. All being well, Furze then expected to receive orders to advance from there up to the fire trenches and then further on to join hands with the 8th Division. He was left waiting, for little news was received for the rest of the day. Snippets of information were passed along the lines whenever anyone caught a rumour on the wind, but Furze placed no importance on hearsay. They were on constant alert due to the Germans' moderately heavy shell fire on their lines, a grim retaliation to the barrage they had been subjected to that morning.

Furze scuttled over to Kirkpatrick, bending low as shells landed close to the front of their trench. "They're going for it now!" he roared above the shrill cries of the explosive rounds.

"Can you blame them?" Kirkpatrick had just passed on an order to a nearby subordinate. "I still haven't heard anything definite from the 8th, but this morning's barrage had to have hit the Germans hard."

"I wish we had some clarity," uttered Furze, "this suspense is dire, and the men feel like fish in a barrel right now."

"I know Furzzy, but there's little I can do…" the Major's response was cut short as a shell hit the parapet of their trench further down from their position. Shouts immediately erupted from the position and Doctor Greenleas, who had been standing close at hand, rushed towards the scene.

"Send a man back with a report!" Kirkpatrick shouted after the Doctor, who waved his hand in a show of acknowledgement as he disappeared. "Take a look at this map Furze, I've been attempting to plot our advances with what we currently know."

As they were perusing the dirty little field map, a soldier appeared from the direction of the recent blast.

"Sir," he spluttered, as he pulled up next to the officers and saluted.

"Private," saluted Kirkpatrick in response, "how bad is it?"

"One dead Sir, fourteen wounded," the Private stated simply and efficiently. The Doctor had chosen his messenger well.

"Thank you. Furze, return with the Private and see to it that the wounded are removed behind our lines."

"Sir," Furze responded, addressing Kirkpatrick with due formality in front of the Private.

"Oh, and check on the parapet," added Kirkpatrick, "I leave it to your judgement as to whether it needs repairing."

Once again, their conversation was cut short as the three of them flung themselves to the wall of the trench. Another shell had landed close to the first and resulted in further shouts and groans.

"Go, Furze!" shouted the Major, and Furze and the Private darted towards the blast.

As they arrived, Furze noticed the Doctor slumped against the wall of the trench. The scene was a mess, with soldiers writhing in pain on the grime of the trench floor.

"See to them." Furze ordered the Private, gesturing at the soldiers as he quickly judged the situation. "Assess the damage and get back to the Major with another report. By my reckoning we'll need ten men and some stretchers."

"Sir!" flashed the Private, attending to his task.

Furze moved to the Doctor who was, thankfully, alive. "Doctor, are you wounded?"

"My arm." Greenleas responded, through gritted teeth whilst attempting to control his breathing. "Compound fracture."

Furze took a look. He knew little about medicine but could tell that the arm would be of no further use, meaning the Doctor would be no help to the wounded men around him. *Damn!* cursed Furze to himself. Aloud he continued, "thank goodness you weren't killed, let's get you and the other wounded out of here."

The Doctor would easily recover, however, his loss at that moment was a severe blow. The likelihood of survival for anyone who received an injury from then on was markedly lessened, as the immediate medical aid that the Doctor could provide was of critical importance. Furze rued the luck of the German aim. Nearly twenty soldiers had been wounded by the two shells, and it took a good deal of time and effort to get them all safely behind the British line.

"Any news on our overall casualties?" he queried one field Doctor, having escorted Greenleas into a medical tent.

"Nothing solid," replied the flustered Doctor, for the tent was teeming with injured soldiers, "but by my reckoning we have suffered some five thousand casualties."

"Five thousand…" Furze grimaced, it was the equivalent of losing every member of the Brigade he served in.

"A farce," piped up an officer near Furze who was supporting a bloodied leg.

"How so?" enquired Furze.

"The 1st Corps, situated to the North between La Bassée and Ypres, and the Indian Corps never even got going. You know the bombardment this morning?"

"Who could have missed it," noted Furze.

"The Germans, it appears," said the officer dryly, "it did little to weaken their defences. The wire was barely cut, and the shells didn't fall close enough to the machine gunners to suppress them."

"Good God!" Furze was incredulous.

"Add all that to the fact their artillery was left generally unworried, and their reserves were able to move freely behind their lines, and you have a royal nightmare."

"That explains our casualties," muttered Furze, "we got hit a number of times by their shells."

He thanked the officer and headed back to The Queen's. The only snippet of good news Furze was able to glean, was that the French had allegedly done well in the South. But even this news was patchy and questionable at best.

The Queen's remained in the support trenches until around 10:30 pm, when news arrived that they were expected to retire shortly. More information on the battle was slowly filtering through to the troops, yet Furze was having a hard time finding any good news amongst the tales of disorganisation and struggle that were being passed to him.

"A mess, Furzzy," Kirkpatrick said quietly to him after reading a note. "Apparently a large proportion of our casualties were caused by our own artillery."

Furze balked at the thought that the gunners had done precisely what he had feared. To be mown down by German machine gun fire whilst struggling through barbed wire was one thing, but to be hit by one's own artillery shells was quite another. He hoped this information was in some way misrepresented, but the air hung thick with resentment and the stench of failure, and he feared the worst. Before The Queen's moved out, a messenger raced up to the Major.

"Sir," saluted the soldier, taking a moment to catch his breath, "orders from the Commanding Officer." He handed the Major a note.

"Thank you," Kirkpatrick acknowledged, before the messenger saluted once more and wheeled away back to Headquarters.

"Incredible," muttered Kirkpatrick, "it seems British stubbornness prevails, the Rifle Brigade is valiantly holding down a footing in the German trenches."

"What are our orders?" asked Furze.

"We're to send a Company up to assist them," the Major stated in a measured tone. He turned to a nearby orderly, "tell Captain Haddon-Smith to take 'D' Company and bring them up to support the Rifles. Their position is on this note."

As the orderly sprang away, Furze marvelled at the determination of the Riflemen, but feared the support effort by 'D' Company was a futile one.

"We're sending them into the lion's mouth, Kirk," he whispered cautiously, not wishing any prying ears to hear them.

"You think I don't realise that?" snapped Kirkpatrick before pausing, regaining his composure. "Furze, what choice do I have."

"No, you're right," Furze responded, realising the error in his comment. In that moment, his friend and Commander needed support, not doubt. "Plus, we should never leave brave men behind. 'D' Company is an excellent choice, the Captain will see them safely home."

11:00 pm.

'D' Company had still not returned when Furze's Brigade made its way out of the fire trenches and back to the support line. He got his men settled and attempted to ease their concerns as best he could with the information he had. They were noticeably anxious, understandably so given that most of the rumours they had heard focused on the day's attack being a failure. Added to this was the feeling that 'D' Company had, by all accounts, been sent on a forlorn hope, so the atmosphere hang heavy with resentment. The soldiers were painfully aware that they would likely be assaulting the same German position in the forthcoming days and were far from encouraged by its apparent invulnerability.

Whilst making his rounds, Furze eventually saw a body of men returning from the Front and relief coursed through his body as he recognised Captain Haddon-Smith at the head of the troops. Furze ordered some tea to be brought up, joining the Captain and his two Lieutenants, Coates and de Rougaunt, once they had settled their weary men. Fuller and Kirkpatrick hastened to them as well, silently registering the ragged appearance of their three fellow officers.

"How was it up there, Captain?" asked Kirkpatrick, handing mugs of warm tea to their grateful recipients.

"A damned nightmare, Sir! A damned nightmare!" The Captain replied, keeping his hoarse voice low. "The Rifles, when we arrived, were doing a sterling job holding their position in the German trenches, but their position was untenable. They only made it as far as they did because their path to the German lines was one of the few which our shells had largely cleared of barbed wire. Even so, they suffered terribly at the hands of the German machine guns, fighting tooth and nail to take that position."

"What was the layout of the German defences?" Questioned Fuller, with intense seriousness.

"Formidable," he replied gravely, taking a sip of his tea before continuing. "Not only have the Germans doubled, and in some places trebled, their wire defences, they have also increased the size of their defensive breastworks to about fifteen feet, and built up a bank of earth behind their trenches for rear protection. On top of this, about seven-hundred yards behind these earthworks and protecting the trench, is a line of concrete machine gun bunkers…"

"Good God!" exclaimed Kirkpatrick, all the officers listened to the Captain's account with heavy hearts.

"Our intelligence said nothing about this from what I remember?" commented Furze.

"Not a damned thing," growled the Captain, "and this became more and more apparent the further the Rifles pushed.

When we got to them, they were pinned down by heavy German machine gun fire, as well as artillery. Apparently, the primary German artillery positions have secondary positions built directly behind them, so that they can move their guns back temporarily in order to deliberately fire on their own lines, suppressing our troops whilst their reinforcements arrive."

Furze looked aghast at Fuller. The complexity of the German defences was astonishing, but what concerned him most was the lack of information the British seemed to hold about them.

"We really could not have arrived at a more critical time," continued the Captain, "for the German reinforcements had just begun their counter attack, their troop movement was swift and effective."

Major Slacke and Lieutenant Garmin hurried in at that point, and the others quickly filled them in whilst Haddon-Smith switched his empty mug for a hip flask of brandy, which he passed around the officers.

"Our arrival managed to create a shock effect, halting the advancing German troops long enough to allow the Rifles to pull out of the German lines. Even then, it was a race against time to retire quickly enough so as not to be overwhelmed ourselves. In practice, we had simply swapped positions with the Rifles, and knew no one was rushing up to support us. Thankfully, the Germans must have assumed we were a far larger force than we were. They halted their initial assault to bolster their forces, and by the time they resumed their attack, we had managed to evacuate with few casualties. My thoughts are with the Rifles, those men suffered heavily today."

"Well done Captain," assured Kirkpatrick, "that was a valiant effort on the part of you and your men. Without a doubt, you saved the lives of those troops."

"It should never have come to that, Sir," snapped the Captain, before composing himself. "My apologies, we executed our orders, and I'm glad we were able to help them."

"No need to apologise," responded Kirkpatrick steadily, "your actions speak well enough. I think it best we all get some rest, for I fear this battle is far from over."

The little group broke up and Furze bid the others good night, departing to stroll the trenches with Fuller. Their current situation greatly concerned him. It was one thing for the soldiers of the Regiment to become disheartened, for the officers could at least attempt to rekindle their motivation. But he could sense the same seeds of resentment fermenting amongst the officers, and that was a dangerous state to operate in.

"Dirty business, Furzzy," commented Fuller quietly, looking around him. "A lack of reliable information, inaccurate artillery, a bolstered German line, and poorly executed troop movements. What could possibly have caused such an apparent farce?"

"The reasons elude me old boy," answered Furze "It has been a terrible day, and I fear further ones are close at hand. I have heard that the 7th Division is to attempt tomorrow what the 8th failed to achieve today."

Fuller stopped in his tracks and caught Furze's arm, pulling him to the side of the trench. "What?! Command can't seriously be considering another such attack, so soon after the first, knowing how well the German lines are defended?"

"It appears so, perhaps they are hoping that the Germans will not be expecting it. Perhaps the Germans were hit harder than we are aware."

"Yes, yes, possibilities always exist but realities are more important," interrupted Fuller, "you heard the Captain, the Germans are well-defended, well-organised, and seem to be expecting everything we throw at them."

"I know Fuller, I know. I'm just attempting to rationalise the attack, make it seem more opportune, more achievable. Perhaps the Captain was unlucky enough to come up against the most heavily fortified section of the enemy line."

"Sometimes I wonder at you Furzzy," Fuller frowned. "But I pray you speak the truth."

"Whatever the situation, we're in for a rough ride," Furze allowed. "Though, I can tell you one thing with certainty."

"Is that so? I'm having serious doubts about the existence of certainty in this dastardly place."

"I'm very glad to have you here with me, Fuller," Furze shot his friend a quick smile. He had been through so much with this man, both at home and at war. They had experienced one another's successes, failures, hopes and fears, sharing each moment of boundless pleasure as well as each raw nerve of pain.

Fuller's brow relaxed and his features softened. "So am I Furzzy, you old sop. Don't go getting emotional on me now, one of us has to keep his head!"

The two friends parted with a firm embrace, this simple action reminding them of the unequivocal bond they shared. No matter the situation, they had always made it through, together.

Companionship

"In the morning the General told us that we were going to have a go at the same spot as the 8th Division tomorrow..."
Monday 10th May.

The next morning was fraught with an intense feeling of foreboding. This was heightened when the General informed them that they would be the next in line to assault the position that the 8th Division had failed to capture the previous day.

"How are we to relay this to the men?" Fuller asked as he and Furze headed back to their trench.

"Beats me," replied Furze sullenly, "I fear that, however we deliver the news, it will be poorly received."

Just then, as the pair were considering their predicament, a runner dashed over and informed them to hold fast. The attack had been cancelled.

"What on earth is going on, Fuller?" Furze queried watching the young soldier hurry on to relay the news to the next group of officers.

"I don't like this at all, Furzzy, our best guess is that the situation is developing so quickly that we have to react instantly to any new development."

Furze nodded but couldn't help registering the concern mirrored on the face of his friend. "And our worst guess?"

"Headquarters hasn't a clue on how to proceed..." Fuller growled.

The Brigade subsequently spent the day resting on a farm behind the British lines, waiting for its next set of orders. For Furze, these came that evening, when he was informed that the Brigade was to move to Essars, close to Bethune and about a twelve-mile ride from the farm. As acting billeting officer for the Regiment, Furze rode on ahead in order to scout out accommodation for the troops. He welcomed the chance to escape the uncertainty of the trenches, even for a moment, and focus on another task. Atop Tommy, he cantered towards Essars, allowing his spirits to rise as his trusty mount sped him towards their night's rest.

He thought fondly of Tommy, as the horse powered onwards. *Ever dutiful, I wonder if you have any idea of the folly of men.*

Essars only consisted of four rotten farms, so this was all Furze had to work with to ensure everyone had an assigned place when the Brigade marched in at about 1:30 am. At daybreak, the General gathered the officers for a second time to inform them that they would be joining with the 20th and 2nd Divisions to attack the German lines more or less opposite La Bassée. Once again, however, the plans were scrapped later in the day. To vent his frustrations, Furze decided to walk over to Bethune where he knew Bobbie Ross had just been positioned. He managed to find his friend with little trouble and Bobbie invited him to lunch with Captain Arthur Hamilton, the Adjutant of the London Irish Regiment.

As the pair entered the Hotel, it transpired that Hamilton had, in turn, invited his Regimental and Brigade commanders to dine as well.

"Charmed, Lieutenant Furze, charmed," greeted the Captain when Bobbie introduced him. "I'll be interested to hear your view on the past few days."

The whole affair turned into an incredibly informative one, with each of the officers swapping the stories they had heard about the failed attack.

"Rotten business about the friendly fire," whispered Bobbie, after Furze had recounted what he had heard.

"Tell me about it." Furze replied quietly, wary of the senior commanders at the table. Although they were agreeable fellows, he had not had a chance to fully weigh up their opinions on the current plan of battle. "When I heard Captain Haddon-Smith relay this news, as well as his experience of the German defences, I was quite taken aback."

"It's not like our gunners to be so poorly directed, nor our intelligence to miss such vital information," assented Bobbie, "lessons learned, eh?"

"I hope so, only time will tell."

The pair then rejoined the conversation around the table, Furze feeling a hint of encouragement at Bobbie's shared opinion of the recent attack.

Thursday brought with it a grey and dreary rain which seemed intent on dampening the soldiers' spirits. Furze and the other officers nevertheless trudged down to the trenches in order to survey the ground across which they expected to attack at any moment. The ground had turned into a quagmire of heavy, sticky mud and the group made slow progress. From what they could gather, they had Thursday and Friday to make their preparations before the assault commenced on Saturday or Sunday.

With this impending inevitability at the back of all their minds, the officers were determined to prepare their lines of attack as best as they could, gathering all the knowledge available to them in order to best serve the soldiers under their command. They knew that, when the time came, they would be called upon to lead their men into the unknown with a steady yet firm resolve. Snap decisions would need to be made, each one either costing or saving lives, either driving their troops forward or causing them to be repelled. So, they noted, observed, scanned, commented on and sketched every detail of the land that lay in front and to either side of their allotted lines of assault. If they could be confident in their knowledge of the land

and the trajectories of the surrounding Allied troops, they would have one less thing to have to consider during the assault.

"How far do you think the German lines are from ours?" Furze queried to nobody in particular, as he was comparing his drawing with the landscape in front of them.

"Not far," answered Kirkpatrick, flicking tiny droplets of rainwater from his notebook's protective covering.

"By my reckoning, no further than one-hundred-and-sixty yards," Furze estimated pensively. "Not too far for our men to cross."

"I'd second that," concurred Fuller, "not a great distance, but it'll be a bugger to cover under machine gun fire."

Furze cast his eye over the intervening ground. "It's not exactly the flattest ground," he muttered, "it looks full of undulations and ditches, and the grass there is very long." He pointed with his pencil, and the officers nearby followed his gaze.

"That'll be hard going, by any standards," observed Kirkpatrick, "we'll need to keep the men close together so as to retain effective command, whilst allowing them to spread out enough so as not to present too great a target to the Germans."

"No easy feat," agreed Fuller, "but we can do it."

To Furze's knowledge, the plan of assault was that his Regiment, The Queen's, would form the front line with the Welsh Fusiliers. They would be backed up by the South Staffords and the Warwicks. Though he dreaded the thought of being the first 'up-and-over' to face the German guns, at least he would know first-hand what was occurring in this assault and not have to rely on snippets of unreliable information to assess the situation. The British were offering a formidable force, that much was certain, but whether it would be formidable enough against the well-defended German lines would remain to be seen.

The torrential rain doused the night and continued into the following day, causing the operation to be postponed once again.

To ease their nerves, nearly all the officers in The Queen's set off into Bethune to dine, and Furze met up with Bobbie, Fuller, and Kirkpatrick.

"How are your plans, Bobbie?" queried Furze.

"Clear enough," responded the young man calmly. "But enough talk of battle. Has Furzzy told you two about the time he appeared in my room in the dead of night, caked in mud and near dead from cold?"

"Has he indeed!" snorted Kirkpatrick. "I think not."

"Well, there's a merry story," smirked Fuller.

"You bugger, Bobbie," Furze exclaimed, flinging a napkin at his friend who laughed mischievously.

"I'm afraid you're done for now old chap," cajoled Kirkpatrick. "I'd be loath to have to order the story from you, as your superior officer."

The group was in a highly contented state of mind, and Furze sat back in his chair, pulling from his coat pocket a hip flask of whisky. "Well, it appears I have been backed into a corner. Allow me a small civility before I continue," and he took a swig of the whisky before passing it around his companions.

"It was back in February, if I remember rightly?" Bobbie nodded his assent, and Furze recounted the time he had shaken his friend awake to the sight of his muddied and disheveled frame.

The group roared with laughter, and Furze took back his hip flask with a smile. Times like these reminded him so very much of life at home, and he welcomed the distraction from thoughts of the grim battle ahead.

"Quite the farce," commented Kirkpatrick, who had very much enjoyed the account of his young friend's past happenings.

"That's Furzzy," smiled Fuller, "ever the sublime verging on the ridiculous."

"We've been through some times, eh Fuller?" Furze looked into the depths of the grey eyes he knew so well. Calm and still as a mill pond on a spring morning. Even on the eve of such uncertainty, Fuller was admirably collected.

"That we have, Furzzy," Fuller agreed, raising an imaginary glass to his friend. "We've seen snow, sleet, rain, sun, and lord knows what else out here. Yet, through it all, we've always managed to find a thoroughly enjoyable place for dinner."

As the group murmured in acknowledgement Bobbie took Furze's hip flask and rose to his feet. "To good friends!" He toasted, looking at each of them in turn.

"The best," joined the others, rising each in their turn and taking a sip of the hip flask as it was handed to them. Joined in the unity of friendship, the men felt as though they could face whatever horrors the world had in store for them. Little did they know the true extent or proximity of such impending lethality.

Furze's Hip Flask
(A gift from his father)

The Battle of Festubert

I

"I advanced with the Commanding Officer who was very soon shot through the arm and head, when I left him he seemed very bad."
Sunday 16th May.

Saturday evening held a compressing heat that mirrored the soldiers' anxiety, and a damp that matched their spirits. Nevertheless, at 6:00 pm the Battalion paraded, the soldiers standing silent and sullen under the steady canopy of rain that beat down upon them. They knew the time had come to head to the trenches and spearhead the forthcoming attack. Though many of the men felt alone, some fearful, others numb, standing shoulder to shoulder with their fellows brought the group some comfort.

Come what may, Furze thought, as he walked past the lines of faces, emotions drawn upon them more vividly than paint upon a canvas, *they will stand strong together.* He shivered, the evening was dire and he was unsure whether it was the cold or fear that made him tremble so. Looking down at his notebook, his shaking hands had scribbled all over the page he had been tallying on. He closed his eyes for a moment, collecting himself, attempting to master the tension that was swelling effortlessly from within his belly.

"Rotten timing," remarked Fuller quietly, who was passing up and down the lines inspecting his men. "Are you feeling alright Furzzy?"

Furze opened his eyes to meet Fuller's searching gaze and nodded, not feeling the need for words. His friendship with Fuller was rooted in something stronger than audible expression.

Kirkpatrick walked over, rain streaming down his broad shoulders. "How are they looking Furze?"

"All present, weather aside, their spirits are a little muted."

"To be expected," Kirkpatrick commented reflexively. His mind was elsewhere, his training kicking in and running the show. "We'll likely move off soon, you know the drill."

As predicted, the order was soon given for the Battalion to move, thus the men marched to occupy their assigned positions. The trenches were thick with mud, at times reaching higher than the soldiers' ankles.

Operationally, The Queen's were prepared for the assault, having practiced the method of attack repeatedly over the past few weeks. Mentally, they were as calm as could be expected given the underlying and incessant tension that shackled the soldiers to one another. Within moments, the order was given to form up opposite a neat line of ladders that had been placed all along the front wall of the trench. Furze observed these simple instruments, so ordinary in life at home, yet so extraordinary in such an environment. Here, they would form the means through which he, and his men, would leave the relative safety of their trench and advance towards the enemy. They leant against the wall; innate, immobile, the soldiers' bridge between life and death.

Everyone was on the alert and the night had exchanged its heat for a biting cold that now accompanied the rain. Furze observed the streams of hot air rising from each man as he breathed out, listened to the suction caused by the mud which clung to their boots, imploring them to stay put. These were good men, good soldiers, dedicated, well trained, ready to do their duty to the best of their abilities and Furze trusted each and every one of them. He felt immense pride in leading and fighting with such strong individuals who had so much life to live - these soaking, shivering young men.

At 11:30 pm, the 2nd Division commenced its attack away to their left.

God-speed, wished Furze, as the sounds of rifle and machine gun fire chattered from that direction, supported by the booming bass notes of the British field artillery. The rain still fell stubbornly, each drop adding to Furze's bucket of trepidation, so he determined to walk amongst the troops to distract his mind, making some final checks and offering encouragement when he could.

"Men." He nodded to a group huddled near one of the ladders.

"Sir," they responded, "any news, Sir?"

"Not at the moment, but you will have heard 2nd Division making its attack."

"Aye, Sir," responded a Corporal. "Was that who it was?"

It did his conscience a world of good attempting to put his soldiers at ease, but it also calmed his own nerves, which had been restless since entering the trench. The British guns had been pounding the German lines relentlessly throughout the night, obstinate in their intensity. The ponderous thud, shudder, thud, shudder, thud, shudder, gave the British troops some element of relief that the enemy was taking such a beating. It nurtured the hope that the going would be easier when the time came to attack their lines.

At 2:45 am, on the morning of Sunday 16th May, the British guns switched their fire to the section of the German lines which The Queen's would be attacking.

"They've switched fire, Furzzy," growled Fuller.

"I know," assented Furze anxiously. "We can't have more than half-an-hour before we begin the assault."

"Are you ready?" Fuller turned to his friend.

"I don't think I ever am," Furze countered, forcing the words from a throat that suddenly seemed parched. "But we're here, and what choice do we have?"

"We'll be all right old chap," reassured Fuller, a ghost of a smile appearing on his face, "I'll see you on the other side." He gripped Furze's arm, his touch lingering a little longer than usual, a little stronger than usual, holding his gaze. Furze thought he felt his friend's hand tremble briefly before he disappeared into the dark.

Furze turned in order to ready the men and found them standing, prepared, before he could say a word. They had been dutifully alert, aware of what the change in artillery fire signified. Gently, the sky began to brighten, shifting from grey-blue to golden-brown. The artillery smoke hung in the morning air as the sun broke over the horizon, and the men felt their energy charge with its appearance.

3:15 am. Major Bottomley blew his whistle.

The whole scene in the trench seemed to freeze, for the briefest moment, as the shrill blast made its swift journey up and down the line. Then the troops, poised and waiting at the foot of each ladder, suddenly sprang into action. 'A' Company mounted the ladders, and dashed frantically towards the enemy lines. As men flung themselves over the parapet of the trench, Furze saw Captain Lang-Browne leading the charge, with Lieutenants McCate, Hillen and Humphreys close behind him.

Please be safe, he prayed, as the troops behind 'A' Company moved forward, awaiting their turn to head over the top. He thought back to when he had first met Humphreys and his mind rested briefly on Austin. His time with the three young Lieutenants in 'A' Company had been a pleasure and he couldn't bear the thought of Humphreys suffering the same fate as poor Austin.

The surging troops looked full of energy and life, with a gallant determination in their eyes and power in their strides. No sooner had the first heads appeared, however, than the Germans dropped hell upon them. Machine guns spluttered, rifles cracked, and bullets whizzed over the heads of the men in the trenches. Clods of earth were ripped from the parapet of the trench, showering down upon the waiting troops below. More terribly, bodies began to join the falling mud. Men rose up to the top of the ladders and lifeless husks came tumbling back down. The awaiting soldiers had to dive and swerve to avoid being hit; fear and disgust mixed upon their faces as they climbed to what they could only imagine was a similar fate. Furze kept a steady head, although his mind was on fire.

"Hold firm men!" He roared. "When up there, give the Germans hell!" The ferocity of the German firepower caused Furze to fear that few of 'A' Company would have reached the German lines. The last men from 'A' Company finally disappeared over the top, and Major Bottomley shouted, " 'B' 'C' and 'D' Companies advance!"

The troops responded instantly as the order was passed along the line and Furze leapt towards a ladder alongside Major Bottomley. He gripped the wooden frame between his chilled fingers, feeling its rough edges under his skin. On his first attempt, his right foot slid off the bottom rung, mud and dirt forming a slippery layer beneath his boot. His second attempt was supported by a far stronger grip, and more power from his shoulders, enabling him to ascend steadily. As he neared the top, his knee gave him a momentary pang of pain and he cursed its timing. Gritting his teeth, he pushed through the discomfort and focused on the climb.

He reached the top, his head emerging over the parapet and meeting the rising sun. As his eyes drew level with the ground, the true carnage of war was laid bare before him.

The scene was grotesque.

'A' Company, leading the charge, had been cut to pieces by the German guns and Furze could not make out the figures of Captain Lang-Browne or his Lieutenants. Mangled bodies presented themselves to him in a writhing, groaning carpet of blood and lacerated limbs. Bayonets stuck to the end of the British Lee-Enfield rifles protruded menacingly from the morbid grips of their fallen owners, and lifeless eyes stared back at him.

There was no time for thought, however, and Furze flung himself into the horror. He reached to his side and pulled his Webley MK IV revolver from its holster. In the face of such bleak destruction, the small firearm seemed completely inadequate, but the feel of its weight in his right hand gave him courage. Major Bottomley appeared next to him, and Furze began running forwards with the Regimental Staff Officers, encompassed by soldiers from 'B' 'C' and 'D' Companies.

The spectacle was impressive, if disastrous. Although the huge body of men surged forwards, the going was rough as the ground was soggy and potholed, causing them to stumble and fall, hampering the speed of their advance. The Germans were reigning down a frightening concentration of fire upon The Queen's and Furze winced, swerving, whenever a soldier in front of him was suddenly wrenched from his path and flung to the dirt by the force of a German bullet. It was a morbid, ugly dance where one incorrectly placed pivot could cost you your life, yet no one knew the right rhythm.

He stumbled, falling to his knees as his right leg disappeared into a pothole hidden by a pool of water. His hand, automatically reaching out to break his fall, fell upon the body of a sergeant from 'A' Company. A bullet had mangled his lower jaw and removed much of the man's neck. He vaguely recognised the poor fellow, but hastily threw the recognition away as his gut clenched in disgust and he scrambled to his feet, launching himself forwards once again.

"Come on men, onward!" He heard Major Bottomley shout from just in front of him. He had fallen a little behind the Regimental Staff Group and forced his legs to power him towards them. His thighs burned. His lungs heaved. Already, his uniform was caked in mud and wiping his hands on his trousers did little to clean them. He approached the command group, feeling a burst of safety at being amongst them once more. As much as he knew he was surrounded by men from the Battalion; they appeared nameless and cold in this environment, so he was pleased to be around people he knew well.

"We need to keep their fire down," Major Bottomley bellowed, "tell 'D' Company to…" but, as Furze watched, a rifle bullet ripped through the Major's arm and, as he stumbled, another found his head. Flesh flew from his body as he fell to the ground.

Rushing to the Major and kneeling to assess the damage, Furze shouted, "Sir, can you hear me, Sir!"

The Major groaned, but his eyes remained firmly shut. Amazingly, given the quantity of blood gushing from his wounds, he was still alive, but seemed in a very bad way. Furze began covering up the wounds before a strong hand grabbed him from behind and dragged him up.

"Leave him Furze, you'll only be cut down as well if you stay put. Let's go!" It was Major Kirkpatrick, now acting Commanding Officer of The Queen's in Major Bottomley's absence. Furze took one last look at his fallen Commander, picked up his Webley and stumbled after Kirkpatrick.

His mind was a blur; one moment Bottomley was racing, full of life, towards the enemy lines. The next, he was lying on the ground with death wrapping its cloak around him.

"Furze, take that section…FURZE!"

He was ripped from his shock back into the present by the exigency of Kirkpatrick's tones.

"Pull yourself together, Furze, I need you!" Kirkpatrick's voice emanated panic and urgency.

"I'm here!" Furze answered, taking hold of his senses and refocusing his attention.

"Take that body of troops and lay down some fire on the left-hand section of trenches," commanded Kirkpatrick. "Fuller!"

Furze was mustering the troops pointed out to him by the Major, when the sound of his friend's name caught his attention.

Fuller flung himself over to the Regimental Staff Group, which was sheltering by the ridge of a shell crater and gave them all a wild grin.

"Some charge, eh?" Fuller spat. "Looking a little muddy there Furzzy."

"Enough yapping Fuller," scowled Kirkpatrick. Though the comment and sight of his friend gave Furze some hope. "Take 'B' Company and get some bloody fire down on the right-hand section of the German trenches."

"Yes, Sir," Fuller answered.

"With that, and the fire from Furze's section, 'C' Company should have a clearer route to the centre of their lines."

"Sir!" shouted Furze and Fuller simultaneously, as they rolled in opposite directions to carry out their orders.

Furze crawled to the nearby troops, who had been running with the staff and were taking shelter in another nearby shell crater. The German fire was wreaking a catastrophic toll on the British troops. To his left, he saw some of the remnants of 'A' Company, led by Lieutenant Hillen, charging the last fifty yards towards the German line.

Come on lads, he thought, as he dived towards his men. At that moment though, a German machine gun rattled through the noise and cut down the entire group that Hillen had been leading. When Furze raised his head in their direction once more, not one man remained on his feet.

"Right men, listen in!" Furze roared, taking charge of the group of soldiers.

"We can't get there, Sir! The German guns are too much!"

"Of course we can, Private," responded Furze strongly, wishing to nip the uncertainty in the bud as soon as possible. "The men from 'A' Company are just ahead of us." He thought of Hillen and his men but threw the thought away as quickly as the troops had fallen. "We need to lay down some firepower on the section of the German trench in front of us. While we do that, keeping the German heads down, 'B' Company will do the same on the right, and 'C' Company will be able to advance."

The soldiers looked uncertain but nodded to show they had registered what he had said.

"After that, we will move up with the Staff group as 'C' Company covers us. Understood?" Furze looked at the Sergeant of the group. Winning his approval would mean the troops followed.

"Yes, Sir," the Sergeant nodded, knowing they had more chance working their way forward under fire than running towards the lines unsupported.

"Good, on my signal." Furze rolled over and looked towards the Staff group, nodding to Kirkpatrick, and noticing Fuller ready further down the line. He got the signal.

"Fire!"

The sound of hundreds of Lee-Enfield MK III rifles roared as one and Furze felt a chill leak down his spine. The firepower from Furze's troops was terrific.

"Cracking stuff men, keep it up!" shouted Furze, as he saw 'C' Company bounding forward. The German machine guns had been silenced momentarily, stunned by the weight of the British attack. Furze's troops were beginning to slow their fire. "Reload, and get ready to move!"

He checked down the line, Fuller was shouting to his troops, who were still flinging their rounds towards the Germans. In a moment, his men would need to reload as well and 'C' Company had better be in a position to support their advance, or they would be left exposed.

Kirkpatrick gave him a signal.

"Prepare to move," commanded Furze. There was a dangerous lull in the British fire as Furze's men collected their strength, Fuller's reloaded, and 'C' Company got into position. The Germans seized the moment and the ground around Furze and his troops erupted under machine gun fire. One bullet caught a soldier to Furze's right and another caught one of the Staff Officers near Kirkpatrick.

Major Slacke commanded 'C' Company, and Furze prayed he had got his troops down in time. As if on cue, he heard a blast of Lee-Enfields to their Front and the Germans ceased their fire once again. That was all Furze required.

"Move!" yelling his command as he leapt to his feet and trusting his men to follow suit.

To their right, he saw Major Kirkpatrick and the Staff Officers doing the same, and Fuller racing ahead with 'B' Company's faster troops. Major Slacke's men were doing a sterling job keeping the Germans suppressed, and only the odd enemy bullet caught its mark. They got level with 'C' Company, just as its troops were beginning to need to reload.

"Timing is everything Furze," shouted the Major, who sported a minor wound to his right shoulder, but was still in command. "We're close to the bastards now!"

Furze glanced over to Major Kirkpatrick, who gestured to him, so he raced over after telling his Sergeant to lay down some sustained fire on the German line. Fuller arrived at the same time, having told 'B' Company to do the same.

"Good work!" Kirkpatrick declared. "Now for the real test. On my signal, all the men are to charge the German defences. We need to maintain this momentum and catch them before they fall back to stronger positions. Inform Major Slacke, Furze."

"Sir!" said the surrounding officers, and Fuller and Furze returned to their troops.

"We're to charge the trench Major," Furze passed on as he arrived.

"Thought so," responded the Major. "Good luck Furze," and he disappeared to ready his men.

"Make sure your bayonets are fixed," Furze shouted, "on my signal, we are to charge the German lines and take their trench!"

The men had come this far and now, despite the terror of the German guns, they just wished to be done with the attack. Furze checked his revolver, the process merely steadying his nerves as he knew he hadn't yet fired a shot. Once more he glanced at Major Kirkpatrick.

The Major bellowed. "Charge!"

Furze followed his call and all down the line British voices roared as troops dashed up from their cover and hurled themselves towards the enemy lines. The German troops opened up, despite the shots coming from the British and the flashes of their weapons set their line ablaze. Furze thrashed forwards, willing his legs to carry him onwards, leaping over potholes, and ripping his boots free from the mud that clung to them. He did his best to avoid the bodies of his fellow soldiers but, occasionally, he had no choice but to trample over those in his path. The thought made him sick, especially when the apparently lifeless husk cried out in pain.

They were making good progress, Furze thought, focusing on the line ahead of him, so very close. Suddenly, a monumental blast to his left threw him to the ground, and he fell hard, his head spinning and his ears ringing wildly. As he attempted to rise, a second blast mirrored the first, and he saw Major Slacke, boldly leading his troops from the front, disappear in a rush of fire, smoke, and blood. He shook himself and fumbled for his Webley. Other soldiers around him were picking themselves up slowly, too slowly. The Germans had tossed some grenades at the approaching troops and they would be lambs to the slaughter if they didn't get moving.

"Come on men!" he yelled, forcing the words from lungs still reeling at the force of the nearby blasts. "Keep at them!"

The troops around him rallied to the call, and Furze led a group of about twenty soldiers right up to the German trench. Further along the line, he saw Major Kirkpatrick approach the trench as well, and thought he saw Fuller jumping in, firing his pistol at an unseen enemy. As they reached the top of the parapet, grateful that the British artillery had successfully cut the German wire, a face suddenly shot up just in front of Furze.

With the face came the long barrel of a Mauser rifle. Furze aimed his revolver and pulled the trigger.

One.

The Webley flashed. The Mauser retorted. Furze felt the whistle of something very close to him but found his legs still carrying him forwards; the face and Mauser out of sight.

More faces appeared all along the German line, but the British troops were upon them and streaming into their trench. Gunshots were heard on all sides, as was the terrible slice and crunch of bayonets meeting metal and flesh. Jumping into the trench, Furze kicked out at a German soldier beneath him and unleashed another round into his chest.

Two.

To his right, a German lunged at him with a bayonet, only to be trampled upon by a British soldier leaping into the trench behind Furze. The soldier buried his bayonet deep into the German's back, twisting as he did so, causing the man to let out a harrowing cry. Another German appeared behind the British soldier, took aim, and fired. Furze swung his revolver towards him but slipped and his shot buried itself into the wall of the trench.

Three.

The German turned and levelled his Mauser. Furze dived, smashing his shoulder into a wooden strut. The German charged at him with his bayonet, and it was all Furze could do to twist his body, contorting it around the bayonet before throwing his weight behind his right hand and bringing the butt of his revolver down hard against the soldier's head. The German stumbled and Furze levelled the barrel of his Webley.

Four. Five.

In his fury, he had pulled the trigger twice. *Better to be certain,* he thought. Further up the trench, he saw two soldiers grappling with one another. Both had lost their rifles in the scuffle, the British man turning to a trench shovel and the German to a short, ugly knife. The German was a larger man, stronger, broader, and had the upper hand on the British soldier. Furze made his way over to them, wishing to get closer before taking his final shot. He stumbled over the ground, ripe with both British and German bodies and slippery with mud and blood. The large German was bearing down on the British man, who was swinging his spade at him wildly.

Hold on, willed Furze, as he approached, but just as he brought his revolver up, the German caught the British soldier's swing and buried his dagger deep into the man's chest. The soldier gurgled, blood dripping from his mouth, as the German man released his grip and turned to Furze.

"You bastard!" Furze yelled, firing the Webley.

Six.

The German, quicker than expected for a man of his size, flung his knife at Furze just as the bullet struck his head. The knife missed by inches, burying itself in the trench wall beside him, but left Furze shaking where he stood.

His Webley was out of rounds, and he fumbled with the mechanism in order to reload his six shots. His hands were covered in mud and grime, causing the fresh rounds to slip from his fingers as he attempted to load them into the weapon. He kneeled to pick up the rounds, wiping them furiously on his soaking trousers in an attempt to clean them.

Come on, damn you, control yourself! He scolded himself, as his hands shook with anxiety.

Suddenly, a noise behind him made him start and, turning, he saw a group of German troops charging frantically down the trench. British soldiers appeared around him, firing at the approaching troops, bayonets level, ready to meet the approaching mass. Furze's fingers were cold, the revolver heavy and he tried desperately to push as many rounds into their chambers as possible.

"Steady men!" He yelled, the sound of his own voice strangely human in such an inhumane environment. Having loaded three cartridges, he slammed the Webley shut and turned to the approaching mass. *That'll have to do,* he thought, and took aim.

The groups met with a clash. Bayonets went scything through the air, and men yelled as bullets and steel found their marks. Furze shot at one German, who recoiled, clutching his shoulder. A British Corporal to Furze's left slammed the butt of his rifle into the belly of an opponent, whilst a German officer levelled his Luger at him, releasing two bullets that sent the Corporal sprawling. Furze fired at the German Officer. He missed.

The officer turned, and Furze met his gaze. The man was hardly older than he was; a young lad in his early twenties. He was clean shaven, with a strong set jaw, jet-black eyebrows and near-perfect white teeth. Although covered in mud, like the rest, his grey uniform fitted him incredibly well and Furze wondered whether he had been a sportsman in his civilian life.

Piercing blue eyes held Furze's gaze for a moment too long, before he realised they were lining him up behind the sights of the Luger. Furze launched himself forwards, grabbing the officer's arm as he pulled the trigger. The pistol jerked the arm away and fell to the ground as Furze's weight brought the two officers to the floor. The German swung a right hook which caught Furze square in the jaw and sent him sprawling. Both men had lost their pistols, and Furze, dazed by the punch, kicked out at the German's chest as he attempted to bear down upon him. The two men recovered their senses and saw the Webley and the Luger lying between them. Time paused, as they weighed up the situation. Furze knew his Webley had one round left, a guaranteed kill at this range, but it was closer to the German Officer. On the other hand, he knew that the German Luger pistol had a capacity of seven rounds, and he had only seen the German fire three.

The Luger was closer to him.

There should be four rounds left in his pistol, Furze thought, his mind racing, *but if I'm wrong, he'll have me.*

The German moved; Furze's mind was set. He plunged forwards, grabbed the Luger, rolled to his side, and fired. Furze's Webley fell from the German's hand into the mud, and the officer slid down the wall of the trench. As Furze watched him, their gazes met once more, the eyes once so vividly blue now a colourless haze. The young man reached for a pocket on the inside of his jacket, and Furze raised his Luger once more, ready to fire if he saw a weapon. But out of the jacket came a small picture of which the man caught a brief glimpse before falling into oblivion. Furze went and knelt by the man, his heart pounding viciously in his chest. Had any of the soldiers around Furze taken a moment to notice his face, they would have seen an excruciating picture of pain upon it. The photo was of a young woman, the officer's sweetheart.

II

Troops from the Battalion were surging around Furze, and it struck him that the British had secured the German position. Even so, the day was not yet won, for their final objective was a German communication trench about one-thousand yards further on.

"Officers, to me!" Furze heard Major Kirkpatrick call through the gloom.

Thank God, thought Furze, immensely grateful to hear the voice of his friend. He jogged over to the voice, telling the troops around him to secure their section of the trench as he did so. Having taken the German first line, he didn't want to fall victim to a counterattack from an enemy who now knew precisely where they were situated.

"Kirk," shouted Furze, as he approached the Staff group.

"Furzzy," the Major responded, the pair dropping all formalities at the joy of the reunion. "Very glad to see you alive."

"As I am you," responded Furze. "That fight was dire, I haven't counted how many men were lost, but it was a great deal. Major Slacke fell, as did Lieutenant Hillen."

"Damn," the Major grimaced, "far too many good men meeting undeserved fates today. We can't settle and assess the damage yet, though, the fight is far from over. We have to advance to the German communication trench."

Furze looked around them, there appeared only a handful of soldiers from The Queen's left.

A Lieutenant Furze didn't recognise, suddenly appeared and saluted, "Major."

"Lieutenant," acknowledged Kirkpatrick.

"I'm from the remnants of The Staffords, Sir, my men are with you."

"Excellent, thank you Lieutenant. Do you know how many of you there are?" Kirkpatrick asked.

"Not exactly, Sir," replied the young officer, though his harrowed look said it all.

If The Staffords have been hit as hard as The Queen's, thought Furze, *they can't be in a good way*.

"No matter, The Queen's and Staffords are stronger together." The Major turned to the officers who had gathered with him. "Furze, gather what's left of 'A' and 'B' Companies and advance on the left."

"Yes, Sir," responded Furze.

"Philpot, take 'C' Company and advance from here through the middle. The Staff will join you."

"Got it, Sir," replied Philpot, who looked absolutely ragged, and was leaning heavily on a rifle he had picked up.

"Lieutenant," Kirkpatrick commanded turning to the young Staffords Officer, "take your men and advance on the right. When you reach the communication trench, secure your position and then come and find me in the centre. That goes for you as well," he motioned to Furze and Philpot. "All officers are to regroup on me once we have captured our final objective, so we can fully assess our situation."

The officers all assented, then rushed away to gather their assigned troops. Furze returned to the section of the German trench he had assaulted and gathered as many Sergeants and senior Corporals as he could find. To his dismay, not a single other officer appeared, though he had sent word up and down the line for them to meet him. He suddenly realised he hadn't seen Fuller at the Major's regrouping, and a pang of concern shot through him.

"It's just you, Sir," said the burly Sergeant who had charged the line with him during the assault. Furze snapped back to the present and took heart in the knowledge he would have the reliable fellow by his side once more.

"A rotten situation," Furze growled, "but here we stand. I admire your efforts, men, in that last assault. You all fought valiantly, and we have one more push to make. About one thousand yards to our Front is a German communication trench. We must secure this location, at all costs, to prevent the Germans from relaying our movements back through their lines."

"Is it just us, Sir?" asked a Corporal.

"We have 'A' and 'B' Company here, on the left," answered Furze, using a bayonet to draw a hasty map in the trench wall, "in the centre, 'C' Company is assaulting with the Staff and on the right, The Staffords have joined our efforts and are assaulting along this line. Our combined numbers make this an achievable objective." He looked to the faces of his men, hopeful that this explanation had emboldened them, if only a little.

"And when we capture it, Sir?" asked the Sergeant.

"We hold it, Sergeant, and make damn sure the Germans don't retake it."

The group nodded, once again bravely resigning themselves to whatever fate had in store. They had followed the young Lieutenant this far and survived, so they found security in remaining with him until the battle was seen to a conclusion.

"Ready the men and await my signal," Furze commanded, and the group disbanded. Once again, his mind turned to Fuller. Kirkpatrick had swiftly re-assigned 'B' Company, the one Fuller had been leading, over to him, and he couldn't help thinking the worst.

Perhaps he was wounded and taken back to our lines, he hoped. Although it was a far-flung hope.

Ladders were placed on the rear wall of the German trench that did not already have exit points, whilst Furze waited for the Major's sign. It came, and Furze shouted, "Move out!"

The thirty to forty troops under his command burst out from the German trench and onto the ground separating them from their objective. The scene this time was wildly different to the one presented to Furze when he had exited the British line earlier that morning. Still pot marked with shell craters, the ground was flatter and, thankfully, not carpeted with bodies. To his great surprise they were not met with an instantaneous wall of machine gun fire either, his troops managing to suppress the light rifle fire that was directed towards them as they powered across the open ground.

The light resistance continued throughout their sprint, the Germans, perhaps, not having expected the British to get as far as their first line. As they approached, Furze took no precautions. "Grenades!" he roared.

The grenadiers amongst his men hurled their charges up and into the German communication trench. Furze waited, poised. The blast sent clods of earth shooting into the air, and he yelled, "Charge!"

Over and in they went, for the second time that day, and a minor close quarters scrimmage occurred for a matter of minutes. There was little resistance even when inside the trench, Furze and his men meeting a handful of Germans still breathing. One British soldier was impaled on a waiting bayonet as he jumped into the trench, but the German soldier who had sprung the grim trap was duly dispatched. At one point, Furze rounded a corner, coming face to face with two Germans. The three of them raised their weapons in turn, Furze having holstered his Webley and kept the Luger, but the Germans flung their Mausers to the floor when six British soldiers rushed up in support of their young Lieutenant.

"Secure them," commanded Furze sternly, blood pounding his temples at the close call, "they could have some useful information on the German lines."

"Sir!", came a voice from behind him.

Furze turned; it was the Sergeant. "Glad you're still with us Sergeant," he smiled.

"We have secured the trench, Sir," replied the Sergeant, "I just caught a runner from the commander, he's down the line waiting for the officers."

"Excellent," replied Furze, glad in the knowledge the Major was still alive. "Fortify this position and put out a watch. We're deep in the enemy line now and a counter-attack wouldn't be unexpected."

"Yes, Sir." Then the Sergeant began barking some orders to the nearby soldiers.

III

Furze hurried over to where Major Kirkpatrick was gathering his remaining officers. "Kirk," he announced as he arrived, "the left is secure."

"Good," replied the Major, wheezing slightly.

"You're wounded!" Furze noticed a bloodied rag wrapped around his friend's neck.

"Oh, it's nothing," dismissed the Major, tightening the rag. "Got caught by a piece of wretched flying shrapnel during that last dash. It won't hold me back."

Furze decided not to press the issue but made a note to keep a close eye on the wound in case it got any worse.

"This can't be all of you?" muttered the Major, incredulous, as he looked around his gathered officers.

Furze took stock himself, there were not many remaining. Major Kirkpatrick was the most senior officer left from The Queen's, followed by Lieutenant Furze. The other remaining commanders were Lieutenant Philpot, from 'C' Company, and Lieutenant Taylor-Jones, from the bombers. Furze felt a lump in his throat. "Has anyone seen Fuller?"

"Not since the initial assault," Kirkpatrick answered softly, shaking his head.

"He got to the trench, I'm sure of that," piped up Taylor-Jones. "My bombers supported his men as they reached the line. I lost him after that."

"Don't think upon it, Furze," directed Kirkpatrick calmly, acutely aware of how close the two were, "for now, let's focus on the task at hand."

Furze knew the Major was right, worrying wouldn't help anyone at that moment, but he couldn't help feeling terrified on behalf of Fuller. *The four of us can't be the only officers who made it through*, he told himself, *the others must be holding firm in the initial German trenches or fighting elsewhere on the battlefield.* The group was distracted from its thoughts by a commotion behind them.

"I'm a Lieutenant God-damn it! Though bloodied and ragged I thought you'd know that much."

Furze wheeled in elation, recognising the voice of his dear friend. "Bobbie! You, old rascal, get over here."

"Stand down Sergeant, let the good Lieutenant through," added Kirkpatrick with a wry smile.

"A miracle to see you Furzzy," sighed Bobbie, bending double to catch his breath. Lieutenant Bobbie Ross looked a state, his uniform caked in mud and his jacket torn and covered in blood.

"Not mine, don't worry," he said to Furze, noticing his concerned glance, "though it got close to being so."

"I'm glad, Bobbie, very glad. You haven't seen Fuller, have you?"

"Afraid not old boy," replied Bobbie, returning a sorrowful look.

A runner then dashed in and spoke quietly to the Major. "Right, I asked for a quick headcount. It appears we have one-hundred-and-fifty soldiers, and the five of us."

"Talk about odds," commented Bobbie dryly.

He had a point, thought Furze. The Queen's now found themselves spearheading the British assault, with just one-hundred-and-fifty-five men.

"Nevertheless, this is where we stand," remarked Kirkpatrick strongly, "and we have taken our objective. Furze, with me. The rest of you, look to the men."

The Major took Furze to the front of the communications trench, to a position facing the British lines where, remaining low so as not to present themselves as a target, the pair took up a position from which to observe the rest of the British assault.

"Our success isn't enough, is it Kirk?"

"Not in the slightest," responded the Major, "look over there, have the Welsh Fusiliers and the 20th Brigade dislodged the Germans?" He handed Furze his eyeglass.

Looking towards The Queen's left flank, Furze observed a fierce firefight raging. "We haven't taken it, the Germans still hold their position on our left."

"Dash it, if our troops haven't taken that trench by now, they never will." Kirkpatrick took back his eyeglass, scanning the line. "Sooner or later, they'll realise we have taken this position, and they'll level Holy-Hell upon us as a result."

"Our left flank is hopelessly unprotected," assented Furze, "our troops will have fortified their positions as best they can, but I doubt it will be enough. Do you see the house and the orchard further to our left?"

"I see them," puzzled the Major.

"We appear to occupy the house," continued Furze, "whilst the orchard appears to remain in the hands of the Germans."

"I understand," breathed Kirkpatrick, tightening the bloodied rag around his neck with a grunt. "That orchard commands our left flank; were they to direct their fire towards us we would be heavily pinned down. That's only a matter of time. Our right flank is currently held and fortified by The Staffords, but further on from them…"

"More Germans." Completed Furze.

"We're surrounded on three sides, we have to secure our position Furzzy, as strongly as we are able." The Major rose. "We've fought too hard to take this position, and shan't lose it without a fight!"

They walked back to the others, briefly relaying what they had seen before the group disbanded under the Major's commands to secure the trench as best they could. Further lookouts were posted to ensure the first sign of enemy movement was picked up and runners were sent back to the British held German Front line.

"Get to Headquarters," Kirkpatrick ordered, before the two runners headed off, "notify them that The Queen's and Staffords have achieved their objectives, and that we await further orders. Give the most senior officer there this," he handed them both identical notes he had hastily written, "that will explain our position."

"Keep your heads down, and stick to the centre," added Furze, "the Germans are currently distracted, so move swiftly, and you'll be fine."

The runners nodded and flashed from the trench. "Brave lads," remarked Kirkpatrick, as he and Furze hurried down the trench, checking on lookouts as they went.

"That they are, Kirk," agreed Furze. "We've lost a great number of good men today, but the ones we have left are determined. Down to the last man."

"I don't want to lose our foothold here, Furzzy," the Major began, as he and Furze continued down the line, "we've a decent footing, with a bit more support from the left…"

As he was speaking, a flurry of German machine gun and rifle fire suddenly erupted upon their position. Whistles and thuds broke the relative calm, and clods of earth were ripped from the trench walls around them. Before the pair could take cover, Kirkpatrick was hit in the head.

Furze glimpsed it, and his heart flew at his ribcage, pounding so hard it felt as if it would rip itself free to seek cover alone. The Major stumbled and fell, just beside Furze.

"Kirk!" he exclaimed, scrambling over the muddy ground towards him. As he did so, he screamed at the nearby troops, "return fire!"

The soldiers, touched as much by the emotion in Furze's command as by the sight of the wounded Major, threw their full weight behind the returning volley. Their Lee-Enfields flung round after round in rapid succession back towards the German lines, the ferocity of their retaliation meaning that, after a minor firefight, the Germans ceased their small-arms fire.

To Furze's great relief, Major Kirkpatrick was not severely wounded as the bullet had only grazed the side of his head. It may have created a monumental gash, but one that would not likely be fatal.

"Kirk?" Furze was holding the Major's head up as best he could. "Get a medical kit over here now!" he roared at a nearby Private. "Kirk, look at me, can you hear me?"

"Furzzy…" responded the Major, "damn it Furzzy, how does it look?"

"You're awfully lucky," said Furze, smiling at his friend's animation, "just a graze." He moved his hand and noticed that the forearm that had been supporting the Major's neck was covered in blood. The bandage there had come undone, and the wound was seeping.

"I feel dizzy Furze, I don't think I can stand," Kirkpatrick's head fell back, and his eyes closed. He was still breathing, and Furze was certain his friend would make it, but only if he got him back to the British lines right away.

"Corporal, on me," he ordered, "get two strong men, and bring them here. They have to get the Major back to the British lines with all haste, his life depends on it."

"Yes, Sir," nodded the Corporal, before bolting away.

Furze took the medical pack that had been handed to him and bound the Major's neck and head. Once this had stemmed the bleeding somewhat, Furze felt a little better, and the Major's breathing became more regular. The two soldiers arrived with a stretcher.

"Right, you two," Furze commanded, "get the Major back to the British lines as fast as you can. He's stable, but he needs medical treatment as soon as possible. Tell the doctors he has a shrapnel wound to the neck and a bullet wound to the head. Understand?"

"Yes, Sir," the young men responded, eyeing the Major warily.

"Good, thank you. The Major has led us this far, let's return the favour. Remember, stick to the centre of the line; our runners have made it through there already. Go!"

Still kneeling, he watched with a heavy heart as the two soldiers dutifully jogged away, carrying the delicate cargo of his friend back to safety. Furze became aware of a pair of eyes upon him and rose. It was Bobbie, who had run up with Philpot and Taylor-Jones as soon as they had heard the news.

"You're in charge now Furzzy," Bobbie began tentatively.

Furze started. He hadn't even considered the position the Major's departure left him in, and now realised the weight of the mantle that had been rudely thrust upon his shoulders. Lieutenant Furze was now in command of The Queen's Regiment of four officers and one-hundred-and-fifty soldiers. He was only twenty-four years old.

His mind raced, and anxiety coursed through him. How was he ready to lead all of these soldiers in any situation, let alone the dire one in which they found themselves? He thought back to the occasions when he had held such responsibility, most recently as the acting Adjutant of the Regiment and the acting commander of 'A' Company before that.

His breathing quickened. He thought back to Austin, his young friend.

You couldn't keep him safe, what makes you think you can keep these men from meeting the same fate? He felt his fists clench, felt the touch of one-hundred-and-fifty eyes upon him, suffered their judgement as each one of them, in turn, disappeared as Austin had done, screaming silently as they were dragged into nothingness. He couldn't do it, he couldn't lead as well as Kirk, as well as Fuller. He had not earnt the right to. His temples pained terribly as his veins thumped furiously; he could barely see.

He became aware of Bobbie's hand which had been placed comfortingly on his shoulder. Measuring his breathing, he stared into Bobbie's eyes, pleading with his old friend for an answer, and found in them a world of emotion. Bobbie knew the turmoil Furze was going through and this knowledge became apparent in a look that revealed pain, care, understanding, fear, and trust.

Trust, Furze wondered, *does he trust me?*

Bobbie's eyes glinted in response.

"So, it seems," Furze replied, gathering his strength. "The Germans know we are here, and I have no doubt they will continue to harass us. Get around the trench, as safely but as quickly as you can, and inform the troops to return fire vigorously when they are engaged."

"Right you are Furze," consented Philpot.

"We have to preserve ammunition," cautioned Taylor-Jones.

"Quite so," agreed Furze, "but we are only one-hundred-and-fifty men and I'd bet the Germans think we are far more. I don't wish to shatter that belief."

"Ah," smiled Bobbie.

"Tell the men to return fire with vigour, but only for brief intervals," continued Furze, "given our Lee-Enfield's rate of fire, I want them to believe we have more troops here than we do, with machine guns in support. The longer we can keep them from assaulting us, the better."

"Good plan," Taylor-Jones agreed, "any word from Headquarters?"

"Nothing, the Major and I sent runners, but they haven't returned."

"Let's pray they do so with haste," remarked Bobbie, "let's be off gentlemen, and get Furze's orders executed."

Furze took Bobbie by the arm as the others shot off. "Thank you," he whispered.

"I'd follow you anywhere Furze," Bobbie replied, each word dipped in emotion, "and I'd hazard that every man here would as well."

"Once you're done, make your way back here," Furze spoke with gratitude, "you're second in command now, after all."

IV

The rest of the afternoon passed with nothing more than minor firefights. The British troops returning a fierce but brief retort whenever they were engaged by the Germans. Thankfully, nothing serious occurred and The Queen's suffered no further casualties as they awaited the return of the runners. Steadily, the light began to fade.

"Sergeant, gather the other officers," Furze ordered, as he spread out a field map. He had commandeered one of the German dugouts for his headquarters, primarily because it had a neat little table in it and a lamp that glowed invitingly as the sun dropped below the horizon. He was concerned, quite naturally, about their position, but what worried him most was the lack of communication from British Headquarters. They may have been holding the line successfully for a number of hours, but he didn't trust the Germans' brooding inactivity.

"Evening gentlemen," greeted Furze, "Taylor, everything alright?"

Taylor-Jones had entered in deep contemplation, not uttering a word. At the sound of his name, he raised his head, and studied his companions. "I've been thinking over our position," he mused, "and, unless you are about to offer us something new Furze, it's only a matter of time before the Germans realise how vulnerable we are."

"Your concerns are my own," replied Furze, who appreciated his honesty. "I'm afraid I have had no word from Headquarters."

"What are our options?" enquired Bobbie.

"From this map," replied Furze, leaning over the small table and drawing his companions' attention to it, "we know we are exposed on our left, the Germans holding the orchard that commands the ground in front of it. To our front, further enemy trenches and, for all we know, massing reinforcements. To our right, The Staffords, but they are being pressed by Germans on their right flank."

"We need support." Observed Philpot.

"Precisely," agreed Furze, "by morning, if we have not heard from Headquarters, one of us will need to dash back across the ground we have covered, and relay our situation directly. We cannot hold this position as we currently stand, so we either need to be reinforced, or retire to the first German line."

There was a moment's silence, as the officers took in the plan. So far, they had sent four soldiers and the wounded Major back to the British line and had heard nothing.

"Come morning we shall determine who goes. In the meantime, check our defences, and double the sentries on watch. As night descends, we become ever more vulnerable, and I wouldn't put it past the Germans to launch an assault."

"Right you are," agreed Bobbie.

"Before we go..." Furze withdrew a hip flask from his pocket. The group's faces gleamed.

"You're a devil Furze," complimented Philpot, as he tasted the exquisite liquor. There was a contented silence as the four young men enjoyed a moment of quiet reflection, allowing their taste buds to whisk minds strained by the drag of battle to happier places.

"It's a beautiful thing," remarked Bobbie, turning the hip flask over in his hands. It was a little larger than one's hand, silver plated, and curved in such a way that it hugged one's torso when placed in a chest pocket. On the front were engraved Furze's rank, initials, and regiment.

"My father gave it to me, the day I first left for the front," explained Furze, taking it back and gazing at it adoringly. "I've had it on me ever since, it reminds me of home, of my family."

His companions watched him, silently, respectfully, singularly aware of the deep feelings behind his words.

"I always fill it with whisky, my father's favourite drink. Back home, he used to take great pleasure enjoying a dram of the stuff with his friends and I, saying very little but utterly engrossed in the conversation. When I share it around with my friends out here, as I am with you just now, I like to imagine he is here with us. A contemplative guardian to us all."

They would all be in need of such a guardian.

As the four officers left the dugout, meeting their respective Sergeants outside, an almighty explosion further up the trench ruptured the silence of the evening. Before the officers had time to react, another two explosions ripped the air around them.

"Shells!" shouted Furze, "get the men into cover. Now!"

"Take cover! Take cover!" shouted the officers and sergeants, as they rushed about amongst the troops.

Furze came across one of the sections of the trench that had just been hit by a German shell. The scene was terrible havoc, and at least five dead soldiers lay mangled across the trench floor.

"Damn them," cursed Furze, "damn them all. Those were direct hits; they know our exact position."

Bobbie rushed over, "high explosives!" he yelled.

"We know…"

"The other two shells caused much the same damage," reported Bobbie, observing the destruction. "I reckon we've lost at least ten men."

"That explains their recent silence," cursed Furze, as the three of them ran onwards, "they must have been moving their guns back to the secondary positions Captain Haddon-Smith saw when he rescued The Rifles. Why didn't I foresee that...?"

As they trampled along the communication trench, shells continued to rain down upon their position.

"Is everyone in?" Furze asked as he entered his makeshift command dugout. He was relieved to see all three of his friends alive and safe, although there were only two Sergeants.

"I lost Sergeant Perkins," said Taylor-Jones, remorsefully. "Got caught by shrapnel that very nearly found its mark with me as well."

An enormous explosion was felt overhead, clumps of earth fell from the ceiling and the lamp on the wall fell to the floor with a crash. As darkness descended, and Furze's Sergeant attempted to re-light the shattered lamp, he took a moment to think over their position. He had never been subjected to such an aggressive barrage. The accuracy of the German aim meant that every soldier had to be fully covered, or even a non-direct hit would catch them with shrapnel.

Every now and again, an explosion was followed by screams and groans. A direct hit. The very thought of the carnage being unleashed by the German artillery chilled Furze to the bone.

He couldn't stand it. "We have to check on the troops," he commanded. The looks from his friends, and the Sergeants, confirmed that they had been thinking exactly the same. As safe as they may have felt in the dugout, there were few of these along the trench and they couldn't sit there whilst the rest of the Regiment was slowly blown to bits.

"When we get out of here, Philpot, Taylor, you head left. Check on how the men are doing, and if there is any cover to be had." Furze ordered, now fully in control of the situation. "When you have made a full round, meet me back here so we can consider our best course of action. For God's sake, keep your heads down."

"Got it Furze," they said, rushing out of the dugout with their Sergeant.

"Bobbie, you and I will go right, doing the same."

Furze, Bobbie, and the Sergeant stumbled, ducked, and slid through the trench. As hard as his soldiers had tried, there was little cover to be found against such accurate fire. At one point, the ground behind them seemed to heave and split, evolving into a grim crater writhing with mud and limbs, as a shell found its mark.

We shall all be killed if we remain here much longer, he thought desperately, and realised he now faced the toughest decision of his command. The Major's last words, "I don't want to lose our foothold here Furzzy…" shot into his mind, and the thought of Fuller, somewhere out there on the battlefield, made him feel sick.

We can't give up this position, not after everything we have sacrificed to take it. But as he mulled this over, another shell hit the line further up from them, and two soldiers flew into the air, their bodies slamming against the walls of the trench before crumpling in a heap on the floor.

"Furzzy!" screamed Bobbie, standing right next to him but seeming a world away.

If we retire, what was all the loss for? What was the Major's sacrifice for? What about Fuller? Furze wondered.

"FURRZY! WHAT DO WE DO?! FURZZY!"

But if we stay, there'll be nothing left of us. Furze caught a glimpse of a nearby soldier, young, no more than nineteen. He lay on the grubby floor of the trench shaking violently, clutching his rifle so tightly his knuckles were sheet white, his eyes locked shut. Furze knew what he had to do.

"Let's go, we have to find the others!" Furze bellowed, relief flooding onto Bobbie's face at the sight of his friend's reanimation. They raced to find Philpot and Taylor-Jones, who looked harrowed as they approached.

"This is dire Furze," declared Philpot.

"I know," Furze acknowledged, "we cannot stay here, it's suicide. We have had no word from Headquarters but, if they were to see the position we are in, I have no doubt they would act as I am about to." Furze drew a breath, then released, "we must retire to the section of the trench occupied by The Staffords."

Taylor-Jones, who had been thinking the same thing, sighed with relief.

"The barrage is directed at us currently," Furze reasoned, "and we should be able to slip over to their section without the Germans noticing. With luck, by the time they complete their bombardment, we will have received orders from Headquarters. We'll send another runner on ahead, notifying them of my decision. If they take issue with my orders, I'll bear full responsibility, but I refuse to see my men blown to bits for nothing."

"Let's get it done," Bobbie pronounced, but no one needed telling twice. The four officers set about moving the soldiers, section by section, the four-hundred yards back towards the position occupied by The Staffords. Furze did not want to think about how many men they had lost to the artillery fire, but he felt a huge relief when he followed the last of his soldiers to safety.

The Staffords made room for the shattered Queen's, and the young Lieutenant from earlier that day greeted Furze with marked relief. "We were watching as they levelled your position," he started tentatively, "but that bombardment…it was terrifying even from here. I'm immensely glad to see you and your men."

"Not as grateful as we are to you for making room for us," Furze declared. He felt utterly exhausted, but there was more yet to do. "I'd get all our men under cover, if they aren't already. The Germans will hopefully still believe we are holding our position, but it won't be long before they realise we have left and shift their aim over here."

The five officers, having ensured The Queen's were well settled, convened in the young Lieutenant's command dugout. The intensity of the shell fire had had a terrible effect on Furze's already battered nerves and he welcomed the company of his four companions. To pacify his concerns, he occupied himself by deliberating with the Stafford's Lieutenant on their next course of action. Remembering how hard The Staffords had been hit after the initial assault, Furze was keen to understand their current state. "How many men do you think you have left?"

"Hard to say," considered the Lieutenant, "no more than one-hundred-and-fifty at best."

"That was our count, before the bombardment," replied Furze grimly, "we lost at least thirty men back there, and haven't re-counted since."

"S'cuse me, Sirs," a young soldier rushed into the dugout, "orders from Headquarters."

"Over to you Furze," retreated the young Lieutenant, "you're the senior officer here. Best my Staffords join The Queen's under you, unless those orders state differently."

"My thanks," murmured Furze, he had all but doubled his command thanks to the letter's arrival. He opened it and sighed. "Gentlemen, The Queen's and Staffords are ordered to retire from our current position, and occupy the part of the German first line we captured this morning."

"That's it?" Bobbie asked.

"There's confirmation that they received our runners, and that they understand our position."

"Do they indeed," roared Philpot, his whole body tensing with rage, "a wonder it took them so long to reply!"

"All the same," cut off Furze, meeting Philpot's glare to subdue his anger, "we have our orders. Taylor-Jones, join the good Lieutenant and take over half of The Staffords."

"Right you are," Taylor-Jones affirmed.

"Then, lead us away. Bobbie, Philpot, we'll take the rear with The Queen's, and make sure everyone gets out alright. The night should provide us with ample cover as we make our way back across the ground; nevertheless, tell the men to keep their heads down."

Orders given, Furze watched every shattered British soldier pass him as they exited the trench. Eventually, Bobbie reached him. "Last man Furzzy," he whispered.

"Thank God." Furze was unable to believe that they had retired without a single casualty. The German guns had ceased their deadly serenade shortly after the orders from Headquarters had arrived and Furze was expecting an assault at any moment. "Let's get out of here Bobbie."

It didn't take them long to reach the first German line they had captured, and they settled into their position quickly. It felt good to be back amongst the main body of British troops, with their flanks secure, and no longer holding an outcrop of territory surrounded by the enemy. They had succeeded in breaking the German lines but could have done a great deal more if only they had been supported on their flanks. At 3:00 am, another runner approached Furze's command group with orders for The Queen's and Staffords to retire further and be relieved by fresh troops.

Parting ways with the Staffords, Furze conducted a headcount, registering two-hundred-and-fifty soldiers, though no further officers appeared. Philpot and Taylor-Jones led what was left of The Queen's Regiment out of the German first line, and onto what had been 'no-man's-land' that morning. Despite the late hour, the moon shone brightly enough to cast an eerie half-light upon the ground they had fought so fiercely over. The move back was appalling. Scattered, like a morbid blanket upon the ground, were the dead and the dying. Furze tried to close his ears to the moans and groans uttered by the severely wounded, which were just too ghastly to listen to. The putrid smell that filled his nostrils made his eyes water.

He thought about Fuller, dear old Fuller. If Taylor-Jones was right, he had reached the German first line, so couldn't form a part of the Hell before him that belonged to the deepest levels of Dante's Inferno, rather than the living world. Every time he took a step, however, he was grimly reminded of the catastrophic losses that had been sustained making their advance, and how his friend was yet to appear.

Bringing up the rear, Furze watched as the gallant remains of his poor Regiment marched lethargically to safety and felt for each and every man. Some strode with their heads high, others limped, and the majority hung their heads on drooping shoulders. All were grubby, bloody, and worn, but they had performed admirably, and he loved them for that.

Deprivation

"It is all too deplorable…I just don't know how I shall get on without them."

Sunday 16th May.

The Queen's sat and rested, each man visibly shaken and absolutely dead beat.

"Philpot, recover the Regimental documents, would you?" Furze requested, his duties as commander far from over.

"Of course," Philpot departed swiftly.

The remaining officers set about ensuring the troops around them were settled, gathering any information on the whereabouts of their fellow officers as they did so. Having collected their wounded back at the German first line as they retired, they were able to glean the fate of many of their friends before re-grouping in the centre of the shattered mass of bodies to assess the damage. The ensuing task was brutal.

The Queen's Regiment had gone into action that morning with twenty-two officers, and seven-hundred-and-fifty soldiers.

"Let's begin with the Staff," Furze said grimly, "Major Bottomley?"

"Wounded," said Philpot.

"Major Kirkpatrick, wounded," Furze noted, his mind racing back to the bullet that had hit the Major in front of him.

"Just you left from the Staff, Furzzy," said Bobbie.

"On to 'A' Company," continued Furze, "Captain Lang-Browne?"

"Dead."

"Lieutenant McCate?"

"Dead."

"Lieutenant Hillen, dead. Lieutenant Humphreys?"

"Dead."

"Humphreys…" Furze muttered, aghast. He hearkened back to the first time he had met the dutiful Lieutenant who had helped make 'A' Company a home. His feelings tugged at him and he determined to find a way to do justice to his memory.

"Did 'B' Company fare any better?" Furze questioned quietly. A lump held in his throat and choked him. 'A' Company's dire casualty list had strained his emotions, but it was the next officer that turned his skin pale and nearly made him wretch. Silently, he stared at the name on the page, a small scratching of pencil that brought him more fear than the sight of a German levelling his bayonet.

"Captain Fuller?"

"I'm sorry Furzzy," said Bobbie, "he's dead. One of the Sergeants in 'B' Company saw him fall."

Furze's stomach turned over, and his hands shook so violently he had to drop the pencil and paper he was holding and clench them together. Tears welled in his eyes, and the world turned to a watery blur. His friend, his dear friend, who had been with him through so much.

Dead.

He couldn't take it in, couldn't face the reality of such indigestible news. The loss was just too deplorable for words.

The others watched, quietly, as Furze wiped his eyes and picked up the pencil and paper.

"Lieutenant Messon?" he continued, his voice quavering but holding true.

"Missing, supposedly dead from wounds."

"Lieutenant Fairclough?"

"The same."

"How about 'C' Company? Major Slake, dead." Once again, Furze faltered, the next name a roadblock against the completion of his dreadful task. "Lieutenant Garmin?"

"Again, I'm sorry Furze," this time it was Philpot, who had been in the same Company as Furze's friend, "he fell during the initial assault."

Stop, thought Furze, *please, just stop this vicious turmoil.* Still numb from the news about Fuller, he made his note and continued.

"Lieutenant Pratt?"

"Dead."

Lieutenant Philpot was the only officer to survive from his Company.

"So, 'D' Company. Captain Haddon-Smith?"

"Dead."

"Lieutenant de Rougaunt?"

"Dead."

"Lieutenant Coates?"

"Alive, but wounded."

"Well, there's some good news at last, Lieutenant Bunkitt?"

"Also wounded."

Another name appeared, emerging from an abyss of despair, another slice to Furze's already lacerated emotions. Eddie, surely not another… especially not one so at peace with the world, so humble a character, inoffensive to the last breath. With the weight of Fuller and Garmin already on his shoulders, Furze doubted he could stand much more. But he had a task to complete and the quicker it was done, the quicker he could retreat somewhere by himself. He felt heavy, his heart made of lead, his hands of rubber.

"From the Machine Gunners, Lieutenant Brookes?"

Bobbie took this one. "Dead, I'm afraid, Furzzy."

The lead heart dropped, as an oversized apple from a branch too thin to bear its weight. Brookes. Garmin. Fuller. All his dearest friends, all his closest companions. All gone, within the space of a day.

I just don't know how I shall get on without them, Furze thought, heavy with the sorrow of three good lives lost far before their time. He stared blankly at the page on his lap, a hollow husk of the man he usually was. Bobbie handed him a fresh tea.

"Take your time old chap," Bobbie suggested, attempting to relay strength whilst his own voice betrayed another soul buffeted by the winds of sorrow.

Silence descended on the miserable group and Furze surveyed his remaining friends; young men he trusted with his life and who trusted him with theirs. It was a landscape of pain. Once more, he forced his eyes to the list of names and his hand to the paper. Mourning had a time and a place, and neither were there.

"Sorry, Lieutenant Heineking?"

"Wounded."

They counted down the list. All in all, in the space of twenty-four hours, The Queen's had lost twelve officers, seven had been wounded or were missing, and only three, Furze, Philpot and Taylor-Jones, had come out unscathed. Bobbie Ross, being part of the Grenade Company attached to their Battalion, was not included on their list. Out of the seven-hundred-and-fifty soldiers that they led into battle, only two-hundred-and-fifty had come back alive.

Having written this all down in his report, Furze could barely hold it together. The destruction, the loss, was unbearable. However, being the most senior officer present he was not yet allowed the space to grieve. As the four officers were finishing up, the 7th Division commander, General Hubert Gough, appeared in their midst. He cast his eyes over the sorry sight of the battered Regiment, registering that a young Lieutenant was all that was left of its Staff.

"Lieutenant?" asked the General, as Furze rose to his feet.

"Yes, Sir, Lieutenant Furze," he saluted, "acting commander of The Queen's Regiment."

Furze struggled with the weight of these words, cursing the events that had caused them to ring true

"Is this all you have left?"

"Yes, Sir," replied Furze, "Majors Kirkpatrick and Bottomley are wounded, but alive. Although I cannot see Major Bottomley pulling through."

The General nodded, noting the strain behind Furze's replies and catching the furious emotions raging within the young officer in front of him.

"Well done, all of you, the bravery and dedication you have shown today does you all great credit, and shan't be forgotten. Yours was one of the only Regiments to secure its objective. Though we retired from the Germans' communication trench, we still hold the section of their first line that you personally captured. That, gentlemen, is no mean feat."

"Thank you, Sir," replied the officers. It was rare for a General to address them so personally.

"Mind if I make my way around the Regiment?" enquired Gough.

"Not at all, General," assented Furze, slightly taken aback, "the men will appreciate it enormously."

"My thanks," smiled the General sadly, "keep your heads high, I fear times like these will be far too common in this war. Courage, of the kind you and your men showed yesterday, is more effective than any artillery barrage."

The officers watched as he offered words of encouragement to their men, creating moments of brief animation among them, even if their faces returned to stone the moment he turned away.

"At least our losses were not entirely in vain, nor did they go unnoticed," commented Bobbie, as positively as he could.

"What I would give, for it not to have cost us so dearly," Furze remarked solemnly, as he wandered away to seek solace alone.

Relief

"Thank God we are out of it – the past three days have been terrible."

Monday 17th May.

Until around 11:00 am the next morning, the remainder of The Queen's were allowed to rest. As the morning sun broke upon the ground, it brushed against the sleeping soldiers who hadn't had the energy to find shelter. They lay, huddled against one another, wrapped in their trench coats, catching whatever rest they could before the day brought what it may.

Furze wandered among them. He hadn't the strength for sleep that morning, terrified of what might appear if he allowed himself to dream. His mind was a Ferris wheel, circulating between dull nothingness and cascades of raw emotion.

Eventually, orders arrived directing them to move up again into the support trenches situated close to Brigade Headquarters. Every muscle in Furze's body ached as he walked over to the remaining officers. Bobbie had departed, shortly after the General's visit, to rejoin his Grenade Company, and Furze felt immensely unnerved by his friend's absence. He rubbed his weary eyes, conscious that his grubby hands were hardly doing them any good but lacking the will to alter the situation. He had tried so very hard to change the course of the battle, to fight forwards and preserve his men's lives. Despite all this, Fuller, Brookes, and Garmin lay somewhere on the battlefield, cold, lifeless and alone. He hadn't the energy to struggle anymore.

"We've to move back up to the Front," Furze stated bluntly, the time for delicacy long past. Given all that these three young men had been through over the past twenty-four hours, they dealt only in brutal honesty and appreciated each other for that all the more.

"So soon!" sputtered Philpot, who had just taken a gulp of tea.

"The men Furze," added Taylor-Jones, "they're spent. Just look at the poor buggers."

Furze could hardly deny this observation. All around them The Queen's lay battered and bruised, bloodied and torn. Those who were not injured had been paired with those who were, and the whole scene was a mess. Nevertheless, that was the nature of war. He knew this, and so did the men. If they were needed on the Front, what choice did they have?

"Up to the support trenches," Furze continued, "close to Brigade Headquarters."

"Well, that's something," grunted Taylor-Jones.

"I doubt we will see any further action, given what the General said earlier that the British assault appears to have been a monumental failure everywhere except for our stretch. They won't want to lose our gains, or the whole offensive will have been for nothing. Likely we'll be told to sit tight in support for a few hours, until fresh reinforcements arrive."

"Let's hope so," chimed in Philpot.

It took all of Furze's strength to muster the men and get them moving again. He gathered the remaining Sergeants and notified them of the plan.

"They'll move, Sir," assured one, aware of Furze's concern. "Many of the lads have lost friends, they'll not want those deaths to be for nothing."

"Good, make sure they know that our efforts are in support of the British holding the German first line we captured yesterday," Furze encouraged.

They worked hard to raise the men's spirits. By this point, a large proportion of the troops were responding automatically, resigned to moving to wherever they were told whenever they were told. A few grumbled, but nearly all were bound together in solidarity and this gave the men the courage to move off with a sense of purpose. Come what may, they would protect each other fiercely. They moved into the support trench, glad that it was, at least, relatively dry. Furze took a dugout for his command point. "Philpot, spread 'A' and 'B' Company along the trench to the left of this position."

"Right you are Furze," Philpot agreed, as he left.

"Taylor, do the same with 'C' and 'D' Company, but to the right."

"Got it," Taylor-Jones replied, and left as well.

Boom! Yells from outside the dugout.

"Damn them, is there no peace!?" Roared Furze, as he ran out into the trench to assess the damage. Thankfully, the Regiment suffered no casualties, even though the Germans levelled shells onto their position for the rest of the afternoon. In comparison to what they had been subjected to the night before, this barrage hardly fazed the men.

Dusk galloped over the afternoon, and a runner entered the dugout as Furze was discussing the new British Front line with Philpot and Taylor-Jones. The 21st Brigade had taken over from the 20th Brigade that morning and was now engaged in its own assault. The cackle of machine gun fire, and the cracking of rifle duels between the British and German troops was raging in the distance.

"What news?" queried Furze of the runner.

"Not good," replied the soldier, "the 21st isn't making any ground. Headquarters says to remain ready to support the assault if needed and asks if you sustained any casualties from the enemy artillery strike."

"We suffered no casualties," answered Furze calmly, "and The Queen's is at Headquarters' disposal should they require our support."

"Thank you, Sir," acknowledged the runner, saluting and rushing out of the dugout.

The three officers walked out into the trench to get air that was hardly fresh but was at least less stagnant than the dugout. Looking up, Furze suddenly felt heavy drops of rain. Within moments, the grim sky had unleashed a trident of water upon them, and it was all the men could do to wrap the collars of their trench coats tight around their necks, huddling low to shelter themselves as best as possible.

"The going sounded tough for the 21st before the rain," Furze observed. "With this downpour, I can't imagine their struggle pushing through mud and grime under a blanket of German machine gun fire."

"Lord help them," agreed Taylor-Jones, "but let's think to our own for the moment though, Furzzy, look."

Furze followed his gesture and understood immediately. Their trench was rapidly filling with water, meaning the entire Regiment would have to resign itself to a dire, soaking, cold, and sleepless night. Despite his incredulity at their continued bad luck, Furze couldn't help but laugh. In fact, he was simply beside himself with amusement.

"What on earth are you laughing at?" asked Philpot, aghast.

"Well, in all honesty," responded Furze, between bouts of uncontrollable hysterics, "could anything more be thrown at us? In the last two days, we have almost been shot, stabbed, and blown up. Now, we are in danger of being drowned!" He fell, once more, into his somewhat delirious joy.

Suddenly the others understood and burst out in fits of laughter.

"Come to think of it, old chap," grinned Philpot, "you're right!"

"Oh, to hell with it all," smiled Taylor-Jones, "we're wet, cold, muddy, and exhausted as it is. What can a bit more rain and mud do!"

"Well bless me," passed a bewildered Sergeant, observing the three young men in rapturous amusement, "I know we're short on officers, but trust us to be left with the oddballs."

The group thoroughly enjoyed this jibe. "Come on," announced Furze, gaining control of himself once more. "Let's check on the men, and see if there's any way we can brighten their sodden night."

The Regiment remained soaking and immobile in its support trench for the whole of the next day until word was received that it was to be relieved that evening. This news spread around the soldiers like wildfire and brought with it an immense feeling of excitement and anticipation.

"Get the men formed up," Furze instructed Philpot and Taylor-Jones. "Taylor-Jones, take the rear, behind 'D' Company. Philpot, take the middle, behind 'B' Company. I'll lead us out."

"About time Furze," pronounced Philpot, "the men are withered."

With Furze at the head of the column of troops, The Queen's trudged out of their boggy trench and onto the road. The solid surface, beneath their soggy boots, brought a spring to the soldiers' steps, as they marched seven miles through Essars, around the northern edge of Bethune, to a village called Oblinghem. Upon their arrival, Furze was immensely pleased to find very empty billets, meaning his troops would have the pick of the comfiest, driest, and warmest accommodation. However, the thought crossed his mind that the reason for this situation was probably rather harrowing.

He shivered. This brought him back to the present and, realising that everyone was caked in mud and wet through, he set about assigning the Regiment its rooms.

"Get everyone into the warm," he ordered the Sergeants, "get them dry, get their kit out to wash, and get them clean. Give them their humanity back."

Before he could settle himself in, however, one Sergeant hurried back to him.

"Pardon, Sir," he began, "but there's a fresh draft of men just arrived."

"Of course there is," sighed Furze at his seemingly endless duties, "let's go take a look." The Sergeant led Furze out to the drill square, where thirty-five men stood, formed up and to attention, their kit gleaming and their faces fresh.

"Thirty-five will hardly replace the five hundred we have lost," muttered Furze to the Sergeant.

"Course not, Sir," replied the Sergeant, "but it's a start."

"That it is," agreed Furze. He spoke to the Corporal who led them, before approaching the group. In contrast to their clean and healthy appearance, Furze cut a figure almost devoid of life. Some gawped at him in horror, others stole questioning glances.

"How are we, men?" Furze boomed, his strong voice snapping them back to attention.

"Good, Sir."

"Fine, Sir."

Various voices replied.

"They look fresh off the block, Sir," commented the Corporal, "but I assure you, they're well trained."

"Excellent, thank you Corporal," nodded Furze. "I am Lieutenant Furze, acting commander of The Queen's Regiment, your new home."

There was a ripple, as the troops' minds mulled over the shocking situation that must have occurred to leave a young Lieutenant in charge of an entire Regiment.

"I shall level with you," Furze continued, he planned to win their loyalty by presenting the truth to them man to man. "The Regiment has had a tough time these past two days. We have lost around five hundred men, and all but three of our officers remain. You join a Regiment exhausted, but proud."

He paused, allowing his words to sink in.

"Why are we proud, having lost so much?" Furze looked into the eyes of the soldiers in the front row. "Because The Queen's was one of the only Regiments to achieve its objective in the last assault. General Gough himself, the commander of the Division, offered his personal thanks to the brave men you will soon call your companions."

More ripples, as the new troops began to understand the situation, and their place within it.

"My men fought through mud, blood, steel, fire and Hell to be here today, and to go home to their loved ones. My friends…" he stopped. He hadn't slept for two days, and his emotions exhausted him. "My friends gave their lives for that objective and for the freedom we enjoy at home."

He took a step towards them and the front row of soldiers braced themselves, looking at him with rapt attention. "I am proud of every man under my command, and I respect them to the utmost." His voice was low, confident, and dripping with command as he stared into the eyes of the troops in front of him. "Allow me to think the same of you all. Welcome, gentlemen, to The Queen's Regiment. You now know what that means."

He then handed over to the Sergeant to dismiss the men and assign them into their various Platoons. With this duty over, Keith Furze finally stole a moment to take his kit to his room, to undress, get warm, and get dry for the first time in two days. He lay on his bed, limbs stiff and immobile. His eyelids fell heavily, drawn down as by an invisible hand and he listened. His breathing was deep and steady. His heart beat slowly. The sound of gunfire was as constant as his pulse, but distant and disconnected in that moment. He was thankful not to have to concern himself with what its targets were.

Though he could not wholly detach his mind from the horrors he had been subjected to, he found peace in his current stasis and his mind wandered to Daw. He wished to be with her, to dance with her, hear her laugh and watch her hair ripple gently in a Spring breeze as they walked in one of London's glorious parks. Most of all, he wanted to hear her talk, and sit quietly, listening to her gentle voice, saying nothing at all.

Thank God, he said to himself, *thank God we're out of it, the past three days have been hellish.*

Emotion

"Breakfast late – everything late...Major Bottomley, Haddon-Smith, Fuller, McCate, Hillen, Major Slacke, de Rougaunt, Humphreys, Pratt. It is terribly sad, but I must try and stick it and think of the Regiment."
Wednesday 19th May.

Furze slept blissfully well, not waking once and enjoying a dreamless night. The next morning, he ate breakfast late, in fact, he did everything late, taking time to appreciate every mouthful, every conversation, every moment, and solidify it all in his mind. Life seemed to hold so great a purpose, after what he had been through, that he didn't wish to waste a single moment from that point on.

At 2:30 pm, Furze received orders that the Regiment was to move to new billets at Bourecq, so he gathered the other officers, and the trio set about readying the men for their impending seven-mile march.

"It's as if Headquarters feels we need the exercise," grumbled Philpot, when Furze told him the distance. "We seem to have made nothing but seven-mile marches since we left the trenches!"

"Nothing like some exercise and fresh air to rejuvenate the spirit old boy," bolstered Taylor-Jones, attempting to liven the mood. They were all tired, and tensions were running high.

"Lord knows it must be a task to keep track of all our troop movements," added Furze. "Especially after such a large offensive. I'm hopeful that we shall gain further fresh troops at Bourecq."

"Some additional officers wouldn't go amiss," noted Philpot, as they dispersed to their usual positions throughout the Regimental column.

They arrived that evening at what Furze thought was a rather charming country village, surrounded by luscious green fields, with not a trench or muddy shell crater in site. It was all immensely peaceful. When the Regiment had settled into its new home, Furze received a letter from a messenger who had followed them from Oblinghem.

He read it over, twice, then called for Philpot and Taylor-Jones. "Major Bottomley didn't make it," he said, downcast. "He died from his wounds in Bethune."

Although Furze had been aware of the severity of the Major's injuries, the news still shocked him, and grazed his already raw emotional wounds.

"God rest his soul," Philpot said, bowing his head.

"An exceptional officer," agreed Taylor-Jones, "does the letter detail his burial?"

"It does," Furze replied, looking over the piece of paper once more, "alas, he is due to be buried this very day. I'll be sorry to miss the chance to pay my respects."

"As will we," Philpot acceded.

The unfortunate news about the Major's passing caused Furze's subdued contemplations to resurface. He reflected that more than ten officers, to whom he had been close, had died during the last battle. His mind ran over their names, Major Bottomley, Haddon-Smith, Fuller, McCate, Hillen, Major Slacke, de Rougaunt, Humphreys, Pratt, Brookes...it was terribly sad and Furze felt his spirits sliding back into the vile abyss of hopelessness that they had been flung into when he had first assessed the Regimental damage. Once again, he fought hard to pull his thoughts together. *You have to stick at it*, he said to himself, *and think of the Regiment.*

Furze had only been in command of the Regiment for four days, but it felt like an eternity to him. Although he was coping with the responsibility, he was relieved when a fresh face appeared in the officers' quarters on Thursday morning. Philpot, Taylor-Jones, and he were sitting quietly playing cards, and enjoying a moment's peace, when a Captain entered. He walked in humbly, taking care not to interpose his presence in their card game, taking up a position near the door. He was tall, lean, with kind eyes that engaged one's attention when his gaze fell upon you. He took off his cap when he entered and placed it delicately on a hook on the wall, allowing his light brown, cropped hair some freedom. Furze noticed him first, as Philpot let out a howl over the hand he had just lost.

"My apologies, Sir," Furze greeted, rising from his seat, "we were engrossed in the game."

The others rose and turned to meet the Captain.

"Please, no need to apologise," the Captain responded, with friendly familiarity, "Lieutenant Furze, I assume?"

"I hold that burden," Furze answered, attempting to infuse some humour into the introduction, though the look he gave the Captain imparted the reality. "I'm the acting commander of The Queen's Regiment. This is Lieutenant Philpot, and Lieutenant Taylor-Jones."

"A pleasure," the Captain greeted each man in turn. "I'm Captain Duckworth, formerly from The Staffordshire Regiment. Having just returned from leave I've been reassigned as commander of The Queen's." He turned to Furze, "I hope you don't mind my relieving you of your burden?"

Furze felt a flood of gratitude at the news that he was to hand back command of the Regiment. It wasn't that he had not come to appreciate, or even to enjoy, the role of commander; in fact, he very much hoped to hold such a position substantively in the future. But at the present moment, having not had time to deal with his own emotional turmoil, he was thrilled to hand that mental strain to someone more senior. Furze also felt charmed at the delicacy with which the Captain had handled the shift in authority.

"Not in the slightest," Furze acquiesced. "It's been an honour to lead this Regiment, but I hand the men to you glad in the knowledge I have taken them this far. The Staffords we fought with in the trenches were valiant soldiers, I'm glad you'll be leading us, Sir." Furze's eyes dropped from the penetrative gaze Duckworth gave him. "I'm just sorry I am not able to hand you more men, we three are the only officers left."

Once more, Furze couldn't help his mind turning to Fuller and Brookes and mustered all his strength to hold his nerve so as not to appear weak and broken in front of his new commander. *If Fuller had been here,* he thought, *he'd be able to hold himself together, to be strong.* But Fuller wasn't there, neither was Brookes, and these two absences left gaping chasms in Furze's resolve.

Duckworth had been well-briefed on The Queen's efforts during Festubert, and their resulting state of mind had been a particularly important topic. Indeed, he had expected far worse than he found, for the evident dedication of the three young officers greatly encouraged him.

"I'll hear nothing of the sort Furze, General Gough himself talked to me briefly of the Regiment's efforts. By all accounts, the men were put through Hell and led out of it courageously. It is I, gentlemen, who is honoured to be counted amongst you."

Duckworth asked Furze to take up the Regimental Adjutancy, a position Furze graciously accepted, before informing the group that two further officers would soon be boosting their depleted numbers. To Furze's surprise, he knew them both and the addition of two more friendly characters was greatly welcomed.

"Were our efforts really noticed at Headquarters?" asked Furze, as he led Duckworth around the Regiment, introducing him to the men.

"More than you may be aware, Furze," replied Duckworth, a knowing glint in his eye.

The Captain evidently had a point, for General Gough visited The Queen's once again on Saturday morning.

"I'll level with you Furze," Gough remarked, as he, Duckworth, and Furze walked towards the waiting Regiment, which had been formed up for his address. "I was both shocked and impressed by the Regiment's condition when I saw you the other night. You all looked ragged, not surprising given everything you had been through. Yet, you all marched straight back into the support trenches when required." He turned and looked at Furze with measured respect. "Not everyone would have been able to achieve that."

He surveyed the gathered troops before him, now clean and rested, but still less than half the number they should have been.

"Men of The Queen's Regiment," Gough bellowed, his sonorous tone capturing the soldiers' attention. "Over the past few days, you have been recovering from what has been a thunderous stage in your war. The losses you suffered at Festubert were harrowing and I feel for the pain every one of you must be going through. Whether injured physically or emotionally, such battles leave scars that only time can heal. Time and camaraderie."

Gough took a breath, scanning the faces of the troops before him. "Look to one another during this sorry time and remember, your fellows did not die in vain. You did not struggle through mud and bullets for nothing. The Queen's took its objective, succeeded where others failed and spearheaded the extension of the British Front line. For this, for your determination, for your courage in adversity, I salute you!"

The General stood tall and saluted the Regiment proudly, the soldiers returned his salute and looked markedly impressed by his words, which had certainly touched Furze to the quick. Gough then took some time once the troops had been dismissed to talk to a couple of them in groups, before making his departure, his visit reminding The Queen's that they hadn't been forgotten.

When he got the opportunity, Furze took the time to ride into Lillers. He took immense pleasure saddling Tommy, feeling the animal's energy beneath his warm coat, and trotting leisurely over to the nearby town. It enabled him to muse, peacefully, without being wholly alone. Tommy, who seemed to have a sixth sense about his owner's mood, would whiney kindly every now and again, ears pricked, throwing his head back gently to remind Furze he knew he was there. The first time he made the journey, lost entirely in his thoughts, he was brought back to reality when a French farmer asked him if he knew where he was. Taking a moment to assess his surroundings, Furze admitted that he was thoroughly perplexed and allowed the old man to direct him in the right direction. Thankfully, Tommy was quick to learn the route so, when his thoughts took over on future trips, he regularly found his destination right in front of him without any recollection of the journey.

In the strongbox of his mind, simmered two thoughts. The first, naturally, belonged to Fuller, Brookes, and Garmin. He had mastered the ability to control his emotions whilst on duty. However, in the stillness of night, he could not help but think back to the battle that had stolen his friends' vibrant lives. Occasionally, when he awoke, he was convinced that the whole dire episode had been a nightmare and fully expected Fuller to comment playfully that he had been talking in his sleep. He didn't feel as though he had fully come to terms with their loss and found it difficult to imagine a future where he had.

The second related to a set of emotions he had hitherto not observed with such strength. The death of so many of his close friends had caused a shock to his nerves and his sense of belonging. Subsequently, he had begun to question his purpose, mulling over the relevancy and importance of certain aspects of his life. Daw, above all else, held a commanding presence in his contemplations. Certainly, he had always known that he cared for her and enjoyed her company, but he hadn't before realised the extent to which she doused his life with meaning.

Such self-reflection had been sparked by the news of Fuller's death, which he had initially reacted to with pity, swiftly followed by remorse and anger, before finally uncertainty. He began to question whether his actions, his life, made any difference at all if those he cared about could vanish so grotesquely. Then, one evening, he struck upon a tiny detail of his nature he had yet to consider. It was that, in moments of his deepest troubles, he would turn for solace and support to letters from home. More regularly still, the letters he chose to digest were from Daw.

Darling Daw, he always thought, as he read over her cheery words, *a constant positive in a world so draped in pain.* It was on such a thought passing through his mind that Furze realised that his life still had meaning. As long as Daw and his family remained united behind him, his actions still held a purpose. Strange as it was to say, he had never before viewed his family as giving his life purpose. He had always fought for them, to make his father proud and to keep his mother safe, but to say they gave meaning to his existence was a novel concept. Turning this principle to Daw opened up another facet of Furze's deep emotional well-being. *What does she truly mean to me?* One question that popped up as he trotted along. *Why now does she appear at the forefront of my thoughts so often?* In truth, he was a little perturbed to be thinking about a woman so far away, living a life vastly removed from his current situation, especially when he had a multitude of other duties to think about. But this was why he allowed Tommy to walk him to Lillers. Dropping all other responsibilities from his mind, for even the briefest of moments, gave Furze the exquisite pleasure of being able to think about Daw and her importance to him, in the context of his recent loss.

Throughout these days of deep emotional consideration, Furze and his remaining friends also attempted to support one another as best they could whilst grappling with their own demons. One morning brought the welcome arrival of Bobbie, who sat down to breakfast with Furze.

"How have you been keeping, Bobbie?" greeted Furze.

"Holding myself together, just about," responded Bobbie. He was calm, but the dark rings under his eyes told sorrowful stories. "I've been run off my feet looking to the needs of the men and that's helped take my mind off things."

"I know how you feel," agreed Furze. "It does all get a little too much to bear from time to time." He caught his mind wandering back to Fuller, Brookes and Garmin, and looked down into his tea.

"Just why I thought I'd come and visit," smiled Bobbie, "would you like to join me on a trip to Bethune for the day? I've booked the staff car in anticipation."

Having watched, helplessly, as Furze's resolve crumbled, friend by friend, following the Battle of Festubert, Bobbie had been rapt with worry. Subsequently, he had been thinking over ways to lift his friend's spirits and the glorious day presented just such an opportunity.

Furze raised his head to meet the inquisitive gaze of one of his last remaining close friends. Thank goodness the war had spared at least one kind soul, for now.

"It would be my pleasure, Bobbie," smiling as he accepted the invitation, and welcoming the wave of gratitude that swept over his friend's face as he agreed. "Thank you for the thought."

They proceeded to leap into the staff car and motored the nine miles to Bethune. The pair meandered around the village, making a point of stopping in at every shop they found just to take a moment to browse its contents. Time held no sway over them that day, safe in the knowledge that their official duties were all in hand. It could have appeared strange that such a routine activity as shopping counted as a treat on the Front, yet, on reflection, the idea was not a significant oddity. The men on the Front craved any pastime that reminded them of their old lives and abnormal situations called for the comfort of normality.

To cap off what had been a thoroughly peaceful day, Bobbie suggested dining at L'Hotel de Lisbon that evening.

"Monsieur Ross?" the waiter enquired in a heavy French accent as they trooped in. "Right this way gentlemen."

"You booked a table?" chuckled Furze. "The place is nearly empty!"

Bobbie took the seat offered to him by the waiter and sat down with deep satisfaction. "Sometimes the things that appear the least significant can have the greatest impact. How are you really, Furzzy?"

Confident that Bobbie understood and had experienced much of what he had been through, Furze allowed his strongbox of emotions to open momentarily.

"I haven't had a moment to fully mourn, Bobbie," he sighed. "I've found myself sleeping poorly, worrying over what my life is coming to, wondering where we shall all end up…"

Bobbie remained silent, observing his friend.

"This war seems to present one with two paths," continued Furze. "Death or unbearable sorrow, and the path we walk along is never one we choose."

"It may appear that way," acceded Bobbie, "but we always have a choice."

"Do we?" Furze countered quickly, becoming ever more animated as his sadness grew angry limbs. "No matter the decisions we make, good people die. Ground is won and lost and still, friends die."

"We're still here, Furzzy…" Bobbie attempted to soothe.

"Who cares!" Furze spat, "what about Eddie, what about Fuller? The Germans killed them and I'll never see them again!"

Furze turned sheet white, aghast at the outburst he had allowed to descend upon his remaining friend Bobbie, who in his turn, sat stock still.

"Forgive me, Bobbie…"

"Please, Furzzy," Bobbie cut him short. "No one fighting in this war needs to ask for forgiveness. We're all just doing the best we can, even if our best can sometimes be appalling."

"Who are we going to be when we return?" Furze voiced a concern he had worried over for days. "I'm scared of the person this place is turning us, turning me, into. What if my parents, or Daw, do not recognise this sorry state of a man?"

"I've thought about that," Bobbie smiled regretfully. "There's no doubt this war will change us, dear fellow, in ways we may never come to realise."

Furze's countenance darkened, Bobbie's answer realising a wealth of fears. "I shouted at you just now, one of my dearest friends…"

"The people that love us will always see past any changes, cutting through to the honest heart of our characters, as I'm doing with you," Bobbie responded. "I'm hurting Furzzy, we both are. I don't know what the future will hold, but you and I have to keep going, together. We owe Eddie and Fuller that much at least."

Mentioned in Despatches 1915
Signed by Winston Churchill

Recognition

"General Gough spoke to me afterwards and said I had done very well on the 16th and that he would see that I received an honour, which very much pleased me."
Saturday 29th May.

Furze awoke on the morning of 27th May, to a buzz of excitement amongst the officers.

"What's causing the commotion?" he yawned at Philpot.

"Snap to it Furze!" Captain Duckworth belted with mock authority as he entered the room. The pair had been enjoying running the Regiment as it recovered. "I have just been informed, by General Gough, that General Joffre will be paying the entire 7th Division the honour of a visit. Today!"

"General Joffre?" Furze's jaw almost dropped from its socket. "Why so?"

"Gough didn't say," replied Duckworth, evidently a little strained by the news. "But I'll be damned if The Queen's doesn't look the finest Regiment in the Division. Furze, we have work to do."

General Joseph Joffre was the Commander in Chief of the French forces and, as Furze understood it, the Allied Forces on the Western Front. With a rich and varied military career, he had held such a position of responsibility since the beginning of the war. As Adjutant, Furze had a great deal to look to and Duckworth near swept him out of the room flinging, as he did so, some orders to Philpot.

"Right," the Captain instructed as they strode outside, "the entire Division is to be formed up in a field near Bas Rieux."

"Gathering thousands of men in one place is no small feat."

"Quite so," agreed Duckworth hurriedly, "which is why we need to make certain The Queen's play their part. Especially as we shall occupy the position of honour at the head of the Brigade.

"So, what's to be done?" Furze queried, adamant that the day would be a success.

"All the Regiments are required to be formed up in their Brigades by midday. Let's have The Queen's in their cleanest uniforms, boots polished, leathers gleaming, and rifles in perfect order. You and I shall conduct an initial inspection before joining the Brigade.

The 20th, 22nd, and 21st Brigades formed up in that order, standing smartly to attention in the large open field. Up and down the lines of waiting troops walked and rode their officers, each one casting searching eyes over every soldier. Boots were hastily given last minute rubs, tunics were pulled straight, and collars flattened. All over the field flew the comments, barks and snaps of the corporals and sergeants who, following behind the officers, acted upon their observations. The scene rendered a shimmering mass of humanity, individual bodies working in harmony to create the expected whole.

Captain Duckworth thundered up the line. "He's arrived Furze, how are they looking?"

"Topping, Sir."

"I'm pleased, Furze, very pleased," Duckworth smiled. "Best get into position. Sergeants! The General approaches, let's have silence."

Duckworth and Furze deposited their mounts and took their positions at the front of the Regiment. Silence fell upon the 7th Division, fierce concentration creating a peace as present yet as delicate as a candle's flame. General Joffre, the Commander in Chief, appeared. In his sixty-third year, small and roundly built, he walked with a confidence and purpose supported valiantly by a large, white, very neatly groomed moustache. He wore a pale blue tunic, with bright red breeches, and equally bright brown gaiters. All heads remained quite still, pointing straight ahead, but all eyes swung to observe the Commander and his retinue.

Beginning on the left, with the 20th Brigade, he walked down the lines, followed by Generals John French, Douglas Haig, Godfrey Thomas, Henry Rawlinson, Gough, and a number of other high-ranking officers. The entire retinue was an immensely impressive sight, representing the combined top military minds of Britain and France. Furze braced himself as the leading quartet approached, hearing them conversing with the troops to his left. Short conversations. "How are you?", "You're looking in good spirits!", "Thank you for your hard work, the King shall hear of your efforts." They passed Furze standing there, staring before him, holding his sword out in marked respect, without saying a word. In that moment, only an ancient Greek statue could have retained better immobility, but it would never have been able to emulate such dignity and composure. As Gough passed, however, he cast a grateful glance at Furze and the latter broke into a tiny smile in return.

Eventually, the swathe of seniority completed its walk, and Gough led Joffre to the saluting base. Gough stood to one side of Joffre, with French and Haig close behind, and the rest further back.

"7th Division!" boomed Gough, "it is very generous of the Commander in Chief to honour us with his visit. You have shown him your best selves, and for this, I thank you. Now, I ask that you show him your appreciation, three cheers for General Joffre – Hip hip!"

"Hurrah!" roared thousands of steely voices in unison.

"Hip hip!"

"Hurrah!"

"Hip hip!"

"Hurrah!"

Furze allowed the cheers to escape from his person with the speed of a swooping swallow; the final bellow of the soldiers resounding splendidly in the afternoon air.

Beginning with the 20th Brigade, each Regiment marched past the General, turning their heads and saluting respectfully as they did so. Once the last man had filed past General Joffre, he speedily departed with his retinue. Time, unfortunately, did not allow him any further conversations with the Division.

This didn't stop Generals Gough and Lawford from making further visits, however, and Furze felt the strength to write to Daw following a particularly meaningful one the next day.

> *My darling Daw,*
>
> *Please write to me soon to let me know you are well, reading your words will greatly soothe the pains of my aching heart. I have lost so much over the past few weeks, so many good friends, so many happy memories that I cannot relate to you here. I would not do justice to the sorrow I feel and the sacrifices that have been made.*
>
> *Instead, know that I am keeping as well as can be expected. The Allied High Command has been keeping us immensely busy recently, inspecting us a great deal and commending the troops for their dedication following the recent battle. Today, Generals Gough and Lawford paid us a visit in order to inspect the new drafts of troops we have received.*
>
> *General Lawford is a man who cuts straight to the matter at hand, quite the*

opposite of Gough who, I own, I have come to respect a great deal due to the level of concern he has shown for our troops. That said, Lawford is immensely knowledgeable. The Queen's is the senior English Line Infantry Regiment, one of the only ones to be composed entirely of serving regular soldiers at the start of the war. He wished to know whether the young, fresh troops would be up to scratch, would live up to the 7th Division's reputation as 'The Immortal Seventh'. He asked me as much and I told him that I have every trust in their ability to do the Regiment proud.

General Gough then greatly surprised me by reiterating how well The Queen's had done at Festubert, noting their strength of resolve especially in the aftermath. He is recommending me for an honour! Although I am very much pleased at this, for it is the first I have received, I told him in no uncertain terms that the men were the ones that kept us all going, that fought through such horror to take the ground we did during that battle. Dear Daw, I could not help but think of all my friends who fell during that assault, and who deserve the honour far more than I do. I might have survived, but I feel enormous guilt at the fact that their loss could have been the awful trade.

I do not know when I shall next make it home, for there is much to do here to rebuild

the Regiment's capability. When I do, my
dear, I will look forward to the moment
when I can look into your eyes, hear your
voice, and hold you once more. I have so
much to tell you, and I am struggling to
articulate everything via these letters.

Know that I have thought about you a
great deal recently and count myself lucky
to be able to do so.

Ever yours,
Keith.

Further parades and inspections occurred until, on Monday, Duckworth sat down next to Furze with a letter in his hand. "What," he quizzed, waving the letter, "do you think I have here?"

Furze, immersed as much in his thoughts as he was in his food, took little notice of the Captain's flourishing. "Oh, I really don't care to guess."

"Come come Furzzy," grinned Duckworth, "it might do you good to lighten up a little. What have I got?"

"A letter?" Furze sighed, hoping his reply would satisfy his friend.

"A letter, indeed!" scoffed Duckworth, relentless in his attack on Furze's morning. "You can do better, it'll be worth your while."

"Oh, blast it! What is the letter about?" Furze placed his cutlery deliberately on the table, folded his arms, looked at the Captain and became intrigued at his positive demeanour.

"Only a letter from Thurlow," elucidated Duckworth.

"Oh," muttered Furze, his interest diminished. Thurlow, although a good friend stationed at Headquarters, was not the author Furze had briefly expected.

"Don't be so quick to judge, he writes with news from General Lawford, the General has requested that you go on a week's leave, right away, as he feels certain you require a rest."

For the second time, in only a number of days, a British General had rendered Furze stunned.

"Well, this is unexpected, but a joy!" An enormous smile spread across his face as he thought about his return home and Duckworth leaned over to him.

"You deserve a rest, Furze," he commented quietly, with a firmness and warmth to his voice that expressed great care. "By God, you've thrown your very being into holding this Regiment together and everyone appreciates that, the men most of all. But you're useless to them, to me, if you don't take proper care of yourself. Get home, focus on your own mind, take time with Daw."

Furze looked at him, the mention of his sweetheart causing his heart to pound so loudly he thought the sound reverberated off the very walls of the room.

"Then," finished Duckworth, "return to us fresh and ready to lead once again."

"Thank you," Furze replied, "you're right, I need some time." It suddenly struck him how exhausted he was. Up until that point, he had buried his worries, concerns, and pains beneath the blanket of duties he had to perform for the sake of the men, for the Regiment. Now that there appeared a week where he would be able to put all that aside, those buried troubles weighed heavily on his soul. The last time he had returned home, he had needed time to recover from his physical injuries. Now, he would need help repairing far more intimate, invisible wounds.

Taking Leave

"General Thomas, who now commands the 1st Corps and used to be in the Regiment, came and inspected us at 12:30 pm. He gave us a splendid address and told us how well we had done in this war."

Monday 31st May.

Before Furze departed, he attended a splendid address held by General Thomas. Standing tall, surveying the men in front of him, Thomas paused to allow the silence around them to grow. The pause had the dramatic effect of making the General appear hugely contemplative, as if he knew the background of every individual in front of him and was deciding how to address each of them in the most appropriate fashion. When his voice eventually pierced the stillness thick with expectation, his words dripped with importance and feeling.

"I have spoken to a few of you. Some, I have simply crossed glances with. Most, I do not know. This can also be said of you about me."

The soldiers in the front row expressed surprise at the General's direct approach.

"Though being the nature of things, this does not mean that I do not understand what you have achieved, or what you are further capable of. I, myself, was a number amongst you once. A proud man of The Queen's Regiment, eagerly aware of the weight of expectation placed upon my men and I by the valiant name we fought under. I am pleased, very pleased, that this glorious name and the reputation that follows it remains intact."

He drifted to his left and began to stroll slowly down the line as he prepared his next thoughts, his arms held loosely behind his back. "Though times change, though our enemy emerges in different forms, though we fight on different battlefields and though the people we know come and go, our name, our reputation, must remain constant."

He turned, looked at the front row of soldiers, and padded back up the line. "The name you fight under gives you purpose. It gives you belonging and it gives you security. More than this, though, it gives you something to influence, something to contribute to; a canvas in life that you can place an indelible mark upon. Those before us did so, those around us do so in their various ways. We must ensure that those after us are able to seize the same opportunity and fight valiantly for what they believe in when time demands it."

The General, his words striking chords with more prevalence than a symphony orchestra, had every eye upon him as he paused once again, before moving to take up his original position in front of the Regiment.

"Those of you at Festubert, I thank you. You gave your strength, your will, and your courage that day, putting your lives on the line. Some of your companions, your friends, paid the ultimate price. Know that I grieve for every single loss and that the respect of everyone at Headquarters has been, and is, with you. Those of you who have just joined this historic Regiment, understand the characters who have come before you, the bravery they have shown and the sacrifice they have paid to allow the rest of us to fight on. I have no doubt that you will continue to bolster the name you now represent and will leave a mark upon this canvas that those after you shall be proud of."

General Thomas raised his hand purposefully, drew his shoulders back and commended them sincerely. "Gentlemen, I thank you all."

The Regiment, as one, saluted back before they were dismissed by Duckworth. Furze thought the whole address had been splendid and greatly appreciated the fact that the General had remarked about how well the Regiment had done in the war thus far.

General Lawford, who had been observing the address, suggested lunch, and spirits were high in the Officers' mess that afternoon. Furze found himself seated next to Lawford and took the chance to thank him for the leave he had arranged.

"Please, don't mention it Furze," Lawford responded. "When I last visited, I was impressed by the spirits of the men and greatly comforted by the quality of the new recruits."

"Thank you, Sir." Furze's tone noted that he was thoroughly pleased.

"Only one thing concerned me," continued Lawford seriously, "and that was how much of yourself you were sacrificing to resuscitate the Regiment."

Furze's brow furrowed, hoping the leave which the General had arranged had not been out of concern over his capability to lead.

"Such selfless dedication is more than any commander could ask for and bodes incredibly well for your future as a leader."

Furze exhaled slowly, unaware that he had been holding his breath, as relief came flooding back to him.

"That is kind, Sir, and I hope to put it to good use in the future."

"Kindness has its place, Lieutenant," noted the General, "what I say is simply the fact of the matter. That said, understand this." Lawford lowered his voice and looked meaningfully at Furze. "A Company, a Regiment, an entire army, is only as strong as its soldiers and by association, its leaders. You have to give your all, in order to command during such times. But you must understand when you, yourself, need to rejuvenate, conserve energy, and recover. If you fall whilst propping up others, because you want to take one more step on their behalf, everyone will come toppling down."

Furze nodded, keenly aware of the importance of the General's words.

"I arranged this leave because the British Army needs The Queen's now more than ever. And The Queen's, well, it needs you. Take this opportunity young man, to appease your desires at home, and return with an understanding of the strength you will need to deal with the responsibility of leadership. Be under no illusion, this war will demand more than anyone is able, or willing, to contemplate."

These words sprang to the truth of the situation for Furze, and he suddenly understood the General's approach. Remove the trifles and focus on the reality of events. Everything, to Lawford, had a purpose and if that purpose did not contribute to the defeat of the German Army, he ignored it as easily as a snowflake in a blizzard.

"What do you plan to do with your leave?" Lawford enquired.

"Well, I shall return to my family first, naturally," explained Furze, picturing his father and mother as he did so. The recollection made a smile grow on his face, which pleased the General. Aloof as Lawford was to trifles, he was not cold to the joy of others.

"You have a loving family, can one ask for anything more?" mused Lawford, with a hint of sadness that Furze detected. The General was slowly revealing more of the personality behind such outward shows of stern ceremony. The more Furze spoke to Lawford, the more he became intrigued by him.

"Then I shall see Daw, of course, my sweetheart," Furze added, measuring Lawford's response. The General's face expressed compassionate pleasure at this comment and the conversation became further animated when Furze began planning how the reunion with his sweetheart would go.

"I think I'll take her dancing!"

"I would suggest the Savoy, old boy," beamed the General, becoming ever more personal as the conversation continued. "I took my dear Lillian there when I was attempting to persuade her that I was a half-decent fellow."

The pair chuckled merrily, as Furze responded. "That's a topping idea, I adore the Savoy. May I ask, General, how long you and Lillian have been together?"

"Ah, alas," Lawford replied, giving Furze a smile dashed with pain, "poor Lillian died almost fifteen years ago...she was a true English rose, with a beautiful heart, but her body failed her."

"Please accept my apologies, Sir," Furze replied, understanding now the General's earlier expression. "I didn't know…"

"No need to apologise son, what has occurred has occurred. It was devastating at the time, but one holds one's head high and gets on with life. I know that's what she would have wanted me to do." Lawford's face then brightened as he recounted the tale. "Over the years one begins to build up one's life again, and last year I married my lovely Muriel."

"I'm very pleased for you both!"

"It was a beautiful day." Lawford looked lost in the memory. "So, take your Daw dancing, Furze, and appreciate her, with your whole self for every part of her, whilst you are still able."

With Lawford's words still swirling around his mind, Furze bade his farewells and leapt into the car waiting patiently to take him to Boulogne.

"Good afternoon!" Furze greeted, with volcanic excitement.

"Good afternoon, Sir," responded the driver, slightly bemused at Furze's energy.

"Ripping day, I hope you'd agree? To Boulogne, with all haste, please."

"As you like, Sir," smiled the driver, as he eased the car and its excitable cargo towards the coast.

He was put up for the night in L'Hotel Folkestone, before catching the boat to England at 10:30 am on the first day of

June. Shouts and whistles were heard as ropes were flung off the vessel by sailors who leapt across the deck like a pack of monkeys. It felt odd to Furze being surrounded by so much activity without being a part of it, but he reminded himself that this was a seafarer's world and took pleasure in simply observing the crew at work.

As the boat surged on, picking up speed and slamming through the waves, the sea air swirled around its passengers. It was cool, fresh, and sharp; carrying a revitalising innocence in great contradiction to the pungent air of the front. Furze took time outside, breathing in deeply, flooding his lungs with greater speed than water does a sinking ship. He scanned the horizon, lapping up the enormity of a vista untouched by mud, trenches, and war. He searched the waves, caught the movement of the swell, snatched at the tip of a wave as it broke on the bow of the boat and followed the flight path of a solitary seagull as its wings skimmed the surface of the water. In his mind, the sea could do nothing to hamper the inevitable progress of a vessel so heavily laden not only with its passengers' baggage, but also with the weight of their consciences.

He closed his eyes and listened. The splash of the water, the whistle of the wind, the grumble of the ship, the murmuring of the passengers…the drone of an aircraft's engine overhead, the blast of a gun, the crack of a rifle… He started, opened his eyes, and shook his head fiercely. Looking up, he spotted three lonely aircraft ahead, but there was no gunfire.

Enough, he thought, *it's alright, Keith, you're going home.*

Family

"Dear Dad and Nevil met me at Victoria – it was so lovely seeing them – both as well as ever."

Tuesday 1st June.

I

The train pulled into London's Victoria station and jolted to a stop, urging Furze from his thoughts. Since landing at Folkestone at midday, he had been consumed with the logistics of catching trains and moving his baggage. Now, having actually arrived home, he suddenly felt nervous. His father would be waiting at the station, likely with his brother. What would they think of him and how would he feel about them?

So much had happened since his departure in January, so much had formed, been broken, and reformed in Furze's core that he wondered if he would appear the same man, the same brother, the same son. What if life at home did not hold the meaning for him that it once did?

The train conductor interrupted his self-doubt. "We've arrived, Sir."

"Yes, quite," responded Furze, without moving.

"Is there someone waiting for you, Sir?" queried the man, conscious of Furze's trepidation.

"My father, I believe, who will be awaiting the arrival of his son." Furze paused. "Although, I'm not sure he will be expecting the man who disembarks from this train."

"Well, that may be," the man answered kindly, "and you're not alone in your worrying. Now, I don't know what you've seen and I don't fancy I want to. But one thing's for certain, the people who love you, hold a love that will never change, no matter how much you do. War brings unspeakable experiences to those who don't deserve them, but never doubt the care of your friends and family. Believe you me, the spirit of the British is one thing the Germans will never break."

Furze looked up at this kindly stranger, an elderly man, who knew nothing of Furze or his experiences on the Front. Yet, somehow, he had managed to encapsulate all his worries in one simple stroke and define so coherently what Furze had been attempting to understand.

"Thank you, my dear fellow," he smiled as he stood up. "Those were precisely the words I required. Your family is blessed to count you amongst them."

"We all know people in the war, Sir," the conductor noted, sadly. "In such times, we have to support one another."

Even with the conductor's words ringing true in his mind, he was glad to distract himself momentarily by overseeing the unloading of his luggage from the train carriage.

"Keith! My dear boy!" sprang a familiar utterance that made him gasp tenderly as he whipped around. It was his father's voice, bursting from the sturdy frame that Furze knew so well. Herbert welcomed his son home with a strong embrace, but Furze noticed the tears in his eyes. Ever attempting to retain a model disposition of strength, Herbert's emotions occasionally swelled far too passionately to be kept subdued.

Nevil stood just behind his father; arms crossed in an attempt to appear nonchalant but with evident joy splashed across his countenance.

"Welcome home Keith," he nodded, extending a hand.

Furze looked at the offered hand and he and Herbert burst into laughter. Taking Nevil's arm, he pulled his younger brother in for as warm an embrace as he had given his father.

"You might be eighteen and a man," chuckled Furze, "but that doesn't mean you can't show your older brother a little affection."

Nevil broke into laughter himself, as the three of them gathered Furze's belongings and headed for the station exit.

"You can't imagine the joy your mother and I felt when we received your telegram, son," began his father. "The news we have been receiving about the Front these past few months has hardly been pleasant..." he searched Furze's gaze with his own intelligent eyes, seeking truth behind the fables.

"I'm sorry, Dad," responded Furze, who was aware of his lack of communication since Festubert and regretted terribly the concern it had inevitably caused his family. "It has been a trying few months." He paused, but his father said nothing, allowing the weight of his words to sink in. "The past few weeks, especially, have been difficult, and I have found myself in positions of responsibility I never thought I would at this stage. But the men have been topping, their spirits continually amaze me and I must admit, keep me going."

"Oh son, we quite understand – I meant the comment more to express our comfort at your health and speedy return. I cannot imagine what you have been through and think it quite appropriate you keep the details to yourself. I've been keeping your mother from the worst of the reports in the papers."

The group lost no time in heading straight home and, when Furze arrived, his mother, Mary, and sister, Dorothy, were waiting eagerly by the front door.

"Keith!" exclaimed his sister joyously, as she rushed out of the house just as he was approaching with his luggage. She, unlike Nevil, hurled herself at her younger brother, wrapping her comforting arms around his neck, showering him with familial affection.

"Diddy! I can't tell you how good it is to see you looking so well," answered Furze, dropping his luggage and returning her strong embrace. "Where is Margy?"

"Oh, Marjorie popped out and will be back this evening. But come, mother really cannot wait a moment longer to see you," raced Dorothy breathlessly, taking his hand as Furze bent to recover his fallen belongings.

His father's firm hand gripped his shoulder. "We'll handle these, son, you go on to your mother now."

The gratitude he held for his father almost overwhelmed him. He had spent so much of the past few months attempting to control his surroundings, where his actions, words, deeds, and decisions affected not only him, but also everyone around him. For the first time in a long while, to his immense relief, someone else was taking control of the situation.

Mary stood in the doorway, her hands wringing a tea-towel which always formed part of her attire when at home. Her hair, still wholesome, had flecked with grey since Furze last saw her and her face had the concern of an age written upon it.

Furze gazed at his mother; Dorothy slipping into the background to give them space. An enormous weight descended upon Furze's chest, he found it hard to breathe in. He wanted to leap with joy, he wanted to rush to his mother and tell her how much he had been through, how much she meant to him, how grateful he was for all of her support over the years. Yet, somehow, all this would have been unnecessary, for Mary saw it all in the eyes of her son as they touched upon her.

"Keith," she breathed, gently, almost silently.

Furze walked slowly towards the outstretched arms of the woman who had raised him and almost collapsed into the embrace he knew so well. At that moment, although he was a man who had experienced cruelty few could comprehend, he was simply a boy in need of care, a son in need of a mother.

"Mother." He held her tightly, breathing in the familiar smell of her perfume mixed with her cooking. His chest heaved, and he allowed a solitary sob to resound painfully in that moment. Mary took his head in her hands and kissed his forehead.

"Calm now, Keith," she murmured, as he pressed his head gently against her hand. "It's alright. You're home, you're home…" As much as her own pain was overwhelming her at that moment, the sight of her son's near-silent catastrophe of emotions shocked her terribly and drove her to be strong for him. Her eyes were brimmed with both tears of relief, and terror over what he had been through.

The sound of footsteps close behind them shook the treasured moment and Furze straightened himself, wiping his eyes in an attempt to regain his composure.

His mother, unable and unwilling to hold back the tears that now fell majestically from her, smiled lovingly at her boy. "Darling Keith, how we have missed you so. How I have missed you. The things we have been hearing from that terrible place! You look so thin." She took a step back to view the whole frame of her son.

"Now, now, my dear," boomed Herbert, following Nevil into the house with Furze's luggage, "the lad is looking perfectly handsome for a soldier in his position."

"Yes, yes, I quite forget myself," Mary started, not wishing to alarm Furze with her concern. "Come, I'm sure you have had a long journey and wish for nothing more than to freshen up and have some tea."

Furze's return caused quite the commotion and whilst he settled himself back into his old room, his mother and sister bustled about preparing tea. Upstairs, he sat on the end of his bed, soaking up the quiet of his room above the sound of the activity below. He looked around him, nothing had changed physically, and yet the space seemed different somehow. Smaller, perhaps, in comparison to the world he had since experienced. He reclined, staring at the ceiling, listening to the sound of his breathing, and concentrating on the rise and fall of his clasped hands resting upon his belly.

Tap! Tap! Tap!

He shot up, muscles tensed, was that a rap at the door, orders from Headquarters telling him to be ready to move at a moment's notice?

The sound hadn't come from the door, but from the window. Leaping towards it he noticed a bird flutter away as he approached and paused, reminding himself where he was.

No orders, he thought soothingly, *nothing to be done.*

Opening the window, he closed his eyes and took in a breath of London air. Far from the fresh of the countryside it was, nevertheless, a pleasant reminder of home.

Naturally, he thought, steadying his beating heart, *it's not the room that has changed at all. It's me.*

Descending the stairs, washed and clean shaven, Furze had regained his composure by the time he entered the family's dining room. From the happy table flew conversation on all fronts, Furze speaking little and listening much, absorbing the love carried by each spoken syllable. Occasionally, he stole a glance at his father who, characteristically, surveyed the surroundings and injected his thoughts only when they were absolutely necessary. His mother's and sister's squabbles over insignificant details brought smiles to his face; the evident pleasure his father gained from the reunited family scene brought him pride and the way his mother fussed over every detail of the meal reminded him happily that there was a world beyond the war. He was aware, however, that his father's gaze fell upon him more often than usual and on numerous occasions he thought his father's face expressed concern, mixed with deep pity and almost fear. In these moments he tried to catch his father's eye yet, each time, his father's face resumed its steadfast expression of calm certainty, one corner of his mouth gently upturned as if to say, *everything is as it should be, no need to worry son.*

"Your grandmother is eager to see you Keith," his father commented, as Dorothy and Nevil cleared the table.

"Oh yes," Mary pitched in, "she has not stopped mentioning it to us since we told her of your expected return. You'll visit won't you, Keith? This afternoon, perhaps?"

Furze never needed an excuse to visit his grandmother, so he smiled at his mother's unsubtle steer. "Of course I shall, have no fear. Nothing could prevent me from making that visit."

"I'll join you," Nevil stated as he stacked some plates, "I could do with the freedom."

Mary's look scolded her youngest son's audacious comment, but with five children she had come to understand the teenage need for personal space. She had also noticed the comfort that had spread across Furze's face at Nevil's suggestion and wished to encourage anything that brought him happiness and security at that moment.

Suddenly, a sharp crash was heard from the kitchen, followed by Dorothy's muttered anger. It wasn't a particularly loud noise, nor out of the ordinary, but Furze snapped up in his seat, face paper white, knuckles clenching the armrests, eyes darting about the room searching for the cause of the disturbance. His mother rushed to his side, even his father rose from his chair, watching his son's face intently.

"Keith?" Mary reached out touching his hand. "Keith, dear, what's the matter?"

Furze drew his hand away from that of his mother. He was aware that he was shaking slightly and that the attention of the room was upon him. His mother's audible concern, his brother's shocked expression. Was that pity in his father's eyes? He despised the worry that encircled him and wished for nothing more than to retire to the solace of his room. He didn't understand why such a common occurrence had caused such reaction within him. He thought back to the channel crossing, when the sound of the planes above had reminded him of the fighting on the Front, and the bird at his window only hours before. *Pull yourself together,* he chastised himself, *you're alive, whilst others aren't. Remember that.*

"I'm fine," Furze responded curtly, standing up.

Dorothy, to his relief, wandered in at that moment, breaking the scene. "I'm sorry about that, I dropped a dish. Silly of me really," she glanced at her mother. "Is everything alright? It wasn't one of the old ones, I promise!"

"Everything is fine," Furze answered, moving towards the door. "If you'll excuse me, I must get ready to visit Grammy."

The family watched him go and Mary moved to intercept him. Quick as a flash and with admirable subtlety, Herbert caught her arm, and looked imploringly at her.

"All is well," Herbert said deliberately to Dorothy, wishing his son to hear, "don't worry about it, Diddy. Keith and Nevil are just about to visit your grandmother."

"But..." Dorothy persisted, far too emotionally aware to be distracted so easily from the scene.

"Leave it to me." Herbert responded more quietly, moving towards the vacuum left by his son's departure.

Steadily, Herbert mounted the stairs towards Furze's bedroom. He moved purposefully, taking time to ensure his ascent did not express undue concern through its haste. The state of his son worried him and although he understood the horrors of war, he couldn't imagine the distress ripping through the mind of such a young man. Herbert was unsure how to approach the conversation, a rarity for such a considered man, yet it was clear that the conversation had to be held. He knocked on Furze's door.

"What is it now?" Furze's voice queried, impatience striking through the woodwork.

"It's me, Keith," replied his father, calmly, "can I come in?"

There was a pause, a dejected sigh, before, "of course."

Furze was sitting on the edge of his bed, staring at his clasped hands with a look of concern and resignation.

"I can't stop them shaking, Dad," Furze admitted, looking up at Herbert. "I thought I would be okay here, at home, surrounded by you all. But it's as though life is only a momentary distraction from the fear I feel from the Front. When something sudden occurs, such as Dorothy dropping that dish, I can't help but react. I might be sitting here, on my bed, but my thoughts are subconsciously of the War."

"It's natural son."

"I don't feel natural!" Furze implored, rising to his feet in evident frustration. "All my life I've been taught to take control of my fate, to master my emotions in order to act appropriately, honourably, astutely. How can I follow your example, make you proud, if I can't even stop my hands from shaking with fear?"

Furze stood before his father, the shaking of his hands having migrated to his entire frame. His whole body appeared a clenched fist of quivering distress. Herbert didn't know the words to unclench such a fist, so he just moved forwards and hugged his son, feeling the tension ebb away as he did so. Standing back and looking into Furze's face, he now saw an open palm imploring his advice.

"You're right, what you have gone through, continue to go through, is far from natural," Herbert acknowledged. "But feeling fear, feeling anxious, that is entirely human. You have been encouraged to master your emotions, to be strong and courageous precisely for moments such as these."

Furze sat back down on the bed, considering his father's words.

"No one expects you to be fearless, but rather to understand that fear will take hold of you throughout your life."

"But how can I hope to be brave, to inspire others, if I fear so much?" Furze's question balancing on the brink of emotional repair.

"My boy," Herbert replied lovingly, "it is precisely because you fear, that you understand what it takes to be brave."

II

Furze and Herbert made their way downstairs to find Nevil waiting for them. Although Nevil still harboured concerns over his brother's reaction to the broken plate, a brief glance from his father was all it took to put his mind at ease.

"Best be off then Nevil," Furze declared, "we both know Grammy doesn't like to be kept waiting."

"Capital, we'll be back later father," smiled Nevil, as the pair trotted out onto the street.

Mary walked up behind her husband to watch them wander away, and Herbert felt her touch his arm.

"Herbert, he's broken. What he has been through to leave him in such a state, I can't, I don't want to understand." She shivered as thoughts of the fighting flooded into her mind.

"He has been through more than most could ever bear," he answered soothingly, "and, I'm afraid, he will go through much more before this war is over. We can't expect him to remain the same."

Mary sniffed, and Herbert handed her his handkerchief. She took it gratefully, pressing his hand tightly, ever comforted by the strength he gave her. "But what can we do, Herbert? I wish to hold him close to me, to protect him, hide him from the world and stop these ghastly occurrences from affecting him as much as they do."

"I know, dear, I know, but we must allow Keith to deal with it in his own way. If he wishes to open up about what he saw, what he did out there, he will. But we cannot force him, and we must not make him feel pressured. We must be the parents he needs in this very moment, not the parents we think we should be."

"You are right, of course, but it is hard to step back and watch one's son break apart before you."

"I know, Mary, believe me," Herbert took his wife in his arms, and held her to him tightly. "Keith is a strong young man. Stronger than you or I know. He'll be alright, you'll see, you raised him to survive this war."

233

Furze and Nevil made it to their grandmother's house swiftly.

"Coo-ee!" came Emma's familiar call, as they rang the doorbell. "My dear Keith, you quite surprise me." She beamed with a look that suggested she had been expecting him all afternoon.

"Grammy!" Furze returned in greeting, "how I have missed you so." He gave her a hug that could have outlasted the siege of Troy, before taking a step back, gazing into her face. She had put on one of her favourite frocks, the turquoise one she always wore on his birthday, and her hair which still retained much of its colour, had evidently been made up with great care.

Having shut the door behind the young men, Emma pressed Furze's hand tightly, a gesture which he returned in kind. "Head through to the living room, my dear, I'll be along with the tea in a jiffy."

As Furze wandered through the tiny hallway to the little living room, he recognised the familiar smell of the tidy home. His grandmother was incredibly house-proud, and kept the place as uncluttered as possible having reached a stage where she knew precisely what she did and did not need to be happy. Her family and friends were of far greater importance than material possessions, and this trait made Furze love her even more. He sank into the familiar, comfortable, old sofa he vividly remembered reclining in as a child. Having experienced so much change, so many outrageous, terrible, inexplicable things over the past six months, returning to a place so stubbornly the same was immensely soothing. His grandmother's living room, with the age-old china tea set she laid before her two dear grandchildren, presented an incubated period of time, unconcerned with the carnage raging around the world.

"It truly is delightful to have you home, Keith," Emma repeated once more, as she tipped the china teapot just enough to allow a steady stream of steaming tea to pour delicately into the three cups in front of her. Although the pot contained leaf tea, as was Emma's preference, not one leaf managed to escape into the cups. Keith watched her perform an action he had seen countless times but couldn't help observe the tiniest of trembles in his grandmother's hands as she poured. As spirited and healthy as she was for her age, this small detail brought to Furze the shocking realisation that, even here, in this seemingly unchanged environment, life still took its natural course. He suddenly felt even more protective of his grandmother than before and started thinking over all the ways in which he could make her life easier.

"Allow me, Grammy," he began, reaching forwards to take the teapot.

"Nonsense, Keith," Emma responded, "you may be a young man, but I'm more than capable of pouring a cup of tea!"

Her eyes flashed, and her tone was sharper than usual. Furze realised he had touched her pride and regretted not having had the foresight to understand that at Emma's age, when her faculties began slowly to fade, retaining her independence was of paramount importance to her mental wellbeing. Her reaction, though, thundered deeply within Furze, for it showed that his grandmother was well aware of the change in her physiology and was, possibly, even frightened of what it might signify. He thought back to his own fear and the conversation he had held with his father that afternoon, wondering at the similarities between them and the way they dealt with an apparent loss of control.

Emma observed the thoughtful look on Furze's face. She had noticed the way he looked at her hands and correctly guessed his intentions when he offered his assistance. In that moment, however, she too, recognised the most simple-hearted fear in the face of her grandson. As proud as she was in the strength she still retained in her old age, there was nothing she would not do to bring happiness to her family.

"Thank you though, my dear," she said softly, handing Furze a cup. "Next time I would be delighted if you did."

"No, no, it was silly of me." Furze smiled, safe in the knowledge that they understood and respected one another's position. "You always pour it best, I would just be handing people cups of leaf."

The trio chuckled and Nevil added, "best get a good helping of the stuff before you return to the Front, Keith!"

Furze's face clouded slightly. He had hoped to avoid this subject as much as possible, but knew it would inevitably surface from time to time. There was little else on the tongues of the British public at the time.

They all talked avidly for an hour or so; Furze navigating away from any questions that strayed too close to his experiences on the Front and his grandmother divulging all of her pastimes since his departure. Throughout the conversation, Emma kept a steady watch over Furze's shifted countenance. She thought he appeared far more reserved and observational than he had used to be, yet she did not press for any explanations feeling that Furze would divulge his thoughts to her as and when he felt ready. Furze, as he had done with his father, caught her contemplative look from time to time and thanked her silently for her delicacy. Eventually, the china teapot, which Furze had always thought blessed with the ability to hold more tea than it appeared possible, ran through to its final dregs.

"Alas, Grammy, we'd best be off, or I fear we might remain here indefinitely."

"You would be most welcome."

As Nevil made his way outside, she once again pressed Furze's hand, and mentioned to him gently, "you always make me a very proud grandmother and I wish I could do more to ease the burden you carry. I feel so useless simply pottering about and just want you to know that I am always here Keith, whenever you need me."

Furze looked at the woman in front of him, his Grammy, a face wrinkled with the wisdom of a lifetime. Mistakes, passions, successes, strains and strength all merged beautifully into the familiar, kindly countenance from which he harnessed so much of his energy. She was far from useless and continually provided more support than anyone else in Furze's life without even realising it. He noticed that Emma's soft eyes, that had seen thousands of days come and go, were damp with tears. Furze's emotions broke rank, he held his grandmother tightly, screwing up his eyes and wishing with all his heart never to lose such a bedrock.

"Grammy," he breathed, struggling to articulate fully through the heaving of his lungs, "you are the strongest person I know and have never been, nor will ever be, useless or powerless. People as good as you give people as broken as me a reason to repair themselves. I love you dearly, so never feel as though you need ever do more."

The brothers departed, waving back to Emma standing on her doorstep as they wandered away. Furze then took his leave of Nevil, as the next trip he intended to make needed to be undertaken alone. His feet padded along the pavement, following a path they had trodden countless times as his mind wrapped itself in deep thought.

What if Daw's feelings for me have changed? he mused.

His legs moved unusually slowly, almost pensively. The route seemed longer that day. *What if she cannot bear the thought of my constant departures back to the Front, what if she notices the changes my family have seen in me and despises my weakness?*

His legs carried him up the Wallis' front steps to their elegant black door; the protective wrought-iron and glass roofed porch drawing him in. His hand hovered over the door knocker, as though an invisible force prevented him from reaching out to the object that would bring him back to the woman with whom he feared he was falling in love.

Once more that day he found himself shudder with fear. Not the kind he had felt on the Front, not a shocking, brutal, cold fear, but an electric, meaningful, valuable fear. This fear gripped his heart, held his nerves in suspense and yet, seemed strangely important, appropriate. Furze had never questioned Daw's feelings for him before and the fact that he had been doing so shocked and pained him. Such hesitation lasted only a moment though for, as he was still hovering on the porch, he heard Daw's sweet and gentle voice inside the house. Her tones empowered him, compelling him to fling such unusual worries aside and knock confidently on the door, darting back as soon as he had done so.

Light steps were heard approaching the barrier between Furze and his sweetheart, and he felt as though time was deliberately dawdling at precisely the wrong moment. His fear had transformed into the boldest energy and he wished, at that moment, to barge straight through the door that stood impertinently in his way. The steps stopped; his heart fluttered. The lock clicked; he straightened his jacket. The door handle turned, slowly, painfully. He stood tall, proud, a man charged by the power of desire. As the door swung open, Furze let out a breath and words, so often his greatest asset, failed him.

"Keith?" Daw looked astounded, and Furze feared, hopelessly, that his worries had been realised. Then, the most honest expression of the deepest passion exploded from within her.

"Oh my dear, Keith!" She stepped out towards him and he took her by the hands, looking deeply into her eyes and damming his earlier thoughts. He knew instantly, that dropping by unannounced had been entirely the right thing to do, and he only wished he had done so sooner. Hazelnut eyes gleamed intimately back at him and he searched every corner of them as he soaked up the moment. They were just as he remembered them; warm, engaging and yet, was there something more? He felt as though they had gained a power over him that he had not yet felt, as if they possessed the ability to pierce the rougher outer shell he had developed on the Front.

"My darling Daw," he eventually managed. He was surprised to find the capacity to develop coherent sentences when his entire focus, in that moment, was on appreciating her presence. "Words cannot express my joy at seeing you once more! Your letters, they were a beacon in many dire situations, I kept them on me, and read them constantly." Now the sentences had begun, he felt neither the power, nor desire, to restrain them. "Not a day has passed when I haven't thought of you, and I'm sorry if my letters have seemed rather low. Things have been intense and..."

Furze shied away from her gaze, feeling his resolve weakening once more, not wishing to appear weak in front of the person whose opinion of him he respected so highly.

Daw, surprised at the flurry of conversation from a man so characteristically in control of his expressions and recognising his anguish at becoming emotional, pressed his hands firmly. He raised his eyes to hers once more. She was looking at him with such understanding, such kindness, that Furze realised she viewed emotions not as a weakness, but as a great strength.

"Sorry," he murmured sheepishly.

"Keith, you have done nothing that merits you offering me any form of apology," Daw responded sweetly. "If anything, I should apologise for sending you so many letters! I'm sure you had far more important things to pay attention to, without thinking about silly old me at home."

"Never! I was grateful for every single one of them. Knowing that you were well, living life, and still thinking of me, that touched me every day."

Daw smiled mischievously, "good, because in reality, I wasn't going to stop." The pair chuckled and Daw's mother called from the depths of the house.

Furze looked at his pocket watch. "I really must dash! I'm sorry to cut this so short, but I couldn't arrive back home without saying hello."

"You have brought me untold joy by doing so. I admit, I was greatly surprised when I opened the door to you, as we had planned to meet on Thursday. You are usually so particular with plans, the spontaneity caught me off guard."

"Yes, I don't know what's come over me," Furze blushed.

"I think it is a fitting new characteristic that I hope to see more of. I shall, subsequently, wait with even greater anticipation for you on Thursday evening."

"I shall fetch you at six-thirty, I pray the days race by so that I can see you all the sooner!" With that, Furze whirled around, and flew up the path, waving back to Daw as he left.

B.D. Wilberforce

Equanimity

I

"On my way home in the evening, I called on Mrs. Humphreys and told her all I knew about her son's death."
Wednesday 2nd June.

The next day Furze awoke early, eager to prepare himself for two important visits he wished to make that afternoon. The first of these he made after lunch, travelling to Highgate where Major Kirkpatrick lived with his wife. Since the battle of Festubert, when Kirkpatrick had been seriously wounded, Furze had not seen his friend. On approaching Kirkpatrick's house, he remembered with pride how Kirk had swept up command, even with a shrapnel wound to the neck, and shivered as he recalled his fear when Kirk had taken a hit to the head and fallen beside him. He had been supremely grateful when it transpired that the Major's wounds would not be fatal and hoped that he would find him in good spirits. Furze rapped eagerly on the front door, wondering how his friend had been spending his time at home, and realised that he had only ever known the Major on the Front, shrouded in war.

"Evelyn?" Furze enquired, as the door swung open to reveal a kindly, yet timid, figure looking inquisitively at the stranger standing in front of her.

"That's me," she replied warily, "how can I help you?"

"My apologies for the disturbance, Ma'am," continued Furze, "we haven't had the pleasure of being introduced, I know Major Kirkpatrick from the Front, he was my Adjutant and briefly, my Commanding Officer at the Battle of Festubert."

At the sound of Furze's voice, there trailed the familiar tones of the Major, though noticeably weaker and more strained than usual. "Furzzy! Is that you dear fellow? Evelyn, do bring the good man in, would you?"

At the warmth with which this was said, and on hearing Furze's name, Evelyn's nerves dissipated and she motioned him inside, introducing herself as the Major's wife. She hung his coat before turning towards him and murmuring hastily, "thank you, Mr. Furze, for fighting so hard to get my husband home to me. He says he would not have made it without you... and I could not bear the thought of carrying on without him." Tears stained her cheeks as she uttered these words.

"He told you of the battle?" Furze asked gently, returning her gaze.

"In part," she responded, carefully wiping her cheeks with a lace handkerchief. "He has spared me the details, but I gathered enough to know it was a terrible fight. You can't imagine how grateful I am that you were there with him. Even so, he returned in such a state." Once more, the emotion choked her.

"Many others played a much greater part than I," Furze mumbled, abashed. "I'm just glad that Kirk made it back. So many didn't..."

She looked up at him, understood his thoughts, and pointed him in the direction from which the voice of the Major had come.

"I'll get you both some tea," she proposed, nodding and pulling her senses together. "He'll be glad to see you."

As Evelyn disappeared into the kitchen Furze made his way towards the Major, worry furrowing his brow as he considered her words. Her husband's close call with death had visibly shaken Evelyn and Furze's mind drifted to Daw. *Did she feel this way when I returned home with my injuries in November?* He felt a pang of guilt. *Don't be so selfish, you're here to think about Kirk, not Daw. Evelyn is his wife, so it's natural for her to be so concerned, whilst Daw is...well...*

The Major's voice cut through his contemplations.

"Furzzy! It really is good of you to drop in, you needn't have done so." Kirkpatrick was standing by the fireplace in his living room. Although on his feet and looking comfortable enough, Furze observed that his friend was still very ill, his hands and legs shaking slightly with the strain of standing.

"How could I not, Kirk! When we last saw each other, you were being carted off to the field hospital with shrapnel in your neck and a bullet wound to the head!" observed Furze, attempting to be jovial but inadvertently reminding himself of his friend's lucky escape.

"Not my finest hour," the Major replied, shaking Furze's outstretched hand and offering him a seat. Furze sat, noticing the relief which spread across Kirkpatrick's face as he reclined back into his comfortable armchair. "That was quite a bad one, eh? To see Bottomley and all the others fall so quickly, I never thought it was possible to witness so much sorrow in one place."

"You responded admirably though, Kirk, to take command as well as you did with just five officers remaining and one-hundred-and-fifty men."

The Major smiled at the kind words and took the cup of tea that Evelyn had just brought them. He took his time, lifting the cup slowly to his lips so as not to strain his neck too much.

"I didn't know whether we would make it, Furzzy," blurting out once his wife had left the room. He looked directly and unfalteringly into Furze's eyes. "We were outmanned and unsupported. All I could think of doing was pushing forward, always further forward."

"The men needed your command and followed you without question." Furze did his best to lift his friend's spirits, which were evidently dashed by the memory of the battle.

"Well, let's just say that I am very glad that you were by my side to take over when I couldn't carry on. I wish I could have ended the battle with you, dear fellow. Do you know, when I was being carried back across that dastardly ground that so many of our friends died fighting over, I felt such a failure. A leader, who was unable to lead... unable to fight..." Once again, the Major drew his thoughts back to the depths of that dreadful scene and became morose.

"My dear Kirk," rejoined Furze, filled with affection for this selfless man, "I would have asked for nothing more than that you had been there with me. You inspired countless men that day and I was proud to follow your example."

The Major looked at him but seemed far from convinced. Evelyn's comment from earlier about the Major's mental health suddenly made sense. His friend was burdened by the shame of having been forced to leave his fellow officers and men behind to fight whilst he was carried to safety, and this was crushing him.

"You failed no one," Furze stated sternly, intent on shattering his friend's unnecessary self-blame. "You continued to lead us all, even when injured and your actions invariably drove the men to successfully take their objective. You were wounded doing your duty, leading from the Front and whilst putting the interests of others well ahead of your own. Without you, Kirk, I don't think we would have made it out of that Godforsaken bloody pit of a battlefield alive."

The brutality of this comment slapped the Major out of his stupor and staring cautiously at Furze as if searching for truth in his words, found his gaze matched in kind by simple-hearted honesty. Furze would not let up and his look spoke volumes about how highly he regarded the man in front of him.

"Furzzy, Fuller..." Kirk stopped, watching as Furze's stern countenance shed to reveal the anguish beneath, "I'm so sorry. When I heard...I couldn't't bear to think what you were going through."

Furze paused, considering the torturous cloak of self-proclaimed shame which he was attempting desperately to rip from his friend's shoulders. He had tried not to think of Fuller since returning home, wishing to concentrate on happier events. Now, however, facing Kirkpatrick and urging him to break free from his own demons, he realised he needed to live by his own advice. His grief over Fuller's loss, though subdued, still weighed heavily on his conscience and Kirk blurred in front of him as he allowed the rush of pain, longing, and confusion to flood out from the corners of the past and into the present moment. He realised then, that this action was and always had been, inevitable if he truly wished to move on.

"I lost him, Kirk." Furze covered his head in his hands. "Brookes and Garmin. They disappeared into the grime, the smoke, the bullets, and didn't make it out. I couldn't save them, I was fighting alongside them, and I couldn't protect them. Such good people, such strong friends, gone, forever."

Kirk realised in that moment the depth of his friend's grief and the sight pained him more intensely than his physical wounds. He had been impressed by Furze's show of strength thus far and even marvelled at how together he had appeared after everything he had been through. His question had made it abruptly apparent, however, that the young man in front of him had only partially returned from the Front and he wished to recover the rest of him from wherever it had been buried.

"You cannot think like that, Furzzy," Kirk answered, this time the one offering support. "You and I both took up roles we didn't expect to that day, and we both acted as best we could given the circumstances. War extracts a heavy toll on everyone involved, and it is all we can do to appreciate what we have left when it is over."

It struck Kirk that, in this comment, he had defined what he himself had been failing to realise since his return. *My poor Evelyn,* he mused, a flood of affection erupting from the thought of his wife*, what she must have had to put up with whilst I was selfishly focused on my own sorrows.*

Furze turned the Major's words over in his mind. He knew, of course, that it was useless to blame himself for events far beyond his control. He knew, as well, that brooding over the past was an unhealthy habit, but it helped to have his friend affirm this and to know that they were both attempting to overcome their own terrors with the other's help.

"Thank you, Kirk, and of course you are right. It was just such a shock. Fuller was my oldest friend, he was always alright, had always overcome the worst of it. His death, it brought home bluntly the dire fact that we don't know how each day is going to go, especially during this war." He clutched his tea and looked at the Major. "Kirk, it petrified me."

II

Furze left the Major's house, pacing with great trepidation towards the second visit he needed to make that day. It was to the residence of Mrs. Humphreys, mother of Lieutenant Humphreys, that he now directed his feet, as well as his contemplative state of mind. Although she would now be aware of her son's fate, he wished to personally relay his first-hand experience of him. Even so, on the doorstep of her house, where he imagined she had stood when she received the gut-wrenching telegram every mother feared, he paused to summon all of his strength.

How best to proceed? he wondered, mulling over whether to be completely honest or to pass over the more gruesome details. Although he had not seen Humphreys fall during the battle, the sights he had witnessed were enough to cause any strong-minded individual some sleepless nights. *If she asks and wishes to know about the battle in full, I shall oblige her,* he decided.

The knocker rapped three times, echoing into the hallway of a house that seemed strangely silent. A shuffle, a keychain drawing back, and at the sight of Mrs. Humphreys, Furze knew that complete honesty was the only answer.

She stood in the doorway to her home, a ghost in all but physical form. Her son had paid the ultimate price whilst doing his duty and no amount of motherly pride in such a sacrifice could ever tourniquet the wound this mortal toll had opened. The sight plucked at the stings of Furze's heart.

"Mrs. Humphreys," he began. "My name is Keith Furze, I served with your son on the Front."

At the sound of his name, Mrs. Humphreys drew herself up a little taller and a small glint of animation returned to her face.

"I wished to offer my sincere condolences for your loss…" he paused, allowing the mother a moment to consider what he had said.

"Mr. Furze, I thank you for your kind words. Oh, I mean it's a pleasure to meet you and thank you, I…well, I'm sorry…" Mrs. Humphreys trailed off, evidently embarrassed at having lost her train of thought, overcome with the conflicting feelings she was then experiencing.

"Please, don't be sorry. I only wished to drop in and relay to you my deepest respects for your son. He was a dedicated officer and…a good friend…" This time it was Furze whose voice trailed off and the conjoined emotions of these two strangers brought them closer together than any formal introduction could have done. Mrs. Humphreys invited Furze in and automatically set about making tea for them both. It had been a while since she had entertained anyone, let alone someone so similar in age and stature to her dear son, and she allowed herself the small pleasure of making a fuss over Furze.

"So, I know you and my son were friends, he wrote to me about you a number of times."

Furze was taken aback, he hadn't anticipated that she would have heard about him before that day, and this knowledge tugged at his soul.

"He never went into the details of what you all did out there," Mrs. Humphreys continued, "but he mentioned that serving with you was one thing he was immensely grateful for… I could tell that he looked up to you enormously."

"It is I who should be grateful, Mrs. Humphreys," Furze answered with complete honesty. " 'A' Company hosted a number of fine young officers, of which your son was one of the finest."

"Was that when you first met him? When you joined his Company?"

"It was indeed, in February, I remember it well." Furze smiled warmly at the recollection and Mrs. Humphreys held that smile, committing it to memory. "I had just been assigned as his interim commander. He, Austin and Jones welcomed me with great warmth, I couldn't have asked to lead better men."

At the mention of Austin, Furze stopped, his throat contracted, and he darted for his tea in an attempt to mask his emotions.

"You were all close, I remember that much from the letters," commented Mrs. Humphreys, touched at the obvious compassion in the young man in front of her. "If you are able, I would love to hear about your time with my son."

Furze looked into the eyes of a woman, a mother whose soul had been torn in two, and who was imploring him to offer her some small remedy for her pain. He could not refuse and began recounting the past few months.

"Having joined 'A' Company, it became apparent that the four of us worked well together. Although in command temporarily, I was still the same rank as your son, Austin, and Jones, yet this never troubled them. They followed dutifully and led passionately. What's more, they offered advice when it was asked for, and challenged when it was needed. They also never shied away from work." It was at this memory Furze grinned. "I remember us taking over a section of the line which, to us, seemed luxurious. Mud only up to our ankles…"

Furze chuckled and Mrs. Humphreys smiled, thinking of how her son used to sit and chuckle similarly in that very chair.

"Even so, we were all up until three the next morning building parapets. That was the way Humphreys used to operate. He led from the front, adamant that he would work as hard, if not harder, than the men he commanded."

"Jones and Austin, did they… are they…?" Mrs. Humphreys could not bring herself to say what she meant.

"Jones, alas, I lost touch with. He was drafted off to a different Regiment and regretfully I cannot say what has become of him. Austin…dear Austin was sniped at the battle of Neuve Chapelle. It harrows me to this day, Mrs. Humphreys. I was standing next to him moments before it happened, and took a letter to his family from him 'just in case'… He was the only man I lost that day, but every death is a death too many."

"And what about my son? Could you tell me how he… how he died?"

Furze once again looked Mrs. Humphreys in the eyes, noticing a calm certainty that had not been there before. She had become emboldened by the honesty with which Furze had recounted Austin's death and appreciated the respect he was showing her by refusing to cover up the truth.

"It was the morning of the 16th May, at Festubert, and The Queen's was taking part in a large allied assault of the German line. In the run up to this action, the Germans had been hitting us hard you understand, so the British command believed a counter assault would slow this advance. They were not incorrect in their reasoning, but the cost was… horrific."

Furze took another sip of tea, breathed, and carried on.

"I was now no longer in your son's Company, but was with the Staff Group. Subsequently, I operated across all four Companies for the duration of the battle. 'A' Company was the first to leap out of the trench and charge the German lines. I remember it so clearly, Mrs. Humphreys. The roars of the men as they flung themselves up the ladders and over the parapets of the trench. Such strength, such bravery. Courage beyond the bounds of human understanding. You know who was at the head of this proud column?"

Mrs. Humphreys, trembling, shook her head.

"Your son. I saw them leap, charge, roar, and disappear. Resplendent, they were, Mrs. Humphreys, in the face of all the terror the German troops could throw at them. I remember hoping, wishing, that they would make it to the German lines alive. But the onslaught I discovered when moments afterwards, I followed, was devastating."

Pausing, Furze looked intently at Mrs. Humphreys and noticed a single tear passing in a gentle rivulet down her left cheek.

"Please, carry on." She encouraged him softly.

"The rest of us followed in the footsteps of 'A' Company and I own, at that time I could not see your son. We pushed forward, eventually taking the nearest German line, and then pushed further on to a communications trench, but at a heavy price. By that time, there were only five officers left out of twenty-two. At this point, there was still no sight of your son and I had taken up command of the Regiment for want of more senior officers. We eventually received orders to retreat, and upon returning to the British lines and taking stock of our situation, found that your son had not returned. He died from his wounds on the battlefield."

Mrs. Humphreys stifled a sob but nodded for Furze to finish his account.

"Only three officers from our Regiment escaped the battle unscathed, and I'm sorry, so sorry, that I wasn't there in 'A' Company with your son. I should have liked to have offered you more about his final moments."

Furze took check of himself, finished off his cup of tea, set it steadily down on its saucer and looked up at Mrs. Humphreys. She sat silently, contemplating the intimate words she had just heard. Other tears had now joined the first but, behind their evident sorrow, was a deep relief.

"My dear Keith," she almost whispered, "your words about my son grant me some small joy. To be offered a window of insight into such an important part of his brief life allows me a little peace. Thank you, for being there for him when you were able. I shall be eternally grateful for that."

Furze felt he had offered all he could and rose to take his leave. Walking him to her front door, Mrs. Humphreys stopped on the doorstep and took both his hands in hers. "My prayers now turn to you Keith, continue to look after your men as you did my son and they, in turn, will look after you. I have no doubt you will out-live this ghastly conflict and when you do, live for all of them. Live for all those dear young men who never made it back to the warm embraces of their poor mothers."

His emotions choking him, Furze strode from Mrs. Humphreys, tears blurring his vision. When he was out of sight he leant against a fence, breathing heavily, with his eyes closed. Fuller. Garmin. Brookes. Humphreys. Fuller. Garmin. Brookes. Humphreys. Humphreys… their names turned over in his mind, overwhelming him with grief and making him giddy. Gripping the fence, Mrs. Humphrey's parting words drifted into his thoughts.

I will live for you all, my friends, he thought, gritting his teeth until the pain sealed his vow. *I swear it, by all I hold dear. I promise you.*

Love

"We sat and talked in the lounge till past 03:00 am. Topping evening."

Thursday 3rd June.

The visits he had made to Kirkpatrick and Mrs. Humphreys eased a heavy burden Furze had been carrying since his return home. He still had not fully reconciled the deaths of so many of his friends, especially not Fuller and Brookes, but the Major's shared experiences and Mrs. Humphrey's parting words of encouragement had allowed him small moments to begin processing the situation emotionally.

Because of this, he felt more confident in his relationship with Daw, at least in respect to being the man she knew him to be. Thankfully, punctuality was one characteristic the Germans could not beat from him so easily, and he arrived outside 48 Holland Park as promised at 6:30 pm the next evening.

"Keith! First rate timekeeping as always," she greeted excitedly, before the front door had opened fully.

"My darling Daw." Furze smiled, taking her right hand and kissing it gently before pressing it firmly with his. "I have been so looking forward to spending this evening with you."

At this, Daw blushed a gorgeous shade of rose sapphire, and they walked arm-in-arm down her front steps to the taxi Furze had arranged. He had booked a table for them at The Piccadilly, in London's West End where, once they had been seated, he allowed himself the chance to relax a little.

As Furze ordered the wine, Daw gazed at him and asked, "has it been a terribly exciting few days?"

"Not as exciting as this, dear Daw" Although she rolled her eyes at his wry romanticism, he noticed the pleasure this compliment aroused in her. "In all truth, it has been a rather trying few days."

"Tell me about it," she requested, looking at him kindly.

"Oh, it's nothing of interest." Not wishing the War to be a third guest at their table.

"Come now, Keith," she urged, "if I can't share your burdens then what use am I?"

He considered the gravity of her words, as well as the imploring look that accompanied them. Thinking back to his departure in January, when he had admitted to her his fear of what awaited him on the Front, he mustered his courage from the trust she had placed in him all those months ago.

"Very well, but promise you'll stop me if it gets too distressing," he implored. "It's a sorrowful story to tell."

She nodded, entirely engrossed in the seriousness of the moment. Something about Furze's attitude and focus gave her the strange feeling that this was a pivotal moment for the two of them.

"I made two visits today, one to a friend and one to a mother. The first was to my friend, Major Kirkpatrick, of whom I became immensely fond when he joined my Regiment back in March. During the Battle of Festubert, it was he who led us to our objective when our Commanding Officer was badly wounded, and it was from him that I took control of the Regiment when he too was wounded awfully."

"Thank goodness he survived."

"Chance smiled on him," Furze said appreciatively, "it did not smile on many others…"

Daw saw Furze's countenance darken, deep furrows impounding themselves on his forehead. This time, she said nothing, for it appeared as though there was a great deal that Furze now needed to relate.

"One of the unfortunate souls that chance forgot that day was a young Lieutenant called Humphreys. The second visit was to his mother."

Daw couldn't help herself and let out a gentle gasp.

"Although I didn't see him fall," continued Furze, oblivious to the gasp, "I was his friend, and wished to give his mother what solace I could."

"Those visits must have been torture," Daw sympathised, attempting to understand Furze's position as best she could. However, she did not expect to discover so vividly the depths to which despair had plunged his tender character.

"They were, but not in the way I expected, Daw," Furze admitted. "Kirk was suffering from the self-imposed shame and guilt of having had to leave us behind and Mrs. Humphreys well, one can imagine her shattered emotions. But both of them, even in their misery, offered me the courage to face and fight my own demons, my own gushing sorrows."

Furze's hands were trembling and he attempted to hide the involuntary movement by rearranging his cutlery. Daw moved forwards, took his hands and steadied them in hers, staring intently into his face.

"Keith, what happened at Festubert?"

"Fuller is dead, Daw," he stated with blunt brutality, fuelling the pain the comment carried with it, "and Brookes, and countless others besides. But those two, my closest friends, snuffed out at once. Thank goodness Bobbie and I had one another in the days after, or I fear we would not have held it together."

The news shocked Daw to silence. She had met both Fuller and Brookes through Furze and had observed in person the care they had held for one another. Fighting back her own tears, she attempted a show of strength for Furze.

B.D. Wilberforce

"I did not wish to upset you," he murmured, holding her hands more firmly. "Such stories are best left where they are born."

"You shouldn't worry for my sake, Keith, I despair over the loss of such close companions of yours, but it is you that I worry for. Are you quite alright?"

Furze looked deep into Daw's eyes, feeling them caress his face, his thoughts, and feelings. "I believe I will be. Following my two visits, I made a promise to savour every moment from now on as though living for each young life lost."

Furze smiled, plucking gentle memories of times past from his friends' shared histories. "Brookes might never again chuckle at a card game, Fuller will never raise another glass in toast to those he cares for, but I see them both in every decision I take, as close in spirit as they ever were in life."

Daw watched as Furze's features relaxed the more he spoke, and realised that he was gently coming to terms with the horrors he had experienced. Glad in the knowledge her company was able to support such a rejuvenation of character, she released his hands as food arrived at their table.

"My goodness, I've been terribly rude," Furze suddenly exclaimed, snapping from his reflections. "Enough about me, I've been itching to ask about your work with the War Relief Fund! What did you get up to when you visited their hospital at Oldway?"

Touched at his recollection, she obliged his question, whilst continuing to observe his countenance. "Oh it's quite a sight, an immensely grand building put to great use!"

Her animation at the recollection of her own war stories made Furze smile, and he encouraged her to continue.

"They are treating hundreds of wounded soldiers, so I asked what they needed most and can you guess what they said?" Daw's face was a picture of humour.

"Medicine?" Furze tried, soaking up her pleasure.

"Socks!" she giggled, and the pair burst into laughter. "So, whilst I was there, I wrote to all my contacts requesting they send what they could spare to Oldway. I hear they received quite the collection."

They passed dinner engrossed in conversation until Furze realised the time, and suggested they head to The Savoy, their favourite place to dance in London. Arriving in good time to find the place teeming with life, they passed through the marbled foyer to the grandeur of the Lancaster Ballroom. From floor to ceiling, the room was a magnificent shade of turquoise, as displayed in the sky on a summer's morning just before the sun rises. The walls were a lighter shade, almost verging on green, whilst the drapes were a royal blue, laced with silver. The five chandeliers floated above the dancers, protecting them from the darkness brooding outside of the enormous floor-to-ceiling windows. The whole scene was a world removed from the war raging across the channel, and Furze paused as he entered. He couldn't help but feel a pang of guilt at his being there, amidst such trivialities, whilst men continued to fight and die on the Front. That feeling lasted only momentarily, however, as Daw took his arm and led him directly into the centre of the mass of dancers. *The room, the music, the lavish décor might represent life's trivialities*, he thought, *but they make Daw seem even more significant by comparison.*

They danced for hours, drifting from one song to the next, utterly at one with each other and the rhythm of the music.

"Did you enjoy yourself?" Furze asked, pensively, as he escorted Daw out of The Savoy just after 3:00 am

"I've had an absolutely topping evening," Daw responded, teasing him with one of his own expressions.

They made their way back to Holland Park, stopping under her porch, Furze looking deeply into her eyes. He had, indeed, had a topping evening and felt as though Daw had managed to unshackle him from some unseen weight. Suddenly, a strange feeling spread from his stomach, up into his chest, and from there shot all over his body. He wished, desperately, to lean in and kiss Daw. Not on the hand, as he had made a habit of doing, but on the lips. The delicate, beautiful lips he had noticed so often that evening.

Daw gazed up at Furze, without uttering a sound, their hands intertwined, their breathing deep and steady. She thought he had something on his mind but feared asking what it might be. Her silence perturbed Furze and he lifted her left hand, kissing it gently before saying, "good night, Daw, I've had a simply marvellous time."

She sighed, the moment had passed. "So have I, will I be seeing you tomorrow?"

"Of course," Furze nodded, attempting to settle his nerves. "I'll collect you after lunch, I'm afraid I have to entertain my aunts tomorrow morning."

Daw chuckled at the thought, "then I'll try my best to make your afternoon all the more enjoyable."

"You need not try, you do so effortlessly," Furze answered, before turning towards the street. Before he disappeared, he looked back, and was thrilled to see Daw watching him from the door. They waved to one another before Furze drifted into the night.

He felt so very alive that he wanted to leap along the road and shout towards the moon. His feelings for Daw were growing stronger and stronger and he was both perturbed and elated by them. He had never felt this way about anyone else before. Every waking moment he wished he was with her, for she made even the most mundane of tasks a pleasure. He craved her attention, desired her conversation, sought a look, a touch from her that signalled she knew of his existence, and valued it.

Is this love? he wondered suddenly, stopping dead still on the pavement. *Could it be?* Furze had never been in what he would consider *love* before. Young as he was, he had had many sweethearts in the past and yet none of them had evoked in him such strong feelings of desire, or happiness, or pain.

That's it! I have never been in such pain when apart from someone before, mused Furze. *When I'm not with her, my heart aches with longing. Whereas when we are together, I fear the moment we will have to part again.*

He began walking on, feeling as though new land had emerged on the continent of his soul ready to be explored.

Love, he thought, *the humblest state of man and thus the hardest to achieve.*

The Orchard

"We walked through glorious woods to Chenies where we lunched, and after reclining for a little in the orchard, we strolled on to a little village called Latimer. It was so lovely – the country looking perfectly gorgeous."

Friday 4th June.

"Goodness, what a night!" Furze said as he collected Daw the next afternoon, "I'm sorry it was such a late evening."

"Nonsense," smiled Daw as she took his arm. "I haven't had that much fun in months, and something tells me you needed the return to normality."

They walked together to Hyde Park, recollecting the amusing happenings of the previous evening until they reached the large central lake that glistened in the delicate afternoon sun. As they stood, soaking up the unimposing tranquility, Furze thought back to Daw's comment earlier that afternoon.

"Does this not seem strange to you?"

"Whatever do you mean?"

"You said that last night was a 'return to normality' and yet, when I listen to that dog barking, see that child's smile, watch that swan unfurl its angelic wings, everything now holds an acute beauty, a deeper meaning than I have considered before." Furze turned to Daw whose face was pebble dashed with rays of sunlight.

"Kirk and I took a ride just before Festubert, and we sat on our horses atop this little knoll surveying the French countryside.

By all accounts that foreign landscape, which we knew so well, was our normal. However, something inherent within us called us elsewhere, back home to the place we had come from. We vowed then that when the War is over, we would sit atop our horses once again, but this time on a British hill."

"I have no doubt that you will," assured Daw.

Furze's eyes twinkled, "yes, but when it does, I won't think it normal. I shall think it extraordinary."

Eventually strolling their way home, Furze found himself once again standing outside Daw's front door wondering what to do. As she made a move to go inside, he panicked, not wishing to lose the moment, and held her hand tightly. She turned her head towards his, her eyelashes flicking inquisitively. He raised her hand and gently kissed it once more.

"Thank you, my darling Daw," he said, with a clenched stomach, kicking himself for once again failing to have the courage to act as he had wanted, "that was another lovely afternoon."

"The pleasure was mine," she whispered, although Furze thought he detected a hint of disappointment in her look, if only for a brief moment.

"I…" he began, struggling to articulate what he wished to express. She waited patiently, a small smile on her face. "I shall collect you tomorrow morning, if you like? I thought we could go to the country for the day." Furze lowered his eyes, he couldn't understand why he found it so difficult to tell her how he was feeling.

"I look forward to it." She murmured softly, "good night, Keith."

As he trod the well-travelled path back to his parents' house, he tried to analyse his state of mind. He had never thought of himself as brave, but neither would he have defined himself as a coward. Yet in this situation, where he wished so deeply to kiss Daw and tell her how much she meant to him, he seemed incapable of bringing himself to do so. What he feared, what held him back, he did not know. As he approached his front door, he decided, for the sake of the woman he held in such high regard, to spend his leave attempting to understand himself more, in order to do justice to her and act more courageously.

Subsequently, when Saturday broke with glorious rays of sunshine flooding through Furze's window, he was intent on sharing another blissful day with Daw.

"My, my, you're in a fine mood this morning," remarked Mary approvingly.

"Quite so," replied Furze, gulping down his tea. "I'm to take Daw to Chorley Wood today, and with such sun it should be a topping trip!"

"What a thrilling plan," Mary smiled. "How is Daw? She is such a delight and seems quite taken with your company."

"Indeed and I with hers, it seems," he sighed mysteriously. "She is doing wondrously well and remains very dedicated to supporting the war effort. I admire her enormously."

"Is it only admiration you feel?" Mary questioned, her kind eyes expressing a lived wisdom Furze yearned for.

"Well, that's the trouble!" he exclaimed. "There is something greater than admiration, a feeling I can't quite articulate to her yet. I want to do something, say something about this to her but I just don't know how. You can't imagine how infuriating the shawl of youth is!"

"Oh, I imagine not," Mary nodded, although her knowing expression stated otherwise. "If I were to make a suggestion, though, it would be to follow your instincts, no matter how novel they may appear."

Emboldened, he collected Daw at precisely 10:30 am. She looked the part in a fetching country outfit that suited her well and highlighted how much thought she had given the outing. This time, Mrs. Wallis accompanied her daughter to the door and cast a searching gaze over Furze.

"Good morning, Mrs. Wallis," Furze greeted her. He very much liked Daw's mother and held the greatest respect for the way in which she had raised Daw. "Thank you for allowing me your daughter's time for the day. How are you?"

"Oh, it's a pleasure," Mrs. Wallis replied, "I'm quite well, thank you. The real question is, how are you, Keith? You look healthy enough, but make sure you look after your mind as much as your body."

Daw's glance silently asked Furze if she should intervene but having spent so much time discussing the War with her, he was steadily becoming comfortable with such questions. After all, he reasoned, most of them were asked out of care for his wellbeing.

"One carries on," he stated. "I shall own my time on the Front has been ghastly, more so than I find it appropriate to express when surrounded by such joy."

Mrs. Wallis watched him keenly, "I know it must be hard to talk about it, my dear, but I appreciate the fact you can mention it to my daughter and I. Being able to do so allows you, and those who care for you," she paused, turning her gaze to Daw, "to overcome almost any challenge."

Attempting to remain focused on her mother's meaningful words, Furze wondered if Daw had mentioned something of his pensive attitude. Nevertheless, he found great strength in these words. It was not just the content he agreed with, for he wholeheartedly supported her sentiments, it was the way in which Mrs. Wallis had handled the situation. She had been both delicate and honest, allowing her emotions freedom of movement whilst retaining rationality.

"Good grief," he exclaimed, checking his pocket watch, "we have to dash! Mrs. Wallis, thank you, I look forward to speaking further next time."

"Enjoy yourselves, my dears," she answered, as she watched the merry couple cascade out onto the street, and off towards Marylebone station where they entrained for Chorley Wood. The little station was almost deserted when they disembarked and wandered in blissful solitude up to the wide expanse of a nearby common.

"Isn't it perfect?" Furze breathed, allowing his lungs to fill with the fresh country air. "To escape the stony city and disappear into such space?"

"Is the French countryside where you are based quite similar?" Daw asked.

"You know, I don't think it is," Furze pondered. "It has many of the same features, but it doesn't make me feel the same way. Nature, to me anyway, is all about how it makes one feel."

"This certainly makes me feel very peaceful." Daw observed as a butterfly drifted leisurely past her outstretched hand.

"It does indeed," Furze agreed, watching her delight in her surroundings. "We become so used to the commonplace wonders of societal life that it becomes easy to forget the intrinsic importance of simply being. Sometimes, I feel that we, as a race, have become too focused on material gain, the result of which is the inevitable and catastrophic, loss of our understanding of our true purpose."

Daw was intrigued, "I agree that wealth, or status, fail to give life full meaning, so what would you say our true purpose is?"

"To exist harmoniously, I suppose," mused Furze, "but not just with those around us. I mean to exist harmoniously with oneself and, by design, with all the people and things you touch through the course of your life."

"How do you mean?" Daw enquired, catching his eye with a flash of her own.

"That existing harmoniously with yourself, your values, morals and characteristics will create a stronger, more honest bond between you and others than an attempted adherence to societal principles. One must understand what brings real joy, genuine kindness, unabated compassion... powerful love and know that this will be different for each individual. We must work out our own personal harmonies, this is our purpose."

Having allowed these thoughts to run riot in the library of his mind, pulling ideas off the shelves and flinging them across his consciousness, Furze returned to the present and looked sheepishly into Daw's thrilling stare. The expression she relayed, however, of total understanding and deep affection, put him at ease.

They continued their walk, having now fully entered the wood situated in the middle of the common. Through the undergrowth, along a little woodland path, they wandered past a family of whittled hedgehogs, Chorleywood House, and a small summer pavilion before emerging from the forest to find a wide valley sweeping gently down before them, at the bottom of which wound the River Chess.

Furze led Daw down the gentle gradient to the edge of the river and they followed its babbling passage up towards the village of Chenies where they hoped to have lunch. To their immense satisfaction, The Bedford Arms welcomed their arrival and soon enough the delighted couple had two plates of hearty food in front of them. For the first time on their walk, the pair talked little, enjoying the general chatter surrounding them and content in one another's company. People came and went from the pub in that leisurely fashion so characteristic of country living, and both Daw and Furze soaked up the tranquil atmosphere with an almost unquenchable thirst.

Eventually, they decided it was best to soldier on with their walk, so they left the pub, following the country road down to the right and into the village of Chenies.

"Do you think you would get bored, Daw, living in the country?"

"Were I to move to the country right away, I would miss the city terribly, but eventually, I would like to move to the country. I think I would envelope myself in a world of activities, and of course, there would be the children to consider." At this she suddenly caught herself, realising what she had just implied, blushed, and swiftly changed the subject.

Furze grinned at Daw's endearing embarrassment and remarked fondly, "I think this would be an excellent place to raise children. I would take them bird watching all over the nearby marshland. Just think, the place would be flooded with insects, meaning the fish and birds would flourish!"

Regaining her composure and testing how far this conversation could go, Daw returned, tentatively, to her discarded thought. "So, do you wish for children?"

"I do, yes. If I should be lucky enough to survive this war, I would feel it the greatest blessing to raise a child. My parents always appear to have gained the greatest meaning from raising my siblings and I, even when we were terrors," Furze grinned.

"Of course you shall survive this war, and you should never think otherwise!" Countered Daw with sincere compassion. "I think you would make an excellent father and I didn't realise you were so fond of birdwatching."

"It started when I was at Charterhouse," explained Furze, enjoying her interest. "In my first few months there I was rather lonely. I wasn't alone in feeling this, in fact, loneliness is probably the one common feature all new pupils share at boarding school." He smiled at Daw, reassuring her that this wasn't a sorrowful story.

"One morning, I was staring out of the window, imagining that I was in my bedroom at home, when a tiny robin perched on the window sill. The boldness of its personality in contrast to its tiny frame held a great allure for me, and from then on I spent as much time as I could studying birds."

"That's beautiful," agreed Daw, "I can see why they attracted you. Perhaps you'll allow me to accompany you one time?"

By this point, the pair had descended into another valley, which connected Chenies to the nearby hamlet of Latimer, where they came across a delightful little orchard, ring-fenced off from the rest of the sprawling marsh. Although keen to press on with their journey, lunch urged them to rest, and they reclined amongst the well-maintained trees for some thirty minutes or so. Lying next to each other, their breathing became regular, and they silently listened to the birds around them. The stream sang its watery tune gently in the near distance and the wind rustled the leaves hanging in a canopy above them. Furze thought about the day thus far, from Mrs. Wallis' comments about facing challenges together, to the discussion about children. He felt incredibly comfortable with each of these topics, pining for the life they represented, yet still, he wondered how such a life was to begin. He wondered what Daw was thinking, as he felt her shiver ever so slightly next to him.

"You're cold?" he asked.

"A little," she answered, sitting up, "may we continue, in the sun? Whilst walking I'm perfectly content."

"I could remain here for years," Furze observed as they left the tiny pocket of peace.

"We should bottle this feeling," Daw remarked cheekily, "and, when we are back in our stone city, unleash it whenever life gets too busy."

As they strode speedily, arm in arm, back towards Chorley Wood station, Furze couldn't help but feel an intense sense of satisfaction. The countryside may have been delightful, the fields, forests, and hedgerows radiating green in the afternoon sun, the sky the purest and most unblemished topaz, but nothing compared to the beauty he saw when he glanced at Daw. Although hurrying back so as not to miss their train, they couldn't help but be continually distracted.

"Keith, look!" Daw exclaimed, upon noticing a flickering butterfly splashed with colour.

Further on Furze, in his turn, would pause, dead still, and whisper, "Hold a minute Daw and look up there." Daw would turn her gaze to a branch, and spot a solitary woodpecker, or another local bird, which had grabbed Furze's attention.

"You really are good at spotting them, Keith," Daw observed, after he pointed her to a bird she would never have spotted otherwise.

"I've always tried to focus on the unobserved, the day-to-day pleasures that bring one genuine happiness. I believe there is a difference, you know."

"Between pleasure and happiness?"

"Indeed, there are many things in life that can give one pleasure. Playing sport, going to the theatre, enjoying some exquisite wine. But these don't, in my opinion, necessitate happiness. One can experience the most thrilling of pleasures, whilst remaining terribly dour."

"So, then," Daw asked thoughtfully, "how does one achieve happiness?"

"If you discover the answer to that question, my darling, you will have helped solve one of humanity's greatest conundrums." He smiled, and she blushed again. "For my part, focusing on the generally overlooked aspects of our existence helps give me purpose, especially in light of all those friends I have lost. Enjoying that morning cup of tea, those twenty minutes stolen to read a book, that bird upon a branch, that delightful conversation with one's grandmother."

Daw knew what he was thinking about. "She's an incredible woman, Keith, don't worry yourself. I've visited her once or twice whilst you have been away, and I can assure you she's in the best of health."

"But her hands, Daw, they were visibly shaking when I last visited her."

"Old age affects us all," she sighed. "In different ways, it is true, nevertheless, it will hit every one of us. As you say, we must appreciate the smaller delights life affords us. For Emma, she draws her happiness from seeing you, and all her other grandchildren, growing up so wonderfully."

Furze nodded, he knew Daw was right, but it pained him to admit his grandmother's frailty to himself. "As ever, you see the world in its best light, Daw. Honestly, I sometimes wonder that I see too much of the negative in every situation, whilst you always see the positive."

"You see things realistically and that is a huge burden," Daw soothed. "It is also a blessing though, as you fight hard to turn challenges into opportunities. To live life blinkered in a state of perpetual positivity is to be continually disappointed. Better as you say, to make the most of each little raindrop of happiness as a good in itself, than to strive for a downpour of pleasure."

Furze stopped and stared at Daw. They had reached a stile, and Daw was beginning to make her way over it, but she halted at the top and looked down upon him. Their eyes locked, Furze shivered. Her words had resonated with him so truly that he had no response and, simply gazed. She trembled, the stile was old and, as she placed her foot down on the lower step, she slipped and fell whooping onto the grass.

"Daw!" Furze yelled, leaping like a gazelle over the stile. Daw was giggling uncontrollably, her chest heaving with the strain of her laughter. Furze grinned stupidly and bent to pick her up. As he took hold of her, she grabbed his arm and pulled him down with her and they rolled in the long grass, coming to a standstill shoulder to shoulder, looking up at the expansive sky above them.

"That was rather silly," Furze declared, still chuckling quietly.

"Life gets too serious if one isn't silly from time to time."

Furze nodded, then noticed that his pocket watch had made an escape. He picked it up and glanced at the time. "The train! Quick, if we hurry, we should still be able to make it."

They almost ran back to Chorley Wood, springing aboard the 7:00 pm train to London only just managing to make it in time. They headed to Furze's house for dinner and Mary greeted them upon their arrival. "My dears, right on time," she smiled, "you must be famished, having spent the whole day outside."

"Quite so, mother."

"Good evening, Mrs. Furze," Daw greeted her warmly, as Mary gave her a kiss on both cheeks.

"Come now, my dear," scolded Mrs. Furze playfully, "you know you can call me Mary."

The evening was a delightful family affair and Furze could not help but smile at the sight of his family's easy acceptance of the woman he had fallen for. His family was equally delighted in his evident happiness, nevertheless, no one was able to shake the underlying and unspoken understanding that all this joy was only momentary. Furze would soon be returning to the Front, and this bone-crunching fact had no trouble making its presence known.

Gardens and Gazes

"In the afternoon I took mother to the Albert Hall to hear Isolde Menges play."
Sunday 6th June.

Furze couldn't help but burst out of bed each morning, given his growing sense of sublime elation. Having spent a great deal of time with Daw since his return, he decided to sweep his mother off to the Royal Albert Hall one afternoon to hear Isolde Menges, an accomplished English violinist, play. Furze knew his mother adored the Hall and he had quite the affinity for it himself. Sitting picturesquely next to Hyde Park, the round-domed, voluminous building exhumed an air of strength and surety in such a time of global turmoil. The pair dressed up for the occasion in some light summer outfits, and it gave Furze the greatest pleasure to see his mother's pride in sprucing herself up for an afternoon of quality time with her son. Having taken a short walk in Hyde Park, they entered the Hall through the northern entrance, and made their way to their seats.

When Isolde Menges emerged on the stage, rapturous applause greeted her composed and confident stance. She bowed politely and then flung herself into her performance. It was a beautiful act, her powerful strokes producing delicate music, racing over one group of notes only to hang as if poised, on others. Furze became lost in the compelling sounds drifting towards him and found it difficult to decide whether to close his eyes and listen to the music, watch Isolde as she played, or sit and observe the sight of his mother, eyes half closed, happiness etched on her face, soaking up every inch of the present moment.

He was painfully aware that his departure to the Front, and that of his elder brother, greatly worried his mother. He also knew that the thought of Nevil going out to join the war was enough to bring her untold despair. As such, it was apparent how much she cherished every moment spent alone with him and he valued such time with her as a result. The sight of her joy at that moment, soaked in the beautiful chorus emulating from the stage, moved him enormously. *I must spend more quality time with her*, he thought as he observed her peaceful countenance, *she deserves nothing less, and certainly far more.*

"Thank you, Keith." Mary expressed her gratitude as they walked out of the Hall, engulfed by the excitable crowd. "Isolde was captivating."

Before Furze could respond, there was a sharp scoff from behind them followed by the pompous words. "It's a shame her parents are Germans, such wasted talent!"

Mary didn't lose a single moment, her morality leaping in as she turned towards the unwelcome intruder. "I don't care if her parents are German, she holds an art for the violin and that is what we should appreciate. The War is pitching enough talented, young individuals against one another as it is without music falling victim to your petty views!"

The man's jaw dropped, and he turned to Furze for support, before stammering an apology when he noticed the pride with which Furze was observing Mary and realised their connection.

"Well, you told him." Furze smiled as they walked away.

"You know full well I cannot stand people being judged, especially on such trivialities as where they come from."

"Quite so," agreed Furze, who supported his mother's view on this matter wholeheartedly, "I'm so pleased you liked her. You seemed lost in the moment at times."

"Oh, I was," Mary answered, closing her eyes momentarily and picturing the performance, "if you visit the Hall enough, you need never actually observe a performance there again, one need only close one's eyes and listen. I know what the place looks like, but it is the acoustics that make it unique."

"Then we shall go again, I'll look at further tickets next time I return on leave," Furze promised. "Time spent like that with you is a treasure."

"You needn't look to my needs so much, remember, I have your father to look after me."

"I know, but I sometimes feel as though I don't see you enough. Life gets so busy, especially when leave is so short."

"My dear son," she added gently, "I adore every minute of your company, but I place far more importance on your happiness than my own. You must spend your time as you see fit, as we only get one chance to live this life and it pains me that the War has denied you so much of your youth."

"It has become rather a habit on the Front to wonder whether each day will be one's last," Furze commented, with a touch of sadness.

"Then you'll live every day far more than the rest of us," Mary comforted, her heart bleeding nonetheless.

Spurred on by his mother's words, he lost no time in visiting his grandmother once again, secretly intending to keep a check on her shaking hands.

"What have you been up to these past few days then, my dear?" Emma asked with a grin, dishing out the meal she had prepared.

"Plenty," responded Furze, "many a splendid walk with Daw, we went to Chorley Wood the other day."

"That is a delightful place to walk, your grandfather used to take me for walks up there myself when we were younger. I imagine it's quite the same," Emma recollected. "I'm glad you remain able to focus on the more important aspects of life and escape from the War."

"I just hope I'm doing her justice," Furze blurted, and then caught himself.

"How so?" Emma enquired, picking up on a subtle emotional nerve.

"Well," Furze continued, attempting to articulate his thoughts, "I wish to give Daw the time she deserves, with the person she deserves."

"Do you think yourself incapable of this?" Emma asked, cutting to the heart of the matter.

"No," considered Furze, "at least not when I am here and when I am my whole and best self." He studied his grandmother's face. "But I will be heading back to war, Grammy, and each time I do there is certainly no guarantee that I shall return. Even when I do, I don't think I'm ever the same man."

His grandmother understood. "Just concern yourself with being genuine, Keith. Give your whole self, in whatever capacity that manifests, and if Daw is not satisfied with that, the onus is on her." Emma took his hand, and although hers was shaking ever so slightly, he could sense her strength in the touch. "You're a dedicated, dutiful young man. But you have to be as confident in yourself emotionally as you are professionally, as a leader. My goodness, you perform when you are under enemy fire, take but a part of that strength and harness it when feelings enter the equation, and you shan't go half wrong."

If only I could summon the bravery to kiss her, contemplated Furze, *it seems easy to do the right thing when there are lives at stake, especially those of one's friends.* He studied her hands, then looked directly at his grandmother. "Are you sure you are healthy, Grammy, healthy and happy? I have seen so many people I love disappear recently, I wouldn't know what to do without you."

Emma clasped Furze's hands more strongly than ever. "Quite certain, dear grandson, life is far from done with me yet. As for you, let your feelings take their natural course, however unsteady that may be. Your grandfather used to call me his sweetheart before we were engaged. I always rather liked that turn of phrase."

The next day Furze met Daw at midday and taxied to Kew. The botanical gardens lounged elegantly in the afternoon rays, and they revelled in the history of the site. Founded in 1840, and with tens of thousands of varying kinds of flora and fauna situated over three-hundred acres, the site sprang to life when brushed in sunlight.

One of the groundsmen, noticing them comment on the architecture of Temperate House, paused from his work for a moment and touched his cap. "Sir, madam, she's quite something, isn't she?"

"That she is," Furze agreed with a smile, the man's weathered appearance suggesting many long years spent toiling outside. "Have you worked here long?"

"All my life, Sir," nodded the groundsman, evidently pleased to be engaging in conversation. "Grew up local, and started working here as a young lad. My old man thought it a proper fancy job when I started, but it brought home my keep, so he didn't complain."

"It must be so peaceful, working everyday amongst such beauty," Daw added, thoughtfully.

"Aye, Ma'am it's the air," the groundsman breathed deeply as he said this, closing his eyes and filling lungs which had no doubt tasted every scent that had ever graced Kew's gardens. "You can't help but enjoy its freshness here."

"So, what is the history of this building then?" Furze queried. "Spend enough time on the Front and one forgets that people are capable of creating such wonders."

"So I understand, Sir, she's the largest Victorian glasshouse in the world," the groundsman answered, casting an affectionate look at the structure.

"Extraordinary," muttered Furze, wondering at the engineering brilliance behind it.

"What's more, if you'll allow me, we have managed to breed rubber trees successfully in these gardens," the groundsman added pensively, hoping he had judged the couple's interests correctly. Thankfully, Daw and Furze were eager recipients of such information.

"Truly," gasped Daw, "I thought they only grew in South America?"

"Truly, Ma'am," the old man responded eagerly. "You would have been quite correct in your statement, but we have managed to breed them here for the first time!"

"My dear fellow, you've brightened our day with your intimate knowledge of the gardens, thank you," Furze grinned, shaking the old man's hand. "May I ask your name?"

Struck at the familiarity, but elated at the interest, the groundsman stammered, "Frank, Sir, and I'm glad you found some use for an old man's thoughts."

"Frank, it's a pleasure. My name is Keith, and this is Daw," Furze turned towards her as she nodded gently to Frank, "my…" he stopped.

Up until this moment, in front of a groundsman in Kew Gardens, Furze had not had to introduce Daw to anyone new. It suddenly struck him that he had not thought about an appropriate term to describe their relationship, and this brought to light all of the thoughts, emotions, and concerns that had been swirling around his mind for the past week. What should he say, that wouldn't appear too intense, but also not too removed? What would Daw expect him to say, and what did the groundsman expect from them? His grandmother's voice cut across the cacophony of internal noise, and he smiled, knowing precisely what to say.

"…sweetheart."

Daw blushed, Frank nodded understandingly, and Furze expressed his thanks before taking Daw's arm and walking away. His heart beat more furiously than a hummingbird's wings as he felt Daw next to him, and wondered if he should say something to explain his pause and the word he had eventually chosen.

Daw squeezed his arm tightly, and all his inner tension dissipated, flushed from him by this gentle gesture of mutual understanding. They broke into laughter and, as they wandered into the gorgeous scenery. Frank returned to his work with a nostalgic smile, remembering the throws of his own youth, when love had wrapped its passionate arms around his young heart.

"Keith, Daw, there you are! Your father and I have searched the whole garden for you both." For a moment, Furze was startled to see his mother and father walking towards them.

Daw whispered, "you mentioned our plans to them over lunch, remember? We invited them to meet us here for tea."

"Of course, well remembered! It had quite slipped my mind," he chuckled. "I did wonder how they found us."

"By my watch, right on time, son," smiled Herbert, who adored Kew Gardens. "It's been a while since I last visited. Have I told you of the time the suffragettes, two years ago, burned down the Tea House?"

The family had, of course, heard the story multiple times, but Daw mentioned she had not, so they all listened happily as Herbert took Daw's arm and regaled her with the fable.

Furze took his mother's arm and the group proceeded towards the place they had decided to take tea. The Tea House story led, naturally, into Herbert's vast library of Kew memories, and Daw was more than happy to be given a seat in this vault of knowledge, pulling tales from the shelves and delving into them with pleasure. Every now and again, she would glance back at Furze who, conversing quietly with his mother, returned her tender expression with a kind-hearted smile. He read the pleasure on her lips, the joy in her eyes, the concentration on her brow, the inquisitiveness in her shoulders, and adored it all.

She is being very, very sweet today, Furze thought, *bless her dear soul.*

Herbert eventually released Daw from his stories and made to depart with Mary, glancing knowingly at Furze as they left.

"How are you feeling?" Furze asked.

"Delighted, Keith," she said, "I don't know how your father manages to remember all those stories!"

"I brought a blanket," he admitted bashfully, "shall we rest under that tree for a while?"

"I'd like that," Daw agreed, and they made their way up a small incline to the tree Furze had indicated. Placing the blanket on the damp ground, the pair lay down next to one another, staring up at a sky spotted with brooding clouds. Their hands touched and Furze took Daw's in his own, the pair secure in one another's company as the clouds contorted above them.

He felt so close to Daw at that moment, their shoulders touching, their hands clasped together, their fingers intertwined as closely as the bodies of passionate lovers. She made him view the world through a more vibrant, positive spectrum. She tempered his anger in times of stress, elevated his passion in times of elation, and infused his world with that subtle tranquility that erupts from the knowledge that someone cares deeply for you and you alone, in such an intimate and reciprocated way.

She is simply ripping! he thought to himself, turning his head towards her.

Yet, they had still not shared their first kiss.

Though they were both young, Furze being twenty-four and Daw being still younger, circumstance had played havoc with their dreams. On top of this, Furze had never been one to rush any decision, especially one where his feelings were involved.

Subsequently, although he had known Daw for some time, the War had only allowed them brief interludes with one another, and he had been enjoying her company so greatly that he had thought little of the romance between them. Equally, he had always been nervous as to Daw's feelings for him and feared making any advance in case his assumption was mistaken.

Finally, after all his deliberations over the past week, he suddenly felt certain that the time was right.

He was to return to the Front on Saturday 12th June, the day after tomorrow.

Under that tree, in Kew Gardens, gazing up at the tumultuous sky beneath which he and his sweetheart lay in blissful serenity, he decided to lay his heart out to her the next day. He could no longer live in the hope that Daw loved him, for he was now certain that he loved her.

B.D. Wilberforce

The Brave Vulnerability of Youth

"At about 03:30 we heard footsteps overhead and then, in a few minutes, a tap on the door and in came Mrs. Wallis who was very sweet – it was a glorious and most amusing experience."

Friday 11th June.

I

Friday arrived, heralding Furze's impending return to the Front, so he took his father to lunch at his Club. Despite the decision he had come to the previous day, conflict was raging around Furze's mind, something that Herbert noticed instantly.

"What's on your mind son, is it your return?"

Furze, looked into his father's seasoned face. "I never could hide anything from you, not that I've ever wanted to. There is something I would appreciate your advice on, more than anything in the world."

"Absolutely son, I'm always happy to offer any advice, even if it may be outdated and utterly useless to you." Furze's father replied with a soothingly experienced tongue.

"Well." Furze was staring intently at the coffee he had been stirring absentmindedly for the past few minutes. "It concerns Daw."

Herbert smiled but said nothing.

"My dilemma, well I suppose it's more of a decision rather than a dilemma, but one which could have troublesome consequences, and yet…oh I'm quite making a mess of things."

Furze went back to stirring his coffee, recollected his thoughts, then began afresh. "I believe that I am in love with Daw, at the very least I know that I have incredibly deep feelings for her. I simply have to tell her how I feel and have determined to do so this evening, or else I shall return to the Front filled with regret and longing. There are enough troubles over there as it is without me bringing some fresh worries with me from home."

"I see," mused his father, gazing thoughtfully at a quite insignificant point on the ceiling. "Well, my boy, love springs upon us in many forms. Sometimes we believe it to be entirely obvious, almost assertively prescriptive, and yet it can shatter into finer fragments than a delicate vase that has fallen from a trusted plinth. On other occasions, love can act as the most tempestuous ocean, calm and inviting one minute, then brutal and unforgiving the next. On rare occasions, love can weave its way into the fabric of our heart without even a whisper, taking hold of its strings and guiding our paths effortlessly. On these occasions, Keith, we need only tread the route laid before us to discover love's destination." He paused momentarily to take a sip of his tea, carefully gauging Furze's reaction to his words.

He thus resumed, "It appears to me, that you know precisely how to proceed with young Miss Wallis, for love in a form unique to you has finally been presented. So, why the trepidation?"

"Dad!" Furze, quite taken aback by how clearly he could express such complex feelings. "Your words touch me to the core and encapsulate all that I have been feeling, except for one thing. I do not know whether Daw feels the same way about me."

"Should this trouble you?" Asked his father, so casually that Furze wondered at the seriousness of his comment.

"Of course! For if she does not, then all is lost. I would not only have misinterpreted her feelings for me, showing that I barely know her at all, I would also lose a dear, dear friend and companion. I have come to value her company, her conversation, her thoughts, her presence in my life so that to lose them in addition to my love, would be crushing."

The older and wiser Furze who had himself, felt the pangs of emotional turmoil similarly in his time, observed with worldly compassion the chorus of his son's aching heart.

"My boy, of course she feels the same way about you. If not in precisely the same terms, at least with no less affection. In addition, it is certainly worth remembering that even were she not to love you, but still care deeply for you, you would be lying to her as well as yourself if you were to keep your feelings from her."

Furze brooded over this perspective. He had up until that point, been wishing to see his own feelings mirrored in Daw. Considering now how Daw might share the same emotions, just express them in a different way, made him pause.

Herbert continued, "individuals have a tendency to surprise even the most experienced of souls with their capacity for affection and it takes a rare conscience, devoid of much emotion, to shatter a friendship based solely on an expression of love."

This statement locked Furze deep in thought. "This does complicate things somewhat."

"How so, son?" Herbert queried.

"Well, previously I was having difficulty understanding how to express my own feelings." Furze paused for a moment to choose the right words. "Yet, once I had discovered my own mode of expression, I simply needed to see Daw act the same way towards me. If as you say, she expresses her affection differently, how will I recognise that her feelings are the same as my own?"

Herbert mulled over this statement, whilst Furze poured some fresh tea.

"Additionally, although it may be unlikely for her to shatter our friendship over unreturned love, you must admit that this will, invariably, complicate things. I can't foresee it retaining all of its colour after such an event."

Herbert began his riposte. "My dear boy, reality is what we make of it. You may if you wish, exist in a reality marred by what has occurred, by what society and others claim is the accepted state of things. I would hazard that this seems a rather bleak existence. You talk of life devoid of colour. I challenge that unless you are true to yourself and take meaningful risks, even when one's heart is at stake, you will live perpetually in a world where you have termed colour a stranger, something not to be trusted."

Furze looked at his father, whose words seemed to tap him on the shoulder and say *this way, there is another, a better path to follow.*

"Keith, my son, you operate at a level professionally and personally that I admire greatly. It has driven you, and continues to drive you, from success to success. Just be wary that the weight of expectation you place upon yourself does not crush you, and that the standards you set for others are not insurmountable. Life is not about success, though we live in a world where this seems to be lauded as the ultimate achievement. It is about understanding who you are and what makes you and others happy, then remaining true to this in the face of every adversity. You know, in your heart, what you need to do. I urge you now not to fear the consequences of the action you wish to take. The War has created enough fear as it is, why allow any more into your life?"

Herbert had allowed the moment to take hold of him, and he looked at Furze with eyes engulfed in compassion.

Furze's mind gripped his father's words, encouraging his concerns to unravel for the very first time. He felt liberated by the conversation, at peace with his feelings, strong as they remained and felt no need to fight his thoughts as though each one was a German entrenched in his mind.

"Dad, your words strike me. How could I have believed Daw capable of lacerating our friendship simply due to my love which if anything, is an expression of the strength our friendship holds? But truly, do you think she may love me too?"

"Since you introduced her to your mother and I, we have greatly taken to her, Keith. We couldn't keep her from our table even if we wanted to, and believe you me, we most certainly do not want to. When you are away, her concern for you rivals that of your mother and she provides the greatest comfort to us all in your absence."

Furze sighed in marked relief, and Herbert knew his son had reached his decision.

"Keith, if this doesn't account for love on her part, she is an angel, and if it does, she is no less divine."

II

Furze's plan was to make his way to 48 Holland Park, take leave of Mrs. Wallis and Daw's sister Alice, then return home with Daw for dinner. What the rest of the night would hold he did not know, and in many ways did not care to know. He was now firmly of the opinion that he would be able to express his love for Daw when the right moment presented itself. As he neared her house however, the clarity of mind, which his father's carefully chosen words had inspired, began to cloud. It was strange for Furze to second guess himself, yet he could not help but wonder whether he had accepted his father's words too swiftly.

Did I just listen to what I wanted to hear? He mused, turning a street corner and pausing for a moment. *Should I return to Dad and question his statements more rigorously?* He almost turned back on himself before realising the ineffectiveness of the indecision coursing through him. *If I made decisions in this way on the Front*, he berated himself, *people would get killed.*

Frustrated, he replayed the conversation at lunch in his mind, and struck upon one passage that he muttered to himself. "Individuals have a tendency to surprise even the most experienced of souls with their capacity for affection."

Furze smiled as he took up his stride once again, thinking, *I simply must declare myself to her*. He then realised that he had managed to contemplate himself all the way to Daw's front door and looked up at it as one would to that of a Headteacher's study. He hesitated, before allowing the honest affection he held for her to lift his hand and knock confidently upon it.

Daw had been expecting him and opened the door without a moment's hesitation. Furze moved forwards and took hold of her hands, "Oh, how I have missed you."

"It's been less than a day, Keith," Daw answered, quite taken at the emotion powering his words. She thought he appeared more open, more soulful, and this touched her.

"I know my dear and yet it seems as though an age has passed since I last saw you. Perhaps it is because I'm returning to the Front tomorrow, or perhaps it is because I have been enjoying my time with you so vividly."

"You really are in a strange mood today, are you quite well?" Daw queried gazing inquisitively at Furze and urging him to allow her access to the vaults of his thoughts that she had been attempting to reach since his return. Pleasingly, she thought she noticed the door to those vaults begin to open. Before he could answer, however, Mrs. Wallis appeared in the doorway to say her good-byes.

Studying him affectionately, she requested, "stay safe my dear, and know that you are always welcome in this house."

"I can't thank you enough for your hospitality, Mrs. Wallis," he responded. "The kindness you have shown me is far more than I deserve. You have raised a wonderful family, and you are all very dear to me."

With that, Furze and Daw walked arm in arm to Furze's home where his family ushered them in with their usual warmth.

As Mary led Daw into the living room asking her opinion on the new blouse she had worn for Furze's send-off, Herbert looked inquisitively at his son.

"Not yet," whispered Furze, "the right time hasn't presented itself."

Herbert nodded, "all in good time, the night is yet young."

Furze paused in the corridor to allow the rest of the family to settle into the living room. "As I reached her house, I found myself questioning what you had said," he admitted in hushed tones.

"I would expect nothing less, I didn't raise you to blindly follow what other people say."

This encouraged Furze. "Quite so, and I thought about the serious consequences that indecision has on the Front."

"There are two fields of war as I see it," Herbert mused, "physical war and emotional war. Inaction can have serious consequences in both fields."

"I know, I know," Furze agreed, "I thought it through and decided your words still rang true. I shall tell her, I promise."

Herbert gave Furze a firm pat on the back as they joined the rest of the family.

"That aside son, how are you feeling about returning to the Front?

"My feelings fluctuate enormously when I think upon it, duty and a desire to be back among my friends draws me on, sometimes making me impatient even to return. Yet, I would rather there was no war to return to. I desire nothing more than a simple life, enjoying the company of you all and that of my friends, without such turmoil. Alas, I can't foresee that coming to pass for quite a while."

Herbert looked over at Nevil, who was laughing heartily at something Daw had just uttered and murmured to Furze, "your mother is terribly worried about him going out there. She's positively beside herself at the thought."

"I can imagine, it will no doubt be immensely difficult for you both with all three of us fighting in the war." Furze knew his parents well. His mother was vocal in her concerns and, although he did his utmost to comfort her by upholding a strong and steadfast persona, his father was a gentle and affectionate man at heart.

"I'm sure he'll be fine," Furze attempted to reassure him. "Nevil is fit, healthy, and has had excellent training. He will do well and, if anything, may even thrive in the army."

"Keith," his father interjected, looking firmly at his son, "not everyone takes to things as well as you, nor leads with such ease. Nevil is a vibrant character, this is true, but I fear for him far more than I fear for you. Am I wrong to do so?"

Furze thought for a moment, realising that his father was asking for his honesty rather than his compassion. "I don't think so, I admit that I am equally as concerned for Nevil as you are. I hope he takes to the life, but the likelihood is that he will not. It's not much of a life to take to. You say that I do, that I lead with ease, but the truth of the matter is that I still struggle with these things every day. It's almost impossible to predict who will thrive in such environments. Looking back, I never would have thought myself capable of many of the things fate has forced me to turn my hands to, hands designed more for playing the piano than fighting."

Herbert considered this comment. His son had changed so very much since he had gone to the Front, and he had almost forgotten that Keith had been a quiet, bird-watching musician throughout his childhood. The highly thoughtful, emotional, serious officer struggling with the concepts of love and war that sat beside him formed a stark contrast to that memory.

"But that's just it, when reality strikes, the Front forces you to perform, leaves you with no choice but to proceed, and in those situations the die is cast. You can only run forward, with your head up and eyes fixed on your blurry destination, hoping the image clears and you arrive safely."

The pair rose as dinner was called and they returned to the blissful scene, Furze grateful to be surrounded by everyone he loved. Only the eldest son, Douglas, and his grandmother Emma, were not in attendance. It had been over a year since the entire family had been together and Mary couldn't help but show her sadness at the absence of one of her children. Thankfully and true to what Herbert had told Furze, Daw added so much to the scene as to be treated as an adopted daughter. She sat opposite Furze, wedged in between Margy and Nevil, who hadn't allowed for any other seating arrangement. Their connection with Daw brought such warmth to Furze's heart that he found himself gazing quietly at her from across the table, marvelling at her engagement within such an intimate family setting.

Every now and again she would look over to him from her conversations, continuing to listen and even contribute to the hubbub around her, but expressing with her eyes a desire to talk to him and him alone. Following dessert, the group retired back into the living room and the jolly conversation resumed. Recollecting his thoughts from earlier, Herbert requested tentatively, "Keith, why not play us something on the piano?"

"No, no, I couldn't possibly," Furze flushed, "the moment is perfect. My awful playing would only ruin things."

"Nonsense!" clamoured Margy. "You play beautifully and it's been so long since we heard you."

"Yes, please Keith," implored Diddy, clasping her hands together in expectant pleasure.

The encouragement of his sisters paired with the silent consent of Daw, convinced him. As he sat down at the family's little piano, a memory suddenly struck him.

"The last time I played an instrument," he said, turning to his family, "was in May, when stationed near Merris. I found a beautiful organ tucked into the corner of the church there and enjoyed a few hours playing it alone."

Everyone in the room was silent, immobile, watching him with rapt attention.

"I thought of two things," he continued, looking to each of his family. "Of you all and the warm memories I have in this room." He then turned to Daw adding, "and of you, dear Daw." Furze blushed, turning back to the piano. "This was what I played with such memories in my soul."

His practiced fingers flew over the keys, leaping about as if each one struck electricity when placed upon the instrument, Elgar's Enigma Variations swooping around the room. At one point Daw sat down next to Furze on the piano stool and he guided her hands as they attempted to play the music together.

At 10:30 pm, when the mood in the room had reached that pleasant warmth of a crackling fire in winter, Daw and Furze decided to embark upon the rest of their evening. Having thanked Mary for her culinary skills and Herbert for his immense hospitality, Daw took her leave of Margy, Diddy, and Nevil in turn, promising to come and visit them all soon. Then jumping into an awaiting taxi, Furze and Daw motored off to central London.

And now, the real evening can begin, thought Furze as he set out with the woman he loved.

III

They made their way to the Savoy, once again heading straight to the Lancaster Ballroom to join the glorious cascade of colourful dancers leading their interwoven paths. The couple merged with the mass enjoying the singularity of their connection to one another in so public a domain. As they waltzed gracefully, Furze looked into Daw's eyes, which smiled back at him with immense intimacy. Gliding in unison, Daw thought she once again recognised that strange look of his, the one that hinted there was something he wished to say. She returned every gaze with warmth, every smile with feeling, and every touch, signalling to him to open up to her.

They continued in such a fashion for a number of dances, then made their way to the dining room for a very late supper.

"Keith, is there something on your mind?" Daw enquired when they were alone. "Is it your return to the Front?"

"In a manner of speaking."

Far from satisfied with this answer, Daw pressed the question. "Come now, we've spent a delightful evening together, with your parents, dancing here. Something has been on your mind all evening," she crossed her arms and looked purposefully at him. "I shan't eat another mouthful until you tell me what it is."

Her direct approach caught him off guard, he didn't feel it was the right time. "Oh, it's nothing Daw, honestly."

"Keith…whatever the challenge, no matter how difficult, let me share it with you."

He observed her imploring look, soaked up her encouraging words, and let out a breath. Her mother, his own parents, even the gardener at Kew Gardens knew that he loved her and believed that she loved him in return.

"I'm finding this very hard, Daw, I don't want to return to the Front. There is so much pain there to return to, so much horror, sorrow, and uncertainty."

"That is perfectly natural," Daw responded, softening her approach at his dejected look.

"But for me, there's more to it than that," he locked Daw's gaze. "it's not simply whether I return, or whether my friends make it out alive. It's whether I return or don't return to you."

Daw held his attention, trembling slightly. "Your comment about thinking of me in Merris…"

"Daw, I think about you constantly, more so when I'm on the Front," he took her hands. "The thought that I might never return, thus leaving you here alone, or that I might return and that you might not…" He let her hands go and picked up his glass of wine.

Daw was both pleased with the progress she was making and perplexed with Furze's timidity. Before she could answer, however, the hotel manager interrupted them.

"My apologies Sir, Ma'am," he nodded to them both. "It's two in the morning, and we really must close for the night."

"Goodness! You are returning to the Front tomorrow. No, later today."

Furze's mind was torn. He had hoped by now to have been able to tell Daw how he felt, however, the moment had not seemed quite right. *Perhaps it is a sign that things were never meant to be*, he thought.

Daw read his mind. "Will you take me home, Keith?"

"I should like to very much," he smiled. There was yet hope.

They bundled into the awaiting taxi and Furze bid the Savoy's doormen and façade adieu, unsure when he would next see them again. Arriving swiftly at Holland Park, Furze caught Daw's arm as they leapt up her front steps.

"Your mother!" Furze whispered.

"Don't worry, when we get in, you head to the drawing room and I'll check on the family."

Doing as he had been told, he padded his way to the drawing room and waited. Daw quickly appeared in the room, closing the door gently behind her, and tip-toeing over to where he was seated. This comedic act of subtlety was too much for the pair and they burst out into stifled giggles as she fell onto the sofa next to him.

"I say Daw," stammered Furze, valiantly failing in his attempts to pull himself together, "should I really be sneaking around your mother's house like this without her knowing? I shouldn't like to appear rude."

"Nonsense, Keith," Daw responded, grinning and holding onto both of Furze's hands tightly, "Even if mother was awake she wouldn't fuss. She simply adores you and holds you in the highest esteem."

"You have an immensely welcoming family."

Daw blushed. "I am rather blessed to have such an open family. Without them, I may never have been allowed to go dancing in the Savoy so freely, and subsequently may never have met you."

"Now that was an evening," Furze remembered, with a wry smile on his face, "I remember quite clearly the moment I first noticed you. I was standing to one side of the dance floor, having just retrieved a drink after my second or third dance of the evening. Talking to a few friends, we were remarking upon the elegance of a number of the couples dancing that evening as well as the inelegance of others…"

Daw stifled her laughter picturing quite clearly the scene Furze described.

"My eye caught your gaze, though only for a moment. So briefly in fact, that I wondered whether it had only been my fancy."

"I remember your look to this day, for I had been looking in your direction hoping you would notice me. Strangely, when you did, it so surprised me that I quite forgot myself and hastened to look away."

"Quite so!" agreed Furze. "In fact, your entire head shot in another direction so quickly I was afraid it might spin right round like an owl's." The pair burst into fits of laughter, before controlling themselves and Furze continued. "Luckily, a close friend had observed the look you gave me and convinced me to talk to you. I thank him continuously, for I fear I would have lacked the courage to believe you were looking at me had he not."

"Keith," Daw's tone was loving, "how could I have been looking at anyone else?"

"Well, somehow I made my way over pondering what I was going to say."

"You evidently didn't think for long enough," grinned Daw, conscious of what was coming next in the story, "from what I remember you said nothing at all! I just took your arm and we danced for the rest of the night."

At this memory, neither of them could contain themselves any longer. Furze burst out into fits of laughter and Daw simply screamed with delight. They let the moment fly, allowed it to burst into every corner of the room, bounce off the walls and ceiling and express all their unrestrained delight. When their laughter eventually subdued, they heard footsteps above which froze the moment. Furze looked at his watch, it was three-thirty in the morning, and he shivered at the thought of having woken Mrs. Wallis. The footsteps made their way down the stairs, reached the corridor, turned towards the drawing room, and approached at a steady pace. The seconds seemed to last an age.

What if she turns me out before I am able to tell Daw how I feel? He wondered, fear gripping his thoughts. He had been engrossed in the moment, absolutely captivated by Daw's conversation and jovial memories and had felt the right time approaching. He braced himself at the sound of a light tap on the door which preceded the entrance of a drowsy Mrs. Wallis. As soon as she saw Furze and Daw, all apprehensions were shattered, and the blissful enjoyment of the previous moment once again descended upon the scene. A smile bloomed on her face as she made her way straight over to Furze, embracing him with motherly affection.

"Keith, what a pleasant surprise!" Mrs. Wallis said, "I do hope the pair of you had a lovely evening. I hadn't expected to see you again before you headed back to the Front, but this is a supreme pleasure, regardless of the hour."

"Mrs. Wallis," Furze replied, "please accept my pardons for waking you. It's not becoming of me in the slightest…"

"Oh, nonsense," Mrs. Wallis cut in, "you are heading back to the Front today, I am glad you are able to make the most of our hospitality."

Furze was relieved at Mrs. Wallis' generosity.

"I look forward to seeing you upon your return, my dear," Mrs. Wallis stated finally as she turned to leave, "I'm positive it won't be too long. Remember, all the thoughts of this family will be with you."

As the drawing room door clicked shut, the couple turned to one another.

"Now, Keith," Daw said, quite seriously, "what was it you wanted to say to me in the Savoy?"

He moved closer to her, their gazes anchored, and with one swift, bold movement, Furze swept dear old Daw into his arms and kissed her for the very first time.

The Return

"Very sad having to say good-bye to all at home – it is absolutely rotten having to return."

Saturday 12th June.

After crawling into bed at 4:15 am, Furze woke only a few hours later to the welcome smell of freshly brewed coffee. He instantly recalled the happenings of the evening before, stealing a moment to savour the quiet happiness he felt.

"Morning son," his father greeting him as Furze appeared in the dining room. "You got in late."

"Did you and Daw enjoy a good evening?" queried his mother, the pair of them attempting to mask their shared interest.

He studied them both, his dear parents seated next to one another in unspoken solidarity. "I told Daw that I love her," he announced. "She feels quite the same."

Mary and Herbert smiled in unison, before his father commented. "We never had any doubt."

The family breakfasted very well before Furze gathered the last of his things for the journey ahead. It was very sad having to say goodbye to Mary, Herbert, and Diddy at home even with Margy and Nevil accompanying him to the station.

He hugged his mother tightly, feeling her hold him just that second longer than usual. "Look after Dad and Daw for me mother, and I'll make sure I get tickets to the next event at the Royal Albert Hall upon my return. I love you so very much."

"My darling," Mary released him to fate. "I'm very proud of you. You're such a strong, emotional man now, even if I shall always see you as my young son in need of protection. Don't you worry, Daw will be welcome here as much as she likes."

Furze turned to his father and hugged him compassionately.

"Be safe, Keith," his father muttered into his son's shoulder. To this steadfast, sure, and sturdy father, his son suddenly seemed so precious, so delicate, and he had to catch his voice before emotion broke it.

"I will, Dad," Furze returned, shaking slightly. "Without your advice, without your sound counsel, I don't know where I would be."

"You would have worked it out eventually," Herbert assured him, his resolve returning. "You always do."

Finally taking leave of his sister, he packed up the taxi and turned to the three of them, waiting patiently on his parents' threshold. Waving his final farewell, Margy, Nevil, and he headed to Victoria station. They arrived in plenty of time for Furze to make all his necessary good-byes. He thanked Margy for being such a good soulmate to Daw, then turned to Nevil.

"When are you set to be drafted out to the Front?"

"Next month," Nevil replied. "I've requested to join The Queen's Regiment, given its reputation."

Although his younger brother was doing his best to put on a show of strength, Furze could recognise the trepidation on Nevil's face.

"You'll be most welcome," he reassured him, "The Queen's would be lucky to have such a capable officer. Keep in touch dear brother, and send me a letter as soon as you know more about your movements."

As Furze was about to board the train, Nevil caught his arm. "Keith, is it usual to be…" he paused, embarrassed at what was on his mind.

"Petrified?" Furze finished for him.

Nevil nodded.

"I'm yet to meet a man who hasn't been, myself included. We can't choose when we are afraid, but we can choose how we react in the face of fear."

"I hope I react honourably," Nevil murmured.

Furze moved to hug his brother, before adding, "you're stronger than me, Nevil. As father once said to me, a path will be made out for you, all you have to do is follow it wherever it may lead. You'll know how to act when the world calls you to do so."

Nevil nodded slowly, and Furze boarded the train feeling absolutely rotten about having to return to the Front. He looked back as it pulled out of the station, catching sight of Nevil standing alone, his hand raised towards the departing train, a flush of pain and compassion upon his countenance.

Furze's journey across the Channel and towards the War passed immensely quickly, and he cursed the efficiency with which time delivered him to danger. The Queen's was stationed ten miles behind the Front line at a village called Les Harasoirs, and he was greeted by a Regiment of men that were muddied, ragged, and evidently spent. The Battalion had come out of the trenches that day, after what had apparently been a week's rotten time opposite La Bassée. Given the lateness of the hour, Furze silently made his way to the officers' billets and got into bed. It was a cold night. His breath seemed to hang petulantly upon the air in front of his face. He heard movement all around him and recalled the blissful silence of home. He reflected on his parents. On Daw.

How rotten this life is, he thought distractedly, turning over and shivering under the thin blanket. There in that war-torn environment, the closest he would get to comfort, to family, was his friends. He moved to get up and seek out Fuller in the next room before he stopped, shocked.

Fuller is gone. He sat on the bed, aghast. The support of his family and his love for Daw had helped him recover from his losses at Festubert, but now finding himself back in the midst of that conflict, the memories made an unwelcome return.

*No Fuller, no Brookes...*he felt incredibly lonely before his mind turned to Bobbie. *Hopefully he is stationed nearby, and Philpot should still be a part of the Regiment. I'll seek them out in the morning.*

He lay himself back down on the bed, his heart aching for the friends he had lost and the woman that he loved. Fuller and Brookes had left him behind, and now he had left Daw at home. *Please, God, let me get back to her.*

The next morning Furze captured a young subaltern to ask about The Queen's. Given the decimated state the Regiment had found itself in after Festubert, he was unsurprised to discover a great many changes since his departure.

"Over the past two weeks?" Queried the subaltern who, himself, was unknown to Furze. "Yes, a great deal of change. I have joined, for one, as have a number of other officers."

"Is Captain Duckworth still in command?" Furze had not received any communication since his return home.

"I'm afraid not, he left last week, upon the arrival of Major Heath from the 1st Battalion, who is our current Commanding Officer."

This news greatly saddened Furze, who was in dire need of a friendly face. "I see, I shall have to make myself known to the Major. Any other changes?"

"Lieutenants Longbourne and Hammay joined last week with the Major, as well as many fresh drafts of troops." The subaltern observed Furze with curiosity. "You were the officer in command after Festubert, is that right?"

"Yes, I held that responsibility before Captain Duckworth took command," Furze responded distractedly.

The subaltern assumed an aura of marked respect, "I know the Regiment looks ragged, Sir, but it's in a far stronger position than when you last saw it. You have my word on that and the men are in good enough spirits, they have just had a tough time of it recently."

"I don't doubt it, thank you for your time Lieutenant, it's good to have you in the Regiment," He touched his cap to the young man and turned to leave.

The subaltern suddenly stopped him. "Sir, I almost forgot, I was told to look out for the arrival of our Adjutant and hand him this letter."

"I see, well tell me his name and I'll see if I can help," answered Furze, looking at the letter.

"It's you, Sir, the letter is to Lieutenant Furze." The subaltern handed over the letter.

"My thanks," he replied, opening the letter as the subaltern departed.

It informed him that he was to return to his former position as Regimental Adjutant, a position he was to relieve from Lieutenant Philpot. At the sight of his friend's name, his spirits soared. At last, someone he knew. He strode over to the building from which Philpot had chosen to conduct his duties and found him barking orders at two haggard Corporals.

Although Furze had only been gone a short time, it seemed as though an age had passed since the two friends had last seen one another. Philpot seemed visibly strained but as Furze's frame filled the doorway and the Corporals hushed at his arrival. Philpot's furrowed brow opened into a show of warm welcome.

"Furzzy! I'm so glad you're back, you're looking healthier than ever," Philpot pronounced, as he moved to greet Furze.

"My dear fellow," smiled Furze, returning the handshake and nodding to the Corporals. "Time at home has served as the greatest balm to the toils of war that any man could hope for. But tell me, how has everything been since my departure? The Battalion, let alone the Regiment, seems replenished?"

"Indeed," Philpot agreed, turning to the Corporals. "Gentlemen, this is Lieutenant Furze, who has returned as our Adjutant. We shall continue this business later once I have briefed him fully on the current state of things."

The Corporals made their introductions then left, visibly pleased to have put the tense conversation on hold for the moment.

Philpot offered Furze a seat. "We now have thirty-four officers in the Battalion, many of whom are young subalterns, but all of whom are capital chaps."

As he said this, the unmistakable sound of artillery fire began pounding from the direction of the Front. Furze inadvertently started at the sound.

"You'll get used to it again in no time, old chap," Philpot chuckled dryly. "We have been giving the Germans hell the past week with our big guns and they have been returning our greeting in kind. Expect this barrage to continue all day."

"It's good to see you," Furze uttered as he recovered. "I was worried I had returned to a Regiment filled with new faces." The longer he spent back on the Front, especially talking to his friend, the more he regained his confidence and command. "I've been meaning to ask, where's Tommy? How has he been?"

"My dear fellow." Philpot rose from his seat. "Tommy has been a beast since your departure, I don't think a day has gone by when he hasn't rued your absence."

"Can you blame him?" Furze jested. "But thank you for looking after him, that means a great deal."

"Don't mention it, I'll just hold it against you until an appropriate moment. Come on, he'll be itching to see you."

The pair strode outside and over to the makeshift stable block where the officers' horses had been put. Furze picked Tommy out instantly, the two white socks on his right legs standing out conspicuously amongst the other mounts. Having gained so much from his father over the past few weeks, the horse that his father had sent him held an even greater significance than before. Tommy caught his owner's scent before Furze had approached and wheeled his head, blinking at Furze, and whinnying imploringly.

"Tommy," Furze greeted softly, reaching out to the animal's long nose. "Hello there, boy, hello!"

Tommy snorted, expressing a small notion of dissatisfaction over having been ignored for so long, then moved forward and gently pressed his head against Furze's chest. Furze breathed in the musky equine smell, wrapped his arms around Tommy's powerful neck, and scratched behind his ears. It felt as though he had returned to the embrace of an old and trusted friend, and Tommy's presence allowed a calm warmth to flood through Furze's veins.

The next two days passed exactly as Philpot had predicted, with heavy artillery bombardments from both sides. On Monday, the Battalion marched towards Bethune to be ready to support the attack being delivered by the 4th Corps that evening against the enemy around La Bassée. The attack commenced at 6:30 pm yet very little news permeated back from the Front line to where Furze's Battalion was waiting and, at midnight, they returned to their billets.

The next morning, Philpot caught Furze with some snippets of news he had managed to catch. "It's not good, Furzzy, the news is that the attack has been a complete failure."

"Damn" Furze growled, "objectively, or in terms of our losses?"

"Both," Philpot sighed. "We appear to have lost a great number of lives, with no appreciable gain in ground. There is to be another attack by the 21st Brigade this afternoon."

"Has nothing changed in our approach to this war since Festubert?" Furze fumed, aghast. "We suffered so much that day for such little gain and it seems we are to make the same mistakes again and again."

"It can be hard to judge the intentions of our commanders," Philpot admitted. "That said, try and get some quality time with Major Heath. I think you'll find him a capable fellow."

Furze welcomed his friend's advice and just such an opportunity presented itself over the next few days, whilst the

Regiment was engaged in digging and fortifying a new line of trenches. One particularly quiet evening, the CO wandered over.

"Good evening Lieutenant," Major Heath welcomed.

"Evening, Sir, happy with the day's work?" greeted Furze.

"Indeed, it's a relief the Germans have been so quiet. Will you accompany me in visiting 'A' and 'B' Companies?"

"That would be topping, Sir," Furze answered enthusiastically, eager to catch some personal time with the new commander.

"Splendid. Finish up here and we shall make our way over. Bring your field glasses, I think we'll be able to observe some rather interesting ground from their position."

Intrigued at this final remark, Furze gave a few orders to the nearby subalterns and followed the CO down the line. They strolled in silence for a few minutes, the Major evidently deep in thought and Furze unwilling to interrupt him.

"We have lost over fifty-thousand men in the past month alone," Heath said at last.

"I knew it had been a dire month, Sir," replied Furze, shocked at the figure. "Still, I had no idea we had lost that many."

"Gas, sordid German chlorine gas Furze, that's what's been hitting our troops around Ypres. You heard about Hill 60?"

"I did, Sir," Furze recalled what he had heard. "The 5th Division and 15th Brigade bore the brunt of it, if I understand it correctly. They fought valiantly, but without the hills surrounding them being under British control their position was untenable."

"Quite right," the CO nodded, "and high ground is the key to controlling the Front. Right now, we are on the back foot at Ypres, but our Royal Engineers may be able to play havoc with their position."

At the highest point along their route, the CO stopped abruptly and peered towards the German lines. He then reached out for Furze's field glasses, which the young man willingly handed over.

"Hmm," muttered Heath, "fascinating," handing them back to Furze. "Take a look towards the German lines there, and tell me what you see."

"Well, the Germans have dug themselves in strongly and put up barbed wire along their line."

"Indeed, what else, what about the land?"

Furze took stock of Heath's comment and trained his eye on the land in front of the German line. Suddenly he struck upon a crater, which he had not seen before, focused as he was on the German fortifications.

"The crater," murmured Furze.

"Precisely! Also, does anything strike you about this feature?"

"It looks out of place, Sir, that's for sure, and the German line seems misplaced because of it."

"That's because it's man-made Furze, by the power of our Royal Engineers. There used to be an area of high ground commanding the land surrounding it just where that crater now sits. The Engineers tunnelled underneath it and successfully blew the hill to high heaven!"

"But the Germans still hold the line," stated Furze, unsure of the success of such a feat.

"They do," concurred the CO, with a glint in his eye, "but that was only due to our failure to foresee the success of the Engineers. We were so taken aback at the spectacle that we didn't advance fast enough and the Germans had entrenched again before we could force them back any further."

"But the principle..." muttered Furze, beginning to understand Heath's thoughts.

"Could be applied to other areas of commanding ground across the Front," Heath finished. "All it takes is better planning, a decent distraction further along the line and a good dose of explosive."

Pondering the Major's words, Furze returned to his duties suitably impressed by the CO's astute observations and allowing himself to relax a little under such an apparently capable commander. That evening, stealing a moment of solitude, Furze wrote a letter to Daw.

My darling Daw,

How have you been these past weeks? I must own that time passes immensely quickly over here, even when one is digging trenches under a canopy of soaking summer rain... I miss you terribly, do write and tell me about your happenings, simply reading your words will allow me to picture you and hear your voice. That alone provides me untold comfort.

Oh, my dear, it was simply awful having to depart from you on that blissful morning. You may never know how much my heart pined to express its love, my love, for you. Given everything that has happened and is bound to happen out here, you showed me the greatest care in a moment of immense turmoil. I hope, in time, that I can be strong enough to bear your burdens, as you have so willingly shared my own.

The situation out here has not got any better and I remain uncertain how the future will go. Please know that I think about you daily, there is rarely a moment when I do not miss your comforting words, your laugh, your smile. All I can hope for is a swift end to this bitter conflict so that I might return to you and hold you once again.

All my love is yours,
Keith

An Unmarked Grave

"We found all the graves of our officers except Fuller, but we placed a cross in the ground where we are under the impression he lay."

Sunday 27th June.

It was Furze's 25th birthday. He recalled this as soon as he awoke, for he had received a number of letters from home all with express instructions not to be opened until the 26th of June. As dutiful as ever, he had followed these instructions, and now very much looked forward to opening them. Involuntarily, his mind wandered to his dear friend Fuller. A pang of guilt struck him at the fact that he was about to enjoy numerous wishes of good health whilst so many of his friends had already seen their last day.

Subsequently, he determined to make a visit the following day to the ground over which the Battle of Festubert had raged. *I owe them that much*, he admitted solemnly, *for giving me the gift of being able to live another year on this Earth.*

He smiled at the memory of his eventual kiss with Daw. *Fuller*, he whispered, closing his eyes, *you wouldn't believe the life that began when yours ended. I can't ever hope to repay you, but I shall always try and remember.*

With this important duty committed to, he stretched his way out of bed and made his way to breakfast. Coffee in one hand and a particularly warm and encouraging letter from home in the other, Furze felt a hand grip his shoulder and turned, delighting in the sight of Lieutenant Taylor-Jones.

"Happy Birthday, old chap," grinned his friend, "that's quite a library you have in front of you!"

"Taylor! Good to see you my dear fellow, do take a seat." He hadn't seen Taylor since Festubert. "It is a veritable pile I suppose, but with a family such as mine, lengthy letters become the norm."

"It's endearing, Furzzy, better to have too many to read than too few."

"Very true, how have you been this past month?"

"Well enough, well enough," but behind the veneer that Taylor put on, Furze could detect a great deal of pain. "I could have done with some leave after Festubert, but it was a good thing to keep some old blood here. There were so many changes in leadership within the Regiment after that battle, that any further losses would have been disastrous."

Furze looked at Taylor with feeling, "I'm sorry for not being there, had I known…"

"Don't be ridiculous, Furzzy!" countered Taylor attempting to wipe the sadness from his features. "You threw yourself into that battle and had a heavy burden of responsibility thrust upon you without any warning whatsoever. You needed a rest, or I fear for how much of yourself you would have given to those around you. I'll be off soon enough, leaving you to clear up the mess I've left."

"It was a horrible battle, Taylor, and the memory of it haunts me still. I don't think I could have carried on as I was. Even at home, I sometimes found it difficult to cope." The pain returned to Taylor's face at Furze's words.

"Everyone lost something that day, Furzzy," Taylor muttered, mournfully. "One either lost one's life or something far more intangible." He straightened and forced a smile. "It's your birthday for Christ's sake! Let's not mention it now. There shall be a time and a place to remember them."

"Now you mention it, I was going to visit the ground over which we fought tomorrow. Would you like to join me?"

Taylor-Jones reflected, then nodded. "Yes, I would like that very much. I need to put my sorrows to rest, and I doubt I would have the strength to visit the scene if you didn't accompany me."

"It'll do us both good." Furze assured his friend.

Thus, the next morning, the pair rose early and went to seek permission for the trip from Major Heath.

"Morning Sir," Furze saluted, as he entered Heath's room with Taylor on his heels. "With your permission, we would like to take a walk over the ground we fought across last month, around Festubert. I admit, rather awfully, that I have yet to pay my respects to the soldiers and… friends who lost their lives during that ghastly action."

"Yes, that was quite a fight. Remind me, what were our losses that day?"

"We went in with twenty-two officers and seven-hundred-and-fifty soldiers, Sir," responded Furze, with a rapidity and precision which surprised the CO. "We returned with only two-hundred-and-fifty men."

"What about the officers?"

"Of the twenty-two, twelve were killed, six wounded, and one was missing in action. Only Lieutenants Taylor-Jones here, Philpot, and myself returned unscathed." Having related the facts so mechanically, Furze trembled ever so slightly as their meaning sunk in and placed his shaking hands behind his back in an attempt to regain his composure.

"Of course, you must go and visit the ground," assented Heath, without taking his eyes off Furze's. What he had observed allowed him to fully appreciate the importance of such a reparative and reflective excursion. "What is more, it is my wish and duty to walk the ground with you and pay my respects to those from this valiant Regiment who came before me."

"Thank you, Sir, that is incredibly decent of you," Furze replied before leaving, grateful that the Regiment had been assigned another respectful, understanding and thoughtful Commanding Officer. He just hoped Heath would last longer than his predecessors. Outside, a hand touched his shoulder.

"Are you alright, old boy? You seemed a little shaken just now." It was Taylor.

"I'm not sure," Furze murmured, plunged deep in thought. "Recalling the numbers back to Heath just now, the way I could just reel them off so automatically brought back memories of Festubert in shocking detail. I remembered Major Bottomley as he was shot and then Kirk as he was wounded. The whole scene was laid out in such vivid detail I feared I was re-living it once again. Like I could still feel the blood on my hands as I tended their wounds one after the other." He looked at his hands. *Nothing*, he reminded himself, *you're not there anymore.*

Taylor's grip brought him back to the present. "We both faced death that day, Furzzy," murmured Taylor, "and whether through timing, luck, or ruddy divine intervention, we survived whilst some of our friends did not. I've replayed those hours over and over trying to sleep at night, pondering how things might have been had I been running a foot to my left, had I not taken cover when I did, had I not pulled the trigger when I…" he trailed off, equally deep in the folds of his memory. "This walk will help, Furze, I'm sure of it."

The pair met Heath at precisely 1:00 pm and the three officers began their walk through Festubert. When they reached the right ground, Furze stopped abruptly, causing the other two to halt and look inquisitively at him. He cast his penetrative gaze towards an orchard, before moving it across the surrounding landscape, his eyes darting between the British and German Front lines that were clearly visible.

"Well, we took that blasted orchard at least!" Furze almost spat these words, before resuming a powerful stride forward.

A little behind Furze, Taylor suddenly struck upon the cause of his friend's distress and explained to Heath. "The German first line is precisely where it was when we launched the attack. It hasn't moved an inch."

"I understand," responded Heath quietly, "meaning our young Lieutenant is currently questioning the value of the many lives spent gaining what appears to be so little?"

"I believe so."

"And the orchard?" queried Heath, thoughtfully.

"Our final objective for the assault was a German communication trench, situated just there," Taylor directed Heath's gaze to the right of the orchard. "We captured it successfully but the Germans held the orchard throwing some terrible counter-fire in our direction from that position."

"But we appear to have wrestled that stronghold from the devil," Furze interjected bitterly, having slowed his pace and caught the end of the conversation. "All the better. I would like to think our attack achieved some measurable benefit at least."

"In this war Furze, no conflict is ever in vain, though it may very well appear so." Heath was keen to strengthen his Adjutant's state of mind. "Even if we fail to take any ground, hitting German morale, preventing an attack they were planning to make, distracting the enemy's attention whilst attacks are made elsewhere, these will all bring tangible benefits in the end."

"Tangible benefits, Sir?" Furze replied, his temper rising. "I'll tell you one tangible benefit, taking the damned German first line, holding it, then taking their second line, then their third, and every blasted line all the way back to Germany!" He paused, aware that he had allowed his anger to get the better of him. He looked across the ground, breathing heavily after his outburst, and attempting desperately to think of something more constructive to say in response to Heath's well-intentioned remarks.

"We'll do it, Furze," Heath affirmed in a voice so calm, so indisputable in its delivery that Furze believed he truly meant what he said. "I don't know how, I don't know when, and although this war perplexes me, aggravates me, makes me downright terrified every single day, I never let this change my opinion. Every order we follow, every act we commit and, as hard as it is to accept, every friend we lose, drives us closer to our ultimate goal. Victory will not be easy, the Germans have decided upon that, but it shall be ours eventually."

Furze felt his anger dissipating and muttered, bleakly, "I know, Sir, I know." Finally, aware of his own moroseness, he added, "and I suppose that, ultimately, our victory has to come from numerous small engagements. Whether successful in themselves, or not."

The trio wandered on, observing the large amount of equipment and rubbish which still littered the ground around the British line. As they walked, they passed the scattered graves of their fellow officers who fell on, or shortly after, the 16th of May, 1915. Friends of both Furze and Taylor-Jones, brothers on the field of battle. Major Bottomley, Captain Lang-Brown, Lieutenant McCate, Lieutenant Hillen.

Furze was keeping an eye out for one name in particular.

Lieutenant Humphreys…Furze stopped in front of the tiny, grubby, inadequate excuse for a grave that lay before him. It wasn't the name he had been searching for, but it pained him greatly. "I visited his mother when I was on leave," Furze recalled, motioning towards the ground.

Heath and Taylor stood in silence, wondering where Furze was going to take the conversation.

"She appeared at the door gaunt and shattered, more spectre than woman."

"Mothers face their own wars when their sons are away fighting," offered Heath. "Unspoken, unobserved wars they may be, but vicious wars of emotion nonetheless."

"She was a prisoner in her own home. Alone, with hardly any details of her son's passing, no knowledge of his bravery, nothing with which to respect his memory."

"You know it has to be that way, Furzzy, at least for now," consoled Taylor.

"I told her," Furze snapped, "when she asked for the details... I told her everything I could. She was so composed, showing the same bravery her son did during Festubert."

Heath was observing Furze's countenance, noting every contour of his cheek, every twitch of his mouth, every flash from his deep, searching eyes. "You needn't have made that trip, it was immensely good of you."

"It was the right thing to do, I had no choice. When I left, she told me to live for him, and all the poor souls who have passed away before their time."

Furze drew his head away from the earth and continued their walk. "That grave is a pathetic tribute to his memory, to any of their memories. So, it remains for us to honour them in our deeds for the duration of this war, and in how we live our lives thereafter."

Further graves followed, carrying with them name after name, memory after memory, mourning mother after mourning mother. Major Slacke, Lieutenant Garmin, Lieutenant Pratt. Still Furze's eyes searched and his heart ached, each pound slamming against his chest as though urging him to release it from the captivity of his human form.

Captain Haddon-Smith, Lieutenant de Rougaunt and, finally, Lieutenant Brookes.

Furze felt bitter distress building up inside him.

"Where's Fuller, where did they bury him?" He could hardly bear the thought that his ever-present friend, with whom he had been through so much and whom life had imbued with the most vibrant of colour, could be so transparent in death.

"I'm so sorry, Furzzy," Taylor almost whispered, "we couldn't identify his body, I thought you had been told."

"I think he lies here, somewhere..." stammered Furze, striding blindly forwards, fighting back the tears which were welling uncontrollably behind his eyes. He frantically cast his gaze across the ground, wondering where, how, his friend had met his end. His eyes landed upon a spot which, oddly, felt like the right place.

"Here," said Taylor-Jones gently, holding out a small wooden cross, "I brought one, just in case."

Furze reached out, took the little emblem, and clutched it fiercely in his hands. Taylor and Heath watched him, silently, as he carefully placed the cross in the ground where he believed his friend had fallen and intricately arranged some rocks around it to hold it in place.

As he stood there, Furze took in the moment. He listened to the sounds around him, the whispered rustle of the nearby trees. He felt the earth under his boots, softened by the recent rain yet firm in its ceaseless support. He breathed in the air, filling his lungs with his surroundings, and noticing the scent of flowers which, for the first time, overpowered the stench of the Western Front.

Life, in that moment, was a rare pocket of peace. He brought his mind back to Fuller, and all his other friends who had been snatched prematurely from existence, their lives forming paving stones on the world's path to peace. As he did so, he turned his thoughts to the people his friends were fighting for, and subsequently to his own loved ones.

For their courage, I shall be bold, thought Furze. *For their duty, I shall lead. For their sacrifice, I shall live. We will prevail in this war, and fight to the bitter end, if need be, to ensure their lives were not given in vain.*

Then, Lieutenant Edward Keith Byrne Furze turned to his companions, his calm demeanour and determination returned to him, two delicate tears glistening as they rolled down his cheeks.

B.D. Wilberforce

Epilogue

An epilogue is not the end - merely the continuation of the story.

Furze will return to continue his fight...

B.D. Wilberforce

The Medals of
Brigadier Edward Keith Byrne Furze
DSO, OBE, MC

Medals from left to right:
Distinguished Service Order (DSO)
Order of the British Empire (OBE)
Military Cross (MC)
The 1914 Mons Star
The British War Medal
The Victory Medal
The 1930-1945 Star
The African Star
The Defence Medal 1945
The War Medal 1939-1945

OBE - January 1946

George R.I.

George the Sixth by the Grace of God of Great Britain Ireland and the British Dominions beyond the Seas King, Defender of the Faith Emperor of India and Sovereign of the Most Excellent Order of the British Empire to Our trusty and well beloved Edward Keith Byrne Furze Esquire Companion of Our Distinguished Service Order on whom has been conferred the Decoration of the Military Cross temporary Colonel in Our Army **Greeting** Whereas We have thought fit to nominate and appoint you to be an Additional Officer of the Military Division of Our said Most Excellent Order of the British Empire We do by these presents grant unto you the Dignity of an Additional Officer of Our said Order and hereby authorise you to have hold and enjoy the said Dignity and Rank of an Additional Officer of Our aforesaid Order together with all and singular the privileges thereunto belonging or appertaining

Given at Our Court at Saint James under Our Sign Manual and the Seal of Our said Order this First day of January 1946 in the Tenth year of Our Reign

By the Sovereigns Command

Mary

Grant of the dignity of an Additional Officer of the Military Division of the Order of the British Empire to Colonel (temporary) Edward Keith Byrne Furze, DSO, MC.

OBE - Letter from King George

BUCKINGHAM PALACE.

I greatly regret that I am
unable to give you personally the
award which you have so well earned.
I now send it to you with
my congratulations and my best
wishes for your future happiness.

George R.I.

Col.(Temporary)Edward K.B.Furze,
          D.S.O., O.B.E., M.C.
12th March, 1947.

Letter of Award
Military Knight of Windsor - March 1955

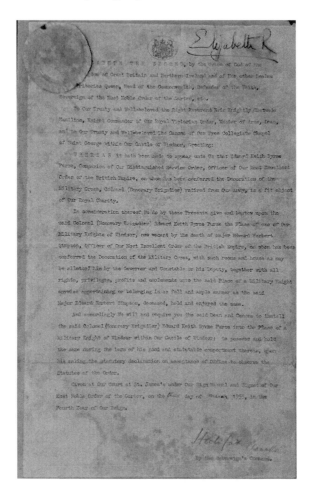

B.D. Wilberforce

Brigadier Keith Furze
Military Knight of Windsor - March 1955

Queen Elizabeth II
Brigadier Edward Keith Byrne Furze
DSO, MC, OBE
1970

B.D. Wilberforce

Postscript

Brigadier Edward Keith Byrne Furze DSO, MC, OBE, was a man I never had the opportunity to meet. He was one of those rare men who inhabit this planet all too briefly but leave, during their short tenure, an indelible mark upon it. I grew up surrounded by stories of his exploits as a boy, as a soldier, and as a family man. He was my great-grandfather and, therefore, someone from whom I could still learn a great deal, given that my mother had known him and his wife as her own grandparents. Who would not, as a young boy, sit with rapt attention and a keen glint in his eye listening to their mother and grandmother talk about trips to see 'Furzzy' in Windsor Castle? For that was where he lived with his wife, in a flat above the Henry VIII Gateway of the Castle, having been rewarded for his long and dedicated service in the British Army, through two World Wars, with the honour of being made a Military Knight of Windsor in 1955.

I have often wondered what it would have been like to have known him. To have visited that stronghold and soaked up the sort of kind, delicate, yet steadfast advice that life's experiences imbue upon the elderly to pass on to the young. However, one cannot dwell on the past, and although I do think about what advice I would have liked to have asked him, I feel I am better placed to ask, instead, how he would have acted in my position when I have decisions to make.

It was with this idea in mind that I chose to relate a small fraction of the life of this man, whom I never knew, to you, the reader. I find that each time I look back on his exploits, whether as serious as leading men towards enemy gunfire, or as simple as appreciating the beauty of a church organ, I learn something new about him. This was a man who led a life filled with happiness, optimism and kindness, even at a time when the world seemed lacking in all of these essential qualities.

B.D. Wilberforce

This book is based on the handwritten diary he kept from the dates of Wednesday 13th January to Wednesday 27th June 1915. I kept to the facts and terminology as closely as I could, wishing to do justice to not only Keith's memory, but those of the brave individuals he names in his account, especially those who never made it home. I only deviated from his written word to bridge the gaps found within the diary, for the literary purpose of the novel. Like many first-hand accounts of this tragic period of humanity's history, some things will be unique to the life and experiences of Keith Furze. Other moments will resound throughout any recollection of that period, as described by others who were unfortunate enough to have lived through it.

I hope you enjoyed it, in a manner of speaking. It is essential when reading such a novel to understand that, even in the bleakest of situations when everything around you seems to be crumbling, there is always one point, one object, however distant, that is not disintegrating, and upon which you can fix your gaze.

B.D. Wilberforce

Military Ranks

Officer Ranks in ascending order of seniority:

1. Second lieutenant – Command of a Platoon of 30 soldiers
2. Lieutenant – Command of a Platoon 30 soldiers
3. Captain – Command of a Company of 50 and 120 soldiers
4. Major – Command of a Company of 120 soldiers
5. Lieutenant-Colonel – Command of a Battalion/Regiment of up to 750 soldiers
6. Colonel – Field Command in a Staff Group of a Battalion/Regiment
7. Brigadier-General – Command of a Brigade, typically 6 Battalions
8. Major-General – Command of a Division of 6,000 to 25,000 soldiers
9. Lieutenant-General – Command of a Corps of two to five divisions
10. General
11. Field Marshal

Non-commissioned Ranks in ascending order of seniority:

1. Private – No command
2. Lance corporal – Second in command of section
3. Corporal – Generally commands a section
4. Sergeant – Second in command of a troop or platoon
5. Staff/Colour Sergeant – Management role of a Company
6. Warrant Officer class 2
7. Warrant Officer class I - The most senior advisers to Battalion Commanding Officers

B.D. Wilberforce

Battles Referenced in Furze Sweethearts and Swan Songs:

The First Battle of Ypres – 19 October to 22 November 1914

The Battle of Neuve Chapelle – 10-13 March 1915

The Battle of Aubers Ridge – 09 May 1915

The Battle of Festubert – 15-25 May 1915

Acknowledgements

Andrew Ritchie, my Dad, is the first individual I would like to thank for his guidance and support whilst writing this novel. It has taken six years from conception to publication, and it was to Dad that I sent my first A4 draft of the book, an unrefined collection of words and ideas that I thought was the finished product. Naturally, being a lawyer, he turned his experienced eye to my work and reviewed it with honesty, clarity, and a lot of red pen. However, as with all things he turns his attention to, he did so with his whole heart and I never have, and never will, question his love, support and care for me and my work. Victoria Wilberforce and Imo Wilberforce, my Mum and Sister, are the next people I have to mention. My Mum is a wonderfully caring woman, someone who has dedicated her life to raising Imo and I and encouraging us to be the versions of ourselves we feel most comfortable being. Whilst writing Furze, I turned to her on numerous occasions for guidance on Furze's characteristics, wishing to pair the person she had known in reality to the man I was presenting fictionally. No son could wish for a finer example of maternal courage, and I hope she knows that, when times got tough writing this book, the thought of her smiling whilst reading the accounts of her Grandfather kept me going. Imo, my dear Sister, is a lifelong companion to me and an inspiration for my creative spirit. I've come to admire her tenacious approach to life more and more as we have grown up together, and can safely say that, although I am the older sibling, she has always had a more mature grasp on the meaning of life. Imo, without the example you set by following your creative passions in fashion and textiles, I may never have seen the value in the words and stories you know I live my life by.

Michèle Smith, Managing Director of Jasami Publishing and my publisher, deserves a special mention. Most of the books I read hold acknowledgements to the author's publisher and writing this novel has made me appreciate why this is. Picture, if you will, something you have created. It has taken a great deal of time, patience, thought, and frustration because we rarely succeed at something the first time around. Imagine, then, your pride when it has reached a state that you believe is complete, a state that expresses you, your morality, your unique skills, and the emotions you wish others to feel. It is at this moment that your work is rejected time and time again by agents and publishers, an industry saturated with thoughts, ideas, hopes and untapped potential. This experience is crushing, brutal, and disheartening even to the most energetic of individuals. However, it only takes one person to trust you, to take a risk, for all that challenge to be worth the time. Michèle provided that trust, she took that risk on my first novel, extending to me a chance to earn her trust, and prove why Furze's story was worthy of being told. Michèle, thank you from the depths of my soul for allowing me to take Furze's place in history and bring it into the present day, to gently remind people that challenge is a part of life and that we can face it all the more strongly when supporting one another, as you and your team have done with me. Your care for others inspires me whenever we talk, and your work with Jasami Publishing contributes to more than just the literary world, it contributes to the social fabric we exist within and makes it more wholesome.

Furze would not have reached the state it is in today without the guidance, expertise, and delicate professionalism of Michèle's team. Creative Director Paula Weir, your enthusiasm for "Furzzy" made my heart smile whenever we spoke, and encouraged me that his character had been captured appropriately upon the pages of the novel. Executive Editor May Winton and Editor Joanne Tahaney, where to begin. I failed to appreciate the criticality of the editing process until I was reviewing your thorough notes on my first and second drafts. Between the two of you, there were no corners of the novel where my inept writing could cower, and I matured as a young man at the same pace that Furze improved as a piece of art. I hope I have done your dedication justice, for without you Furze's story would never have reached its published state. To Photographer Joy Dakers, all credit must go for the inspired front cover, which managed to capture the historical background of the novel in a modern, heartfelt way. Finally, Kirsty Lawson, Videographer, Photographer and Marketing Intern as Jasami. You have been a real pleasure to work with and I've been awestruck by your videos, interviews, and photos throughout the marketing process for Furze. You represent the inventive challenge and potential apparent in so many young minds today, which society so rarely allows to flourish for fear of the change you will inevitably bring. I have no doubt you will bring enormous and positive change to whichever industry is lucky enough to count you among its members, and I hope you never lose your endearing spark and poise to tackle the unknown.

Nearly all of this novel was written in local cafés across the broad spectrum of locations I have called home over the past few years. From the Gail's on Abbeville Road in Clapham, to Noranne, Cassidy and the staff at Cafe G. just off Peckham Park, one café deserves a special mention. The Steamie, in Glasgow. Stevie, Wendy, you run a warm, friendly, and intimate little business within which I have always felt welcome. Although I took up your space for hours at a time each weekend for at least a year (how could I not, you serve the best salmon and eggs in the world), you were always pleased to see me and your staff, especially Megan and Ben, are a continuous joy to work amongst. Without the creative space you have nurtured, I would never have been as inspired as I was to bring the characters in Furze to life.

Finally, some of the dear friends who bring me to tears with their unerring support for my alternative ideas, and who always see past my many flaws to the caring person I try tirelessly to be. Miranda Aldersley, without you the toughest times I have experienced in my early twenties would have left me dejected and directionless. I think constantly back to the numerous brunches we have enjoyed in Soho when I have had emotional, frustrating or hilarious stories to tell, and your ability to listen to other people's woes is a rare and beautiful characteristic. You have guided me through every heartbreak I have experienced, and it is with your supportive words in mind that I infused Furze's own courtship of Daw Wallis with my emotional turmoil. You are a tremendous marvel, and a heart at one with my own.

Oliver Higginson and his wonderful wife Megan Martin. You lived with me when we first moved to London together, saw me through the undulations life threw at me when I first came out as gay, and helped me to recognise the parallels between Furze's life challenges and many of our own. Both of you represent, to me, the pinnacle of spirited determination in your pursuit of acting careers. You work tirelessly on the things you care about and believe are meaningful for society, and your love, support, and commitment to one another is what I based Furze's relationship with Daw on. You are both delightful companions, serious professionals and, above all else, immensely silly people at heart, and this is why I love you both so very much. Never stop dreaming!

To Lyle Calnan, Andrew Fraser, Alex Knight and Ted Gibson. My oldest friends, my most comforting companions, although our lives change so much as we grow older, our souls will never walk different paths to the ones that brought us together all those years ago. You are my Fuller, Brookes, Ross and Garmin. I couldn't imagine a life without you all, and based much of how Furze approaches his friendships on the hilarious times we have all had together. Remember, my friends, how much good you inspire in those around you, for we never tell our friends how much they mean to us until it is sometimes too late. Our connection is so often unspoken, but I hope this small tribute to the enormous part you play in my life allows me to tell you, in Furze's words, how deplorable life would feel were you not in it.

Rose Noble, Oliver Horton and Tom Davison. From the moment I met you at Bristol University, we were destined to influence each other's lives. You are all, undeniably, the most dedicated people I know to the causes you represent, yet you never allow the diversity of your interests to influence the people you care for. Rose, your pursuit of a career in film and TV production has been a great challenge and my heart has ached every time you have faced setbacks. Nevertheless, you have never stopped believing in yourself and the good in others. Oliver, your job in the highly intense setting of a global bank has certainly tested your patience and strength of mind, yet I have never seen your work come between you and your friends. Tom, dear Tom, your career in the military is something I admire and respect you so very much for. You represent the honour my Grandfather held through his time in the Royal Marines, the ferocious commitment to his friends that Furze showcased through his diary, and I sometimes wonder how two people separated by a century could hold such similar and rare qualities.

Finally, Tom Harvey-Smith and Noma Moyo. There was a moment, when we all enjoyed lunch together following Tom's return from Australia, and we had all moved on from jobs at a firm that was grinding down our creative spirits. We drank in that moment, grateful to have all been brought together by difficulty because of the bonds of friendship it formed between us. At that lunch, and many others afterwards, your boundless imaginations have given me countless phrases which I included in this novel, and our trips to the countryside and the mountains revitalised my mind and body when it needed it most. As you both represent so well, even the most enthusiastic extroverts need a little me-time to revive, just as Furze found when he took his leave at home.

Furze Sweethearts and Swan Songs would not be the novel you see before you without these particular influences, and many more besides. As Albert Camus would say, life will always have the capacity to become absurd, and I deal with absurdity, much like Furze did, by listening to my family and friends – the people I love just as Furze loved his Dad, Mum, siblings, Fuller, Brookes, Garmin, Ross, Kirkpatrick and Daw Wallis.

About the Author

B.D. Wilberforce is best characterised by his optimistic enthusiasm and curiosity for life; maintaining the mantra that to appreciate the quality of the present moment is one of life's more important practices. To help achieve this, he adores delving into expansive thought by enjoying many a serene evening exploring the passions, hobbies, and ideals of his friends and family. It is from these enriching conversations, generally encouraged by a glass of red wine, that Wilberforce builds many of the emotional experiences which form the touchstones of his novels. People, and the way in which they inhabit their time, are the essence of his writing style, and ensuring that authentic voices are heard by the reader is a pivotal focus. Wilberforce's life is fuelled by meaningful friends, classic novels, and dashing runs, although he never feels more at peace than when he is on the summit of a Scottish mountain in the Highlands.

B.D. Wilberforce

Furze Sweethearts and Swan Songs

Jasami Publishing Ltd

www.jasamipublishingltd.com

78578069R00198